BILLY JENKINS

EUROPE'S KING OF THE COWBOYS

A NOVEL

HUGO N. GERSTL

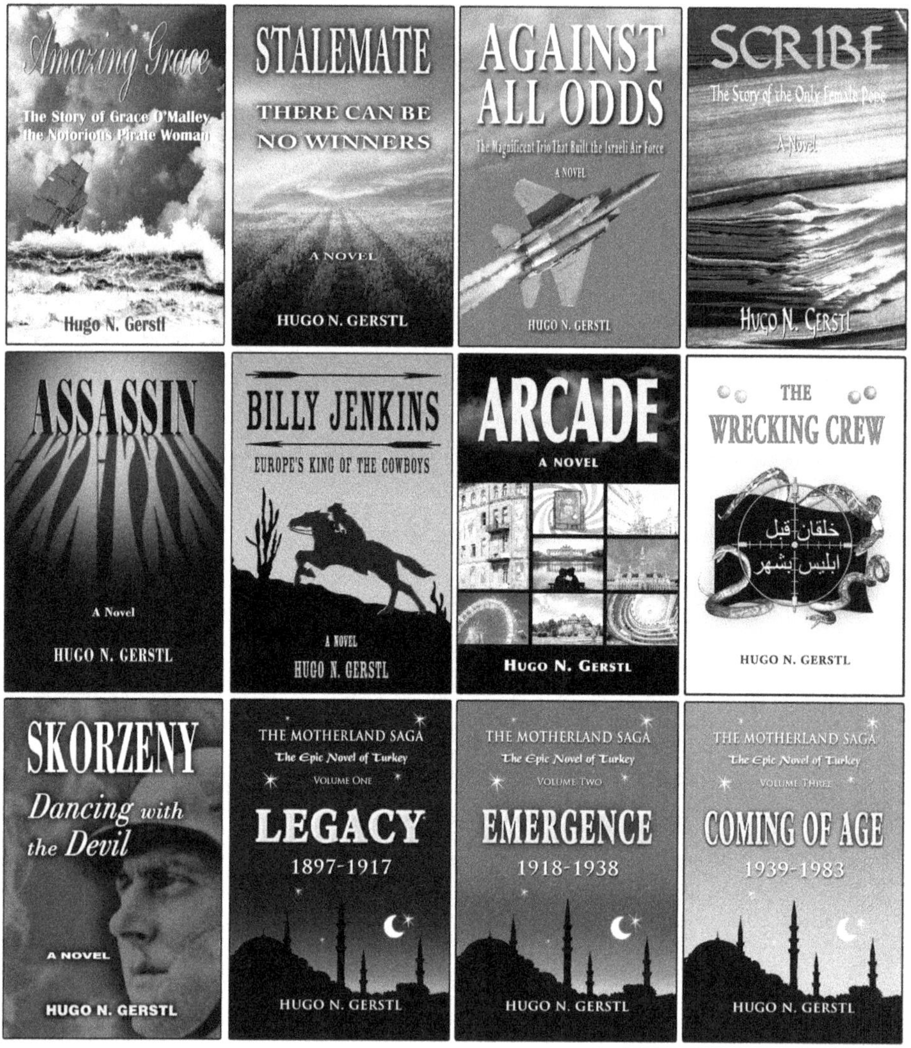

BILLY JENKINS

EUROPE'S KING OF THE COWBOYS

A NOVEL

HUGO N. GERSTL

PANGÆA
PUBLISHING GROUP

Billy Jenkins: Europe's King of the Cowboys

ISBN 978-1-950134-04-5
Pangæa Publishing Group
www.PangaeaPublishing.com

This book is a work of fiction. With the exception of certain anchors of fact, all the characters in this book are the author's creation. As in all novels, much of what occurs in this book originated in the author's imagination. Any similarities to persons living or dead or to events claimed to have occurred are purely coincidental.

Cover design and typesetting by
DesignPeaks@gmail.com

For information contact:

PANGÆA PUBLISHING GROUP
25579 Carmel Knolls Drive
Carmel, CA 93923
Telephone: 831-624-3508/831-649-0668
Fax: 831-649-8007
Email: info@pangaeapublishing.com

This book is a sequel and a salute to

Gary Jennings' *Spangle*
The greatest circus novel ever written

~ ∫ ~

To Dick and Claire Gorman
Mike & Ruth Baltes Stuntz
and In Memory of Braxton Stuntz
Alan Furst, successor to Eric Ambler
and one of the finest writers in the world

~ ∫ ~

And always

For My Lorraine

GLOSSARY OF AMERICAN AND
EUROPEAN CIRCUS TERMS

Advance man – goes out ahead of the circus, reserves the tober, arranges for publicity

Bianca (**Bloomer House**) – an almost empty house

Blow the stand – pick up and leave the show

Blues – plain, plank seats on bleachers – the "general admission" seats, as opposed to the Starback seats (see *infra*).

Bull – circus elephant; actually a female – easier to train and less combative than the male

Cache sexe – a small pad used to cover the genitals of both men and women circus-performers so that the audience cannot clearly see either the man's bulge or the woman's "cracks" when they are dressed in leotards.

Chapiteau (**Big Top**) – the main circus tent

Cherry pie – extra work laid on at no extra pay

Convict – Zebra

EMERGENCY OR DISASTER: The Governor or the Equestrian Director raises his arms in an **X** above his head. The band *immediately* plays Mendelssohn's **Wedding March.** This signifies emergency or disaster and the chapiteau is cleared out *immediately*

Equestrian Director – Ringmaster

Exotics – show animals that are not native – not familiar to the jossers

Faking privileges **–** food purveyors, slum purveyors, dancers, singers, etc. who are not part of the circus, but who follow the circus everywhere and have permission to conduct their business on circus grounds.

First of May – any new recruit or temporary circus performer.

Governor (**Main Guy**) – the proprietor of the circus.

Grouch bag – a circus performer's – usually a woman's – savings. This was to guard against the fickle ways of fate or a man, and was often the only "retirement" available. It could mean anything from a bag full of coins or diamonds to a bank book.

Holdback – every new circus hand always has his first three weeks of wages withheld, not to be paid until the end of the season. It's an old custom, partly to discourage the good hands from defecting to some better paying outfit, but partly also a philanthropy to ensure that the drunkards and wastrels among the crew have at least money to get home on when the show closes.

Hump – camel

Jocko – monkey, chimpanzee, ape

Joey: Happy-faced clown, named for Joe Grimaldi, the first famous clown in England, 1810 – 41

Join out – join the circus

Joint, butcher, etc. – independents who peddle edibles, potables, slum, every sort of thing – at circuses. They are not part of the circus but have *faking privileges (supra)* to conduct business on the circus grounds

Jossers or *Flatties* (**Rubes**) – commoners, audience

Klischnigg – a contortionist, usually a woman. Other names for this phenomenon are India-rubber woman, human serpent, or boneless lady. Because of their very soft bone structure, they normally live very short lives and die of lung disease.

Liberty Act – horses doing tricks around the ring *without* riders or harness, and often without the sign of an animal trainer cracking the whip

Lungia (**Rope Fall**) – boom that supports tricks in the ring

Lupino Mirror – exact duplication of mirror image by two performers

Making one's nut – earning at least one's daily expenses

Pista (**Ring**): the area where an act is performed

Posting paper: affixing advertising posters to lampposts, poles, etc. where the circus is to go next

Risley act: foot jugglers and upside down acrobats, usually from the Orient.

Roustabout – common worker who does set-up, tear-down, dirty work

Sfondone (**Straw House**) – packed, more than a full house, a turnaway house

Slanging buffers – a dog act

Slum – cheap souvenirs on sale on the midway

Starback seats – the best and most expensive seats in the house, folding chairs instead of bleachers – strategically positioned where the inhabitants can see everything that goes on.

Swazzle – a bogus gadget sold on the circus midway

Tober (**Pitch**) – the field where the circus show plays

Toby – a sad-faced clown

Voltige – a particularly violent type of horseback riding used in the circus where the rider may jump from one horse to the next – even under the horse

Water dog – sea lion
Zeke – hyena

> If you are with the circus, you are always "***on the show***," <u>not</u> "*in* the show"

As you watch the huge tent, its multicolored pennants waving gently about in the balmy afternoon breeze, reflect on the variety of people, audiences and performers alike, that the circus has attracted: people of so many different racial or national characteristics, modes of dress, customs, languages, and temperaments.

And all the time, bearing some losses and additions to its company and equipment, the circus had stayed the same. Everywhere it goes, it takes with it the familiar sounds of canvas flapping, ropes and poles creaking, rigs and harnesses jingling, heavy wheels rolling, animals whuffling or snorting or rumbling; the familiar odors of those animals and their feed bins and their droppings, aromas of hay and tanbark, of greasepaint and the sweat of hard work, the sharp smells of burned gunpowder, hot lamps, and chemicals; the familiar sights of garish banners billowing, and the tents brilliant in daylight or glowing after dark, and the *pista* full of action and color, or, afterward, empty and asleep in dreams and memories. And always, everywhere, those least and tiniest things in the circus, but those things that say unmistakably "*circus*" – flashing their bright glints to pick out this or that face in the crowd, and dappling with their reflections the faces of their own wearers – the spangles…

> *The circus is a floating island. It moors for a time on any and every kind of coast, and briefly brightens it with spangled light. Then it floats away from the landbound and commonplace, remaining always uncommon, undimmed, and unchanged by any encounter.*

PART ONE

1898 - 1909

1

The springtime sun had finally broken through the endless gray days of the northeast German winter as Isaiah Hobbs, still an imposing six-foot tall and thin – although he had to admit he was lately feeling every one of his sixty-seven years – ambled along the right bank of the Elbe. They had made parade into Magdeburg two days ago and the circus was now playing to *sfondone* houses in the Elbaue Kulturpark. He thought back to when he'd joined up with what was then known as *Zoltan's Titanic Treasure Trove of Wonder.* He'd succeeded to the governorship of the show by default after Zoltan's death back in 1871. For the past twenty years it had simply been called *Zoltan's Great American Circus.*

"As I was sayin' Colonel Isaiah, looks like the winter's finally over."

The voice cut into his reverie. Hobbs looked at the huge bear of a man, an inch taller than he was, bald as an egg, with a scraggly gray beard, who still looked like he was capable of lifting a horse – which, in fact, he'd probably done a hundred times during his career. Zeke Willis had been his best and closest friend for fifty years, and still was.

Ever since they'd joined the army – the *American* Army back in 'forty-eight – in Mexico.

"Alisa's still a goddammed good-looking woman at forty-three, high yaller or not. And loyal …"

"That she surely is, Zeke," Hobbs said, taking a long drag from the cigarette before dropping it to the ground and stamping it out. They came to a small hillock overlooking a place where the river widened. The two men sat down companionably on one of several benches along the waterfront.

"Isaiah?"

"Mmm?"

"Tell me, man to man, friend to friend, do you ever think back to those few days you had with the Empress?"

"Amelie? Only about a hundred fifty thousand times since Balaton. She's got to be over sixty by now. You know, she never let *anyone* take her photograph or paint a portrait of her after she turned thirty-one."

"They say she was the most beautiful woman to ever wear a crown."

"I can tell you she was the most beautiful woman ever to wear *nothing at all,*" he said, standing up. "Shall we head back to the tober for tonight's show?"

Zeke nodded and they did, and they'd gotten halfway back when they were accosted by a lad of about thirteen, who was a head shorter than Hobbs. He had curly blond hair and eyes so blue they looked unreal.

"*Enschuldigen, bist Sie der Herrscher von das Zirkus, Herr Hobbs?*"

"Yes, I am the Governor. *Sprechen sie Englisch, Jüngling?*"

"Yes, sir. The man with you must be the famous strong man, the Quakemaker."

"Used to be, son. Just plain old Zeke Willis now," the big man replied. "And you are …?"

"Erich Otto Rudolf Rosenthal," the boy snapped, clicking his heels together smartly in quasi-military style.

"I'm pleased to meet you, Erich, but shouldn't you be in school? It's only …" Hobbs extracted a cheap steel pocket watch, one of the few things he'd kept from Zoltan's days, and looked at it. "My mistake," he apologized. "It's four-thirty. Is there something we can do for you?"

"Yes, Herr Hobbs. I would like to join out with the *zirkus*."

Isaiah's eyebrows lifted, but, like Zoltan, he'd been through many such surprises, and, like Zoltan, *he* was surprised that very little surprised him anymore.

"Just like that. How old are you?"

"Thirteen years." He hesitated, then said, "On June 26, two months from now."

"You live in Magdeburg?"

"No, sir. I was born in Magdeburg. My most recent home was fifty kilometers from here. Before that Berlin. My father is the Jew, Georg Rosenthal. I'm told my mother, Anna Fischer, was not Jewish."

"*Was* not Jewish?"

"She left my father when I was five. I haven't seen her since."

Hobbs glanced sharply at his second-in-command. *The circus had always picked up strays – not the least of which had been himself. What's one more or less?*

"You said 'join out' with the circus. Where'd you learn circus lingo, Erich?"

"My father was on the Sarrasani."

"Pretty big show," Zeke said. They were now only a few hundred meters from the pitch. "What'd you say his name was?"

"Georg Rosenthal – Süssmilch." The boy responded.

"Sweet milk," Hobbs said. "He was a passable joey with Sarrasani and with the Donnert before that." He turned and faced the boy. "You don't seem to be too fond of your father."

"Herr Governor, I hate my father. For the longest time after my mother was gone, he would leave me with governess after governess while he was on one show or another."

"That's to be expected. You must know what circus life is like."

"Yes, but *I* never went on the circuit with my father. He'd come back to wherever I stayed, once a week or so. He always brought a woman."

"You feel he ignored you?" Zeke asked.

"I *know* he ignored me. From the moment he came home, he and whatever woman was with him disappeared into the bedroom. I didn't see either of them until the following morning, when he went back out on the road and she came out of his room looking rather disheveled."

"You called him, Rosenthal-the-Jew," Hobbs continued.

"He's always complained about how hard it is to be a Jew, like that's some kind of badge of honor, but I don't think he's had it hard at all. Life has been a game for him. Maybe I was nothing but an accident that resulted from that game."

"What would he say about your running away to join the circus?"

"Probably 'Good riddance!' One less burden for him, and honestly, neither one of us could care less."

Their conversation was interrupted by the nearby trumpeting of elephants.

"One of our three bulls," Hobbs said. "Brutus, Caesar, and Antony."

"Wouldn't it be better to have at least one girl so they could … you know … have baby elephants."

"Might," remarked Willis, taking a last satisfying tug at his pipe. "But in this case, they're all girls."

"But you called them 'bulls'?"

"Erich, *every* elephant who performs on *any* circus is called a bull, even if 'he's' a cow. In all my years on the circus I've seen maybe one male elephant. The females are smarter, gentler, a lot easier to train, and a damned sight more sociable."

"So their real names aren't really Brutus, Caesar and Antony?"

"Nope. Brutus, our oldest elephant – she's about fifty – is really named Peggy. Caesar is Mitzi, and Antony, who's only a kid of twenty, is Steffi."

As if on cue, the three pachyderms appeared. The lead elephant was ridden by a wiry old dark-skinned man who looked to be somewhere between seventy and death.

"Hey, Abdullah!" Willis shouted up to the man. "Got a new fella' wants to join out. Not much older than you were when you came aboard. How old were you anyway?"

"Don't rightly know, Massa, um, *Sahib* Zeke," the darker man rejoined. "That's 'cuz I don't rightly know how old I am now."

"His real name's George," Willis said quietly to the boy. "Forty years ago, he was a freed black buck in Philadelphia. Zoltan spotted him on a street, gave him a new career and a new name. He's been on the show longer than anyone I can remember. He and Zoltan had been together when Colonel Isaiah – the Herr Governor – and me joined out."

As the lead bull approached Hobbs, Willis, and young Rosenthal, she stopped in her tracks, lifted her trunk up and down in the boy's direction, and softly whuffled what sounded like a respectful greeting.

"Well, I'll be damned," Zeke said, his eyes widening as he looked toward Erich.

"Who would have believed it?" Isaiah Hobbs echoed.

"Believed what?" Rosenthal said, aware that not two but three pairs of eyes were on him. The third pair belonged to an attractive mulatto woman in her mid-forties, who'd appeared out of nowhere, propelling a sturdy and maneuverable wheelchair.

"Whoo-ee, Guv'nor," she said, addressing Hobbs. "You know what dat means."

"I do indeed, Cinderella. Why don't you break the news to our newest First of May?" he said, using the universal term for a new recruit. "His name's Erich."

"He may call hisself Erich," she said, "but he be's Billy to me."

"Can't have two Billys on the same circus," Hobbs said.

"Ain't gonna' be no two Billys, Guv'nor Isaiah," she replied. "You ain't done that Buckskin Billy rough ridin' for fifteen years. He be's a new Billy."

"Erich, I fear I've forgotten my manners," Hobbs said. "Permit me to introduce Elvira Simms Pemjean, wife of our cat trainer, Jean-Francois, Le Démon Debonnair."

"Frau Pemjean," the boy said, bowing courteously.

"Aww, hell, Billy, call me Elvira," the woman said. "C'mon over here, honeychile, and let this Nigger lady give you some lovin'."

Embarrassed, he came obediently to the woman. Elvira wrapped her arms around him and hugged him to her breast, slowly rocking him back and forth in front of everyone. Hobbs could see tears well up in the boy's eyes, but he said nothing. After awhile, Elvira released young Rosenthal. "Y'all don't know what those menfolk were fussin' about, do ya'?"

"No, Frau Elvira," he said.

"There's an old circus tradition been around for more than anyone remembers. If'n a bull comes up to you and salutes you – shakin' her trunk up and down and purrin' – that means y'all is gonna' be a big, important man in the circus and one day y'all's gonna' own your own show. And old Elvira knows one more thing – y'all's gonna' be one of the most famous *cowboys* that ever lived. I don't know how y'all got here, Billy, but you sure done come to the right place at the right time."

"And if there was any question about you joining out, Peggy sure done answered it," Zeke said.

"Well, Erich Otto Rudolf Rosenthal, or Billy, or whatever else you want to call yourself," Hobbs said, "looks like you've got a new home. Welcome to *Zoltan's Great American*!"

2

"I first met Alisa thirty years ago when she was thirteen and an abused house slave," Hobbs told Erich. "Even though slavery had been outlawed and the War Between the States had been over for more than a month, her mistress would have none of it. And she never let her slaves believe they were anything *but* slaves. Zoltan had to convince the girls' mother that we weren't stealing her family when we told mama and her twin girls, Alisa and Elvira, to meet us at the far side of the mistress's property and not return to the house. Even though Alisa and Elvira look alike, Alisa's as different from her sister as night is from day."

"*Auch eine schwartze?*" the boy asked.

"*Mulattin,*" Hobbs responded equably. "A lovely, brilliant human being who's made more of herself, given her beginnings, than anyone I've ever met."

"You are not married?"

"No, we chose to be together without benefit of clergy because Alisa's sensitive enough to put my feelings first.

"Another woman?"

19

"Yes. A long time ago. She was twenty-three when …" Hobbs coughed roughly, and Erich knew enough not to pursue the subject. Hobbs continued, "You'll be staying in our wagon until we can find you more suitable sleeping quarters."

~ ∫ ~

Sunday morning breakfast on the tober was a tradition Isaiah had begun shortly after he'd assumed the stewardship of the circus. Promptly at nine o'clock, the entire troupe, from the Governor down to the lowest-ranking roustabout, met in the center of the midway for a few moments thanking God, or whoever, for the week past. Then, as one, they toasted the memory of Zoltan, the man who'd started the circus half a century before. The cooks served up a buffet that would easily have fed twice the number of circus stalwarts. Hobbs insisted it be what he remembered as an *American* breakfast: fried, scrambled, boiled and poached eggs; ham, endless rashers of fatback and a kettle full of sausage; loaves of freshly-baked, still warm bread, served with mounds of butter and strawberry or raspberry jam; hotcakes with maple syrup; fried potatoes mixed with onions, red and green peppers; every kind of in-season fruit that could be imagined; orange juice, milk, buttermilk, sparkling wine; and gallons and gallons of steaming hot, strong coffee.

After breakfast, the performers would take whatever was left over to orphanages or children's hospitals in the *stadt, dorf,* or *burg* where they happened to be playing that day. While there, they'd put on a free performance for the wide-eyed children that some of those poor urchins would remember for the rest of their lives. By two o'clock, they'd be back on the *tober,* dressed and ready for the afternoon show.

"You called Elvira 'Cinderella,' Herr Hobbs," Erich said. "Is that because she is bound to the wheelchair and you want to lift her spirits?"

"Not at all, Erich. Elvira Simms was one of the most beautiful and athletic aerialistes on any circus – she could have done a star turn with any of them – Knie, Renz, even the Orfei would have been glad to have her. While she constantly entertained the *jossers* as a *comic aerialiste,* she was truly a *performer's* performer."

"A *performer's* performer?"

"Yes. Anybody can work up an *audience* trick in a couple of days. To work up a *performer's* trick may take a couple of *years.* It's the difference between the showy and the artistic. One's like a minstrel show, the other's like a ballet or a symphony. An ordinary audience will go wild over something that *looks* difficult or dangerous. But only other performers and a few very discerning spectators will appreciate a trick that *is* difficult but *looks* easy, because it is done with skill and grace."

"But she is *verkrüppelt.*"

"A great tragedy, but one that is, unfortunately, not uncommon in our circus world. It happened back in eighteen and seventy-one. The Communards and the forces of the French Republic were fighting for the control of Paris. Cinderella was in the very middle of one of her most spectacular tricks when a huge cannon fired within half a mile of the tober. Thank God, she never felt anything after she fell. She was only eighteen at the time."

"*Gott im himmel,* a *schande!*" the boy gasped. "Her life and her circus career ended when she was only five years older than me!"

"Might have," Hobbs replied, sardonically, "but circus folks are family – we're really all we have in the world – and we fight harder than most to keep it together when one of our members has a misfortune. Within a year of her accident, we'd built a contraption that holds Elvira so secure that she still rides dressage in the ring and looks as though she's fully in control. She even wore her spangled Cinderella léotard until a couple of years ago, when she got a bit hefty for that. And when God saw how that girl fought back, He gave her a very great gift, too."

"What's that?"

The older man lit an Italian *sigaretta* and took a deep, satisfying drag before he continued. "Many years ago, when I first joined up, there was a very, very old Spanish gypsy on the show. She must have been close to ninety. Zoltan told me she'd been on the first show *he* joined, when he was little more than your age. She had the power to look into the past and predict the future. Whether it was a *schwindel* – a humbug – I never found out, but it turned out to be accurate too many times to be a fake. After Elvira's accident, the *mulattin* seemed to have acquired that old gypsy's power – like when she said things yesterday she couldn't possibly have known about you. Especially about you becoming a famous cowboy. I wouldn't take that part to heart, unless you're planning to move to Texas," he said, chuckling. "Regardless of what you might have heard, that's a place I would not recommend."

"You've been there, Herr Hobbs?" the boy asked eagerly.

"That I have. South Texas, anyway, when we crossed the border into Mexico. Flat as a wooden box, dry as a wooden box, and you can grow just about as much grass on it as you can on a wooden box. Got a big river, the Rio Grande, that divides the U.S. of A. from Mexico and more longhorn cattle than you'd ever believe, but aside from that, there's not much there."

"I can vouch for that, son." Zeke Willis had come up behind them, his arms laden with a huge kettle of food which he loaded onto a nearby wagon. "In summer it's hotter than a – " A sharp glance from Isaiah instantly caused the big man to switch from what he was going to say to the much tamer "than the Sahara Desert. Bugs and mosquitoes. Let me tell you, in all my born days I ain't never got stung so much or itched in so many places."

"Have either of you ever heard of Buffalo Bill?" the boy asked.

"Cody? Who hasn't?" Hobbs replied. "Outside of Phineas T. Barnum, who died a few years back, he's probably the best known showman in the world."

"My father took me to see his show once," the boy said dreamily. "Sitting Bull, Annie Oakley, General Custer's Last Stand..." Each time he mentioned a name, Erich pointed his right index finger at his palm, highlighting the memory. "That's the real reason why I came to you first – because yours is an *American* circus."

"Come into my office for a few minutes," Isaiah said. "I have something that might interest you."

They walked the hundred feet to Hobbs's office wagon. Once inside, Hobbs pulled up the cover of his roll-top desk and handed the boy a large poster. Erich's eyes widened until they seemed to be bulging nearly out of their sockets. The poster read, *Buffalo Bill's Wild West and Congress of Rough Riders of the World.* At the bottom, in strong, easily legible handwriting, the boy read, "To Isaiah Hobbs. Any time you're ready to join forces, so am I. W. F. Cody."

"*Mein Gott,* Herr Hobbs," Rosenthal said. "You ... you *know* him ... and he wrote this to *you* ..."

"Yes, Erich, and now I'm giving it to you. It's an old circus tradition to give a really promising First of May something more meaningful than a handshake."

"But, but Herr Hobbs, I can't accept this. It is the most valuable gift anyone has ever given me," he mumbled, dumbfounded.

"Take it as a favor to me. Who knows? One day you might give me an equally valuable gift."

"What could I possibly give you that would come close?"

"Well, Son, that's something we both might want to think about."

Later that morning, when the Governor was preparing for the afternoon show, Erich went to the wagon where he'd slept the night before. His hands trembled as he sat on the bed and unrolled what to him was a sacred relic. Once again, he read Buffalo Bill's encomium to his employer.

~ʃ~

On the way back to the wagon he shared with Alisa, Isaiah walked to the edge of the stand. He gazed at the crescent moon, which hung low in the western sky. In the few solitary moments he had to himself, he thought about the life that had been somehow miraculously thrust upon him the day after the Confederate American States collapsed and he, a Lieutenant Colonel in the Army of the South, had suddenly been left without a career.

The circus is the oldest art there is — performing. We strike light across the air, but like light on air, we leave no mark, no trace, no history. Poets leave thoughts, artists leave visions, even warriors leave deeds. We do nothing but entertain, and we don't pretend to do anything more significant. We come into humdrum communities where pinched little people lead commonplace lives, and we bring them a bit of novelty, a touch of the exotic. For the space of a day perhaps, we give these people a look at gloss and gossamer, danger and daring, a laugh and a thrill they may never have had before. And then, like a dream or a fairy tale, we are gone and forgotten. Others may want to be remembered. We only want to be enjoyed.

3

"Are you sure it doesn't bother you that I'm here, Herr Pemjean?"

"Mais non, certainment, jeun ami," Le Démon Debonnair responded. "We cherish every young person who wants a future with *le cirque.* One of the first things you must do is to find out what rôles interest you," the animal trainer said.

Jean-François Pemjean had already been in the pista, practicing with the circus' two lions, for half an hour. Unlike the red-devil costume he wore on the show, he was wearing street clothes. Outside the cage, he held the trident and the whip which he brought into the arena when he was performing.

"How close may I come, Herr Démon?"

"Three meters from the cage should be fine. Please remain as still and quiet as possible. I would prefer *les chats* do not lose their concentration so *I* may keep my head in one piece on my shoulders." He laughed jovially, but Erich took the request with utmost seriousness.

The two lions prowling around the cage, *Leo* a huge male, and *Juno,* a slightly smaller lioness, were both in their prime. When they showed their massive teeth and occasionally growled or snarled, goosebumps ran down the boy's spine.

Pemjean entered the cage firmly but casually. "*Gut morgen, Kätzchen,*" he greeted them. The female nodded and the male yawned. Pemjean snapped the whip with a loud *crr-ack*, which came nowhere near the animals. They started trotting around the cage. Pemjean made sure he was always facing them.

"*Platz!*" he said, loud enough for the cats and the boy to hear him, but by no means shouting. As if on cue, each of the beasts lay down. "*Mach todt.*" One of the two lions rolled over on its left side, the other rolled over on its right. They closed their eyes, playing dead.

"*Schön Machen,*" Pemjean commanded. The king and queen of the beasts sat up dutifully on their haunches and lifted their forepaws.

Pemjean cracked the whip and the two lions started trotting around the cage again. After they had made three circuits, Le Démon Debonnair held his trident out at the height of his waist. The cats slowed to a walk, the male on one side of the trident, the female on the other side of the rod, each about ten feet away from it.

"*Leo, Hoch!*" Pemjean said in a quiet, but commanding, tone. Leo reared back slightly and jumped cleanly over the trainer's trident, coming to within three feet of where Juno stood, then walking around behind her. "*Juno, Hoch!*" The lioness jumped over the trident from the other direction. Pemjean repeated his commands twice more, with the same result, then held out his whip at a level between his waist and his shoulder.

"*Hoch, Kätzchen!*" In a spectacular display, the two cats jumped over the whip together as though they were a matched pair of horses. Then Juno walked back to the opposite side of the whip. "*Einmal, Hoch-HOCH, Kätzchen!*" This time, the two lions did the seemingly impossible. Without pause, they leaped over the whip simultaneously, the male on the left, the female on the right, but going in opposite directions.

"*Sehr gut! Platz, kätzchen.*" Both lions returned to a prone position and Pemjean exited the cage. Neither the lions nor the trainer was even breathing hard.

"Herr Pemjean," Erich said, "that was truly amazing. You are a Frenchman, are you not?"

"*Mais oui,* but of course."

"Yet you spoke to the lions in German."

"No matter where in the world you are, German is the language of circus animal training, mainly because that language seems to have been *made* for command. Animals are regularly traded. Animal trainers grow old or die or they get traded, too. This way, any cat in the world on any circus in the world understands what it supposed to do. A Russian trainer once told me it would take at least two Russian words to give a big cat a command that could be given in German with one – and might have to be given in a hurry. A syllable's fraction of a second can mean life or death when you're working with lions or tigers."

"How do you manage to tame a huge lion when you, yourself, must weight far less than half of what that animal weighs?"

"An excellent question, boy. But first let me correct something you said. There is *taming* and there is *training*. In Europe, we always prefer *training*."

"How do you train a cat to do tricks?"

"A cat never learns a *trick*." Pemjean explained. "A cat learns a *habit*. Two things make this possible: One is that a man has *patience*. Second, a cat is *greedy*. So you use *your* patience and *his* greed to develop a habit. You must be absolutely consistent. The cat must do *exactly* as you want him to do. It may seem hard for you to believe, Erich, but all cats are playful."

"They are?"

"Yes. I visited Natal Province in South Africa a few years ago. Some *Setswana* guides allowed me to go with them when they followed three lionesses on a twilight hunt. Don't look shocked, *ami*, we all had guns and the lions had long ago learned that human beings were neither their natural predators nor their natural prey. We were not important to their lives."

"Lionesses? Females?"

At that moment, as if emphasizing the point, Juno gave a loud roar.

"Yes, Erich. It's almost always the females who do the hunting. Even then, as large and swift as they are, they only catch their prey once in every five attempts. We watched from behind a bunker. In the midst of their prowling through the trees, these three beautiful lionesses rolled and slapped and played with one another just as you might play with a kitty cat. An experienced lion trainer uses that knowledge. We watch and see what a big cat likes to do naturally, then we encourage the animal to exaggerate that. Finally, with luck, we convince the cat to make a habit of it."

While he had been talking to the boy five handlers had wheeled in three smaller cages. The first cage was empty. They opened the doors to that cage and moved it close to the door of the large performance cage. While the lions were still lying on the ground opposite the door to the large enclosure, the handlers opened that door so that the entryways to each cage immediately adjoined one another.

"*Heimwärts,*" Pemjean called out, while the handlers held out two pitchforks, each bearing a small piece of lean, raw meat. They pitched the meat into the holding cage. Leo and Juno raised themselves up and trotted into the smaller enclosure. As the handlers shut the door behind the lions, other roustabouts moved each of the next two cages into place. Three Bengal tigers entered the arena.

Pemjean entered and put the tigers through their paces. They, too, seemed quite familiar with their trainer. Every so often one or another of them would make a *chuff-chuff* sound, neither a growl nor a roar. Pemjean held out hoops that were on fire and commanded the tigers to jump through them.

To the boy's surprise, all three tigers, in turn, jumped cleanly through the hoops, not the least bit afraid of setting themselves afire. After the performance of several other tricks – no, *habits,* the boy corrected himself – Pemjean once again left the cage. This time, Erich applauded loud and long.

"How … how did you get them to jump through the fire?"

"They didn't."

"But I saw with my own eyes …"

"You *thought* you saw them jump through fire." Pemjean walked calmly into the large cage, took the hoop he'd been using, and came back to where Erich stood. "All cats love to jump – kitty cats, lions, tigers, it doesn't matter. So a trainer starts to develop the habit by holding the hoop close to the ground and having the cat jump through it. Every time he does it successfully, the cat gets a small reward, usually a piece of raw meat.

"As time goes on, the trainer raises the hoop higher and higher until it's as high as the trainer's shoulder. Then it's time to train the cat to jump through the 'flames.'" Pemjean lit the hoop and flames surrounded the top of the circle.

"There are no flames at the sides or at the bottom!" Rosenthal exclaimed.

"Correct. If there were, the animal would singe its fur and never go near the hoop again. Nor could I hold the hoop because it would burn my hand. But only the top quarter of the hoop is lit. To the cat, is makes absolutely no difference if the hoop is 'on fire' or not. He never feels the heat, since it moves upward above him, and he never sees the fire because he's concentrating on a habit he has learned over a long period of time. From however far away the cat is from the audience – and there is also a cage to alter the audience's perception – it *looks* like the entire hoop is ablaze."

The boy stood up and stretched, his muscles tense from watching the trainer work.

"You make it look as though it is not at all dangerous, but I look at these huge beasts and …"

"Don't let appearances deceive you, my young friend. When a cat goes stiff, rigid, then he is dangerous. When you are working with a cat, always remember you are looking at *five* mouths – one full of teeth and four full of talons. Never approach a cat timidly – always firmly – and never approach a cat unexpectedly, never from behind. If a cat bites you, he can let you go, but if a cat claws you, he *cannot* let go, even if he wants to. When a cat reaches to grab something, the tendons extend the talons and fix them in a hooked position. So there is no way he can do anything except rip out a good deal of flesh. Cats, like humans, can be either left-handed or right-handed. Above all, you must *never* take chances – a cat watches for every weakness and takes quick advantage. Make no sudden moves."

"But a cat is so much larger than a man, Herr Démon."

"You know that and I know that, but one of the very few advantages a man has is that a cat does not know that. You must always, *always* stand tall. If you are taller than them, cats will think you are larger and stronger than they are."

"What if, God forbid, you fall?"

"Pray that you never fall, but if you do, roll immediately onto your stomach. The big cat may – *may* – if you're lucky, reach out his paw without the talons extended, and try to turn you over, where he knows you're most vulnerable. In the few seconds he is doing that, this will give the handlers time to race into the cage and distract him, and you might survive. Another thing to remember: if a cat starts to charge you, the most tender spot on a cat is his *nose*. If he attacks you, hit him on the nose and he will usually back off. Anything more you'd like to know, young Herr?"

"Just one thing, Sir. When cats are content, they seem to purr. Can lions and tigers do that?"

"Lions cannot. Only cheetahs and cougars can purr and they cannot roar. Tigers make a rough sort of *chuff-chuff*, like you heard while I was in the cage. Well, I am going outside the pista to take a brief smoke."

As Pemjean left the tent, Erich, looking after him in awe, did not notice that a pair of eyes – the tightly squinted eyes of someone smaller than him, glared maliciously at the boy from outside the tent, furiously jealous of all the attention the newest First of May was getting.

"You may think it's all sweetness and light in the circus world, my young friend," the owner of those eyes hissed. "But you'll find out soon. Oh yes, you'll find out soon enough."

~ ∫ ~

"There are three types of clowns."

"Three, Herr Allmann? I know of two. My father was a Joey, the kind with the happy face. Then there's the Toby, the one with the sad, droopy look and painted tears."

Six clowns ran about the pista in street clothes, stepping in buckets, performing somersaults, juggling, and even climbing the slant rope. They ranged in age from no more than eighteen, to a graybeard in his mid-sixties. Yet, they moved with fluid economy, even when creeping or tiptoeing. As he watched, four clowns backing up from different sides of the pista, none seeing the others, moved toward each other. When they were less than one step from colliding, each suddenly froze in place. Then they each circled to the right for ten steps. At exactly the same moment, they started circling back to the left until they came to the precise position in which they'd been when they'd almost collided. They froze again. Then each backed another half step. They were now no more than a few inches from one another's backsides. Suddenly, they jumped in unison and each started running helter skelter toward that part of the ring from which they'd originally come.

"Clowns are much more important to a circus than merely being funny. They distract the audience while other acts are setting up. In the event of an emergency, even a tragedy, their antics mask what is happening. A clown won't hesitate to march into a lion's cage and distract the cat. Clowns have saved many a trainer's life." As he spoke, Allman, a Joey of early middle age, practiced pratfalls.

"There are six basics in the clowning art," Allman continued. "Stupidity, trickery, mimicry, falls, blows, and surprises. A clown is not a person and not an object. He is what *happens*. A good clown always pays the closest attention to what best amuses the audience, Joey ribaldry or Toby pathos, the horse laugh or the weary smile, Joey cunning or Toby helplessness, pure pantomime or a pista full of props, Joey knockabout or Toby melancholy. The clown finds his particular bent, his métier, his magic. Then he *makes fun of it*."

"You said there were *three* types of clowns, Herr Allman."

"Ah, yes, the *Whiteface*. Comparing a *Whiteface* to a mere clown is like trying to compare Leonardo da Vinci to a child trying to draw for the first time. A *Whiteface* is the most ancient, most esteemed, traditional, and ever-changeless character in a European circus. No matter what circus or where in the world it is playing, a *Whiteface* is the most respected and usually the best paid performer on the show. They are so rare and in such demand it takes a circus several years to find one genuine Whiteface with classical training. *Zoltan's American Circus* is fortunate. We have *Fünfünf*. He's been teaching me the ancient art for the past three years. You are in luck, young Rosenthal. Here he comes now."

Fünfünf – literally "five-by-five" – entered the pista. Unlike the other clowns, he was fully costumed. He was a short, broad apparition of no apparent sex, who wore a one-piece loose costume of bright red satin, lavishly adorned with silver sequins. It had tight, wrist-length sleeves that rose in high peaks at the shoulders. From these peaks, the costume hung as straight and waistless as a smock, until it forked into a pair of short, broad pants that ended just above the Whiteface's bare knees. The costume made Fünfünf's torso look almost perfectly square. Below it, he wore slippers and calf-high stockings, both snow white. Likewise, above his torso, the clown's entire face was white with greasepaint. His eyebrows and eyelashes were blacked. His mouth and both his ears were painted bright red. He wore a brimless, conical white hat which, blending into his forehead, made him rather resemble a bald pinhead, except that the cap was jauntily tilted just a bit to one side. The white, black, and red makeup was both droll and demonic.

Throughout his act, when his face was not comically-evilly impassive, it showed only two expressions: his eyebrows were raised in disdainful hauteur or his red mouth grinned sardonically wide.

Erich trembled involuntarily as the *Whiteface* performed. His bizarre makeup and dress was imbued with the tyrannical authority of antiquity. The boy could not help but laugh at the *Whiteface's* antics, but he felt an urgent need to run – to the nearest bathroom, to the safety of Hobbs' wagon, to a place where he could be sick, *anywhere*. The seriocomic figure of the *Whiteface* was eerily familiar – a recognizable nightmare from childhood of that funny-frightening, grinning goblin, spook, or bogeyman which he'd never really encountered, but who was always lurking – just under the bed, just outside the window on a cold, snowy night, just outside the door, or just inside the closet: the view of what Satan would *really* look like, the one who would come to "get you if you don't behave."

As suddenly as it had started, the act was over. Erich let go of his breath, feeling relief as the tension drained out and the *Whiteface* exited the tent. Not long afterward, a man so old he must have been there at the beginning of time shuffled into the tent. He was as short and as broad as the *Whiteface*, but he was not fearsome at all.

"Erich, I'd like you to meet my mentor, my teacher, and my idol, Herr Jörg Pfeiffer. Last year, he received the highest civilian award that could be bestowed by Kaiser-König Franz Josef, the *Goldener Hahn*."

"I am pleased to meet you, young Herr," the old man said, his voice as crepacious as his skin. His handshake was remarkably firm. "I am told you are Süssmilch's son.

"You know him, Herr Pfeiffer?"

"I know *of* him," Pfeiffer said diplomatically, venturing no more information. "I understand he left the circus to become part of the café circuit."

"Herr Pfeiffer will be *eighty-nine* on his next birthday," Allman said reverently.

"I am not eighty-eight. I am four times twenty-two," Pfeiffer rejoined.

"How long have you been on the circus, Herr Pfeiffer?" the boy asked.

The old man started counting on his fingers while squinting his left eye and looking up at the ceiling." I came on the Donnert when I was fifteen," he said, his mind going back "It's now eighteen ninety-eight…"

"Eighteen twenty-five," the boy said wonderingly. "Seventy-three years. Herr Pfeiffer, you must have been performing at the beginning of the world!"

"Not quite, but certainly a goodly while, young man."

"Were you always a *Whiteface*?"

"No, I started out as a roustabout – helping to put up and take down the *pista*, shoveling truckloads of elephant, lion, camel, and horse *scheiss*. From there, I graduated to slant rope walk, then to trapeze aerialist – old style. I was forty when I fell off the trapeze. I lost my timing and, more important, my nerve. That was the year before Franz Josef became Emperor of Austria-Hungary. By that time, I had been on the circus for twenty-three years and I didn't know any other life."

His eyes clouded over and Erich could see the old man was wandering back through time. "I was on the Krone and they had a *Whiteface* – Gregor Petrovic, a Czech. By then, he was in his mid-seventies and plagued by arthritis, but he was always a good, kind, and happy man. Gregor saved my circus career – he taught me to be a *Whiteface*, so that, in the end, I became a greater performer than before."

"When did you join the *Great American*?" Erich asked.

"Eighteen and sixty-seven. Back when it was Zoltan's show. No matter what they call it today, it's still *Zoltan's* show. When I joined on, it was still a small circus. Zoltan told me I was the costliest artiste he'd ever hired. He paid me less than half of what I normally made, but I saw a lot of promise and it's been my home for the past thirty-one years. Another circus would have retired me years ago, but Isaiah Hobbs, who took over for Zoltan, is one of the finest human beings I've ever met. Of course, even though I'm still a young man in my own eyes, I feel my own goblin starting to peer out from under the bed."

"Does the specter of death frighten you, Herr Fünfünf?" Allman asked.

"No, it does not. I'm proud I've been able to pass on the tradition to you. You're just about ready to make your own entrance as a *Whiteface*. Turning to Erich, the old man said, "It's a glorious day, young Erich Rosenthal. I wish you the happiness I've had in my own career, may it be as long." Pfeiffer shook the boy's hand and, smiling, turned to leave the tent.

As he did so, he suddenly slipped on a bucket so small it could not be distinguished from the wooden railing a couple feet away. The old man didn't seem surprised by the unexpected motion, and seemed to sag rather than fall straightaway to the ground. Everyone was startled when his head hit the railing with a muffled *crr-ack*.

Erich screamed and tried to help the old man sit up, but it was of no effect. Pfeiffer breathed no more. Within moments, Isaiah Hobbs, was at Erich's side, holding him in his arms and trying to comfort him.

"I should have seen it," the boy mumbled. "I could have moved faster. He … he would still be alive."

"I very much doubt that, Son. Jörg Pfeiffer was the oldest living man I ever met. I'll wager an autopsy would show he was dead before he even fell to the ground."

"But we don't know that."

"No, and we never will. None of us ever knows when the last moment comes. It's one of the mysteries God doesn't reveal to us."

"You believe in God, Herr Isaiah?" The boy looked up, wiping his red eyes with a swipe of his elbow.

"Let's just say I believe in *something* higher than we are. Although truthfully, after … after someone who meant more than the world to me became ill and died, I didn't believe in *anything* for years."

"If you don't mind, Herr Isaiah, I really don't feel like watching the circus this afternoon. I think I'd like to be alone in the wagon, if that's all right with you."

"I understand, Erich. Do you read?"

"I can read."

"That's the right answer to a different question. I didn't ask if you *can* read. I assumed that. I asked if you *do* read – for pleasure."

"I have never done so. There were never many books around any of the places where I lived."

"If you have a book to read, you are never without a friend. This would be a good time for you to start having a friend." Isaiah Hobbs reached into a rucksack and withdrew a well-thumbed book. He held it up so the boy could see it.

"*Winnetou, The Apache Knight,*" Rosenthal read the title out loud. "By Karl May."

"Cowboy stuff," Hobbs said. "This would be a great 'friend' to start you off."

4

Four days later, the circus had broken down the tents and loaded them and the rest of the circus equipment into a series of heavy wagons. As always, there was the excitement of the next stand, the next hill over the horizon. Their destination was Potsdam, seat of the Prussian kings and reputedly the most well cared-for city in Brandenburg Province.

Alisa and Erich rode atop the wagon they shared. Isaiah rode a white horse at the head of the wagon train. During the day, he frequently rode back and forth to make sure everyone on the circus was not overburdened.

"If we're playing in winter, we charter a train to go from one tober to the next, but during the spring and summer, Isaiah likes to travel the way circuses have traveled since ancient days in Rome," she continued.

"You and the Herr Hobbs never married, Fräulein Alisa?"

Looking a trifle sad, she said, "Not that I wouldn't have done it in a heartbeat."

"I've heard him talk about another woman, but he never mentions her name. Does it hurt you if I ask about her?"

"Only distantly. She was truly such an angel that I could never speak badly of her, any more than I could hope to take her place in

Isaiah's heart," Alisa said, donning a bonnet to keep the sun's heat off her head. "Have you given any thought to what you want to do in the circus, Erich?"

"Are you trying to change the subject because you don't want to talk about the lady?" he asked seriously.

"No, Erich. She died more than thirty years ago. She was the best aerialiste I ever knew, and when I first met her, she was the most stunningly beautiful woman I'd ever seen. It all started when she lost her balance on the high wire for a split second one day. The old gypsy woman had predicted that Autumn – that was her name – would cause no dissension, only heartbreak, and she was right."

"What happened?"

"She contracted a rare nerve disease that was known to only a very few doctors. They were powerless against it. Beautiful young people like Autumn suddenly turned very old and grotesquely ugly." Isaiah told me the first doctor they saw told Autumn she would live for only a very short time. So for the next two months, she and Isaiah lived as though every day would be her last. The old gypsy told us, '*Not everything beautiful has to be pretty.*' During that time, even though she was no longer capable of doing any work on the show, Autumn spent days teaching me just about everything I know today. When they got to Vienna, Isaiah couldn't wait to take her to a man reputed to be one of the two or three experts in the world when it came to that disease.

"The great doctor had no appointment open for three weeks, but somehow Zoltan got them in within a week. The doctor was very kind but very direct. He told them Autumn would live for many years, to a normal old age, but that she would never be *normal*. The changes to her face and body would become worse. Occasionally, when things got too painful, they could surgically cut some of the more pronounced growths – sort of like pruning a tree.

"I remember that Isaiah looked as though he'd gotten a reprieve from a death sentence, but Autumn seemed to be in another world altogether. She shot herself in the head that night – a single shot with a small nine millimeter pistol."

"And he never took up with anyone after that?" Erich asked.

There was now much more traffic on the macadamized road than there had been earlier, and Erich could spot some of Potsdam's taller buildings as they came within a few miles of that city.

"There was one woman – he wasn't in love with her, and none of us ever begrudged him, particularly when we saw her. She was taller and her hair was more a bronze color than Autumn's, but otherwise she could have been Autumn's twin sister. If I mentioned her real name, it might shock you. But enough of the past," Alisa said brightly. "Isaiah told me he wanted you to see everything that went on so you could decide for yourself what you want to do. Where would you like to start?"

"I had no idea until I read the *Winnetou* book, Herr Hobbs loaned me. Now ..."

"Karl May?"

"Yes. Fräulein Alisa, you're from America, are you not?"

She clucked her tongue and the horse picked up its pace.

"I am, Erich, but not from *that* part of America."

"Did they have cowboys where you lived?"

"No, they had *slaves* where I lived. That's the way I started out."

"Oh," he said, obviously disappointed.

"But Isaiah got me started reading Karl May books, too. I've read ten of them."

"Are there more?"

"Several."

"I think I'd like to be a cowboy someday. I could ride horses and shoot six guns and save people, and ... and..."

"Oh, Erich, it's not at all like the Karl May books. Isaiah told me being a real cowboy is mostly drudgery – mending fences, checking barbed wire, breathing in the dust and the stink of dry, flat land – . Have you ever thought of becoming a *circus* cowboy like Buffalo Bill Cody?"

"You mean he wasn't a real cowboy?"

"As far as I can tell, he never herded cattle."

Isaiah Hobbs had ridden quietly up to them and been listening to their conversation. "You actually could become a 'circus cowboy,'" he said "You could bring Karl May's books to life for a lot bigger audience than if you stayed out on the plains for months at a time."

"The Governor is being modest," Alisa said. "If you really want to be a circus cowboy, he could teach you skills most 'real' cowboys have never learned."

"Could you, Herr Hobbs?"

"Might," Hobbs drawled. "So you really enjoyed *Winnetou The Apache Knight*?"

"More than any book I've ever read."

"I'll trade you the one you've read for another," he said, winking at Alisa. "Once you get started reading, it doesn't matter *what* you read. It only matters *that* you read. We'll start your training as soon as we set up."

5

"Herr Rosenthal?"

"I don't believe we've met." Erich looked down at a man no taller than a meter in height.

"We haven't. I am Pedro Hernandes Ortega y Alcantar," he said, bowing formally. "Professionally known as Major Maximus. You've no doubt heard of me?"

"I'm sorry, Major, but I have not."

"No matter. I was the most famous performer on this circus before I left for a short break."

Except for a pencil-thin moustache, the dwarf's face was clean-shaven and, Erich noticed with mild disgust, powdered. He wore an Austrian *lederhosen* outfit, which made him look like a parody of a young boy.

"Are you coming back on the show?" Erich asked politely.

"When I have completed working up my new act," Maximus said. "Not before. I trust Isaiah Boggs is still the Governor."

"Hobbs," Erich corrected.

"Ah, yes. It has been some months. I fear my memory is not what it once was. Would you perhaps like a cigarette, Herr Rosenthal?" Maximus asked.

"I think not, thank you," the boy replied coolly.

"You find it strange that I would offer a cigarette to an upstanding young man of, what, sixteen?"

"Thirteen."

The dwarf slapped his right hand against his cheek. "Really? You seem so mature, I would never have thought you were so young. I apologize for my lack of manners."

Billy puffed up proudly. Perhaps he had misjudged the little fellow, who was obviously a gregarious sort.

"Would you permit me to make it up to you?"

"I see no need, Major."

"Please. Allow me to escort you through the streets of Potsdam," he said, taking Erich firmly by the upper arm.

"I really must be heading back to the tober," Billy said, somewhat uncomfortable at the way the *zwerg* seemed to be taking control.

"Nonsense," the dwarf rejoined. Then he said, in a confidential tone, "Have you ever seen a man and a woman …?"

When he described what he was talking about in more vivid detail, Erich felt repulsion, recalling the time he'd seen his father. Now, however, that revulsion mingled with the voyeuristic thrill of forbidden fruit.

"I'll show you what I mean when we're in the middle of the *stadtpark*." When they arrived at a remote section of the park, Maximus reached into a pack he was carrying and extracted a soft-cover book wrapped in brown butcher paper. He handed the book to Erich.

When Rosenthal opened the book, he is face turned crimson. There were smudgy photographs and erotic drawings which left nothing to the imagination. Although the people in the photographs were, for the most part, unattractive, there was one beautiful young woman whose body itself was a sensual invitation.

"You may tear out that picture and keep it," Maximus said. "I'm sure you'll discover hidden delights just thinking about what she'd be like."

"I ... I can't," Erich stammered.

"You can't think of what it would be like?"

"No, no, I could never take such a thing back with me. I live in the same wagon with Herr Hobbs."

"And that hot-blooded *mulattin*?" the dwarf said, leering.

"I never thought of Alisa Simms that way," Erich said stiffly.

"Perhaps not, but she's a handsome woman. I'm sure you can imagine what the Governor does with her when you're not around."

"Major Maximus, how *dare* you?"

"How dare I what, Herr Rosenthal?" the midget said innocently. "I think as men you and I need not mince words. Are you telling me you weren't excited by that photograph?"

"Well ..."

"I have many others. Keep that one as a souvenir. Perhaps we may meet again." With that, the dwarf clicked his heels, bowed, and took his leave.

~ ʃ ~

Erich's initial embarrassment gave way to fascination. As one week gave way to another, the midget turned up in various unplanned places, each time luring Erich into more adventurous pursuits. Erich began to spend time away from the circus on various pretexts.

During those times, Maximus handed the boy ever more provocative photographs of different women, some of them young girls, not much older than Erich, with small, pubescent breasts and only the slightest escutcheon of pubic hair. One day, Maximus suggested that they go to a party at a private club in one of Potsdam's more disreputable districts. Erich, reckless with anticipation and lustful feelings, agreed.

The "club" was a small basement apartment. When Erich entered, he noticed six people, four men and two women, seated at a table. The men were plying the women with absynthe, and the women giggled a lot, as if they were enjoying a wicked and forbidden game. One of the men stood up and nodded at the dwarf.

"Ah, Major Maximus, you're just in time. Did you bring the, umm, medication?"

"I did," he said, handing a vial of powder to the host.

"Good, good," the man said, rubbing his hands together. "Girls," he said, turning to the two women, who looked to be in their early twenties, "our friend the Major has brought fun powder so our party can begin."

During the next half hour, Erich watched, fascinated, as two of the men and the two women retreated into an adjoining room, where there were two double beds. The couples quickly disrobed. Erich felt his member stiffen with excitement as he viewed the women engaging in what had only been suggested by the photographs Maximus had given him. From behind him, he heard harsh breathing and guttural noises. Turning, he saw that the dwarf had covered the bottom half of himself with a towel and was doing things to himself under the towel.

Erich's conscience told him he should leave immediately, but another part of his mind refused to budge. In the end, he remained until the "party" wound its way down to an exhausted end. On the way back to the tober, he refused to speak to or even look at Maximus.

~ ∫ ~

Erich, who had never sat astride a horse in his life, learned the rudiments of riding under Elvira Simms' supervision. He was an eager, adept pupil. His initial reticence quickly gave way to a determination to learn this new discipline as quickly and thoroughly as he could. Although Elvira knew his name as well as anyone on the circus, she continued to call him Billy. He didn't try to correct her.

"The reason the Governor started you workin' with me isn't because I'm a cripple, but, like you, I'd never sat a horse in my life until I joined on the circus. How's the saddle feel?"

"Hard and it's rubbing my thighs."

"It's gonna' hurt for the first few days until you get used to it. Colonel Isaiah wants you to learn to ride on a Western saddle. Now somethin' beginners always do and they shouldn't. You're doin' it now."

"What's that?"

"You're holdin' on to the horn, that big knob right in front of you."

"But that makes me feel much safer."

"Yeah, and it tells the horse you be afraid of him. That ain't never the message you want to give. That horse, he's nothin' but a big, stupid animal on top of four skinny legs. He's gotta' know who's boss and you gotta' let him know who's boss – and the boss has gotta' be *you* 'cause you be's smart and he be's dumb. Real cowboys, they hold onto the reins, not the horn."

"Then why have the horn in the first place?"

Isaiah Hobbs, who'd been watching the training session, spoke up. "The horn serves a very useful purpose. Cattle are a damned sight bigger and heavier than you. If you lasso one of them and all you've got to work with are your bare hands, you're going to get pulled off that horse mighty quick, and *you* might be the one who gets branded. But if, after you rope the animal, you wrap the lariat around the horn of the saddle, you've got the entire weight of the horse to push against that of the steer."

"Like a brake?"

"Exactly. Many circus riders prefer the English saddle, but if you're going to be a circus cowboy, you have to *look* the part. That's why I want you to train on the Western saddle."

After the first week, Erich, who'd been riding one of the oldest and gentlest rosinbacks on the show, had gotten over most of his saddle sores and was eager to advance to the next stage. Hobbs wisely held the boy back, but graduated him to one of the show stock, a dapple grey gelding.

The circus had been granted a privileged tober on a flat bluff in Babelsberg Park, from which even a casual observer could spot the outskirts of Berlin, eighteen miles away. The setup was ideal. Because of the long stand which the *Great American* had scheduled in Potsdam, a *würstelprater* – a midway strewn from one end to the other with foodstalls, drink stalls, slum and swazzle sellers, *schuplattler* dancing girls in dirndls, games of chance, patent medicine peddlers, entertainments of a less moral sort, and other entresorts – sprang up within three days of raising the circus' main tent.

Erich rose early each morning, when the summer sun had just crested the horizon, saddled his dapple grey, and walked the horse around the ring. He learned that every circus ring in the world was exactly forty-two feet in diameter, ever since the Englishman Ashley had started the first modern circus and decided on that diameter.

"It has to be standard everywhere," Alisa told him. "Otherwise, the horses and other animals couldn't be traded about and perform in one circus after another."

"There would be ungodly confusion if all rings weren't the same size," Hobbs added. "Not just for the animals, but for the performers as well. A rider's horse at performing pace takes exactly twenty-two steps to go once around the ring. The horse knows that. So does the artiste, and so do the musicians. The horse and the rider know just where each of them is during each trick – every step of the horse, every movement of the rider – and the band music can keep perfect tempo, too."

Erich was now reading Karl May adventure novels at the rate one a week. Between waking up at dawn, his hard physical and mental work, helping the roustabouts set up each day, watering the elephants, and collecting tickets at the door during performances, he still found time to read each night.

Hobbs had started paying Erich – not well, but more than enough for his needs. For the first time in his life Erich Rosenthal had extra money to spend during his time off.

~ ∫ ~

"I think it's time for your next lesson," Maximus suggested to Erich one day, a week later."

"What do you mean?"

"You've been *watching* long enough. I think it's time you learned by *doing*."

The boy said nothing as they continued walking downtown.

"Do you know what I'm talking about?"

"You mean one of those women at the club?"

"No, no. I have a friend who lives in the eastern district, a married woman, but very compliant. For not very much money …"

"I've heard of such women," Billy remarked.

"You're thinking of a common whore, my friend," Maximus said. "Charlotte's not that kind at all. She just appreciates a small present now and then."

The woman lived in a much classier flat than the one in which the club was housed. She was barely on the wrong side of thirty, plump, but not obese, and seemed eager to meet Erich. After a few preliminary words, Maximus left the two of them, "So you can get to know each other better."

No sooner had Maximus departed, Charlotte said, "Erich, you seem rather ill-at-ease. Would you like a glass of wine to relax you a bit?"

"I think I would enjoy that very much, Frau …?"

"Charlotte would be fine." She went into the kitchen, and brought back a decanter and two wine glasses. She poured one for each of them, sat on the large sofa, and invited Erich to do the same.

As they spoke about small things – the weather, the growth that was going on in the city as Potsdam reached ever closer to the Prussian capital – Erich felt the room growing quite warm. The woman reached over and started softly massaging his shoulders. Far from relaxing him, Erich's growing excitement was obvious. Charlotte smiled lasciviously.

"I'll bet you'd like to see me in something a little more revealing," she said suggestively.

The boy, tongue-tied, said nothing but nodded dumbly.

"You stay right here, you naughty young lion. I'll be back in a few moments."

"Your … your husband …?" he managed to stammer.

"Don't worry. Heinz is away in München all week, leaving poor little me all alone." She sighed. "He's leaves me so often …"

Moments later, Charlotte emerged from the bedroom wearing a silk gown and, so far as Erich could tell, nothing else. The robe was tied loosely and Erich could see the creamy mounds of her breasts. She sat close to him on the sofa, stroking his knee. "Do you see anything you'd like to touch?" she asked, her hand moving farther up his leg.

He felt his breath catch in his throat as she loosened the gown still further, leaving nothing to the imagination. As if in a trance, he started to reach out toward the heavenly twin rises.

At that moment, Erich heard a sound coming from the front door. His look of lust turned to one of sheer horror. A man of forty stood in the doorway, accompanied by a burly fellow in a police uniform.

Charlotte screamed, quickly gathering her gown around her. "Heinz! I can explain everything!"

"No need to explain, my dear," the man said. "My eyes can see very well what is going on – as can Officer Moltke's."

"He … he burst in on me while I was napping! Thank God you're here. He would have had his way with me!"

Erich did not know what to do or say. Without thinking, he bolted through the door and out into the street. He ran down one street to its intersection with another, mindlessly trying to distance himself from the scene. He didn't know how long he'd been running, but tears were streaming down his face when he finally found himself on a familiar avenue, a mile from the circus. From there, he could see the big tent and the streamers atop the chapiteau gaily waving.

Major Maximus appeared, seemingly out of nowhere. "Calm down, Erich," he said.

"I … I …"

"You can't go back to the tober just now. They'll know exactly where to find you."

"How did you know?"

"I saw what happened. I tried to warn you, but it was too late."

"You followed me here?"

"It wasn't hard to figure out you'd eventually find your way back. I took a shorter route. You must stay with me until we can decide how best to handle this situation."

"But the Governor …?"

"Erich, think!" the dwarf said, wagging his forefinger. "This is an emergency. What would he think if the police suddenly descended on his show? Even closed it down while they investigated the morals of the performers?"

The boy started crying uncontrollably. He had not a remote thought of how to handle this horrendous situation. All he could see was the world crashing down on him, spending months, perhaps years in a jail cell, humiliated before the whole world, bringing shame to those who'd been so good to him.

"There, there," the little man comforted him. "I've dealt with this kind of thing before. There is always a way out. Do you have money?"

Erich nodded. "S…some."

"I trust you are drawing regular pay from the *zirkus*?"

"Yes."

"That will be very helpful in resolving this little problem. Come to my quarters and we'll discuss this calmly and rationally."

The dwarf's flat, which consisted of one room, seemed small and cramped, even though there was almost no furniture in it: a small cot, a cheap wooden table, and two chairs. A stone sink held a few chipped, unwashed dishes. There was a sour smell throughout the place. "Sorry it's not the Four Seasons Hotel."

During the next hour, the little man told Erich that he'd met the husband on occasion, and he seemed like a reasonable fellow. "And, of course, like every policeman everywhere, I'm sure the officer who was with him can be made to see that it might be more profitable for him to turn a blind eye and not report this to his superiors."

"Offer him a bribe?"

"I wouldn't call it that. Simply trying to convince the good officer that there are more pressing crimes to investigate. *Real* crimes."

"But I am paid very little, Colonel Maximus."

"I'm sure you could find access to a bit more money. Borrow if you have to?"

"I couldn't possibly do that. I couldn't let anyone know."

"That presents a bit of a problem, Erich. The circus brings in a great deal of money each day, does it not?"

"I wouldn't know," Erich said.

"But you could find out," the midget rejoined. "And when you did find out, I'm sure you could …?"

"Are you suggesting that I *steal* …?" Erich said angrily.

"Someone in your position can hardly complain about morality," Maximus said, a bit smugly. "Besides, you need take only small nip. Do you know where the Governor keeps his cash box?"

"In a desk drawer in his wagon," Erich mumbled, embarrassed.

"Good. A little here, a little there. Hobbs is so wealthy he wouldn't even notice."

"So I'd just need to take a little?"

"For now. The problem is that once you pay, they'll expect you to keep paying."

"No different from being in jail ..."

"But at least you're free to work and travel. Without anyone knowing what happened."

6

By the end of his third week on the show, almost no one called him Erich. It seemed everyone, including the Governor, called him Billy, the name coined by Elvira Simms. Soon, he began to think of himself as Billy. In that way, he distanced himself from that other, darker life.

One day each week, he'd absent himself for the day and go into town. No one asked where he went. During those times, he would visit Maximus's small flat, leave a tidy sum of money with the dwarf, and depart. They rarely spoke. It was as if they were conspirators in web of silence that must not be broken.

During the next fortnight, Billy became proficient at controlling his mount during the trot, the canter, the full gallop, and, on one or two occasions, an all-out run. His exuberance got the best of him, and he started shouting what be imagined to be the noises cowboys would make, high-pitched "Yeee-haaa's," made-up Indian chants, and blood-curdling war cries – at least they were blood-curdling to him.

Most often, Isaiah Hobbs rode beside him. Billy marveled at the dexterity his mentor displayed, even at his advanced age. "It's not so much a matter of physical strength or agility," the Governor told him. "It's more a habit than anything else. Next week, we'll start a new phase of your training."

~ ∫ ~

"Billy, I've got a favor to ask," Hobbs said one day.

"Anything, Governor. You know that."

"During the past several weeks we've been exceptionally busy, yet the receipts don't seem to be as much as they should be." Billy said nothing, hoping Isaiah Hobbs did not see the look of fear that momentarily clouded his face. "Everyone on the show seems to like you," Hobbs continued. "I wonder if you could keep your eyes and your ears open to see if someone – the ticket seller, a roustabout, whoever, might be dipping into the til."

"I ..."

"You don't have to say anything, Billy. I just mention it in passing."

~ ∫ ~

"He suspects, Major Maximus. I can't go on this way."

"I'm afraid you don't have much choice, Erich ... I mean Billy. I see you've taken to calling yourself that name now. Even more reason to keep your deep, dark secret a *secret*."

"But I could get caught," the boy said.

"You could," the midget said. "Either way the choices don't look good."

"But you said ...?"

"I said nothing," Maximus replied. "It was *your* decision to put yourself in that position. *I* merely listened and pointed out certain things."

"You said you'd help me." Billy's tone was desperate.

"And I did," Maximus answered. "You're not in jail, your circus has not been humiliated, and the outraged husband has not cut off your hands or your private parts."

"What can I do, Major Maximus?"

"Nothing. In for a *pfennig*, in for a *groschen* as they say."

~ ∫ ~

On his thirteenth birthday, Hobbs and Alisa handed Billy a large wrapped package. The boy opened it with trembling fingers. "*Mein Gott*," he said, "this truly says 'America' more than anything I've ever had." He feasted his eyes on the pair of Levi's jeans.

As if that were not enough, the Governor proudly pronounced his charge ready to move on to the next step: trick riding and *voltige*. "Maybe not as spectacular as some wild riding," he told the boy, "but *American* is different, and the European jossers love anything exotic."

"Voltige riding, Herr Hobbs?"

"A French word for mounted gymnastics. In voltige, you vault off the horse's back and run alongside it, holding onto a handgrip attached to the harness. Or you might turn cartwheels and somersaults, then spring back up to assume a rear-facing position, before you scissor around to the front."

"There are different kinds of voltige," Alisa added. "'Voltige à la Richard,' where the horse is unbridled and unsaddled, 'Voltige a la cowboy,' where you use a lariat. The most violent kind of voltige is *tcherkesse,* 'Cossack' riding, where you lie across the horse's back with your ankle in a loop attached to a band passed around the horse's midsection. While you're almost upside down, you grab handkerchiefs and other objects from the sawdust floor, while the horse gallops around the ring."

Erich looked nervous and uncertain.

"Don't worry, Billy, Isaiah didn't learn to do some of those tricks until he was almost forty, and that's a lot scarier than learning when you're thirteen."

~ ∫ ~

"I think we're getting close to identifying the thief, Billy."
Billy turned pale. "Who do you think it is, Governor?"
"I don't know yet. But we have hired a private investigator."

~ ∫ ~

Billy's mind was in turmoil as he headed toward Maximus's flat late that afternoon. He had made up his mind. No matter what, he intended to tell Maximus this would be his last payment.

As he was walking along the *Hochstrasse,* he observed a strange sight. Fifty yards away, Maximus, Charlotte, her husband, and the police officer, now out of uniform, were coming toward him, walking together. They were so engrossed in their conversation that they didn't notice the boy. Frantic, Billy searched for and found a nearby alley filled with several large garbage cans. He ducked behind two of the bins.

As the four adults came closer to the alley, they were laughing and appeared to be enjoying themselves immensely. They were in no hurry to get anywhere. Billy overheard snatches of their conversation.

"Payday," the "policeman" said. "What time's the kid due?"

"Half an hour," Maximus replied.

"What a find!" Heinz said. "The gift that keeps on giving. Maximus, your idea of renting the flat for a day was brilliant. Charlotte, you are such a wonderful actress! Horst, you were the best of all! You of all people dressing up like a constable. Oh … my … God!" He guffawed loudly.

As they came closer, Billy could hear more clearly.

"It's almost time to cut him loose," Maximus said. "He tells me that old fraud Hobbs is getting suspicious. He's scared enough he could tell him, and then there'd be hell to pay."

"Maybe," Charlotte said, "but it's been 'money for jam' for all of us since that day I bared my titties. I hate to cut it off…"

They picked up their pace as they passed the alley. But Billy had heard enough.

~ ∫ ~

That evening, when he returned to the tober, Billy sought out the one person he trusted more than any other. "Elvira, I need to talk with you," he said forlornly.

"'Bout what, honey?"

"Things."

"Money things? Blackmail things?"

The boy rocked back on his heels, stunned. "You … you know?"

"Don't know. Suspected, though. You been acting awful funny the last few weeks. Wanna' tell ol' Elvira everythin'?"

"Yes," Billy said miserably.

"Come to Jesus, Darlin' and y'all shall be saved – or somethin' like that."

~ ∫ ~

"I think you better tell this to Colonel Isaiah 'n' my sis. Mebbe old Ezekiel, too."

"I thought this was just between us," Billy said.

"It is, if that's the way you want it to be, honey. But I think you done worked yourself into a damnable mess and if circus is really family, we should all be working together to straighten it out."

~ ∫ ~

"I'll be damned," Zeke whistled. "That little bastard Ortega y Alcantar's back on the loose. The leopard sure hasn't changed his spots."

"What do you mean, 'back on the loose' Herr Zeke? He told me he used to be on this show and took a short break."

"I'll say he took a break," Isaiah said. "Worked on the show for six months, then took a two year break in the state prison when they finally caught him. He was lucky he wasn't shot."

"Why is that?" Billy asked.

"He was one of the most twisted people I ever met," Isaiah continued. "The fact that the circus traveled made it hard to learn what was going on. It turned out, when he wasn't performing, he was dressing up like a schoolboy, even powdering his face, while he was going into town, molesting – hell, *raping* – little five- and six-year-old girls who didn't even *know* he was doing it. He was truly the most disgusting excuse for a human being I've ever met," the Governor concluded.

"But I stole from you, Herr Hobbs," Billy said, his face tearstained. "I betrayed your trust."

"That you did, Billy," Isaiah responded. "But you're all of thirteen years old. You were frightened and you simply didn't know how to handle what you'd gotten yourself into. It'll be most interesting to see what our friend Pedro Hernandes Ortega y Alcantar has to say for himself."

~ ∫ ~

The midget spat out a string of malicious epithets, the least of which was "*Verkrüpelt* fucking *Néger.*" Elvira sat in her wheelchair, quiet and unperturbed.

They had agreed to meet in the *stadtpark*, Zeke and Elvira representing the circus, Maximus and "Officer" Moltke representing the erstwhile blackmailers.

"You realize we could have you arrested. Given your colorful history, you might go away for a long time."

"Ah, the great Quakemaker has learned how to speak instead of just grunt," Maximus said. "Still rutting with cows and elephants instead of women, big fellow?" he continued, trying to incite Willis to lose his composure.

"Still sticking you *hujek* into little girls?" Zeke rejoined calmly.

"Lady, gentlemen," Moltke said smoothly. "I thought we'd agreed to come here to try to work out a deal."

"Deal?" Maximus exploded. "They want the money – *our* money – back. Lest you *zirkus volk* forget, we have *four* witnesses, including the lady herself, that your young hoodlum tried to have his way with her."

"They'd never believe you. With your record …?"

"No one's asking that they believe *me*. But *zirkus* is no more credible than a whore or any other carnival lowlife."

"So we are at an impasse?" Zeke said.

"*Mein Gott*, the idiot has learned a word with more than one syllable," Maximus smirked. "Fortunately for you, I am in a generous mood. I have an offer to make."

When he explained his offer, Elvira, without waiting for Zeke to respond, said, "We accept."

~ ∫ ~

Isaiah Hobbs raised his eyebrows. "Let me get this straight. He asks to do one performance. We promise to invite a representative from three major circuses. His associates post the money we've given him in the Potsdam branch of the *Deutschebank* three days before the show and they hand us sworn declarations stating what really happened. And each side releases the other."

"That's about it, Isaiah."

"The show will take place Thursday week in the afternoon. Maximus will follow *Le Demon Debonnair?*"

"Yup."

"Strange," Hobbs murmured. "He's never been in a cage with *any* animal or taken a lesson from anyone. Now he's gathering a menagerie of plain old everyday alley cats, taking them to his flat and *painting* them with yellow and black stripes, just like tigers."

"That's what he told me, Isaiah."

"And he says he's going to mimic the *Demon* Debbonair's act, only he's going to do it all in miniature – miniature cage, kitty cats instead of lions, miniature whip, miniature animal trainer's costume, even down to his pista shoes?"

"Are you aware the police are investigating complaints that he's up to his old tricks?"

"You mean screwing *babies*?"

"Uh-huh."

"God, I'd love to see that slimy bastard get his comeuppance one day," Zeke said.

~ ∫ ~

The afternoon of his performance, Major Maximus, dressed in extraordinary finery from top hat to highly polished pista shoes, sat on top of his miniature cage wagon, which was pulled into the center ring by a small pony. The cage was full of cats, at least fifteen of them, all clinging frantically to the bars, their mouths wide open and yowling. Every cat's fur was matted with paint smudges. They were not happy.

Finally, Major Maximus hopped down from the wagon and went to the door at the rear of his cage, slashing with his midget-sized whip to beat back the cats clinging to it.

Allman stood next to Isaiah Hobbs. "You can't let him do this, Governor!"

"It's not as if I didn't warn him," Hobbs said, "It was his own idea and he took a lot of trouble over it. Why should I stop him? I remember Zoltan once told me something about this act being popular back in medieval times."

Allman looked horrified. "Back in medieval times, the most popular entertainment was *public execution*. One way of execution was that the criminal would be tied inside a sack full of cats, and the cats would fight to get out …"

While they were talking, Maximus had gone into the cage and clanged the door shut behind him. He whipped the cats down from the cage bars to the floor. When he had them all cowering at his feet, he flung up his arms in the 'V'. The band music stopped on a victorious chord.

Then one of the cats sprang high from the pack, raking at Maximus's face as it flew past him, leaving a big red scratch across his cheek.

The audience laughed at that, but suddenly, over the laughter a child's voice could be heard shouting clearly, '*Papa! That's the little boy who made me naked!*'

Maximus heard it and he stood uncertainly among the snarling and spitting alley cats, his face suddenly so pale that the scratch across it gleamed vividly. The child was still excitedly crying out, and the audience was murmuring in confusion.

Inside the cage, Maximus went into a spasm of fury. As if he were beating off his small accuser, he whipped desperately and viciously at the cats, but not for long. Now, one cat did not spring, *all* of them did. Maximus stayed upright for a time, but he was invisible inside a seething, writhing, caterwauling mound of black and yellow, and his own screams were muffled. Then the mound collapsed to the cage floor, but continued to wriggle and scream and yowl. People started shoving to get down from the stands and away from the scene.

Just then, a policeman, who'd been investigating the complaints that a boy from the circus had been molesting little girl children, came running into the pista and stuck his truncheon between the bars of the cage, trying ineffectually to beat at the furry, heaving heap. Several roustabouts with sticks came running to do the same. One of them brought a bucket of water and dashed it into the cage, but even that did not deter the maddened cats. They went on with their clawing and rending. Now blood red was added to their black and yellow coloring.

Somehow, one of the men milling around the wagon thought to unlatch the cage door and fling it open. That was all the cats had really wanted. They poured out in a single surge of black and yellow and red, then became separate streaks darting in all directions. Those in the audience who had not already been struggling to get out of the tent did so now, when the bloodied cats exploded among them.

When it was over, Isaiah Hobbs, Zeke Willis, and those who had remained in the pista, looked in at the sickening sight that was left on the blood-puddled floor. What they saw was Major Maximus's toy whip, fragments of his clothing, none larger than a handkerchief, and a raw, ragged, pulpy blue-red slab that might have been freshly delivered cat's meat, except that it still wore tiny, highly polished shoes.

7

"A *countess* who does voltige?"

"Well …" Hobbs murmured. "We don't happen to have her Imperial Majesty in residence, so a plain old countess will have to do." Alisa looked at Hobbs sharply. He continued, "When I first joined on the circus, a gangly thirteen-year-old, Brenda Lee Crowley, was just learning the ropes. She'd always said she would marry a high-ranking nobleman. Five years later, she was one of the world's great beauties and the toast of Paris. She really did marry a nobleman, Gaspar, Count du Bourges.Gaspar was killed in the Franco-Prussian war less than a month after they'd married. That made her a very wealthy widow. She could easily have retired in luxury for the rest of her life."

"Brenda Lee literally begged us to come back, not that she had to 'beg' very hard at all, since she was the undisputed star of the show, and she's been with us since," Alisa said. "But she's forty-three, the same age as me, and she won't be keeping up her voltige much longer."

When the three of them got to the pista, Brenda Lee was already going through a brief morning routine.

Erich stared unabashedly at the woman. "She's forty-three? Impossible! *Twenty*-three I would believe." This time the sharp look from Alisa was aimed not at Isaiah, but at the boy. Still, Alisa had to admit, from thirty feet away the striking woman with shoulder-length blonde hair and tight, youthful figure, dressed in a skin-tight leotard, could easily pass for a girl in her twenties.

As the three of them watched, Brenda Lee posted on one of four matched horses who were trotting smoothly around the ring. None wore a saddle or bridle of any kind. Brenda stood on one leg, kneeled, jumped to a standing position, then lightly somersaulted from the back of one horse to the back of the horse following behind. After a moment's pause, she somersaulted back to the next horse, then back to the one on which she'd been posting. She went through numerous other equally difficult routines, displaying grace and athleticism until the trainer signaled the session was at an end. Just before her mount stopped, Brenda Lee leapt off the gelding and raised her arms in a "V" above her head.

Billy clapped so hard his hands were sore. "Bravo! Bravissimo!" he shouted.

"Thank you, Kind Sir," she said. As she came closer, Billy could not see a forty-three year-old woman. He was so blinded by puppy love and the glamour of this fairy-tale princess-come-to-life that he could only blink stupidly.

"Mam'selle," he said, blushing and bowing deeply.

"Oh, pshaw," the apparition said. "You're on the show, same as me. I'm no Madame or Mademoiselle, I'm plain old Brenda Lee. You must be the new fellow, the one Elvira calls Billy."

"But I have been here for two months and I've never seen you. I would never have forgotten …"

"You wouldn't have had a chance to. I've been in Paris for the past three months. I only got back last night. Isaiah tells me you joined up in Magdeburg. The last pitch I played before I left was Hanover, and I can tell you *that* place was as cold as a witch's tittie. Sorry if I offended you, Billy, but after three solid months of courtseying, acting dignified and demure, and doing everything expected of the widow-countess du Bourges, I felt I would simply burst if I didn't have a chance to get back to straight talk. I was raised on the circus. From the time I was five, I learned to call a spade a shit shovel."

Billy said nothing. He'd heard men talk like this frequently, but never a woman, and never so beautiful a woman.

"I was as shocked as you when I first heard her speak that way, and she wasn't even thirteen at the time," Hobbs said. "You grow up very quickly in the circus world. I learned early on that those on the show never ask about another man's politics, his religion, his morals, or any of his other superstitions. Even if Brenda Lee lapses back to the language of her earliest days, I can assure you, she's a truly gracious and a great lady. Get used to her, because she's going to be your voltige teacher."

"You look a little frightened by all this," Brenda Lee said. "Are you? And don't you dare bullshit me."

"Well, ummm, yes, Fräulein … Mademoiselle …"

"Brenda Lee. It's a good thing you are frightened. I'd be a lot more worried about working with you if you weren't."

~ ʃ ~

As June turned to July and then to August, Billy surprised himself at how naturally he took to voltige riding. Five days a week he'd practice in the pista. On the sixth day, he'd ride to a remote part of the city park, where the circus was pitched, and practice on his own.

"What's a liberty act?" he asked the trainer one day.

"That's where the horses are in the ring alone, without riders, without anything to interfere with the sheer beauty of their bodies, even, as far as the audience can tell, without a trainer. They appear to do all kinds of movements, dancing, in unison, cross-steps, reversing direction, changing their gait – and it always thrills the jossers. To make it even more dramatic, we use either *Pinzgauer Tigerschecken* horses – which are white Austrian horses spotted with black, like Dalmatian dogs – or we use *Friesians,* which are shiny black all over, with wavy long manes, ground sweeping trails, and little wavy plumes of hair at their fetlocks, like wings on their feet."

"Those huge draft horses?"

"Yes. We get two jobs out of them for the price of one. They're hefty enough to pull the circus wagons when we're not traveling by train, and they're gorgeous enough to use in the liberty act."

By mid-August, Isaiah had started Billy working with the western lariat and the European trick rope. "As a cowboy performer, you're going to need at least three disciplines in your act: riding, roping, and shooting."

"*Shooting*, Herr Hobbs?"

"That will be the third thing you'll learn and probably the most fun."

"So I'll be able to protect the circus against 'bad guys?'"

"That's a little *too* much Karl May. We'll start working on shootist's tricks next week."

~ ʃ ~

"Brenda Lee, today we start our young cowboy on the road to being a shootist. Could you help me out?"

"Omigod, Isaiah, it's been years!"

"Twenty-four to be exact."

"Whatever. Billy, come over and stand by me. It's school time!"

As the boy watched, Isaiah held up an old-fashioned brassbound carbine and struck an overstated "V" pose.

Assuming her best ersatz ringmaster's voice, Brenda Lee bawled out, "As his first display of virtuosity, Colonel Ramrod has only one shot, so only one chance to hit the moving target, ladies and gentlemen. I will allow you five seconds to place any wagers you may care to make among yourselves."

"Colonel Ramrod," now significantly older than the first time he'd tried this trick, frowned studiously and pretended to check over his weapon.

"Mam'selle … *throw!*"

Brenda scaled a ceramic saucer straight up in the air toward the tent's peak. Isaiah had been holding his carbine at port arms. He almost leisurely brought its butt to his shoulder, cocked the big hammer, pretended to sight as if he were really drawing a bead on the little pale object, but merely fired in its general direction. So loud was the blast of the carbine that the saucer seemed to dissolve silently into powder. Brenda Lee applauded as delightedly as if she had bet on the shot.

"Colonel Ramrod" put his empty carbine down, then unholstered a pistol. He scowled at it, examined it, twirled the cylinder, counted the caps, and seemed to be occupying himself with preparing the gun for serious business. Brenda Lee took five saucers to the opposite side of the ring and stuck each saucer's rim into the ring's curb so that it stood upright.

"Notice, ladies and gentleman," Hobbs said in a commanding voice, "There are five targets and I have only six shots with which to hit and shatter them." He settled the pistol back in its holster on his right hip, its walnut grip facing forward, the holster's stiff leather flap unbuttoned and raised. He walked to the edge of the ring farthest from the target, then held both hands a little way out from his sides, a little below waist level.

Brenda Lee had been quietly talking to Billy. Now she nudged him gently, and he shouted, "*Fire!*"

What followed happened so quickly that the pistol's *blam!* seemed to put an exclamation point to the boy's command. The first saucer in line disintegrated. Isaiah had flicked his left hand across his body the holster, whipped out the revolver, and thumb-cocked it as it came up level in front of his face. Then his left hand had dropped away, leaving the pistol apparently levitating there just long enough for his right hand to flash up, seize it, aim it, and pull the trigger – all of that done so fast as to appear simultaneous with Billy's barked order. Hobbs spun the gun around his finger in its trigger guard so it did a graceful twirl, then plunked it down into the holster.

He shot the next saucer from a kneeling position, the next with his left hand holding the revolver, the next shooting from the hip without appearing to take aim at all. In between, he wiped his palms on his trousers, swiped the back of a hand across his forehead, and knuckled his eyes, as if the strain and deliberation were almost too much for mortal endurance. Only one saucer remained standing. Isaiah picked up a hand mirror, which had been lying on the same table which had earlier held the saucers. He turned *away* from the saucer at the opposite end of the ring, glanced through the mirror which reflected the whereabouts of the saucer. Sighting the pistol back and forth over his shoulder, he finally nodded, as if he'd found the position he wanted. Then, with another loud *BL-LAM!* the final plate shattered, pulverized.

"Teeth?" Hobbs asked Brenda Lee.

"Why not?" She walked to the far end of the ring.

"Ladies and gentlemen," Hobbs called in his showman's voice, "I must beg you now for your absolute silence and stillness. For I will now attempt to shoot directly into the face of this brave and beautiful young woman in such a way that she can *catch the ball in her teeth*! Please! Absolute silence. Those who cannot bear to watch are requested to leave the chapiteau this moment. Also any who are liable to swoons or epileptic seizures. I must not be discomposed by any sound or movement."

Brenda Lee stood at the opposite end of the ring with her hands on her hips, her head erect, with a farewell-cruel-world expression on her face. "Are you ready, Mam'selle?" Hobbs queried. Brenda slid her eyes sideways.

"Colonel Ramrod" spread his feet apart and assumed a solid, tense, braced posture. He aimed carefully – *low*. After a long, suspenseful pause, Hobbs fired. Brenda Lee rocked backward the tiniest bit. Her hands left her hips in an uncertain, steadying gesture, as blue smoke blurred her outline, even from Billy. Then she smiled, her mouth slightly parted. She raised her hand to her mouth, plucked a bit of lead from between her teeth, held it up, and tossed it to Billy.

"Examine it, young man!" Hobbs called out. "The ball shows clear evidence of its terrific impact on the Countess du Bourges's fragile teeth." The ball was clearly spent.

Afterward, Hobbs explained to the astonished Billy how the tricks were gaffed.

"I loaded the carbine with bird shot for knocking the one dish out of the air. In order to demolish that saucer, all I had to do was to fire a shot anywhere within thirty feet of it. As for the pistol, it really was loaded with *five* balls. From that distance it doesn't take a particularly astute marksman to hit those targets – that's something you'll learn quickly."

"But what about the sixth shot? The one the countess caught in her teeth?" the boy asked.

"The pistol is a six shooter. There were only five balls in the six chambers. There was only powder in the remaining chamber."

"You fired an *empty* chamber at the countess? But I *saw* a spent shell with my own eyes."

"That you did. When Brenda Lee walked over to where she was standing, your eyes were on me, so you didn't see her quietly pick up a spent shell from where I'd shot the dishes. She palmed that shell, and just before she placed her hands on her hips, the shell found its way into her mouth."

"But I saw blue smoke come out of the gun."

"True. Because I used only a light load of powder in my pistol, I topped up each chamber with a little cornmeal before I rammed in the ball. It burns as it goes out the barrel behind the ball, and it burns out the residue from previous shots, so it helps keep the barrel clean."

The bemused Billy turned to both of them. "Are you saying all circus tricks are fakery and witchcraft?"

"No, Billy," Brenda Lee said gently. "But sincerity does not make for showmanship."

"I've been on the show for almost five months," Billy said. "How long before I'm ready to try my hand at performing?"

"It won't be long now," Hobbs replied. "Brenda Lee and I will work up a routine for you, which you must follow very strictly – at least for the first few performances. We'll be breaking down the show in two weeks. After that we have a few brief stops before we settle in for the winter."

~ ∫ ~

During the last day of the breakdown, Elvira sat morosely in the wagon she shared with her husband. She did not eat, which was odd for her, and she cried incessantly, which was even odder for the normally imperturbable woman. Pemjean approached Elvira's sister and said, "Alisa, I think your twin is seeing things she won't even disclose to me. Perhaps you might talk to her."

Alisa went to Elvira's wagon and found the wheelchair-bound woman lying face down on her bed, sobbing. When Elvira spoke, it was muffled, as though she were talking through a piece of gauze. "Oh, Sis, I been dreamin' the most terrible dreams, and they's always the same. A big windmill with black and white arms is sittin' on a hill, turnin' round and round in the wind. Then the arms start comin' off, one at a time, until there ain't none left, and when I wake up, it's as if I been ridin' them arms all night, and I be dizzy and sick at the same time, but I can't even throw up. I'se *skeered*, Sister. I'se *so skeered*."

"What do you think it means?"

"The end of the world." She trembled. "There's more I ain't tol' *no one* about. Mister Isaiah come to me in these dreams and he be lookin' normal, then he turns into a skeleton with a grinnin' face like a dead man. And the same thing happens to you, Sis. Then there's this gold crown in the middle of the air and you and Mr. Isaiah is fightin' over it, each of you pullin' it one way or the other. Somebody comes up to y'all with a dagger and stabs the crown and it melts into blood. Then that young boy, Billy, his head be all in white like a halo and he's growin' taller and taller, and he be's kissin' each of us goodbye."

8

During the three days they played in Leipzig, *Zoltan's Great American* played to well-attended, not *sfondone* houses, but Billy remembered these shows for the rest of his life, for this was the first time he actually performed, albeit in very small and anonymous roles. The wardrobe mistress had fashioned a small clown suit for him. While the other joeys and tobeys were running and jumping and cavorting, Billy performed rope tricks. He lassoed a fellow clown around the waist and dragged him around the pista, to the hearty laughter of the audience. He roped another clown by the leg when he chased a third clown who'd hit him over the head with a rubber mallet. Billy also rode atop one of the elephants in the come-on and in the closing parade.

"I did it! I did it!" he crowed to Hobbs and Alisa that evening. "Now I really *am* a circus performer!" The following morning, he practiced with renewed vigor in perfecting his real act, which he felt was coming closer every day.

Dresden was situated on both sides of the Elbe River, in a broad and lovely valley. Erich was dazzled when Brenda asked him to walk about the city with her, while the rest of the circus was setting up. "By next week at this time, we'll be in Prague," she said.

"I've never been outside Germany. I've always wanted to travel, but I never had the chance. Have you been to Prague, Counte – Brenda Lee?" he asked, still feeling uncomfortable addressing the beautiful noblewoman by her first name.

"Three times. I've found it more beautiful each time. I was prepared to love Prague ever since I first heard *Vltava* when I was in my twenties."

"*Die Moldau*," Erich said, proudly displaying his knowledge. "It's one of the most beautiful melodies I've ever heard. I wonder why the Colonel Hobbs wanted me to see the city this morning."

"Don't know," she responded. "Maybe because we'll only be here for two days and maybe because it's the last place in Germany you'll see for awhile."

They returned to the tober shortly before noon. As they entered the midway, the band burst into a spirited rendition of the English-American folksong, *Billy Boy*. The boy's eyes widened as he saw a large iced cake with the words, "*A Star is Born*."

"For me?" he asked.

"It is," Brenda Lee told him, kissing him lightly on the lips. He almost swooned with delight. "There's more," she said.

Isaiah Hobbs approached him mock angrily. "Where have you been, you lazy lout? The wardrobe mistress has been waiting for you all morning and the show starts in three hours. She'll barely have time to make sure you're properly outfitted."

As he walked in a trance toward the costumer's tent, a ripple of applause accompanied him, but it was nothing compared to what awaited him inside that tent. What he saw made his eyes bug out and his jaw go slack. "Well, try it on, then," the wardrobe mistress, a dour Scotswoman, said archly. "Lord knows ye kept us waitin' long enough."

In front of him hung the most perfect cowboy outfit he'd ever seen. He had no idea that any similarity between what cowboys actually wore on the range and the circus cowboy show outfit was purely coincidental. He grabbed the white ten-gallon hat, which fit him perfectly, and a checked red and blue bandanna. Suspended from a hanger, he touched the silver-colored satin shirt, with matching spangles and pants, and a wide leather belt sporting a Texas-size belt buckle. He couldn't fathom what the initials "B.J." standing out in gold relief from the rest of the buckle signified, but it was probably the manufacturer's name. Buckskin chaps and very light leather boots completed the outfit.

Still not believing this was real, Billy tried on the outfit.

"Not bad," the mistress said. "A pull here, a tuck there, and you'll be just fine. Plenty of time to finish it. Go wash up, then get back here an hour before you go on."

Billy had never been in the changing tent before. Eager to be part of the circus family, he unquestioningly pushed through the swinging door of the tent. And froze. Brenda Lee was in the tent, and she was wearing *absolutely nothing*. His gasping intake of breath distracted her from what she was doing, and she turned to face him. "Oh, hi, Billy," she said nonchalantly.

The boy was too confounded even to turn politely away, but frankly stared and finally stammered, "I'm so … so sorry, Countess."

"Nothing to apologize for. I was just changing to a new outfit for the come-on. Sweat is worse than moths for eating holes in clothes. Got to rinse them out right away, What's the matter, Erich? Surely you know what sweat is?"

"Well, uh, sure."

"Ah. Then maybe you never saw a female naked before."

He blushed a bright crimson. "I could never in my wildest dreams imagine anything so beautiful."

"Thank you, Billy," she said, and sincerely. "Perhaps it's not true anymore, but it feels good to be admired by such a *young* gallant. Meanwhile, you go ahead and look all you want – there's no harm in that." Then she laughed, as she realized he wasn't looking entirely at *her*. "Oh, you're looking at this thing." She held up the small pad she had just removed from inside her discarded tights. "Every circus artiste wears one. Men, too, only in their case it's to make the bulge at their crotch less noticeable. For us females, it's to cover our little cleft, so it won't wink at the audience. It's called a *cache-sexe*. That's French."

She tucked the pad between her legs, swiftly slipped into clean clothes from the skin out, and flitted out of the changing tent. The boy said nothing, only wondrously shook his head. After taking a brief sponge bath, he returned to the wardrobe mistress's tent, where she helped him with his final fitting. She clucked approvingly, then sent him on his way to get ready for the opening spec.

As he and the Governor rode in side by side, Hobbs spoke quietly with him. "Are you nervous, Billy?"

"Gott, yes," he said, feeling his palms go clammy.

"Don't worry. You're bound to make mistakes. Heck, *I* still make mistakes. The gun may jam or the recoil may jerk the pistol up so it doesn't hit the target. A thousand things can go wrong, and sometimes do, but never forget, *you* are doing the jossers a favor. You are bringing joy and entertainment to them. Just to the best you can. That's all anyone can ask of you. If, for some reason, you make a mistake, ignore it. Pretend it was supposed to be part of the act. Regardless of what you do and how you do it, spread your arms in a big 'V.'"

"I'll try, Herr Hobbs."

"No matter what you might feel like doing today, do *not* – *absolutely do not* – deviate from the program we've worked up for you. The lariat's first, then the shooting, then the riding, but only when I announce you. One last thing. You may be very surprised when I announce you for the first time. It must not take away from your job, which is to perform *exactly* as we've gone through it. Don't let what I say and don't let any extraneous noises distract you."

"I'll try to make you proud, Governor. For everything you've done for me."

"You don't have to make me proud of you, Billy. I already *am* proud of you."

The first part of the program crawled by. The thirty minutes seemed like thirty hours as he waited outside the chapiteau, watching the well-orchestrated mix of hilarity, thrill acts, and suspense. Then, time condensed and the next ten minutes seemed like ten seconds. He smelled the sweat and sensed the huge man as Zeke Willis gently touched him on the shoulder. "Start walking in now."

He did, and he thought his ears were betraying him as he heard Isaiah Hobbs go through his impossible *spiel*. "Herren und damen, boys and girls, you are now in for a real treat! *Zoltan's Great American* travels the world finding new talent for the sole purpose of thrilling *you*.

"Earlier this year, our scouts went to America – to *Texas* – where we found a blond, blue-eyed American boy. He'd been kidnapped by the wild Apache Indians, led by Chief Crazy Horse himself. They intended to hold the lad for ransom, but their evil plans were frustrated by none other than Wild Bill Hickok. That fine American lawman brought the boy back to Laredo when he was only three years old, but by that time, alas, his mother had died of grief. So Wild Bill Hickok himself gave the boy his own first name and taught the boy everything he knew. He had two of *his* friends, Butch Cassidy and the Sundance Kid, teach the lad everything *they* knew. Before long, the youngster could outdraw, outshoot, and outride all three of 'em. While he was planning his campaign to take revenge on the wild Apaches who'd kidnapped him, our circus scouts spotted him, heard his story, and convinced him that before he took his revenge on the wild Indians, he should first dazzle our European audiences with his brilliance.

"I can talk about him all day and it won't do him justice. Here he is – at only thirteen years old – appearing for the first time in Europe – the *wunderkind* of every cowboy in Texas, the one, the only …." Here there was a loud drum roll. "***BIL-LY JEN-KINS!!!***"

Remembering Hobbs's admonition to ignore everything but his act, Billy entered the ring to much more than polite applause. He worked one lariat, lassoing objects as small as a rubber ball. Then he drew a second rope out of his belt loop. Using his left and right hand simultaneously, he accurately lassoed items as diverse as a cup and a josser's cane at the same time. When Brenda Lee threw a hoop ten feet into the air, he roped that on the fly. As he was drawing that hoop in, he sent his lariat spiraling toward a clown who, at that moment, was mock-lighting a huge rubber cigar. Before the clown knew what was happening, the cigar was yanked from his hands.

At each trick, the audience's applause grew louder and longer. Finally, after his most spectacular trick, whirling *two* lariats in each hand and hauling in *four* objects, he stopped, smiled, and threw up his hands in a wide "V" to thunderous applause.

"***BILLY JENKINS***!!!" crowed Hobbs, as the boy ran out the circus tent, came back, threw his arms up in another "V," and ran out again while the ringmaster was announcing the next act.

At the end of the first half of the show, "Billy Jenkins" came on again, this time for his shooting exhibition. While his first performance had been frenetic, this time he was far more deliberate. He remembered Alisa's admonition: "There's a very subtle device of dramatics I learned over the years: When every other person in a crowded tent is in hectic motion, the audience's attention is riveted on the one figure who remains perfectly still. Remember that and whenever you want, you can seize the audience for your own – better even than if a spotlight were on you. That can make a difference between a mere performer and a real star."

Billy recalled how Hobbs has used this dramatic turn to his advantage during the first morning when he'd trained with the Governor and with the beautiful – the *scandalously* beautiful – Countess Brenda Lee du Bourges, who had now come out to act as *his* assistant during the shooting exhibition. They went through the same routine he'd learned from Hobbs that first morning, and he powdered the saucer with buckshot easily.

When he did the five-ball pistol shoot, an image of the nude Brenda Lee flashed before his eyes just as he was getting off the first shot, and he missed the target, which unnerved him. He hurried the next four shots, and they struck true, shattering all but one of the plates. The ball-in-teeth act went off perfectly.

When he left the Big Top, Zeke Willis pounded the boy on the shoulders. Peggy / Brutus trumpeted her congratulations, moving her trunk up and down. Even Elvira had gotten over her morbid mood long enough to wheel over and say, "Billy, you done real good!"

Billy eagerly awaited his turn as the "horseman of the ages." Unknown to any of the artistes on the show, he'd devised a truly spectacular trick he intended to use if – when – the crowd demanded an encore.

The cowboy voltige came off smoothly. Hobbs had warned him, "If they want more, we'll call you back. Do *not*, however, do *anything* different. Stay with what you know, nothing more."

The audience stomped and cheered and gave him a standing ovation, shouting, "*Mehr! Mehr! Mehr!*" Some were chanting in rhythm, "Bil-ly! Bil-ly! Bil-ly!" Still others shouted, "Encore! Encore! Encore!"

"All right, Billy," Hobbs said. "It's obvious they love you. Give 'em what they came for, but remember, do nothing you haven't practiced. This is not the time to take unnecessary risks."

Billy had no intention of taking any unnecessary risks, but he wanted to give Hobbs, Alisa, and particularly Brenda Lee, a surprise he'd been practicing secretly in the park in Potsdam. He felt strong and confident as he strode back into the pista, lariat in hand. He patted the horse's withers and cinched the rope tightly around the horse's midsection. He mounted the horse slowly, focusing attention on himself.

At his command, the dapple grey started trotting, followed by three other matched horses. As he looked about the tent, he saw Brenda Lee's eyes go wide. Hobbs sliced his hand across his chest, mouthing the word, "*No!*" But Erich knew something the others didn't – he was sure of himself, secure in what he was doing. He tossed his bandana and his hat to the ground, making sure they were inside the pista.

As the horse started trotting, Billy slid one leg, then the other between the rope cinch. Billy lay down on its back. He was just about to reach down to retrieve his hat, the largest object, when the cinch came loose. The last thing he remembered was the ground rushing up at him. Then everything went black.

9

In between his bouts of unconsciousness, Billy caught snatches of conversation. "Concussion. Extremely fortunate he didn't fracture his skull." "Broken leg, but it's a simple fracture and not green bone. Three months maybe four." "Broken ribs, nothing you can do but let them mend on their own."

On the third day, he struggled back to consciousness. "Where am I?" he asked the tall, heavy-set nurse.

"*Krankenhaus Dresden.*"

"But the circus is supposed to be in Prague."

"*Ja, ja,* the Americanischer Zirkus to Prague it went four days ago."

The boy's heart sank. The nurse remained in the room. As he focused more and more on his body, he saw that his leg was in a full cast, and there was a tube in each arm.

"We have been injecting you with a codeine compound," the nurse said. "Your leg is raised to ensure proper circulation while it is healing. You had a mild concussion."

A horrible thought assailed him. *Elvira Simms.* "Will I be *verkrüppelt?*"

"No. You'll be on crutches within a week and you should be walking within three months. Your friends have dropped by every few days. A lovely *mulattin*, a large, older gentleman with a bald head and a thick beard, others as well. A distinguished-looking man left some books for you."

"So they *do* intend for me to rejoin them?"

"Yes. Your grandfather, Herr Hobbs, said he hoped that would be very soon. The *zirkus* will be in Prague for the next two weeks. Ah, here is the Herr Doktor Klassen. He is the leading orthopaedist in Dresden."

The doctor's prognosis was favorable. "You were a very lucky young man," he told Billy. "Had you been a few centimeters closer to the edge and cracked your head on the wooden berm around the ring you might not be with us. Fortunately, the young woman closest to the pista, Madame de Bourges, jumped onto one of the horses and drove it to the center of the ring. The other horses became confused and stopped. Although your leg had already snapped, you were still hanging over your horse. Had he not stopped you'd have continued bouncing and striking your head."

~ ʃ ~

Billy had already been propelling himself on crutches for two days when Zeke Willis came to visit. "I'm ready to get going if the Herr Doktor approves," he said. "I have a lot of catching up to do."

"Not so fast," Zeke said. "You got plenty healing to do first."

"But I want to earn my keep and I'd like to see if someone on crutches can still rope and shoot."

"Looks like you got lots of circus blood in you already. We perform when we're sick, we perform when we're sad, hell, we've gotta' be pretty much dead to stop playing for an audience."

"Is the Governor angry?"

"Naww, a little bonk on the head is nothing more than a pimple on the rear end of the circus."

"I mean, is he angry that I disobeyed him when he told me not to deviate from the routine?"

"I doubt it," Zeke said, lighting up a big cigar. "When him and me were talking about it afterward, he said, 'Better a warning shot early than getting blasted out of the water later. Best lesson a young piss-and-vinegar artiste can learn.'"

"How long does it take to get to Prague from here, Herr Zeke?"

"Four-and-a-half hours."

"So quickly?"

"Yep. We'll be travelin' on one o' them new high-speed passenger trains. They can hit sixty kilometers an hour!"

As they detrained, Hobbs was waiting for them. "Well, Billy Jenkins," he said, "you've had a good rest. I'm glad you've decided to come back to work. Tomorrow morning, we start a new routine to keep you busy while your leg is healing. We've got a great tober in *Riegrovy Sady*, the largest open space close to the city center."

~ ∫ ~

"*Dámy a pánové! Vážení hosté!* – Ladies and gentlemen, esteemed guests! This afternoon, we have a very special treat for you!" Billy barely heard as Hobbs projected his usual flummery about the boy's abduction and his rescue by Wild Bill Hickok.

"What a load of twaddle," Brenda Lee said, winking at him. "If you were born in 'eighty five, Crazy Horse and Wild Bill would have had to make a mighty long trip to come back and rescue you, since they'd both been dead for nine years by that time. Crazy Horse would have been scalped before he led a bunch of Apaches, since he was a Lakota Sioux and the Apaches lived a thousand miles away in

Arizona. Butch Cassidy and the Sundance Kid were only ten years old at the time."

"Is *any* of it true?" Billy asked.

"Yeah – and your name is Billy Jenkins." She smiled her dazzling smile. "It'll be interesting to see how he deals with your little accident."

Billy listened as Hobbs raised his voice. "Before we could stop him, the young boy took out after the Apaches to gain his revenge. He'd gotten halfway through Apache country when four full-grown savages ambushed and viciously attacked him. The boy singlehandedly fought off two of 'em and took their scalps! Look closely at his chaps. You'll see those scalps hanging from them – now I'll admit they *look* like leather, but that's only 'cause they dried out on the trip across the Great Ocean." There were cheers and congratulatory shouts and handclapping.

"But the two remaining savages used rifles they had stolen from the U.S. Army and shot this brave young man in his leg, shattering it in five places!" There were groans and even cries of outrage. "Fortunately, a detachment of cavalry came to the aid of the stalwart young man, saving his life." Again, cheers.

"Four weeks ago, after they'd put his leg in a cast, they were about to give up all hope that he'd ever walk again and they were preparing to amputate, but the brave lad begged the doctors, 'Please, gentlemen, send me to *Karlovy Vary*, where I'm told that all the great heroes of the world came to take the cure." The jossers nearly fell over themselves applauding at the mention of this most famous Bohemian spa.

"My friends, your applause is justified. The miraculous spa did indeed work wonders, and he is here with you this afternoon, not completely cured, but well on his way. Without further ado I give you the Prince of the Cowboys, **BIL-LY JENKINS!**"

Billy was restrained in his roping act, but his story had so moved the audience that they would have applauded wildly simply because he'd had the courage to enter the tent. He lengthened his shooting exhibition by sitting down when he fired his carbine at the thrown plate. Brenda Lee threw five gourds in the air, one right after the other, and he pulverized them in quick succession. For his display of shooting a row of standing plates, he lay down on the ground and shot at the first one. Two clowns helped him up. As they carried him around the ring, he shot another. Then he drew a second pistol from another holster, and holding one gun in each hand, he simultaneously shot two more saucers. Finally, he looked through the mirror, facing away from the target, while he calmly shot the last plate.

Brenda Lee danced over to the opposite side of the pista, ready to gaff the shell-in-teeth trick. Billy, however, seemed to pay her no attention as Hobbs gave his warm-up palaver about attempting to catch the live ball in her teeth. While he was giving his announcement, the ringmaster calmly lit a *sigaretta*, as though the risk to Brenda's life was the last thing on his mind. Billy turned slowly toward the Governor, aiming his gun directly at the Governor.

"*No!*" Hobbs exclaimed, raising his voice.

"*No! No!*" the horror-stricken audience shouted.

Hobbs took a long, nervous drag of his cigarette and its ash was a bright orange-red. A boy with a gun against an unarmed man. It would be no contest. Billy grinned – a malevolent grin – as though he were about to get even with the Governor for some real or imagined slight. Hobbs held his arms out. The next moment, there was a shattering blast and Isaiah reared back as the cigarette dropped from his fingers. Slowly, dramatically, he bent down to retrieve it, and as he held it up, the audience could clearly see that the cigarette had been shot cleanly in half.

"Now, Billy, why did you do that?"

"I saved your life, Governor!"

"What on earth do you mean?"

"Colonel Hobbs, you always told me that smoking is bad for your health. I simply wanted you to be healthy, so I thought I would put your *sigaretta* out!"

A loud *BOOM* from the bass drum underscored the laughter that erupted from the audience. After he calmly "shot" Brenda Lee in the teeth, to more wild applause, Billy bowed modestly and looked all around the chapiteau, savoring his return to the ring. His eyes were drawn to a figure in black in a face-hiding veil. Whoever it was, applauded gently and slowly. When Billy returned for the closing spec, the figure had disappeared.

The apparition appeared the following day, and the day after that, each time sitting in a different part of the tent. On the fourth day, Billy mentioned this strange image to Brenda Lee, who looked long and hard in the direction of the veiled person. When the figure rose and started moving toward the exit, Brenda Lee's hand involuntary flew to her mouth. "Uh-oh," she said softly.

Neither Billy nor Brenda said a word to Isaiah Hobbs, but next day, as though there was a wire between the ringmaster and the figure in black, Hobbs looked in that direction. He froze in mid-sentence and turned pale. His normally taciturn face broke into a grin. Far above them, as she was finishing her trapeze act, Alisa Simms looked in the same direction as Isaiah Hobbs. She looked harder, then started trembling uncontrollably.

Feeling the electricity that suffused the chapiteau, Billy asked the person nearest him, Zeke Willis, "What's going on here?"

Zeke started to say he didn't have the faintest idea, then turned in the direction the rest were simultaneously facing. "Holy shit!" he swore. "It can't be! It just can't be!"

As if acknowledging the looks they were all giving, the figure in black nodded once and directed a delicate five-finger wave toward Hobbs.

And Elvira Simms, strapped into her contraption and riding one of the Friesians around the ring, said quietly. "It's a' comin' now."

10

"Billy, this is the Gräfin von Hohenembs," Isaiah said, politely taking her hand.

"Your Grace," the boy said, bowing deferentially.

"The Baroness is … is an old and dear friend," he said, and Billy noticed a slight tremor in Hobbs's hand. "You must excuse my surprise, Your Grace, but it has been …?"

"Twenty-seven years, Hobbs úr," she said softly. "Balaton."

"Excuse me, Baroness," Billy said. "We have a countess on the circus. Could you explain to me the difference between a Countess and a Baroness?"

"Billy," the Governor said, deftly changing the subject, "it seems every nobleman or noblewoman in Europe claims some title or other. I believe the Baroness von Hohenembs is more interested in learning about your plans for the future."

"That is true, Herr Jenkins," the woman said. Billy could not help but notice she had not removed her black veil. "You are how old? Fifteen?"

The boy preened beneath her gaze, "Thirteen, Your Grace."

"Oh," she said, nodding her head and bringing her hand slowly to her lips. "My Rudi was only a few years younger when I met your Colonel Hobbs."

"Yes, ummm …" Isaiah said uncomfortably, searching for something to lower the tension he felt. "Billy's a rider as well as a roper and shootist," he continued.

"Yes, yes, the wild Apache Indians. Hobbs úr, you seem to have acquired Zoltan's gift of bluster. I suppose Billy's not your real name, either?"

"How would you know such a thing?" the young boy asked, surprised.

"Because you're German – Saxony or Brandenburg from your accent. I've never met a German named Billy Jenkins." She laughed. "Don't worry, Billy, your secret's safe with me. The Indian attack … you fell off a horse, no?" He blushed furiously. "I'll let you in on a little secret of my own, Billy. Many years ago, I fancied myself a bit of a horsewoman. I can't even number the times I fell off one of those beautiful beasts. It's an occupational hazard."

"Did you ever think to join on a circus, Your Grace?"

He could not see the look behind the veil, but she answered, "Yes, Billy Jenkins, when I was your age I very much wanted to join the circus. My life took a … a different direction."

~ ʃ ~

After he had gone, Hobbs looked longingly – at her. "Amelie, Amelie …"

"Not Autumn?" she asked, lifting her head but not her veil.

"No, not Autumn. Would you prefer 'Your Imperial Majesty?'"

"Not really. Walk with me. Please."

"I remember a young woman so imperious she *ordered* me to walk with her."

"That was many years ago, Isaiah. Much blood has flowed under the bridge since then. If I ask you …?"

"Amelie, it would be my deepest honor. Where should we walk?"

"*Stare mesto*, the Old Town, *Vaclav Namesti*? It doesn't matter. Someplace where there are lots of people and I can disappear into the crowds."

It was a fifteen minute walk to the heart of Prague. They walked slowly, reminiscing, two once-lovers, now old friends, each of whom had seen better days and a multitude of bad times since.

"It was most considerate of you to change the subject when I mentioned Rudi," she said. "I still can't understand …"

"Some things we can never understand," he said comfortingly.

"We did have fun, didn't we?"

"A lot more than fun, Amelie. And we were both of sufficient sophistication that I didn't demand to be the only man to possess you."

"You weren't even a little bit jealous, Isaiah?" They turned a corner into Wenceslas Square. In the early evening, it sparkled even brighter than the circus midway.

"I can't say I wasn't, Amelie. With the possible exception of Autumn, you were – you are – without question, the most beautiful, exciting woman I've ever been with. Several months ago, Zeke Willis asked if I ever thought about you. I responded truthfully, 'Only about a hundred fifty thousand times"

"And your lovely *mulattin*, Alisa?"

"Different altogether. She saw you. I didn't know what to say to her. I can only hope she forgives me."

"You sound like a bad boy being caught with a naughty secret."

"I feel that way."

"Ah, Isaiah," she said. "You don't know how good it feels for an old, worn-out crone to hear such words. Shall we stop for coffee or a small aperitif?"

"Your wish is my command, Your Imperial Majesty."

He held the chair out for her and she seated herself gracefully. After he'd ordered for them both, he asked, "Amelie, is it true that you've refused to have your portrait painted or your picture taken for the past twenty-five years?"

"Half-true, like anything else. Oh, Isaiah, you've no idea what it's been like. I've heard all that garbage that means so much when you're young: the most beautiful woman ever to wear a crown, the fairytale princess. For all the glory and the adulation, I'd have given it all away to have *some* happiness."

"You had Andrassy and a score of others. Whatever else was said, you were – are still – one of the most desirable women that ever lived."

"Yes, there was that," she sighed wistfully. "Four children whom I was hardly allowed to see while my mother-in-law was alive. I hope she rots in hell!" she said bitterly. "Megaliotis, of course, was too chicken-hearted to stand up for his *wife*. He was content to drive me into the arms of Hungary, and into the *arms* of Hungarian men – and you, of course. And the greatest tragedy of all."

Hobbs looked down at his hands, hardly daring to speak.

"It had been over for a long time anyway, but six-and-a-half years ago –.I couldn't bring myself to come near him after Mayerling – he took on a 'special friend,' Catherine Schratt, who's twenty-five years his junior."

"And you've been mourning ever since Mayerling? You don't have to answer, Amelie."

"Oh, Isaiah, I haven't heard that name in ever so long. Sisi, of course. The people took to that name."

"Amelie," he said again, taking her hand.

"Isaiah, please don't speak in that tone. I'm an old cow – a grandmother who hardly ever sees her granddaughter."

There was a rich, reverberant silence between them. An attentive waiter refilled their glasses and brought them lemon cakes.

"Where are you staying, Amelie?"

"*Hradcany.*"

"I should have known. Would it shock and repulse you if I suggested that we take a hotel room in town for a few hours?"

"You're joking."

"Never more serious in my life."

"But I'm fat, my breasts probably hang down below my stomach, and my face …."

"Would it not be *my* privilege to discover that?"

"Isaiah! Hobbs úr!" she said, but in a way that was contemplative rather than scolding.

"I remember that when we were in Balaton, you made love like no other woman I've been with before or since …"

She said nothing for several moments, savoring the last of her light wine. She seemed to be considering Hobbs's bold proposition. *One hundred fifty thousand times, he'd said.* She'd thought about him from time to time as well, nowhere near as frequently, but still …

"You realize we mustn't be seen together."

"I know."

"Have you a place in mind?"

"The Letna. Quiet, unobtrusive, and located in the diplomatic quarter. We could take a sedan to the area, divide, and then …"

"Come together?" She laughed for the first time in years at her double entendre.

~ ∫ ~

Later, when they lay resting side by side, the room suffused with the musky scent of their lovemaking, she looked over at him, her eyes aglow. "Thank you, Isaiah," she said quietly. "I may be far from the way I once was, no longer young, beautiful, or even desirable, but you certainly made me feel that way."

"Until tonight, Alisa had been enough for me, and of late we've become much more friends than lovers. I'm at the point where I no longer seek out the sole possession of a love, only the tranquil enjoyment of it at intervals. I've come to enjoy the sober splendor and gentle warmth of a September sunset, which does not buffet me with the springtime storms of resentment or jealousy."

"You've become quite the philosopher, Isaiah."

"And *you*, my dear, have become a most accomplished poet. When I first read what you'd written ten years ago, I thought I was reading Heine."

She blushed, and happily, all the way from her forehead down. "I never suspected you would read such stuff."

"Because I'm an American or because I'm a 'he-man.'"

"A little of both, I suppose. I'm quite flattered."

He lit a cigarette and sat up. "You should be. I picked up one of your books in Wien, simply because I saw your name on it and it stirred some wonderful memories. Then I read *Nordseelieder* and *Winterlieder*. They were charming." Hobbs looked at his pocket watch. "Close to midnight. I don't know if your friends at *Hradcany* Palace will miss you, but it might be hard for me to explain my absence from the tober."

Her Imperial Majesty stretched like a cat and smiled. "I don't suppose …?"

"I would love to, dear Amelie, but as enticing as you are, I truly don't know if I'd be up to it. And I've been told it's always better to depart while you are a novelty and interesting, rather than after having become a fixture and stale."

Once dressed, they chastely kissed one another. When he opened the door to leave, she was dabbing at her eyes. "Hobbs úr …?"

"One never knows," he said quietly "But I'll certainly not say goodbye. *Auf Wiedersehen,* my Empress."

"And Queen," she said, lightening their mood somewhat. "We cannot forget my beloved Hungary. *Auf Wiedersehen*, Isaiah Hobbs."

11

"Do you love her, Isaiah?"

"No, Alisa, of course not."

"Aren't you curious as to how I knew?"

"Not really. I've learned over the years it's impossible for a man to hide something from a woman. That's why I've never tried to lie to you."

They were sitting in their wagon the next morning. Billy was in the chapiteau working on his roping act. Neither Hobbs nor Alisa had slept well the night before. Alisa's eyes were puffy from crying. Isaiah was just plain exhausted.

"Why?" She sounded bitter, but neither surprised nor angry.

"When the empress and I were last together, I was thirty-nine and she was eight years younger. Amelie – Elisabeth – came into my life at a rather sensitive time. Last night both of us tried to recapture what, if anything, we had left of our youth. It's sad, really, but I think it helped ease thoughts of our own mortality a little."

Alisa reached over and squeezed Isaiah's hand. "I never could compete with Autumn, Isaiah, even though God knows I wanted to," she said softly. "Did you tell her imperial majesty about us?"

"She knew. I also told her I loved you. I'm not asking you to forgive me, Alisa."

"I know, Isaiah." She half-smiled. "It is nice to know you love me. Nicer still to know that you love me even after ..."

That night they both went to bed early. In the middle of the night, they both awoke, cemented Alisa's forgiveness of Isaiah in the most intimate way, and afterward drifted off to a blessed sleep. The following morning, Alisa awoke with a slight headache. It was not bothersome enough to tell Isaiah about it, so she didn't.

~ ∫ ~

In the latter part of August, *Zoltan's Great American* moved south, playing a series of short stands in Graz, Maribor, Szeged, and Pecs, until the troupe reached Zagreb, a lovely old city of fifty thousand, situated on the Sava River.

"This place must have doubled in size since we were last here," Hobbs told Alisa as they strolled through the *Donji Grad* section of the city."

"That was twelve years ago," she said.

"I'm so pleased you're here with me."

"It *has* been a lovely couple of months. Maybe we both needed a jolt. There's one thing that's been bothering me, though. The morning after we 'kissed and made up,' I awoke with a headache. I thought it would go away, and it did, but it's gradually started to come back more often and a little stronger each time. Lately, it's become a daily thing and I've started feeling nauseous and a bit dizzy as well."

"Are you telling me you think ...?"

"No, Isaiah. I've had my last two periods regularly."

"Migraine?"

"I don't know. I've become concerned that it might affect my ability on the trapeze. Don't look at me like that, Isaiah. It's not Autumn all over again."

"Still, we should get you to a doctor. There should be many good ones available."

Doctor Morganstern was a tall, thin, studious-looking man, who exuded competence and genuine concern. After taking Alisa's history, he examined her thoroughly "You say you suffer dizziness when you have these pains?"

"Not all the time," Alisa said calmly.

"We must go through a series of tests to rule out all reasonable possibilities."

"Do you think I could have brain cancer?" Alisa asked, clearly frightened.

"From what I've observed, it doesn't appear likely. However, I can't say yes or no definitively until we've done some fairly intensive testing," Dr. Morganstern replied. "I don't mean to frighten you unduly, but I suggest the tests should begin as soon as possible. Are you available tomorrow?"

"We have a show tomorrow," Alisa said.

"The Governor and his star trapeze artiste will have to be absent," Hobbs said. "You are far more important to me than a show. Zeke Willis has always wanted to try his hand at ringmastering."

"Good. Fräulein … Alisa," the doctor said. "I will write you a prescription for medication that should alleviate much of your present pain.

He did, and they had that prescription filled at the hospital pharmacy. Within two hours, Alisa had regained her spirit. "The pain subsided an hour ago. If the medication worked that quickly and completely, I don't think the prognosis could be that harsh."

"I agree. It seems we circus folk are the world's greatest optimists, and most of the time we have a lot to be optimistic about."

Hobbs took Alisa out for a delicious dinner of stuffed calamari, mussels, clams, sardines, an assortment of seasonal vegetables, eggplant, stuffed grape leaves, and a light wine. When they returned to the wagon that night, Billy was already asleep in his now-walled-off, separate quarters within the wagon. Alisa was ebullient – a combination of her first day in over a month of relief from her pain, and the softening influence of the wine they'd had at dinner. Hobbs was as gentle as could be with her, but soon their warm embrace signaled to each of them this would be a night for tender lovemaking. And it was.

Next morning, when Hobbs awoke, he saw that Alisa was still under the covers, not moving. He dressed quietly, so as not to disturb her. When he got to the circus's breakfast line, he was peppered with questions as to what the doctor had said and how Alisa had felt last night.

"Oh my gosh, I forgot, we have an appointment to go back to the hospital this morning to begin her tests. I'd better go and roust her out of bed, I'll be back shortly." After he'd returned to their wagon, he approached the bed. "Alisa," he said softly. "I know you'd love to sleep in this morning, but we're supposed to go back to Doctor Morganstern for testing."

When there was no response, he called a little louder. When there was still no indication that Alisa had heard him, he went over to the bed and shook her gently. When she did not respond, Hobbs shook her harder. Then, he noticed she was cold, and that she was not breathing.

"Alisa!" His shout turned into a strangled scream.

~ ∫ ~

"She suffered a cerebral aneurism during the night. The merciful thing is that she felt no pain. She died gently, as though she had simply fallen asleep and never awakened."

"What is a cerebral aneurism, Doctor Morganstern?" Isaiah asked dully.

"A weak spot in a blood vessel of the brain The vessel balloons out and fills with blood, putting pressure on a nerve or surrounding brain tissue. In this case, it was probably a large aneurism that ruptured. Cerebral aneurysms can occur anywhere in the brain."

"She was so young … "

"Herr Hobbs, brain aneurysms can occur in anyone, at any age. They are more common in adults than in children and more common in women than in men. They occur most commonly in people between the ages of thirty and sixty years."

As he thought back guiltily to the night before she'd first experienced the symptoms, the Governor asked, "Could mental stress have brought it on?"

"My experience has been that external tensions have absolutely nothing to do with either the development or the resolution of the aneurism, Herr Hobbs."

"So it's not my fault," he murmured to himself. Still, he was saddened and he knew he would miss her wise and loving companionship for the rest of his days.

~ ʃ ~

Those days were not to be long. On the morning of September 11, Billy burst out of the wagon he shared with the Governor.

"Herr Zeke, Herr Zeke!" Billy shouted urgently. "Colonel Hobbs has stopped breathing!"

The strongman and Brenda Lee quickly joined Billy in Hobbs's wagon, but it was clear they were too late. Hobbs, who was now beyond mortal help, was seated at his desk, where he'd been reading the morning paper. He looked as if he'd just lowered his head to the desktop to take a brief nap. Brenda Lee gently pulled the front page of the *Wiener Tageblatt* out from under Isaiah's elbows. "Oh, my God!" she gasped, then nudged Zeke and pointed to the headline, which was double-size and draped in black.

EMPRESS ELISABETH ASSASSINATED IN GENEVA!

Our beloved Empress, Elisabeth Amelie Eugenie, 60, affectionately known as "Sisi," was stabbed in the heart with a nail file by a young anarchist, Luigi Lucheni. She had been walking along the promenade of Lake Geneva about to board a steamship for Montreux with her lady-in-waiting, Countess Sztaray. Unaware of the severity of her condition, she still boarded the ship. Bleeding to death from a puncture wound to the heart, Elisabeth's last words were "What happened to me?" The strong pressure from her corset kept the bleeding back until the corset was removed. Only then did her staff and surrounding onlookers understand what had happened. Reportedly, her assassin had hoped to kill a prince from the House of Orléans and, failing to find him, turned on Elisabeth instead. Lucheni said, "I wanted to kill a royal. It did not matter which one."

Less than ten years ago, Elisabeth's life was shattered by the death of her only son. The then-thirty year-old Crown Prince Rudolf and his young lover, Baroness Maria Vetsera, were found dead at *Mayerling*, Rudolf's hunting lodge in Lower Austria. …

~ ∫ ~

Isaiah's funeral, which was attended by a very small gathering, took place on a dour, foggy morning two days later. Zeke Willis delivered the eulogy.

"Our friend and fellow trouper Isaiah Hobbs, Lieutenant Colonel, late of the Army of the Confederate States of America, has made his final teardown. He has hit the road for the long run to the final tober on his route sheet. Those who knew Isaiah best understood that beneath his serious demeanor lay a soul which understood and accepted his fellow human beings more than most....

"Once he joined up with the circus, Colonel Hobbs never looked back," Brenda Lee added. "Like all of us, he felt on his face that old familiar breeze that blows always from the far places and beckons, 'come see what I have seen.'"

Once again, Zeke took up his eulogy. "Lord, he was my best friend. Such a man does not need our commending, even to the All Highest. But when he gets there, Lord, do sit down from time to time and have a jar and a jaw with Hobbs and with Zoltan. Of course we are mindful that You are the Governor of the grandest circus of them all – Yours being the whole world here – artistes and players, jugglers and acrobats, rope-dancers and risk-chancers, mountebanks and musicmakers, freaks and roustabouts, slum-joint keepers and brawlers and confidence men – and every kind of menagerie animal there is – all of them prancing around Your great round pista or lining Your capacious midway or gathered in Your multitudinous pavilions. Maybe, Lord, alongside the immensity of that circus, this one seems no more than a mud show. Nevertheless, Isaiah Hobbs can tell You a thing or two, Lord, and not just tober gossip and outrageous yarns and bawdy jokes – though You'll enjoy the hearing of those to be sure. My friend Isaiah can also slip You a handy word of advice, now and again, that will help You keep Your troupers and crewmen working their best ... and being happy at their work ... and all the while loving the Governor of them all. Amen."

Brenda Lee concluded by saying, "When Zoltan died, we buried him under the pista and we said what they used to say in the circus of ancient Rome. We haven't used those words since he passed, but Lord, we use them with reverence now, for Isaiah Hobbs deserves them." She dropped three pink rose petals on his grave as she repeated the threefold benediction: *Saltavit ... Placuit ... Mortuus est.* He danced about. He gave pleasure. He is dead."

12

"Ferdie and Freddie Spencer, Governor, identical twins and closer than brothers should be, if you know what I mean," they said, introducing themselves. The two men, both in their late twenties Willis surmised, were of middle-height, slight build, and looked alike in every other way he could see.

"I don't care about your sexual preferences. What do you do in the pista?"

In response, the roustabouts helped them unload their wagon and set up their own traps, including a large trampoline, parallel high-and-low horizontal bars, rings, and a stationary pommel-horse. After ten minutes of watching their act, Zeke was convinced that whether they had sex with one another or with baboons, it made no difference. In the ring they were magic, performing triple somersaults in mid-air simultaneously, doing incredible one-hand spins and flips on the pommel-horse, and whirling through the air so fast on the parallel bars and rings that they were mere wisps of gold and blue and his eyes could not even discern which was which and where they were at any given time. When they returned to where Willis was standing, they were not even breathing hard.

As they walked around the perimeter of the chapiteau, the Governor asked about their previous circus experience.

"Obviously they don't care for our kind in Jolly Olde as you must know from the Oscar Wilde trial last year. We were on the Blackpool Tower Circus for six months, then over to France, which is much more tolerant of our sort. Most recently the Ringfedel."

"Ah, yes, the beloved Ringfedel, the whore of the industry," Zeke remarked wryly. "How long with them?"

"A year," said the one in gold.

"Why did you remain with them so long?"

"Because we have another nasty habit – eating," the one in blue, who identified himself as Ferdie, said.

"I doubt you'd have trouble finding employment with any circus," the Governor said. "Still, as detestable as the Ringfedel is, they always manage to get top acts on their way up or on their way down, and they put on a damned good show. Conduct books?"

"We left the Ringfedel without their consent. Their security people keep all the conduct books to avoid that very thing."

"That presents a problem."

"Why, Governor?" the other twin, Freddie, asked. "You'll be playing only in Germany this summer. There'll be no need to cross frontiers."

"You've done your homework well," Willis said. "Whatever we pay you, we insist on the holdback."

"Of course, so long as you don't hold back on food."

The brothers were well acquainted with the holdback. Veteran artistes and roustabouts alike were aware of this circus tradition. Every new circus hand always had his first three weeks of wages withheld, not to be paid until the end of the season. This was partly to discourage the good hands from defecting to some better paying outfit, but partly to ensure that the drunkards and wastrels among the crew had at least money to get home when the show closed.

After they had come to agreement, Isaiah introduced them to the rest of the troupe, not mentioning their preferences and proclivities. Within a month, the *equilibrists* had advanced to third act from close, just ahead of Billy Jenkins' voltige.

Billy had grown taller, more robust, and far more confident during his year with *Zoltan's Great American*. One day, he asked Willis, "Herr Zeke, I wonder if you could answer me a question?"

"Go ahead, Son."

"I was thinking back to Major Maximus. How could someone that awful have gotten a job with the circus in the first place?"

Before he responded, the big man lit up a meerschaum pipe. "You've learned a lot in the year you've been with us, Billy. The answer to your question is one of life's more callous lessons. A circus troupe is exactly like any group of people anywhere. They have their complaints, their gripes, their anger, and their natural ugliness. All human beings, even the best, are like that. Without a target for that anger, keeping the circus together would be a nightmare. They need someone who they can honestly feel is *worse* than they are – more reprehensible, more despicable. Over the years, I've learned that when there is one or more 'targets,' the others are more easily able to control their rage at one another. Major Maximus was that target when he was on the show. Sometimes the 'target' is not necessarily a bad person. It can be someone – anyone – as long as he or she can be a perfect 'victim' – someone whom the rest of the troupers don't feel badly about mocking or deriding or hurting. That's not to say it's *right*, that's just how it *is*."

Billy looked thoughtful for a moment. "Did you ever think what would happen if a whole *country* became that way?" he asked rhetorically. "If an entire state thought to torment a whole group of its people?"

"It's happened before."

~ ∫ ~

One evening in July of 1900, shortly after Billy's fifteenth birthday, Zeke Willis approached him. "Billy, what would you say to me selling the circus?"

"Sell *Zoltan's*? You *couldn't!* Where would we all go?"

"Or we could merge with another circus," he said, thinking out loud. "Most of us who were on the show when Zoltan passed are gone. Last year, Pemjean retired and took Elvira with him. Brenda's Lee's still a remarkably handsome woman and a damned good *equestrienne*, but it's time for her to change direction. That leaves me, and there sure isn't much call for a seventy-year-old strongman. I've got enough in my grouch bag to make it through the rest of my life."

"What about me?"

"You're at the beginning of your road and you're already a seasoned circus artiste. You'd have absolutely no difficulty joining on with a bigger show. You've got an original act, original for Europe anyway. One of the reasons I thought to merge was to make sure you and the animals had a place to go. The other performers should be able to find work easily."

Once Billy had gotten over the fear of an unknown future, he actually looked forward to seeing where his new home might be. As the month wore on, he and Willis talked more and more about finding a suitable match. "In its day, *Zoltan's* was a *big* circus. Even though it's about half the size it once was, we've always managed to stay profitable." He chuckled.

"What's funny, Governor?"

"I remember when I joined up more than thirty-three years ago. Zoltan once said, 'With us, it's chicken one day, feathers the next.'

No one was ever as optimistic as he was, and no one had a way with words like he did. I remember when we left the States to come to Europe and the huckster in charge of our sideshow complained to Zoltan that we'd run out of attractions for his show because of the deaths and defections of some of its members. Zoltan told him, 'Don't worry. There are plenty of freaks to be found in Europe, some of them wearing crowns and coronets.'"

By the early September, Willis had started formal negotiations with the Berlin-based Circus Renz. The once mighty Renz, which had been entertaining European crowds for fifty-one years, had been reduced to a remnant of its former self since the death of its founder, six years ago, for much the same reason *Zoltan's Great American* had declined: its loyalty to its performers was legendary. As those artistes passed their prime, there was simply not enough money available to hire new acts until the old performers either retired or died.

The Renz's strongman had recently died at forty-nine, so it had no weightlifter. Zeke had forgotten more tricks than most weightlifters ever learned, but he was into his eighth decade, stiff, and fat. With Alisa and Elvira Simms gone, and Brenda Lee about to retire, *Zoltan's* had several fine horses but no attractive women to ride them. The Renz's nags were dying out and they had four equestriennes. The proprietors of the two shows quickly agreed it would be a true merger, with no cash exchanged. Both sides would honor the other's commitments to its older performers.

By the first of October, Zeke was in high spirits and asked Billy to join him for lunch on Brno's huge main square. Willis led them to Švejk's pub, a large, smoky room with narrow spaces between the tables. Lunch was a gulyaš soup, followed by roasted chicken and boiled potatoes. "All right, Billy," Zeke said, as he started quaffing a tankard of Schultz Moravian stout. "Yes or no to the Renz?"

The boy's eyes lit up. "A thousand times yes!" he said eagerly. "But why should my opinion matter?"

"Because both sides agreed that you are perhaps the most important to the future of both circuses."

Billy blushed with pleasure. "But how would they know?"

"They've been quietly watching our acts and we've been watching theirs. We've had numerous discussions afterwards."

"I've not seen the Renz anywhere nearby."

"They've been south and east of us. After they finish their show in Székesfehérvár this afternoon, they'll tear down. We leave Brno tomorrow afternoon for Bratislava. A week from now, we'll announce the formation of the *Zoltan & Renz Combined Supercircuses*."

~ ∫ ~

"We're less than forty miles from Vienna." They'd just arrived at Bratislava, still officially called Pressburg. Zeke was looking at the city map posted at the entrance to the railway station. "We were supposed to meet Herr Glocken, the Renz's Governor, at the southern side of the *Starý most*, the new bridge over the Danube, at three o'clock."

"It's now six, Herr Zeke. I hope he understands that our train was delayed."

"I'm sure he does. Our advance man, was to meet us at the station. He must have told Herr Glocken of our delay. Let's check with the stationmaster. He probably left us a message."

They did and he had. "I have gone to tell Glocken of the delay. If your train gets here this evening, please join us at nine o'clock for a late dinner at Hotel Europa. Hire a carriage."

Zeke asked the stationmaster directions to the hotel. That functionary pulled out a city map which replicated the one they'd looked at before. "It's not too far from here, but I strongly suggest you hire a fiacre, particularly if you have luggage."

"We only brought a small handcase each," Billy said. "The rest of our baggage will arrive with our troupe tomorrow."

"Still, you might want to consider a private conveyance," the man replied. "It will be dark within the hour. The *bahnhof* area is not the safest part of town."

"Safe?" Zeke said. "On that there map, it looks like no more than a kilometer from here to the Europa. We've been sitting in a cramped train for hours and we could both use the exercise. Besides, you're talking to Billy Jenkins, Prince of the Cowboys, and the Quakemaker," he continued.

"Yes, Mein Herr," the stationmaster said wryly. "But the quake must have taken place quite some time ago."

Willis glared at the man, then said, "We might need something to eat to give us strength to make that short walk."

"Suit yourself," the stationmaster said. "There's a café just outside the station."

An hour later, fortified by a light meal, Zeke and Billy started walking in the direction of the Hotel Europa. As they progressed, the streets became narrower, sleazier, and considerably darker, permeated by the odor of stale beer, urine, and frying onions. Billy looked questioningly at the larger man.

"Don't worry, between the two of us we can handle ourselves against any two …"

"But not five," a surly voice came from behind them. Billy felt the unmistakable sensation of a hard, pointed object being pressed into his back.

Zeke turned in the direction of the voice. "Looks like you've got us surrounded," he addressed the man who'd first spoken. "What are you lookin' for? Money? Ain't got much of that. You're welcome to look in our satchels."

"And catch us off guard, *grosse alter*," the man, who looked to be about twenty said. "What do you think, we were born yesterday? We'll watch. *You* open the bag."

Zeke did, and showed their attackers there was nothing there but a single change of underwear and a shirt.

"The boy?"

Billy opened his handcase.

"*Scheiss!*" the leader said. "Off with your clothes then."

"Why?" Zeke asked.

"Harder for you to follow us. And Blondie here," he said, indicating Billy, "looks like he might be a nice little plaything. We might even watch you play with each other." One of the other toughs snickered.

Zeke moved in the direction of the nearest man. "Uh, uh, uh," that ruffian said menacingly. "You might be a big old fart, but this here knife more than equals the odds. Now *move!*"

When Billy had slowly pulled down his pants, the leader said, "Your underwear, too." Billy dropped his drawers. "Look at that!" a third tough said. "Blondie's a fucking *zid*! Did you know that, big fellow? That you've been hanging around with a Christ-killer? Hey, leader, maybe I've got a better use for this knife." He moved tantalizingly slowly toward the terrified boy.

Suddenly, there was a loud *crr-ackk*, not a gunshot, but loud enough to cause all action to cease. Zeke, Billy, and the three attackers who'd closed in on them shot looks in the direction of the sound. What they saw amazed them all. The two other toughs were lying on the ground. One was unconscious. The other was writhing in pain. Standing over them was a boy nearly six feet tall, not more than a couple of years Billy's senior.

"You have a problem with *zids*?" he remarked calmly to the three tormentors left standing. "Let's see," he continued. "We are now three against three. You fellows have knives, we have none. We have two satchels, you have none. Oh, yes, and we have three pairs of balls, which is probably more than I can say for the three of you."

With that, the newcomer coolly strolled up to the gang leader, grabbed his arm, and made a slight whirling motion with his right hand. An instant later, Billy's attacker hit the ground with a thud and was flat on his back As Billy pulled up his pants, the large young man advanced on one of the two remaining villains. That fellow turned, abandoned his associates, and ran down an alley, followed closely by his accomplice.

"Gentleman," the tall boy said, "you must be strangers in these parts. I apologize for the behavior of these lowlifes and hope you will not have a bad impression of Pressburg. I'm surprised to find two men, even one as powerfully built as you, walking in this area at night. But I forget my manners. My name is Samuel Lichtenfeld. As you may have gathered, I'm a *zid*, and not ashamed of it. You are …?"

"Ezekiel Willis, and this young man is Billy Jenkins."

"Not a Jewish name."

"Né Erich Rosenthal."

"Changed your name to avoid being thought of as a Jew?" the larger boy asked.

"No. It's the name I use when I perform in the circus."

One could have heard a coin drop on the street, such was the silence that greeted that statement. Finally, Lichtenfeld broke the silence and said in an awed voice, "You … are … with … the … *circus?*"

"Yes," said Billy. "Why? Are you now sorry you saved us?"

"N-no, it's not that at all. For the last five years, all I've thought about is joining a circus. Ever since my *Bar Mitzvah*, two years ago, my father encouraged me to follow my dream if that's what I really wanted. You can't be much older than me. Do you think you could … umm, tell me what life is like with the circus?"

"That would be a fair trade for your saving our lives," Zeke said. "Aren't you a bit large for your age, Samuel – may I call you Sam?"

"Or Sammy, whatever you want, Herr Willis."

"Sammy, then. I'd have taken you for at least eighteen."

"You're *my* age?" Billy said in amazement.

"Fifteen. You?"

"The same. But you are … that is you look like a *man*."

"Some people get bigger earlier. Don't hold it against me." Turning to Zeke, he asked, "Herr Willis, how large were you when *you* were fifteen?"

"A damned sight smaller than you," Zeke answered. "'Course by the time I was *sixteen*, I'd shot up some."

"Where are you staying?" Samuel asked.

"I don't rightly know," Zeke replied. "We're supposed to meet Herr Glocken at the Hotel Europa for a late dinner."

"Georg Glocken? The Governor of the *Renz*? I'd have volunteered in any event to walk with you to the Europa, but now for sure it would be my pleasure. Might I?"

"Of course," Zeke said, thinking, *God works in mysterious ways. We're about to merge with the Renz. Both circuses are starving for young performers, particularly a strongman. Now, out of the dark comes this young feller wants to join on a circus in the worst possible way. Maybe this is part of a bigger plan.*

13

"O.K., Sammy. You're now a part of *Zoltan-Renz*. I think I've got just the job for you."

"'O.K.,' Herr Willis? What means that?"

"It means all right. I wouldn't have expected a German feller to understand that. You are from Germany, aren't you?"

"Hungary," Lichtenfeld replied.

"It's an American slang term that started with some newspaper in Boston sixty years ago. I kinda' got used to it."

"O.K. then," Lichtenfeld said, smiling. "You said you have a job for me?"

"Unless you want to use your strength to put up tents and shovel elephant shit all your life, we gotta' make you a performer. How about being a circus strongman?"

"A *strongman* Herr Willis?"

"I learned to do it when I was almost three times your age. No reason you can't."

"Don't you have to be *very* big and *very* strong to do that?"

"Helps. But you got a good start on that already. Besides, I don't know if you've noticed or not in the time you've been on the show, but this here 'Combined Circuses' doesn't have a strongman. Leastwise, not one younger than seventy years."

Billy, who'd been listening to this conversation, said, "Herr Zeke, you said you learned to be a weightlifter when you were older?"

"I did. From an old guy named Ignatz Roozeboom, a south African Dutchman who used to travel with Zoltan back in the day. Hell, he did *everything* – lion trainer, horse trainer, bareback rider, strongman ..."

"South Africa ..." Billy's eyes took on a dreamy look. "Gold and diamonds and explorers ... and ... and *Africa*. Mein Gott, I'd like to go there some day."

"They got circuses down there, too." Turning back to Sammy Lichtenfeld, he said, "Get a good night's rest, 'cause tomorrow we start your training."

~ ∫ ~

"Sammy, you know what a muscle is?"

"Sure, Herr Willis." The strapping lad flexed his biceps proudly.

"That's one set of muscles. But the body has different kinds of muscles, and you must learn their different abilities if you want to be a circus strongman. Some are long muscles, some are short, and some are broad. Long muscles, like in your arms, they're for throw and for lift. Broad muscles are for heavy strain. You know what the trapezius is?

"Sure. It's that swing, way up in the air where the acrobats –"

"Not exactly. The trapezius is the muscle here." He slapped the boy's upper back. "That's a broad muscle, the trapezius, the toughest muscle in the body. Under it is the splenius muscle." He hit the Samuel's neck with his open hand. "Also broad and tough. Now, let's begin. You've picked up heavy things before?" Zeke bent at the knees and got his hands under a nearby iron cannonball.

Lichtenfeld nodded. "I know you've got to get the power of your legs and back into it. You don't just lift or you can rupture yourself."

"Correct." Zeke straightened up with the ball in his hands. "Now, when you get it this high, you can throw it up." He did so, tossing the ball some distance in the air. Samuel Lichtenfeld stared wide-eyed. Willis had as easily lifted and tossed the forty-pound weight as though it were a plaything. Then Zeke stood up and let the ball thump to the ground. "You don't catch it in your hands from so high up, or you'll break something. You catch it on your neck."

"On my *neck*? Not to be disrespectful Herr Willis, but are you crazy?"

Zeke made no reply. He hefted the ball again, stood up, threw it three feet into the air, bowed his bald head, and caught the thing with a meaty thud on the back of his neck. He jiggled his upper body just slightly to balance the ball there for a moment, then let it roll over his shoulder and caught it in his arms.

Lichtenfeld gasped. "My God, I'd rather bust my stomach than break my neck!"

"You don't have to do either, Sammy. It just takes practice. You build up a pad of splenius muscle, it takes the blow. The trapezius muscle takes the weight. I'll teach you how. Bend your head."

Lichtenfeld did so. Willis gently laid the ball in the declivity between the boy's occiput and the nape of his neck. "Put your hand there. Feel it. The ball must land in the curve between the back of the head and this first knob of backbone. *Never* hit that knob, or you'll never move again."

"Jesus!"

"I thought you were Jewish."

"I am, but what else would you expect me to say?"

"You'll get used to it. It just takes practice," Zeke said, lifting the ball off him.

"How do I practice, Herr Willis?"

"The first time – heck, the first *many* times – put the ball on top of your head, bend your head, let the ball roll, and catch it on your neck. After a while, toss the ball a little bit in the air over your head, bend, and catch it on your neck. Toss the ball a little higher each time. That you can do by yourself, Young Hercules."

"*Young Hercules!* That sounds wonderful!"

"Enough self-congratulation. You're going to earn that name. For now, show me how you begin. Pick up the ball." Zeke let the ball thud to the ground again. Lichtenfeld squatted properly, knees on either side of it, got his hands under it, and stood up. "No, no, no, Sammy. You make it look too easy. Make believe it's ten times heavier. Strain. Work up a sweat."

"But Herr Willis, I can't sweat on command!"

"True, but nobody knows that. Carry a rag. Wipe your face and your hands. Shake your head in doubt. It *looks* real to the jossers."

Samuel, feeling rather silly, pretended to be mopping away beads of worry and determination.

"Good. You're too young to grow a big beard, which is unfortunate, 'cause it looks good on a strongman. For now, we can shave your head."

"*What???*"

"Shave your head. The scalp sweats more than any other part of your body. A shiny wet head makes you look like a real strongman."

"But I'll look so … *old*."

"People get used to a young man with a bald head."

"There's sure a lot more to this than I figured," Lichtenfeld muttered.

"Anything good is worth working for. Even looking ugly for. Now, put the ball on your neck and practice balancing it there. Walk around like that all the time. It will make your muscles strong. But *never* let the jossers see you practice."

~ ∫ ~

"How's he doing, Zeke?"

"He's taking it very seriously, Georg," Willis said to his co-Governor, Glocken.

"I see him walking a couple of hours a day at the back of the tober, hunched under a cannonball. I can't wait to see him do his breakout. When do you think that will be?"

"Right after Christmas," the Quakemaker said. "Young Hercules – that's what I think we'll call him – even reminds me of the way I was in *my* younger days. Heck, Guv'nor, you've got the same gift of gab as Zoltan had. I can't wait to see how you introduce him to the public."

~ ∫ ~

The intermission was a torment for Sammy Lichtenfeld because he had been scheduled for the second half of the program. "Don't worry," Billy said to him. "You'll do fine. Even if something goes wrong – and it certainly did with me – you'll be back for more. It's the dead of winter. Osijek is a tiny little dot on the map and you're doing these folks a big favor just being here."

"Easy for you to say," Lichtenfeld remarked. "You're a seasoned trouper."

"I'm the same age as you. Herr Zeke once told me, 'No actor was ever an actor until he started acting.' One more thing, Sammy."

"What's that?"

"I go on right after you. If anyone even *thinks* of hooting, I'll shoot 'em."

That broke the tension. The two boys laughed as the intermission came to an end.

Whether he had been nervous or apprehensive or downright terrified, Young Hercules put on a commendable display of showmanship.

To a loud fanfare, Georg Glocken gave his fulsome introduction. "Good people of Osijek, we now have a very special act. ... This tremendous human being was discovered by a scientific expedition exploring Patagonia, which means 'The Land of the Giants' in the Argentinean language. As hard as it is to believe, this young giant is only *ten years old*. The scientists set a trap for him and he fell in. The fully developed adults of his country would simply have climbed out of the pit ..." This palaver went on for some time. "And now, clad like his namesake Hercules, in the skins of a savage lion he slew with his bare hands ... the world's strongest man under twenty-one years of age ... *YOUNG HERCULES!*"

Samuel Lichtenfeld strode in through the tent's back door with a tread almost as majestic as one of the elephants, which came in right behind him. A bass drum pounded with each step. The elephant was hauling a rope net, in which three cannonballs dragged along the ground, clanking heavily. The elephant took care to walk slowly, leaning forward as if the weight were a load even for the behemoth.

Young Hercules followed all the advice Zeke Willis had given, began by heaving and puffing audibly as he rolled the iron balls from the net to the ring center. Zeke had arranged for one of the newfangled electric lamps to shine a shaft of light directly onto Sammy's shaven head.

After much rag-wiping of his hands and repeated small adjustments, the muscular lad struggled mightily – and took the better part of two minutes – to lift just one ball in both hands. While the audience ooh-ed and aah-ed, he put down the ball and did some more wiping – hands, head, chin, even armpits – slowly lifted the same ball again, tucked it under one arm, stooped, and with even fiercer effort lifted a second ball with the other hand. The audience erupted in applause. Lichtenfeld swiveled that hand around to tuck the ball under that arm, so he was holding the two balls between his elbows and his waist on either side. That left his hands empty. When he stooped again, he was just barely able to grasp the third ball with his fingertips. By the time he had struggled erect, two balls under his arms and the third precariously held by the extended fingers of both hands, and then put them down, young Samuel Lichtenfeld no longer had to pretend to be sweating.

The conclusion of the act went just as well. Zeke Willis walked into the ring, himself dressed in skins, and slowly climbed an eight-foot high A-frame ladder. Young Hercules grunted and sweated and heaved the ball up to the huge bear of a man, who struggled mightily to set the ball at the top, where the legs of the ladder joined. The two of them engaged in a dialogue of grunts and gestures. Finally, at a signal, the bass drum rumbled from the orchestra from soft up to loud. Lichtenfeld made a chopping gesture and went down on his hands and knees. He was sweating now so profusely that the beads were visible as they dropped from his face to the ground. His eyes were bulging. As the drum crescendoed to one thunderous *boom!,* Zeke Willis pushed the ball off the ladder. In the sudden silence that followed, its hitting Young Hercules' neck sounded like a sledgehammer whacking a side of beef.

Sammy Lichtenfeld gave a mighty grunt, but his head stayed on, his neck stayed intact, and the cannonball stayed steady there. After a suspenseful moment, keeping his head bent, he erected himself onto his knees, then slowly onto his feet. The iron ball stayed put. He waited for the applause, which rose around him. Then he let the ball roll over his shoulder and down his extended arm. At the last instant, he flipped his hand so it was palm up, and the ball came to rest on it. Then he dropped it so the audience could hear its convincingly heavy thud on the ground. The entire tent was now a paroxysm of noise and stamping of a hundred of pairs of feet as Young Hercules raised his arms and assumed the **V**-pose.

~ ∫ ~

"Hurtin' a bit, Sammy?" Zeke asked solicitously the next morning.

"A bit, hell," groaned young Lichtenfeld. "I believe I *did* break my neck yesterday. Damn my showing off!

"Not to worry, Young Hercules," Zeke said. "Our company physician will promptly fix you up."

A little man with a neatly trimmed mustache and goatee came scurrying up.

"What's good for a busted neck, Herr Doktor?" Lichtenfeld asked him.

"Lint, liniment, and laudanum. I will use the lint to dab on the liniment while you swig some of the laudanum."

14

Brenda Lee had agreed to stay on with the combined *Zoltan-Renz* show solely to train the four new equestriennes, who ranged in age from eighteen to twenty. As Billy's sixteenth birthday approached, she was still remarkably attractive. Her face was starting to show age lines when one got within a couple feet, but her body still retained its youthful tightness and her small but pronounced breasts stood erect.

Although Billy had been with the show more than three years and had worked with the Countess du Bourges every day, he'd not lost a shred of his puppy love for her. Now, as he neared five feet ten and his body had filled out, his fantasies about her had taken on a distinctly *un*-puppy-like bent. "How long do you intend to stay with the circus?" he asked her, one day in April.

"Zeke asked me the same thing last September, when Zoltan's merged with the Renz. I told them I'd give it another eight months. He asked me for a little more," she said lightly. "So I told him, 'Quakemaker, I'll tell you what. I'll give it 'til the day after Billy's sixteenth birthday, then I'm off to Paris for keeps.'"

"Oh," he said dejectedly. "So it's only a couple more months then?"

"Guess so." She patted him on the shoulder. "Why, look at you, Billy Jenkins. In these past few months you've shot up so you're practically a man, and a damn good looking one at that."

"I always wanted to catch up with you," he blurted. "Now it seems I never will."

"Good heavens, Billy. Why would you want to catch up with an old woman?" Then she sighed as she said, "It seems like only yesterday when I was fourteen. By then I'd been on the show five years. It was only a mud show, but it *was* a show and I had ten years with Zoltan – he was like a grandfather to me. In fact, he was probably the closest thing to a *father* I ever knew. He and my mother ..." She stopped in mid-sentence. "She'd be more than seventy by now. I wonder ...?"

"You had problems with your parents, too?"

"I never knew my father, so I couldn't tell you. My mother did some strange things, but in the end I was pretty cruel to her and drove her away. She was on the circus, too. Madame Solitaire. And she really did have a hard, sad, solitary life."

"So you never knew your father, I never knew my mother, and we ended up hating the ones we were stuck with."

"When you're young you tend to see things in black and white. You never know 'til you're much older that there's a deeper, more subtle meaning to the words 'right' and 'wrong,' and the lines blur."

As April gave way to May, Billy became more depressed as he realized the time when he could talk with Brenda Lee was rapidly drawing to a close. More than that, his urge to do much more than talk to her occupied most of his waking hours.

One day, while the circus was traveling between Reutlingen and Freiburg-im-Breisgau, Billy asked Zeke if the older man would mind if they rode together atop one of the circus wagons. "Absolutely not, Billy. I'd love the company."

During the journey, their talk turned to intimate matters. "Herr Zeke, for the past three years I could always turn to you for wise advice."

"I appreciate that, although I don't know that I'm all that wise. Shucks, when you get to be my age, ain't nothing you can do anymore *but* be wise. Might I try and guess what this conversation's going to be about?"

Billy blushed furiously.

"I thought as much. You've probably heard the same rumors everyone else around the tober's been hearing: your friend Sammy Lichtenfeld's been seen squiring many women – and I don't only mean the young ones on the show, but some of the older jossers as well, and some of 'em married."

"Well, yes, but I didn't feel I could talk to him."

"If you're asking if I've been with women, the answer is yes I have, even though I never tied the knot. If you're asking me if the old saying, 'In the dark all cats are gray' is true, I can tell you it is not. Every woman I've been with – and there haven't been all that many – is different. But one thing I've learned is that the more you can pleasure them the more they *will* pleasure you."

"How does one …?"

"Don't expect me to answer that, Billy. The first introduction I had was with an older woman." Billy blanched. The only attractive older woman he knew was Brenda Lee, and surely …

Zeke continued, "I was a little older than you and she was a married woman back in South Carolina. Quite old. I'd say she was maybe even thirty, and she was quite hefty. I had no idea what to do, but she taught me."

"Did you find it disgusting to put your … you know … in her …?"

"Not at all," Zeke said. "*Not at all*. It was the most pleasurable experience I ever had. Once a man has had it, and so my first woman told me, once a woman has had it, life seems to revolve around when you're next going to get it."

"I've heard that sometimes men and men ... and women and women ..."

"Oh, yes, like our Spencer brothers. And I knew two extraordinarily beautiful red-headed women 'way back when – I could happily have tied the knot with either of them ... Some people find *that* disgusting, but I say live and let live. I take it you're still a virgin?"

Billy blushed again.

"Nothing to be ashamed of. Every man and woman starts out that way. I'm sure there are good and moral women all over the world – more of 'em in the United States where I come from than here in Europe – who pretend sex doesn't exist, or if it does, it's to be suffered through as a way of having children, and *that's it*. What they don't realize is that good, modest women are built no different from any other kind."

"Do you feel uncomfortable that I'm asking you these things?"

"Heck no," Zeke replied. "I feel good that you asked me. There are lots of fellows your age who brag a lot, especially when they *haven't* done anything. They snicker and preen like roosters, but it's all for show. It's kind of like circuses. You've probably noticed that *Zoltan-Renz's* posters and the posters of all successful shows are restrained. Once you have the real goods, you don't have to do empty bragging. Leave the flummery to the would-be's and the has-beens and the never-will-be's. Remember this, Billy, if you kiss-and-tell, and if you name names, word gets around. Be discreet."

"Can ... can I ask you something *really* confidential, Herr Zeke?"

"I don't see why not." The road on which they were riding was steadily climbing, and they could see both the heavily wooded Black Forest and the beginning of the northern Alps.

"The Countess du Bourges ...?"

"Brenda Lee? Boy, you've been making calf eyes at her ever since you joined on the circus. She's more than thirty years older than you. But she's still a damned desirable woman. I'm sure in her day many a youngster your age had those very thoughts about her."

"She'll be leaving the show the day after my birthday."

"Will she now? Something symbolic to be said about that."

The wagon approached the outskirts of Freiburg and they spoke no more.

~ ʃ ~

"Flowers, Billy? How thoughtfully sweet of you. And clover pink, 'my' color from a long time ago in Paris. How could you have known?"

"I listened to circus talk a while back. When Herr Hobbs and Alisa were still on the show."

"It's sad," she said. "Life goes by more quickly every year. So many have come and gone. Now Zeke and I are the only two left. We'll be gone before you know it."

"But you are still … you are very, very beautiful."

"And you are very charming, young Billy Jenkins. Even though I can see the difference between what I am and what I was when I look in the mirror, it's nice to hear."

~ ʃ ~

It was Billy's sixteenth birthday and Brenda Lee's last day on the show. The last stand was in Colmar, which was in the Alsace, but which was now controlled by Germany. "Here's where it all started," Willis remarked to the small assembly as they walked through a street that was little wider than an alley. They came to an old two-story stucco house that had a low dormer attic under the eaves. In response to the questioning looks from Sam Lichtenfeld and Billy, Zeke continued, "Rue du Lycée number eight. Where The Governor was born."

"Herr Hobbs?" Billy asked. "I always thought he was born in America."

"I meant *The* Governor, Billy."

"*Zoltan*," Brenda Lee said softly.

"I thought it fitting," Zeke said, looking at her directly. "The guard changes once again and the torch is passed."

That evening, they ate a simple French country dinner at an inn from whence Brenda Lee would depart the following morning for Paris. After dinner, the remainder of the group, with exception of Brenda Lee and Billy, quietly departed the inn.

"Looks like it's just you and me, Billy," Brenda Lee said.

"It's your last night on the show, Countess. I ... I've saved my money from the circus and bought you a farewell present if you don't mind."

Now it was Brenda's turn to blush as he handed her a small jewelry box. Her eyes widened as she opened it and saw a graceful heart-shaped pendant with a single small diamond in the middle. "It's beautiful, Billy. I will wear it proudly," she said. "Would you help me put it on?"

He did, with trembling hands. He thought he felt the slightest tremor at her throat.

"Shall we stroll through the streets of Colmar?" she asked. "If this is going to be the last place I go with the circus, I'd like to make the memory last."

"Maybe we could walk by Zoltan's house again? I saw the special look in your eye and I knew this place held wonderful memories for you."

"I wish you would have known Zoltan," she said. "He'd have liked you."

"Was Zoltan his first name or his last name?"

"None of us on the show ever found out. I remember at his funeral they asked me and I told the troupe he'd always been nothing but 'Zoltan' to me. It was so odd. Every trouper on the show had two or three different pista names, besides their real ones, and he never even had a *whole* name."

After awhile, the evening had turned chilly. Billy took off his coat and placed it over Brenda Lee's shoulders. "Ah, a true gentleman," she said. "Perhaps I'd best be getting back to the inn."

When they got to the inn, Brenda said, almost casually, "I have a birthday present for you, too. I left it in my room. Come, I'll give it to you there."

They entered the bedroom. Looking around, Billy saw a huge matrimonial bed, a chest of drawers, and a nightstand with a large, wide candle, which provided soft light for the room. Brenda Lee gently closed the door to the room. The candlelight caught the diamond at her throat and reflected the glow in her eyes.

"I'd like … that is … might I kiss you just this once?" Billy choked. *Poor love-smitten boy,* she thought. *What harm would it do?* "All right," she said softly. She figured she'd let him kiss her, count to five, and it would be done. His kiss was almost innocent in its intensity and she mentally counted to three before she found, to her immense surprise, that her eyes had closed and she was kissing him back, her tongue willfully flicking in and out of her mouth, caressing his.

She had no idea how long the kiss lasted, but they were both shaking when it was over. "Shall we try that again?" she said, trying to keep her voice lighter than she felt.

The second kiss was more passionate and lasted even longer than the first. While her eyes were closed, she felt his hand fumble at her corset. "Billy," she breathed. "We mustn't … we can't …"

"Why not?"

"Because you're so young. It would be so wrong …" She relaxed, closed her eyes again, and said, "even if it feels so good."

His response was to move his hand to her shirtwaist again, more forcefully this time.

"Wait." *There's nothing really so wrong with this. He's a man. I'm a woman. It's the most natural thing in the world. Why not let him see it all?*

She gently took his hands from her shirtwaist and put her index finger to his lips. He stood there transfixed, not knowing what to do or say as she removed first her outer clothing, then her underclothing. Her smallish, pink-tipped breasts stood out proudly, beckoning his hands to touch, to squeeze their nipples, to enjoy the greatest intimacy a man and woman can share. While he stood there, she took his hands in each of hers and moved them to her breasts. He did not need further coaxing and his hands, then his lips, moved of their own accord. As she felt the chilly warmth of that old feeling assaulting her, she started moaning softly.

They went on this way for some while before Billy said, somewhat ashamedly, "I … I don't know what to do from here. You are the first … ever …"

That knowledge seemed to excite Brenda Lee yet more, and she tugged at his belt, loosening it before lowering his trousers and after that his drawers. Now *her* hands and lips found what they were looking for. He may have been only sixteen, but he was certainly of sufficient size that she knew that once they lay in the large bed together, it would be a field of battle on which both sides would emerge victorious.

With a *whoosh* of breath, he climaxed in her mouth so quickly it surprised her. "Now you do the same for me," she said breathlessly, reaching down and removing the rest of her clothing, but for the single-diamond pendant which she still wore around her neck. She lay back on the bed. Billy unbuttoned his own shirt and when he was naked, she pulled him to her. His fingers and tongue were quickly and naturally adept, and now her moaning rose to a shrill crescendo as her spasms came stronger and faster.

For the briefest moment, she thought about how *young* he was, but then she became a mindless, demanding female animal. "My God, I'm coming, I'm coming, I'm *coming!*" The last was a mingled scream and moan as she thrashed madly on the bed, her nether parts hot and wet, soaked more than they had been in a long, long time.

They lay side by side, breathing softly for only a few minutes before he felt himself growing rock hard under the ministrations of her fingers. Unable to comprehend what was happening, he reached for her breasts again. This time, she couldn't wait and pulled him on top of her. He entered her tight, slippery cavity and for the second time in a brief period, he could not help himself as he shot his fluid into her. Moments later, she erupted with the same gasping scream-moan as she had before.

Afterward, they slept, but not for a long time, and when they awoke, they made love again, and after they had slept awhile longer, yet again, until, by next morning, they were both sated and exhausted, as well as exhilarated. When they awoke, Brenda Lee raised up on one elbow. Her breasts seemed larger in that posture. His eyes lit up again, as he looked into her green eyes, which were now suffused with the embers of a distant, simmering fire.

"I love you, Brenda Lee," he said dreamily.

"To be more accurate, you love what we *did*," she said in a voice still half-asleep.

"No, I love *you*. I'll always love you."

"And I you, Billy. For letting me be your first, and for pleasuring this woman more than you know. Now, do you want to keep talking or do you want to do something else before we have to get up and go down the hall for breakfast?"

Afterward, they washed and dressed, each drinking in a last vision of the other, trying to etch what they saw permanently in their minds. And when, after breakfast, they parted, she squeezed his hand and said softly, "Happy Birthday, Billy Jenkins. *Au revoir.*"

15

When Zeke Willis quietly passed away at the beginning of March, 1902, the last tie connecting Billy to *Zoltan's Great American Circus* was severed. Billy had heard from Brenda Lee several times during the first three months after they'd parted. He answered each letter professing eternal love. But, as often happens, the term "absence makes the heart grow fonder" was overtaken by "out of sight, out of mind." Their correspondence grew less frequent and more platonic and when, six months later, the Countess du Bourges wrote him that she'd taken up with a widower closer to her own age, any jealousy he felt was muted by the fact that he and Sammy Lichtenfeld were enjoying the company of other females as well.

By mid-1902, both young men had established themselves as fair game for every so-inclined woman, young and not-so-young, who came within their vicinity. Each had continued to better his act, both professionally and sexually.

Young Hercules never forgot the old Quakemaker's admonition: if the ball falls on the knob, you'll never walk again. He took to bending iron bars with his bare hands.

"Now *that* looks difficult," Billy told him one day, while they were strolling and sampling the cheap foreign foods – Chinese, Indian, Turkish – in Frankfurt's Leipzigerstrasse.

"It could be, but the place where the bars bend has been carefully hinged, so small and precise you'd have to be less than a foot away to see the joints, and even then, they're tight enough that it does take *some* effort to squeeze them together."

"What about wheeling a cart loaded with people by a chain held between your teeth? Or the tug-of-war with one of the bulls?"

"Professional secret," Lichtenfeld said, winking at his friend. "Just like a good part of your act has gone to the birds."

"You know, Sammy, once you win them over, falcons, hawks, and golden eagles are more faithful than many ladies I've met," Billy said equably.

"Between shooting, roping, riding, and training wild birds of prey, you've become the consummate circus cowboy. You've certainly expanded your horizons."

"To where? Germany? Hungary? Holland? Here I am, 'the Prince of the Cowboys,' and I've never even left the Continent."

"Aren't European women dazzling enough to keep you satisfied? Now that Queen Victoria, bless her dear old heart, has passed away, it seems they've released a lot of moral brakes. They say the new *Überbretti* Cabaret in Berlin is wilder than anything they have in Paris."

"Is that the only thing on your mind?"

"That and this great food. The beer's not bad either. You're really serious about getting off the Continent?"

"If I were a *real* cowboy, I'd at least have *visited* America."

"The land of the cowboys."

"It *used* to be the land of the cowboys. The Wild West, the great frontier. I've read that the day of the cowboy has ended in the U.S. First the modern railroads, now motor cars." He sighed. "Nowadays, if you want to see the America that *was*, you have to go to Buffalo Bill's show. Even that is mostly a bunch of old guys sitting around, trying to recapture their youth."

"Have some *shish kebab*," Sammy said, changing the subject. "*That* came from the Ottomans when they rode through the steppes of central Asia on the way to Turkey."

"Thank you," Billy said, taking the skewer of grilled lamb.

During their time on the Renz, the young men had crossed paths with several shows. As in any profession, they learned which ones to trust and which to avoid. Young people everywhere tend to congregate with their own, and it was no different with circus performers. Aside from experimentation, some frankly sexual, genuine friendships developed among artistes. The brothers Spencer, who had not lasted very long on the Renz, had been replaced by a pair of gorgeous young blonde Lesbian lovers, who were wonderfully adept on the flying trapeze.

Often, when Sammy and Billy tired of females pursuing *them*, they'd spend evenings walking around whatever town they were in with Rosa and Riane. The girls appreciated Billy's and Sammy's company because no one looked askance at them when they were escorted by such impressive young swains.

Just as Sammy and Billy were coming to the high end of Leipzigerstrasse, Rosa and Riane were starting down the other side of the street. "Share a beer, sweetheart?" Billy said in his most *ersatz* charming tone.

"Gee, did ya' hear that, Gertie?" Rosa said, using her nickname for her lover. "I think Mister Thrill-a-Minute is trying to charm me out of me knickers. Share a beer my arse, mate. If ye're too bloody cheap to stand me to my own I'll just keep walkin', I will." Rosa Davenport was slightly-above-cockney English.

"Yeah, Rose Petal, I'll bet I can get the big guy to spring for my lunch. What do you say, big fella'? Care to treat a Swiss Miss to a meal?"

"Sure," Sammy said. "Anything to avoid our cowboy moping around and complaining that he's never been outside Europe and how badly he wants to go to a land of endless skies and vast frontiers." He punched Billy in the shoulder.

When the four of them were seated at an outside table and had been served their beer and würstel, Riane asked, "You really want to get out of Europe for awhile, Billy?"

"More than anything," he replied. "Now that the days of the real American Wild West seem to be over, there's hardly any place left in the world …"

"You might be in luck," she said. "The Knie, a reputable Swiss show, and the Hagenbeck, which you know of course, are putting together a traveling troupe to play South Africa. With the war winding down and reports of the English concentration camps, they can't seem to find many volunteer performers, and … Are you all right, Billy?"

He was coughing uncontrollably from the beer that had gone down his windpipe. When he was finally able to stop his hacking, he managed to say, in a pinched voice, "S…South Africa? Ever since the start of the Boer War I've always wanted … Do you think Herr Glocken? …"

~ ∫ ~

"You're sure that's what you want to do?"

"I've never wanted anything more in my life, Herr Glocken." He looked down toward the ground. "I feel embarrassed leaving the Renz for another show after all you've done for me. All you have to do is say the word and I'll stay."

"I'd say the word," Glocken said, "but winter is the off-season for the Renz. I don't mind saving the money and I'm willing to take the chance you'll be back." He puffed at a long cheroot, so different from Hobbs's cigarettes and Zeke Willis's pipe. "You've never caused the show any trouble. You've always more than pulled your own weight. I'll happily write a note to the Hagenbecks and to the manager at the Knie on your behalf. What about your friend?"

"Sammy's constantly telling me he gets all the excitement he wants ... in other ways. Herr Glocken, I can't thank you enough! I promise ..."

"No promises, Billy. It's easy to make a promise. It's sometimes much harder to keep that promise."

16

"My God, I've never seen anything so beautiful in my life!" Billy exclaimed to Sophia d'Angelo as they stood on the deck of the *Graf von Nolte*. The ship, which had left the late fall clouds and frigid temperatures of Bremerhaven behind a month ago, had just entered Table Bay on a balmy summer morning in December, 1902. The trip down the west coast of Africa had been busy but uneventful. The Hagenbeck-Knie *World Circus of Marvels* had made arrangements to have the necessary show stock – horses, an elephant, and, for Billy, an assortment of raptors – available as soon as the troupe arrived on Cape Colony soil.

Billy had met Sophia on the first day out. The dark-haired, dark-eyed aerialist had been attracted to him, and he to her, immediately. The shipboard romance had kept them entertained, and frequently happily exhausted, during the southbound journey.

"Cape Town's supposed to be the most gorgeous landfall in the world," Sophia said, gazing in awe at the three-thousand-foot-high flat-topped mesa, Table Mountain, which rose immediately behind the city. "There's no 'table cloth' to obstruct our view," she continued, referring to the clouds that covered the mountain in heavy fog many days each month.

The green-black water was mildly choppy. The whitecaps, the splendid whitewashed city, and a number of southward-marching peaks – Signal Hill, Devil's Peak, Lion's Head, the Twelve Apostles, and more than fifty other sharply-etched mountains – presented a dramatic picture that would be seared in the young man's memory for the rest of his life.

Karl Kürtner, the thirty-year old director of the traveling troupe, was the complete antithesis of the stereotype pompous Swiss burgher: a mane of red, frizzy hair surrounded an open, ruddy, freckled face. He was slightly built and his body seemed to be in perpetual motion. He addressed his charges as they debarked onto Port Street. "All right, my friends, now the fun begins. We'll be giving six performances a week, two on Saturday, and one each on Monday, Tuesday, Wednesday, and Thursday. That'll leave you two full days of free time each week, although I must caution you that the Cape Dutch do not cavil to much activity on the Sabbath day. You may never get this far away from home again, so make the most of it."

"Herr Kürtner, where do we pitch the tober?" one of the performers asked.

"On the other side of Table Mountain – a rather useless piece of wastleland owned by Cecil Rhodes called Kirstenbosch. Nothing there but a bunch of oak trees. It's overrun with weeds and more pigs than you've ever seen, eating acorns and whatever else grows there. It might have been better to show closer to the city proper, but Kirstenbosch seems to be the only place close to the city with almost unlimited room. Every other place is hemmed in by the ocean or the mountains."

During the next several days, the troupers found *Kaapstad* a wonderfully exciting city. As Billy walked along the city's residential streets, he found the feel of the city to be both similar to, and at the same time very different from, Germany.

"Cape Dutch architecture," Kürtner told him. "More like Holland than any other part of Europe, but more spread out, since the Cape Colony has more space than the Low Countries and Denmark combined. Oh! Look at that, will you?"

A parade was passing by. Three dozen men and women, lighter-skinned than the local Bantu population, but darker than whites, all dressed in garishly-colored outfits, the men wearing top hats, came jiggling and bouncing, and shimmying and shaking by, playing all manner of brass instruments. They were trailed by five drummers, two beating bass drums, and three pounding out the rhythm on snares attached by straps to their necks.

"Cape Colored." Kürtner said. "Mixed black-and-white or Asiatic-and white."

"*Mulattin?*" Billy said.

"Yes. They'll make parade for any reason or no reason, simply to have a good time. That reminds me, we'll need a band and I can't think of a better kind to have. It'll add a native touch to our show." He hastened over to the middle-aged man who seemed to be the leader of the band and returned moments later, a huge grin on his face. "Wonderful!" he exclaimed. "Hagenbeck will be delighted! I got fifteen of them for a quarter of what we'd pay in Europe! They'll tour with the troupe as long as we assure them safe passage back to Cape Town at the end of the stand."

After five days of rehearsal with the show animals and the band, the troupe was ready to make parade from the City Centre to the tober in Kirstenbosch. Most of the hundred thousand Cape Towners crammed the streets and alleys, cheering, clapping, and thoroughly enjoying themselves, buoyed by the warm, sunny day, the "Cape Doctor," a fresh wind that had blown all the sooty, stale air out of the city, and the novelty of what they were seeing.

While Kürtner had worried that some of the more staid and sober Calvinist inhabitants would take offense at the tight, scanty, and very revealing fleshings, sequins, and spangles worn by the nubile young women atop the prancing Percherons, if there were any such bluestockings in the crowd, they were not noticed, because what few of them the performers saw were clapping and stomping as eagerly as anyone else.

The first three weeks' performances were *sfondone* – "straw crowd sellouts" – and a goodly number of jossers truly were content to sit on the piles of straw in front of and around the available seats. The troupe eagerly gave the audience their money's worth. Because of the small number of artistes, several had to double up on their acts. Billy alternated with Kürtner as ringmaster. He had no trouble communicating with the audience since, during his time on *Zoltan's Great American* and later on the *Zoltan-Renz*, he'd become proficient in English, French, and Italian – the latter thanks to Sophia – as well as his native German, and he had a sufficient command of Dutch to make himself understood.

Billy peppered his *voltige* and shooting *pista* acts with his newly acquired birds of prey. He used his turn as ringmaster to perform an ever more audacious number of roping tricks. One of the most well-received of these was when he roped a member of the audience who was sitting in the front row, and dragged that unsuspecting man or woman to the center of the tent.

The handsome young cowboy was besieged by showers of *fynbos* and other local flora during the performances. The jossers were even more taken with the Italian girl than they were with Billy, for the majority of the audience was made up of English, Australian, New Zealander, and Canadian soldiers far away from home, and the available – and young, beautiful – girls were few and far between.

On days off, Billy and Sophia traveled around the Cape Peninsula, voraciously soaking up the sights. It was a three-hour climb to the top of Table Mountain, but the young people were invariably rewarded by the stunning view from the summit to the City, Robben Island out in the Bay, the mountain sentinels that ended at the Cape of Good Hope, and north to the barren Cape Flats. Sophia fell in love with the *dassies*, tailless squirrels who resided atop Table Mountain. Those creatures invariably begged or cadged whatever snacks the lovers were nibbling on at the moment.

Three weeks after the first performance, in mid-January, 1903, Billy borrowed a gelding from the show's stock and rode down to Cape Point, where he intended to spend the night before returning to the tober the following day. "Want to come with me, Sophia? They say it's gorgeous down there. The Atlantic and the Indian Ocean come together and the two currents clash into each other *sideways*."

"No, thanks. I'm told the place is overrun with *not* particularly friendly baboons. Would you mind if I passed on your invitation just this once?"

"So the resident males can see you in all your stunning beauty without your ever-present escort?" he said, mock jealously.

"Have a good time, Smarty," she said jovially. "Just remember, I don't need a pet baboon to share our wagon with us."

The countryside on the ride down the western side of the Cape was mountainous and marked by the Atlantic Ocean on Billy's right. From sedate, manicured gentility to sometimes raucous beach towns, to miles of empty, ghostly quiet countryside, Billy could not recall feeling more at peace than he did on his southward journey. From time to time, he would let the gelding have his head, and the horse would gallop or canter or run for a distance before stopping to crop a patch of nearby grass or take water at a natural pond.

By mid-afternoon, Billy arrived at his destination, a steep, high cliff, from which he had an unobstructed view of the coastline and the sea, several hundred feet below. The crash of the surf was loud and the salt-spray smell of the two oceans coming together was aphrodisiac in its wildness. Billy intended to stay there until nearly sundown, then ride back along the eastern side of the Cape for the night's lodging.

He'd been walking atop the ridge for some time when two men on horseback approached him. By the cut of their clothes and the way they sat their saddles, they appeared to be townsmen. Billy nodded to them and they to him. One was about thirty and bearded in the Afrikaaner fashion. The other was clean-shaven, perhaps ten years older. "Good afternoon, Meneers," he said respectfully.

"Good afternoon," the younger man said. "You are the famous circus cowboy, Billy Jenkins? You needn't look shocked, Mister Jenkins. My friend Raynes and I have been following you for some hours."

"You're not highwaymen, I hope?" He smiled to show he didn't think they were.

"To the contrary," the older man said. "I am Daniel Rayne, Cecil Rhodes' clerk, and this," he said, indicating the bearded younger man, "is Jan Christian Smuts, State Attorney to *Oom* Paul's government."

"Rhodes? Kruger? The two opposing leaders?"

"I'm afraid that's no longer true," Smuts replied sadly. "Lord Kitchener's in charge of the Commonwealth forces. The Old Man no longer knows who's in charge. Not him, in any event, because the Boers can't do anything except mount guerilla raids here and there, just enough to make the British nervous."

"The war has become an international embarrassment to us as well," Rayne added. "Can you imagine, a so-called 'civilized' country scorching the earth of a bunch of simple farmers and keeping their women and children in concentration camps? The whole world portrays Britain as a bunch of uncivilized brutes. What other country in history has done such a thing? Who could think of such monstrosities?" Rayne continued, his face reddening. "Mr. Jenkins, you're a German, are you not?"

"I am."

"Could you imagine a civilized nation such as Germany even *conceiving* of concentration camps, sequestering people in a small cordoned-off area just to keep control while it prepares to murder them?"

"Certainly not," the young man replied. "How utterly barbaric!"

"It was never supposed to be that way," Smuts said, dismounting. "Come, let's sit for awhile. You may be used to hard riding, but I'm a lawyer and, at this moment, a desperately uncomfortable one." He motioned to a nearby rock bench. "Many years ago, Mister Rhodes and I tried to form a bond between the English and the Afrikaaners. It broke apart after the Jameson Raid in eighteen ninety-five. Things have gone downhill from there. Rhodes and I haven't spoken since then. Now, he's dying and Paul Kruger's dying, and the English and the Afrikaaners are farther apart than ever."

"That's exactly what the bloody *kaffirs* want," Rayne said, joining them on the bench. Everyone seems to forget there's four Blacks to every White, and the Blacks have this insane idea that *we're* trying to take *their* country. We have the arms, but we're using them to kill off *each other*! *Shaka* and *Dingane* must be dancing in their graves."

"How does this concern me?" Billy asked.

"Some of us on both sides are quietly trying to set up negotiations for peace," Smuts said. "As far as we're concerned, the British can *claim* they own all of South Africa, so long as they let the Afrikaaners govern the Transvaal and the Orange Free State. But there's distrust even among our own. We need a courier, someone who's *visibly* neither British nor Afrikaans, someone who's completely disinterested. An American would be perfect for the job."

"I'm not American," Billy said.

"True," Smuts said. "I didn't say *you* were perfect." He smiled at Billy. "But from a distance, who'd need to know? You speak English with an American accent."

"What would you expect me to do, Mister Smuts?"

"Nothing that would put you in harm's way. Deliver messages between intermediaries wherever the Hagenbeck-Knie is playing. Occasionally, ride into the countryside on a day off, where you'd meet someone else and pass messages."

"Does Herr Kürtner, know about this?"

"He doesn't, but Carl Hagenbeck knows. I understand you've always wanted to go to the United States, but were never able to do so. I think you'll find parts of the Karoo very much like the American west – a big, wild desert, empty except for the occasional outlaw. Ah, *that* lit your eyes up, I see."

"Will I get to hunt outlaws?" Billy asked.

"Most likely not," Rayne said. "These fellows believe themselves to be freedom fighters. They're never been known to go one-on-one with a stranger, and their tales can often be quite convincing."

"Will I get to meet a Zulu warrior?"

"Only if you get to Johannesburg and he's working in the gold mines. The Brits last fought them more than fifty years ago down in Natal Province. They haven't really been a factor since then." Smuts took out his pocket watch and flipped open the cover. "It's close to five," he said to Billy and Rayne. "I hope you hadn't planned on making it all the way back to Kirstenbosch by nightfall. Even though it's midsummer here, it usually gets dark shortly after eight-thirty."

"I hadn't planned on it, Meneer Smuts. I thought to ride up the eastern side of the Cape."

"As long as you turn west after Fish Hoek you'll be fine. I wouldn't venture into the Cape Flats after dark – *kaffirs,* mob rule and such. We'll talk again in a couple of days. We're indebted to you, Billy Jenkins. Hopefully, you'll be able to play a part in bringing this dreadful tragedy to a fitting end."

~ ʃ ~

The sun was setting over the mountains to the west as Billy rode leisurely into Fish Hoek. Tomorrow the circus would be playing two shows and he wanted to get back to the tober by mid-morning. He did not want to camp near Chapman's Peak because he had heard that many guerilla raids originated in the mountains. It was only a few miles from Fish Hoek to Muizenberg. He planned to ride as far as that suburb and spend the night there, making an easy morning ride to Kirstenbosch.

Muizenberg turned out to be farther away than it looked on a map. Billy spotted an inn halfway between Kalk Bay and his intended destination. He hadn't realized how famished he was until he'd stabled his horse, paid for his night's lodgings, and followed the enticing aromas into the inn's dining hall. Although the clerk at the front desk had told him dinner was still being served, the room was empty except for a tall, gaunt-looking man of indeterminate age and a black waiter, who was desultorily polishing some cups in the opposite corner of the room.

At Billy's signal, the waiter looked up and came over to the table. "Meneer? Sir?" he inquired politely.

"Dinner?" Billy asked.

"Yes, Sir. You're not from these parts?" The waiter's voice was well-modulated. His English was not what Billy had come to expect from the *kaffir* roustabouts who were performing the menial tasks on the show.

"I'm with the circus playing at Kirstenbosch."

"Hagenbeck-Knie?"

"Yes."

"Only one thing on the menu tonight." The gaunt fellow had ambled over to where Billy and the waiter were talking. "It's good, though." He held out his hand. "Pieter de Aar," he said.

"Billy Jenkins."

"British?"

"American," Billy lied.

"Wonderful people, those," de Aar said. "Caesar, get the young man some of that slop you call dinner." Turning back to Billy, he said, "It's actually damned tasty, but you don't want to let those fellows get ideas that'll make them uppity."

Dinner was ambrosial: sirloin of roasted beef, boiled potatoes, carrots, and a savory stew that contained cubed meat and vegetables.

"*Varterbloemetje Broedie*," de Aar said. "Water lily stew."

Billy dug into his meal hungrily. Within a very few minutes his plate was empty. Without asking, Caesar brought out a heaping platter of cream puffs topped with chocolate and a large tankard of a steaming hot, red-colored beverage.

"*Roibos,* red bush tea. We Bantus have quaffed it for centuries. Much healthier than black tea."

Billy sipped at the tea, which was sweet with a slight aftertaste. After a while, he felt tired and a little dizzy. "I think I'll go to my room, now," he told the waiter and the Afrikaaner. He bade them good night. As he made his way down the hall to his quarters, Billy's last thought before he passed out was a suspicion that the water lily stew had not agreed with him.

17

When Billy awoke, his head felt like it weighed several kilos. As his eyes struggled open, he realized he was in an entirely different setting than the night before. His bed was a narrow cot in a rustic farmhouse. Bright, harsh shafts of sunlight came through a large window into this room. His mouth felt parched and dry. His eyelids were sticky with accumulated sleep.

"Ahh, the young master is awake."

"Caesar?" He turned and saw the black man he remembered from the inn, now clad in a multicolored robe.

The man laughed mirthlessly. "I forgot, you would know me as Caesar, Meneer Jenkins. The subservient waiter at the inn. The *kaffir* I believe you'd call me."

"*Kaffir?*"

"Nigger, if you prefer. It means the same thing. In Afrikaans or in English, it means a 'soulless one.'"

"I wouldn't know," Billy responded, sitting up. His body felt salty, sticky from dried sweat. "In the circus all men are the same."

"A nice thought," the black man said, his tone neutral.

"Your name is not Caesar, then?"

"No. Dingane Buthelezi."

"Like the Zulu chief?"

"My grandfather."

Billy was now fully awake. As he surveyed his surroundings, he said, "I'm not in Muizenberg?"

"Correct, Meneer," de Aar had entered the room, dressed in tattered workpants, a long-sleeved woolen shirt, and well-worn hobnailed boots.

"Your name is ...?"

"Pieter de Aar. I told you correctly the first time."

"Is there somewhere where I can ...?"

"Hell, boy, go on outside and pee your insides out. There's an outhouse if you need privacy, but there ain't nothin' but sheep within a twenty kilometer radius."

When Billy went outside, the heat hit him like a blast furnace. He finished his business and hurried back into the house. "It must be forty degrees out there!"

"Pretty damned close," de Aar responded.

"If I'm your prisoner, can I at least have something to eat?"

"Prisoner?" Buthelezi said. "I'd hardly call you that. You're free to leave whenever you want."

Billy looked the two men calmly. "Free to leave anytime I want, and it's more than twenty kilometers through the desert to the nearest habitation of any kind. Were you planning on having me escorted by military convoy?"

Buthelezi laughed, this time good humoredly. He nodded at de Aar, who left the room and returned a short time later with a plate filled with grilled lamb chops, scrambled eggs, warm bread, and a pot of tea. "Drugged Roibos again?" Billy asked.

"No," de Aar said. "Just plain old food this time."

The three men went out onto the shaded veranda. In every direction he looked, Billy could see low, dry scrub land with hills in the far distance – very like he imagined Texas would look. "How long have I been unconscious?"

"A day-and-a-half," de Aar responded.

"Would you mind telling me where we are?"

"North of Oudtshoorn, southwest of Beaufort."

Billy eagerly forked down the lamb and eggs. "How did I get here? More important, *why?*"

"We saw you talking with the Englishman Rayne and the traitor Jan Smuts the afternoon before you stopped at the inn," Buthelezi said.

"How did you know I'd stop there?"

"We didn't. When we saw you continuing north after Fish Hoek, we figured you'd get tired halfway to Muizenberg. There's only one reputable-looking inn in the area. We bribed the desk clerk and the rest was easy."

"How could you have seen me talking with Smuts and Rayne? I saw no one. I'm sure those two would have seen something amiss."

"As far as they're concerned," de Aar said, "a black man is nothing more than a part of the countryside and a Afrikaaner peasant farmer is no better."

"You seem quite civilized for a pair of kidnappers."

"Meneer Jenkins …"

"Call me Billy. You fellows are in charge. Mister Buthelezi, you certainly don't seem like the savage Zulu warrior I read about in the German newspapers."

"Sorry I don't fit the image. There aren't many of us who've graduated Cambridge."

"How …?"

"Even though the Brits were responsible for the wholesale slaughter of my people, they've always mouthed platitudes about 'fair play.' My grandfather was the highest chief in Natal Province. The English thought it would atone for what they did if they sponsored Dingane's grandson into the upper echelons of British education. I stress 'education,' because fitting into English *society* is something else, particularly if your skin is black."

"And you, Meneer de Aar?"

"I'm exactly what I look like. A dumb-ass Dutchman farmer who lost a wife and two daughters in the delightful English concentration camp."

"And the reason you've invited me here?"

"Smuts and Rayne talk of peace. They've no doubt told you how horrified they are at what they've seen and how they only want to bring what they call 'the troubles' to an end. I imagine they want you to observe things, pass notes, be their eyes and ears, help write their history …"

"So they've told me," Billy said.

"We've no way to counter their pretty talk," Buthelezi said. "They can *tell* you. All we can do is *show* you."

"What do you mean?"

"You fancy yourself a cowboy, Billy Jenkins. What say we saddle up for a ride?"

Half an hour later, Buthelezi, Billy, and de Aar, rode alternately at a sedate walk or full gallop through what Billy perceived as "cowboy country." Within an hour-and-a-half, they'd showed him five huge patches of burned ground, but no buildings. "Those homesteads were my neighbors': Two families named Riebeck, one named Retief, one named van Rensburg, and Hendrik Pretorius, who was my closest friend. They weren't at war with the British. They never wanted war with anyone. They just wanted to be left alone. During the last three years, all five men were shot at close range. Their farmsteads were burned to the ground and their womenfolk and kids, thirty-four in all, were rounded up and taken to concentration camp. One of 'em, little Paul Retief, was the only survivor."

Billy remained silent, but it was hard to mask the horror on his face. De Aar continued, "The English came over the hills with modern guns. All the farmers had were seventy-five year-old shotguns, good enough to protect their herds against wolves, but not meant to kill other men. Didn't matter. In their eyes, the only good Boer was a dead Boer. The females and kids would only grow up as Afrikaaners, so why not kill the lot now and be done with?"

As they turned back toward de Aar's farm, Billy asked, "What were they fighting over – land?"

"Don't know," de Aar responded. "I didn't see one place where they built up anything or even where they settled down. They didn't want any of this wasteland for themselves. They just wanted to make sure none of *us* settled the area and polluted their sacred Crown land."

"But I read that the Boers didn't treat the Bantu tribes any better than the British. Smuts told me that before either of the Boer Wars, the Trekkers and the English were talking about uniting against the blacks."

"Correct," Buthelezi answered. "As far back as Biblical days, a common saying was 'The enemy of my enemy is my friend.' Aside from not being the 'dumb Niggers' and the 'stupid Boers' the English think we are, we had enough strategic sense to realize that once the English had pounded my people into the ground in Natal, it was only a matter of time before they'd expand into the Transvaal. It made their job – and their justification for their actions – far easier when the gold reef was discovered in the Witwatersrand."

As they re-entered the house and de Aar prepared cold lamb sandwiches for them. Billy remarked, "A marriage of convenience, then?"

"You could say that," de Aar said.

"And that doesn't bother you, Mister Buthelezi?"

"Not at all," the black man replied. "We Zulus believe the whites will play their colonialist games for awhile, but there will come a time when everyone will realize that four out of every five human beings in this country have black skin. By that time, maybe we'll bond with our own brothers and present sworn enemies, the Xhosa, the Tswana, and the other thirty-three Bantu tribes, and realize we can take back control of the land by sheer numbers."

"And you don't mind that, Meneer de Aar?"

"Hell, I'll be dead and buried half a century from now. I don't really care who owns the land then, 'cause I won't be around to see it. Thanks to the goddammed English, I don't have anyone to whom I can hand off the land, so I may as well stake my claim with the Bantus, who'll at least leave me alone during my lifetime."

The three men were silent for several moments, savoring their lunch. Finally Billy said, "Meneer Smuts told me the English were embarrassed in the eyes of the world. He and Rayne suggested the English could claim they owned the Cape Colony and Natal Province, but the Afrikaaners could govern the Transvaal and the Orange *Vreistaat*."

"How generous of them," de Aar said sourly. "But peace without justice is not peace. Who compensates us for the twenty-five *thousand* women and children they killed? Who brings this murder of an entire people to the attention of world opinion? *No one*, that's who. We're just a bunch of dumb niggers and dumber-ass backward farmers. The English want to erase us as a people. The world doesn't give a damn 'cause there's so few of us. Gold and diamonds are a damned sight more important than human lives."

"Meneer de Aar," Billy asked carefully, "do you believe there can be no peace until all the Afrikaaners and as many British as the Boers can kill are dead?"

"Might be nice," de Aar said, stubbornly.

"What would that accomplish?"

"Retribution."

"And more needless suffering."

"Can you think of a better way, boy?"

Again, there was a heavy silence. "Should I pass notes as Smuts suggests?"

"Makes no difference to us," Buthelezi said. "We don't have the right to compel you to do or not to do anything. Best thing you could do would be to share with the world what you have *heard* from others, but also to share with the world what you have *seen* with your own eyes."

"I'm not a journalist and I'm not a politician. I'm a circus performer. *We* may be judged harshly or kindly, but it is not for us to do any judging. We don't take sides. We are a *circus*. Our only mission is to entertain, whether we show before the blessed or the damned."

"You see a great more of the world than most, Billy Jenkins, and you'll see and talk with those who will, in turn, see and speak with others. The news from our shattered land may not be pleasant, but it should be told. Ill news has healthy legs."

"I can't promise you anything."

"We don't ask you to," Buthelezi said. "All we ask is that you weigh the truth in your own mind. It's straight out in that direction," he said, pointing, "twenty kilometers to the nearest British garrison. They'll help you get back to your show. When you see Rayne and Smuts again, let 'em know we're not all barbarians and that you were treated fairly."

"Even though the end of 'inviting' me here justified the means?" He smiled to let his hosts know he bore them no anger.

"Would you rather we'd simply poisoned you, so you wouldn't have been a messenger for either side?" This from Buthelezi.

"You may or may not trust Smuts, but I believe he is sincere. He wants to end the bloodshed. Whether you see him as traitor or saint, would it hurt you to talk with him?"

~ ∫ ~

Billy had left de Aar and Buthelezi at five in the afternoon. The weather had cooled down to a tolerable level. He'd traveled about fifteen kilometers when he heard the sound of horses galloping toward him. Turning, he saw a squad of British soldiers hailing him. He moved to the side of the trail and waited for them to pass, but they slowed and the leader addressed him politely.

"Excuse me, Sir, might you be Billy Jenkins of the Hagenbeck-Knie Circus?"

"I am."

"Thank God you're alive! Commandant Wilson got a call from your Herr Kürtner that you'd gone missing two days ago. You've no idea how worried our commander was. Lord knows we're getting enough bad publicity about those concentration camp allegations – all overdone, of course. The last thing we needed was more bad publicity that we couldn't ensure the security of the Crown's guests. You're certain you're all right?"

"Absolutely, Captain. Thank you for your concern."

"No thanks, due, Mister Jenkins. It'll be our pleasure to escort you back to civilization. You'll be pleased to know we dealt with your captors, Mister de Aar and some no-account *kaffir* who probably hasn't even got a name. They were holed up in some rathole excuse for a farm – a blight on the land if you ask me. No matter. We burned the damned farm to the ground and the two agitators as well. So now we can chalk up our good deed for the day: we've killed two bad guys and saved a good one."

~ ∫ ~

The *Hagenbeck-Knie* played to *sfondone* houses in Kirstenbosch well into early March. "Always leave them wanting more," Herr Kürtner told them.

By then, the troupers were more than ready leave Cape Town to see as much of the huge, lovely, and tortured land as they could. From the "mother city," they entrained for Stellenbosch, the "daughter city," second oldest European habitation in Cape Province, only a few hours distant.

The show played in Stellenbosch for one week, after which they entrained to Kimberley, home to the world's largest diamond mine. Billy had seen a few German movies – the latest entertainment – which purported to display the way towns in the American West must have looked thirty years ago. With its five tawdry saloons, a general store, a chemist's, and the usual selection of dentists, doctors, and lawyers, all jostling for space on the town's main street, Kimberley looked very much like a honky-tonk town he envisioned would be frontier America.

He'd been standing on the street, hands in his pockets, imagining himself to be the gunslinger of the Old West, when he noticed a familiar figure coming toward him.

"Meneer Smuts?"

"It is. I'm surprised after what happened you'd even want to talk to me."

"What happened wasn't your fault. Now that Rhodes has died, there hardly seems to be a reason for the war anymore," Billy said.

"Hard to believe."

"What, that he's dead?"

"Yes, and at only forty-nine. Never married, no children, and probably the richest man in the world. Meneer Jenkins, would you mind telling me what *really* happened? The Afrikaaners are now calling me the biggest arse-kissing traitor of the war and the Brits have brushed off what happened as an unfortunate bit of a cock-up."

When Billy had told him the entire tale, Smuts seemed mortified. "I cannot tell you how ashamed I am. Mostly, I regret that Pieter de Aar went to his Maker thinking of me as a turncoat. I wish he'd lived to speak with me as you suggested. I can only promise you – it would do no good if I tried to promise *them* – that I will make a full report to the Negotiating Committee and demand a serious investigation."

True to his word, Smuts demanded a full explanation of what had occurred. The British High Command, more to mollify him than anything else, since Smuts reportedly had important connections with the Crown Foreign Secretary, conducted a cursory investigation and immediately transferred the suspected troopers, who claimed they had been attacked by a Boer and a *kaffir*, out of the Cape. Each soldier was given a verbal reprimand and a medal. No other action was taken. The High Command proposed to pay £100 each to the families of Pieter de Aar and Dingane Buthelezi, but, unfortunately, no surviving family members could be located to claim the compensation.

~ ʃ ~

By the time the British and the Boer government representatives signed the Peace of Vereeniging in Pretoria, Transvaal's Afrikaaner capital, setting the seal on British domination in southern Africa, Rhodes had been dead for two months. A month-and-a-half later, *Oom* Paul Kruger died at seventy-nine. Shortly afterward, the concentration camps were dismantled. Over thirty-five thousand Afrikaaners had died or had been killed, more than half of them women and children in the camps. Under these tragic circumstances, even one death would have been too many.

18

In July, 1903, the troupe left the ridge on which Johannesburg was situated, and turned south. They rode through the high peaks and wild beauty of the Drakensberg Escarpment, then descended into Natal Province. Just outside Umhlanga Rocks, the land flattened out until they reached vibrant, colorful Durban.

A hot, sweet aroma permeated the city. Billy, Sophia, and Kürtner followed their noses to the huge Indian market, where they sampled curries and unfamiliar foods of every conceivable color and blend. The market was a raucous cacophony of sounds and languages, some mellifluous, others guttural, spoken by black, brown, yellow, olive-skinned, and ruddy-colored men and women of every age.

Billy found a place in the middle of the market where the three of them could sit down. When a turbaned waiter approached them, Billy promptly ordered *somozas,* curried lamb, basmati rice, *nan* and *papadam*, mango chutney, two sweet yogurt drinks and a salty one.

"I'm impressed," Kürtner said, as they dove hungrily into their savory meal. "Where did you learn about such foods?"

"In the Malay districts of Cape Town and in Frankfurt's Leipzigerstrasse. The world is full of wonderful things to see, smell, and taste."

"And touch," Sophia said, possessively caressing his arm.

"Where are we pitching the tober, Herr Direktor?" he asked.

"Just inland from the beach. I think we should go over there and see how the roustabouts are doing with the set-up."

Billy, feeling flush, paid for their meals. They'd gotten halfway to the pitch when they came upon a contingent of policemen armed with truncheons and clubs, beating up on an equally large group of Indians. The Asiatics were stubbornly standing their ground, but they were not fighting back. When Billy inquired politely of the nearest constable what was going on, the uniformed fellow said, "Nothing you'd be interested in. Bunch o' bloody curry munchers think they can take over this town."

"Excuse me, Officer, but they don't seem to be resisting you."

"No they aren't. That's the way they all act. They just stand there like a bunch of smarmy idiots with their, 'Yes, Officer, No, Officer, I'm sorry, Officer' garbage, all the while snickering at us and waiting 'til nightfall, when their gangs set upon decent white folk. Mind, I don't care when they beat up on the *kaffirs* – they save us from that dirty job – but can you *imagine* they want to be able to vote for city government representatives."

Sophia spoke up. "What's wrong with that, Officer?"

"Missy, you wouldn't ask if you knew these people. There's no problem if they stay down in Lenasia, where they belong, but they're getting more uppity than the kaffirs. They've started crowding the trams so there's no room for proper white people. Have you ever stood next to one of them for any length of time? The smell of curry reeks from their pores. Disgusting it is, that's what I tell you. No, Little Miss, you'd do well to keep your distance from them."

"But I don't see – "

"Miss," another constable, who had come up, said curtly. "Officer O'Jameson asked you nice and polite to mind your own business. You're not local here, so you don't understand these kinds. Now, be gettin' you on your way."

Billy did not appreciate Sophia being treated in such a peremptory manner and said as much to the second officer.

"All right, you troublemakers," the officer said. "If you're not inclined to move out on your own, I'll help you along." Taking a truncheon, he shoved Sophia so hard she fell to the ground, badly skinning her knee.

Billy, now furious, started to unholster his stage gun. Kürtner leapt in front of him and quietly said, "No, Billy. That will only make matters worse."

At that moment, a short, ascetic-looking man about Kürtner's age, stepped into the space between the police and the three circus artistes.

"Officer, you are entirely correct that this is none of their business, but they have the same white skin as you and they deserve your respectful treatment." The man wore a silk turban and a western-style suit and tie of expensive cut. Turning to the circus performers, he said, "I deeply regret that these officers who are sworn to uphold the law are acting in such an unmannerly way. I apologize to you most sincerely on behalf of my fellow citizens."

"Fellow *citizens*? Fellow *citizens* did you say, you lowlife curry muncher hunk of shit? I'm ashamed to be on the same *street* as you, let alone in the same city."

Billy, Sophia and Kürtner were amazed that the Indian gentlemen displayed neither anger, impatience, nor loss of his dignity. "Officer, these good people are not part of our dispute. Kindly let them pass. I will walk with them to ensure that they safely get to where they need to go." He bowed politely and beckoned the three to follow him.

As they were walking, Billy, still outraged, said, "How could you let them get away with insulting you so? You had a similar number of men, yet not once did you fight back. Why?"

"That would be reverting to the old rubric, 'An eye for an eye.'"

"Those bullies certainly deserved that."

"You are, of course, right, my young friend, but if you think of it in larger terms, 'An eye for an eye' makes the whole world blind, and to what purpose? There are many causes I am prepared to die for, but no causes I am prepared to kill for."

"You truly believe that?" Sophia asked.

"I do, young lady," the Indian remarked. "When I despair – and there are certainly more times than not when I dread the injustices I see around me – I remember that all through history truth and love has always won. There have been tyrants and murderers. For a time they seemed invincible, but in the end, they always fell. They *always* fell."

"I can't say I agree with you," the circus director said, "but we certainly appreciate that you've gotten us out of a very uncomfortable situation. Would you consider being out guests at tomorrow's performance?" He peeled off a dozen of the best tickets and pressed them into the smaller man's hands.

"Why ...?" the man flushed with pleasure. "I have always loved the circus, ever since I was a small boy in Porbander."

"India?" Kürtner said.

"A coastal town in Gujarat province. I haven't seen a show since I was twelve – twenty-two years ago. I surely thank you, Sir. One day I may be able to properly repay you. Might I suggest at the very least that you join my goodwife Kasturba, myself, and our four children for a proper Indian dinner tomorrow evening?"

"I didn't know you had such a large family," Kürtner replied, handing the man five extra tickets.

The following afternoon, their new Indian friend, accompanied by a dignified-looking woman in a white robe, who was taller than her husband, three youngsters ranging from eight to fourteen, and a toddler of two, swept into the tent. On their entrance, every Indian in the audience stood up and applauded.

The show started off well. The Indian populace went wild over all three elements of Billy's act – shooting, riding, and most of all his falconry. During intermission, a swarthy Indian man came up to Kürtner and spoke quietly and respectfully. Billy couldn't hear what they were discussing. After three or four minutes, the manager nodded and pointed out the chapiteau's door to the dressing tent.

When Billy inquired what that was all about. Kürtner responded, "He asked if three of his friends might perform during the second half. He said they would not charge anything, but would consider it a privilege to repay us for our kind treatment of his people. When I agreed, he asked if there was a place where the men could change. We've been a little thin on performers since our velocipede team, decided to blow the stand after Jo'burg. I figured I'd put 'em on midway through the second half of the show. They'll do no harm, even if they turn out to be rank amateurs."

"Any idea what they do?"

"Antipodists," Kürtner replied.

"What's that?"

"You'll see."

The three little men, who were of indeterminable age and exceedingly thin, were obviously well-known to the Asiatics in the audience. The jossers clapped and cheered even before the men came tumbling into the pista. Each wore loose-fitting shiny satin tunics and trousers, one green, one red, and one yellow. When they were introduced, they took an extravagant number of bows.

Then, before the astonished Billy Jenkins, two of them fell supine on the ground, in opposing directions, and stuck their legs in the air.

The third man jumped straight up from the ground, curled himself into a ball in midair, and the other two began kicking him back and forth through the air between them, making him spin first one way, then the other. While they were in the midst of this thrilling act, the man who'd been negotiating with Kürtner brought out a six-foot tall ladder, which he placed between the two supine kickers. Without skipping a beat, they now kicked the third man higher – straight over the ladder, which he cleared by a meter – and as he came down, the other kicker boosted the third man back.

Billy may have thought he'd seen it all, but he hadn't. While the third man was somersaulting and rolling over the top of the ladder, their manager removed the ladder and threw first one ball, then a second, toward one of the kickers. Now, there were three objects in the air, one man and two balls, each moving so fast the eye could hardly follow them.

Suddenly the balls were gone. Now only the three men remained. The action shifted again. As the flying balled-up man approached the nearest kicker, he hit the ground with a slap and the kicker now leapt into the air and became a balled-up flyer himself, while the former "ball" took his place as a kicker. At each second kick, there was a shift, then another shift. The three men were now jumping and kicking and spinning so high and so fast that Billy could not distinguish between the perpetual-motion streaks of red, green, and yellow. Suddenly, in precise unison, the three antipodists landed on their feet and simultaneously threw their arms up in the classic **V**.

Billy clapped his hands 'til he felt them growing raw. As he gazed at Kürtner, whose face was glowing, the director said, in awe, "I'll be damned. A Risley Act, and a helluva good one!"

"A Risley Act?" Billy asked.

"Foot jugglers, upside down acrobats. Named after an old-time English circus performer, but it's really from the Orient. We've *got* to have them! I'll speak to their agent after the show."

At that moment, there was a horrified gasp from the crowd. Both Billy and Kürtner instinctively looked upward toward where Sophia was performing. The aerialist had just swung into midair, flying from one trap to the other, when one of the two ropes holding the far trapeze broke loose from its moorings. Sophia made it to the trapeze, but now it was dangling by the single rope. She was clinging to the trap for dear life. Although she was small and lithe, the single rope would not hold even her weight for more than a minute or two. The spotlight remained hypnotically on Sophia, suspended thirty feet above the floor. Everyone – audience and trouper alike – realized that a fall, if not fatal, would cause life-threatening injuries and end her career.

The roustabouts ran into the pista bearing a four foot-by-four foot safety net to blunt the impact of her fall. In only seconds, six of them held the net below her. Meanwhile, unseen by anyone, the three antipodists silently ran over to the area and positioned themselves in a triangle around the net. They lay down on their backs, facing upward, their eyes focused on the stricken trapeze artiste. Without taking their eyes off her, they made small adjustments to their positions on the ground.

Moments later, the metal hinge holding the trapeze snapped. The swing came away, tilting perpendicular to the floor, hanging by only a thin strand. Before she could react, Sophia was jarred off balance and fell toward the ground.

The roustabouts tried to follow her trajectory and place the net where she would most likely land. The big top was so still one could have heard a coin drop from anywhere within the chapiteau. The crowd heaved a collective gasp as Sophia hit the net well off-center, clipping an edge of the safety device. While this broke her immediate fall, she half-rolled, half-bounced off the end of the net.

As Sophia fell toward the floor, her flight was suddenly stopped in mid-air and she was spiraling uncontrollable *upward*. An instant later she was hurled in another direction, this time not quite so high. The crowd caught on before either Billy or Kürtner knew what was happening. The jossers shouted, stomped the ground as one, and clapped their hands as Sophia was catapulted from one pair of legs to another. The antipodists had assumed control of the situation and slowed things down until the terrified girl could see she was safe. When she did, she spun a graceful somersault, landed on her feet, and dramatically, if tremblingly, extended her arms in a **V.**

As she lowered her arms, Billy and the ringmaster rushed to her side and held her up as they gently walked her toward the tent door.

~ ∫ ~

"That was an incredibly close call," their host said that night at dinner. "If only our Indian forces could react so quickly in an emergency."

The three circus troupers had ridden with the Indian in a large, open-air carriage to Lenasia, the Indian section of Durban. They were surprised by the modesty of the man's home. Although each of the older children had his own closed-off alcove, the adults and the toddler slept in a small room, furnished with only a low double bed and a tiny crib. The furnishings throughout the cottage were spare. A light odor of curry permeated the residence.

"Circus life is not too different from the military," Kürtner replied. "We're frequently on the move. Like soldiers, we adhere to strict discipline on duty. The main difference between a circus and soldiering is we don't operate by manuals and rigid regulations, so we have infinite scope for improvisation and ingenuity. There are no two days alike with a circus. We expect the unexpected: surprises, obstacles, setbacks, and occasional stroke of good fortune. Dealing with such things makes a person fit for any eventuality. You said your 'forces?'"

"A misnomer, Herr Kürtner. Actually it's called the the Natal Indian Congress. I helped found it to attempt to unify the Indians of this province so that what happened to me when I first came to Durban wouldn't be repeated over and over again."

"If you don't mind my asking, Signor, what was that?"

"Quite a few mishaps, Signorina Sophia," he responded. "When I first came to this land, I was thrown off a train at Pietermaritzburg after I refused to move from the first class to a third class coach. I had purchased a valid first class ticket, and I saw no reason I should be refused admission solely because I was Indian. When I traveled farther on by stagecoach, I was beaten by the driver for refusing to travel on the footboard to make room for a European passenger. I was barred from many hotels for no other reason than that I was, as the constable told you yesterday, a 'curry-muncher.'" He laughed, not without an edge of irony. "When I tried to gain admission to a hotel restaurant, I was told, 'I'm sorry, sir, we don't serve Indians.' On the spot, I responded, 'That's all right, I don't eat them anyway.' I thought it was quite funny, but some toughs nearby overheard it and I got another beating."

"Couldn't it have just been some hooligans?" Billy asked.

"Initially, I thought so, but when I came to Durban, I was told the same kind of story over and over again by my countrymen. No, Herr Jenkins, it was either government policy or it was done with active government encouragement. When the magistrate of a Durban court ordered me to remove my turban and I refused, I was thrown into jail for three days. Not much of a sentence, but those incidents and others like them caused me to question my people's status within the British Empire, and my own place in English society. That's when I concluded there was strength in unity."

"You speak like an educated man," the circus manager said.

"Oh, yes," Kasturba, his wife answered proudly. "My Mohandas started studying law at University College in London when he was eighteen, five years after we married."

"Five years?" Billy asked. "But that means you were only thirteen when …?"

"No. I was twelve, *Mohandas* was thirteen. It was arranged by our parents. Even though we went through the ceremony, we didn't come together until he was almost seventeen. Before he went to London, my husband had to promise his mother he would not eat meat or drink alcohol, and that he would not be promiscuous." She giggled.

Her husband continued. "I didn't *completely* obey my vow to my mother. I took dancing lessons for a little while and once I tried my landlady's mutton and cabbage. It was awful. After that, it was very easy for me to be a vegetarian."

"Everything we've been eating is delicious," Sophia said. "No meat at all?"

"None," Kasturba replied. "We eat such a variety of food we don't even miss meat. Mohandas was called to the bar by the Inner Temple. He rejoined us in Bombay, but he was not successful. Nine years ago, he accepted a contract from an Indian firm and we've been here since."

Mohandas' wife retired to the kitchen and returned bringing cinnamon-laced rolls dipped in honey, a yogurt-rice pudding, and a steaming pot of aromatic Darjeeling tea. Meanwhile, an animated exchange was going on between her husband and their guests.

"So you're an editor at the *Indian Opinion* newspaper, you practice law, you are the chairman of this province-wide movement, *and* you spin and make your own clothes on a charkha?"

"Yes, Herr Jenkins. There are many in our community who do so much more," their host replied modestly.

"Ummm…" Billy continued, fumbling for the right words.

Kasturba's eyes lit up mischievously. "That, too. As you can see, we have four children. Our first one died after only a few months."

Billy blushed and Sophia shot him a sidewise glance.

"Actually," Mohandas said, "I no longer practice actively in the system. Aside from the fact that I have yet to see Indians treated fairly by British 'justice,' I don't think it's right to seek redress for personal wrongs in a court of law. People should try to keep talking to one another and work things out between themselves. Like yesterday afternoon."

"The gendarmes were assaulting your people. You had sufficient numbers to rebuff them, yet you did nothing," Kürtner said.

"What good would it have done?" Mohandas replied. "Had we fought back, the violence would simply have escalated. The English would have returned with a larger force, then we would have come back with a larger force, and so on. Have you heard of Edward Lear, Herr Kürtner?"

"I can't say that I have."

"*The Owl and the Pussycat?*"

"I know that one," Sophia said. "The Owl and the Pussycat went to sea in a beautiful pea-green boat …"

"The same," the Indian replied. "He wrote over a hundred famous limericks, funny, often nonsensical, little rhyming poems that had much more than a shred of truth to them. One in particular comes to mind:

> "There were once two cats of Kilkenny
> Each thought there was one cat too many
> So they fought and they fit
> And they scratched and they bit
> 'til excepting their nails and the tips of their tails
> Instead of two cats, there weren't any."

The evening passed quickly in vigorous, intelligent conversation, the host and his wife stressing their belief in nonviolent resistance, the circus performers polite but unconvinced that this philosophy would accomplish anything more than reduce the Indian population of Durban to being a permanent underclass. As hosts and guests bid each other good night, they promised each other to keep in touch – a promise which, like so many in life – dissolves in the mists of a future which goes by all too quickly.

Mohandas presented each of the troupers with a small gift, a silver Indian coin, and his calling card. As they walked home, Billy asked Sophia, "Would it be impolite of me to simply toss his card away? I don't think we'll ever see him again."

"You never can tell, Billy," his girlfriend said. "I love to keep *cartes de visite*, and I know lots of people who do the same. I have more than a hundred of them cluttering up some drawer back home in Italy. What harm can one more do? Besides, maybe he'll end up famous some day and I can show the card around to prove I met him."

"If he keeps believing that non-violent resistance nonsense and doesn't eat more than he does – did you see how he only picked at his food through the entire evening? – he'll probably be dead long before he has a chance to become famous in his *neighborhood*, let along anyplace else." Billy glanced down at the card again, then, more to placate Sophia than anything else, placed the card in his pocket.

That night, just before he went to bed, Billy looked at the card again. "Mohandas Karamchand Gandhi," he said softly. "We'll probably never hear the name again."

19

In December, 1903, the Hagenbeck-Knie troupe concluded its tour of South Africa. Kürtner returned to the Circus Knie in Bern, awaiting his next assignment. When Billy and Sophia arrived in Frankfurt, they experienced a host of new technological marvels. Sophia thrilled to the voice of Enrico Caruso, captured on the newly popular phonograph. Billy browsed a large bookstore which displayed the latest popular books. He immediately purchased and read Jack London's *Call Of The Wild*.

Two weeks after they'd landed, Sophia ecstatically broke the news to Billy that she'd been offered the opportunity to join on the *Circo Orfei* in her native Italy. She could not contain her excitement. "Darling, it's the chance of a lifetime. The Orfei's more than two hundred fifty years old, the premier circus in all of Europe."

"But what about us, Sophia? I thought …"

"Oh, Billy," she said. "There's no question I'll always love you. But you're eighteen, I'm nineteen – we have our whole lives ahead of us. And we're circus – we both knew that when we joined on."

"We could find work together."

"But this is the *Orfei*. If I were to turn it down now, I'd never get another chance. Don't you see, this is the pinnacle every circus artiste attains to?"

"So your career is more important than me ... than us?"

"Oh, stop talking like a child." An uncomfortable silence hung heavily between them. They walked three blocks before she finally said, "It's not as if I was the first woman you've ever been with. We knew that when we started."

"Yes, but I never thought you'd put yourself ahead of me."

"Put myself ahead of you? What is this, the female gives up everything for the man? Is that what you're saying?"

"I don't want to lose you."

"Lose me? As if I were some sort of possession? As if you don't trust me to make my own decisions?"

"I didn't say that."

"Well, what did you say?"

He had no answer. When he suggested they calm down over dinner, she said, "I'm sorry, Billy, I'm just not hungry tonight."

"Let's go back to our room, then."

"If you don't mind, I think perhaps we should sleep in separate rooms tonight."

"Just like that."

"It would only be worse for both of us. Like two married people knowing they were going to get a divorce and attempting to sleep with one another one last time." Her eyes were glistening with unshed tears, but she kept her voice firm.

"I love you, Sophia. Marry me, then."

"Marry you? As if that would somehow take the place of my achieving what I've always dreamed of?"

"I love you."

"I'm sure you do, and in my own way I love you, too. But marriage is out of the question. Let's part now, while we're still friendly enough that in a few years …"

He grabbed both her hands in his and stood, staring into her eyes, as if by that action he could convince her to abandon her plans, to stay with him. They stood that way for a very long time. Neither spoke. Finally, it was Sophia who broke the silence. "We need not say goodbye, Billy. Let's simply say *Auf Wiedersehen.*" She dabbed at her eyes, turned, and walked resolutely away.

~ ∫ ~

Billy didn't sleep that night or the next. Although he could easily have joined on with his previous employer, and could well afford better housing, he moved to the dingiest hole he could find in Frankfurt and started buying cheap wine. Soon he was drinking three bottles a day. When that didn't sufficiently dull his senses, he found a way to purchase cocaine. Throughout his alcohol and drug-laden brain, images of Sophia passed through his mind. Sophia in the graceful curve of her swing from one high trapeze to another. Sophia in a paroxysm of lust as they came together. The feel of Sophia as they slept like two spoons and he cupped her breast in his hand.

Soon, money became a problem. He pawned what little he owned. With the last of his savings, he made his way to Berlin. His father had a café there, *Süssmilch.* As much as it disgusted him to beg from the man he hated, he had fallen so low he had nowhere else to turn. When he appeared before his father, he was disheveled, half drunk, and hadn't bathed in over a week. The man looked at Billy as though he were some sort of disgusting maggot.

"Father?"

"Oh, so now it's 'father.' For the past eight years I didn't even exist in your life."

"Did I exist in yours?"

The older man walked over to a long walnut bar and started polishing it with a damp cloth. "Whether you realize it or not, yes, you did. I had to work hard, in many places I didn't want to work, so I could provide for you, keep a roof over your head."

"Many roofs, father. Many, many roofs, and many, many women."

"What business is that of yours? After your mother left me …"

"My mother *left*?"

"You heard me. Walked out when you were not even five years old. Said she couldn't stand a life always on the road."

"And that justified your screwing every woman in sight?"

"Silence!" the older man roared. "You have no idea … *she* left *me* and she left *you* as well! I suggest at the very least you have some coffee to sober you up."

"I don't need anything from you," the younger man said.

"Of course not. I almost forgot, you're Billy Jenkins, the famous circus cowboy. Ran off, joined the circus, changed your name, turned your back on your religion …"

"Shut up, old man!"

"Ah, yes. That's the way you show respect to your father."

"I've never denied you're my father."

"You've never admitted it either. You hid everything in the closet, as if, by covering enough of the garbage up you'd never have to see or smell it."

"I said *shut up!*"

"Or you'll do what? Hit me? Shoot me with one of your circus guns. Do you even *have* a gun anymore or have you pawned everything you owned?"

The oppressive silence tortured both father and son. Neither was prepared to break the silence. Neither was prepared to give an inch. Neither was prepared to find fault of any kind in himself.

Finally, it was the older man who spoke. "You can stay with me for as long as it takes to clean yourself up and dry yourself out. You can eat my food. We may not like one another and we may never have a relationship, but you are my son, whether you want to admit it or not. I will deposit five hundred *marks* in an account for you. Whenever you are ready to leave, I will hand the passbook to you. That should get you by for a few months until you can hopefully get on your feet again."

~ ∫ ~

Billy stayed at his father's apartment for a month. During that time, he tried desperately to cadge money from people on the street, but the pickings were niggardly. His father had secured all his money and valuables in a safe place, so it was almost impossible to steal more than minimally from the older man. Billy was unable to afford cocaine. He suddenly found that wine so irritated his bowels that he would either sit on the toilet half the night or retch his insides out. Georg Süssmilch Rosenthal studiously ignored him.

There was a paucity of reading material in Rosenthal's moderate flat, but his father still subscribed to *The Era*, the circus trade paper distributed throughout Europe. Billy went for the paper each week it came. At the beginning of October, his eye seized on an article in the lower right-hand corner of the front page:

"ORFEI TRAGEDY! ANOTHER AERIALIST FALLS TO HER DEATH! YOUNG ARTISTE WAS IN HER FIRST YEAR WITH FAMED SHOW.

> In a history plagued with tragedy, the Circo Orfei lost yet another performer when 19-year-old Parma native Sophia d'Amelio plunged to her death during a rehearsal of the show in Milano last week. Although not yet a star, the press representative of the circus said she showed immense promise and audience appeal …"

On that day, Billy stopped drinking, took a long, hot bath, and cried himself to sleep. Two days later, he approached his father and said stiffly, "I regret that I have been a burden to you. If your offer is still open, I will *borrow* the five hundred *marks* you said you had put away for me. But I will not be beholden to you any more than I expect you to be beholden to me." He handed the older man a writing. "I will pay you back with interest one year from today."

The elder Rosenthal nodded, took the note from his son, and watched with mixed emotions as Billy Jenkins, né Erich Rosenthal, walked out of the door and out of his life.

~ ∫ ~

The next eight months were the most difficult Billy had ever experienced. He had pawned his guns, his lariats, his show paraphernalia, and his cowboy outfits in Frankfurt. When he returned to Frankfurt, he found lodgings, a single room in a sleazy hotel near the *Hauptbahnhof,* in an area where no one knew who he was. He kept to himself. He worked two jobs at a time, one cleaning sewers as a day laborer, the other serving as night clerk at the hotel, where he took half pay, trading the other half for his room and meager board. Within three months, he had reclaimed his clothing and professional gear.

Billy had Sunday off each week. He used that time to relearn the basics of his shooting and roping acts. There was no ammunition in the guns, nor did he want there to be, because he practiced in a nearby park, and any untoward noise that would call attention to himself would almost certainly have attracted the local constabulary. Thus, his practice in "shooting" was limited to picturing in his mind what was happening, sighting nonexistent "targets," and performing exercises designed to limber his long disused body.

Roping should have been easier, since his apparatus was easily at hand. He had not reckoned that his hand-eye coordination, which had been razor sharp a year ago, was now sadly debased. Week by frustrating week, he believed he was slowly regaining his skills, at least with the lariat, and, he thought, with the guns, although he would never know until he shot live ammunition at real targets. The voltige riding was something else again. As for his bird-of-prey act, despite his impatience to return to the *pista*, he knew this would be a long time in coming, for he had not so much as a single canary.

Still, he stubbornly continued polishing what talent he could. By his twentieth birthday in June 1905, he thought he had managed to return to pretty much his pre-dissolute condition. His sixteen months "off" had aged him, but he was still passably handsome, with golden hair and pale blue eyes.

He first attempted to return to the *Zoltan-Renz*, only to find that Glockner had died, Sammy Lichtenfeld had left the show, and hardly anyone remembered him. The show had fallen on hard times. He was politely, but firmly, told that the circus was laying off artistes rather than hiring them. He was not even given an audition. As he went from major circus to moderate circus throughout Germany, he found that his reputation had preceded him – alas, not his reputation as the Prince of the Cowboys, but rather his reputation as a drunken stumblebum, who had disappeared off the face of the earth. Only one show, the successful but unpalatable *Ringfedel*, gave him an audition. While his roping was competent, he only hit the target fifty percent of the time in his shooting exhibition. His formerly brilliant riding abilities were so degraded there was no way anyone could trust him to ride voltige. Thus, Billy Jenkins suffered the ignominy of being turned down by the *Ringfedel*. He knew such a rejection assured he would not find work with any reputable circus of size in Europe.

After paying off the note to his father – five hundred-fifty marks including interest – he used half of his remaining funds to purchase an ancient, but still serviceable, gelding from the *Zoltan-Renz*. In open fields adjacent to small towns, he started practicing his riding and shooting in earnest. By November 1905, when the weather was turning colder, he had less than a month's worth of savings left, but he had recouped most of his former expertise.

Knowing he'd have to begin on the bottom rung of the ladder *somewhere*, he finally located work with the *Gran Circo Spettacoloso Wallachia y Moldavia*, which, despite its pretentious name, was a mud-and-goat show that toured southeastern Rumania, occasionally dipping down into northern Bulgaria. The pay was two-thirds what he'd been paid as a sewer worker in Frankfurt, and he understood he'd have to suffer the three-week holdback, which took him to the end of his financial rope, but it *was* a circus, and the proprietor promised to provide bedding in a wagon shared with four smelly crewmen, peck consisting of *mamaliga,* buckwheat groats, occasionally stew with a few pieces of stringy meat, and all the coffee – or chicory – he could drink.

The artistes on the *Wallachia y Moldavia* had almost all seen better days – indeed, better *decades* – and this was the last stop on the line for them. A large percentage frequently joined the roustabouts in drinking themselves into oblivion on the cheapest *slivovica* or ingesting the local *hashish*-like droppings, which were so impure and dangerous that the show suffered at least one "disappearance" a month. But it was a place to start. And a place to practice. And a place to reconnect with his calling. And Billy, knowing he was only one step ahead of the alcoholics and addicts with whom he worked, ensured that he never once took so much as one drink or otherwise abused his body.

Billy taught himself rudimentary Rumanian by reading as many newspapers as he could. In this way, he kept up with the news of the day. He learned that in America, Wilbur Wright had successfully flown a heavier-than-air powered airplane. Even more exciting, a motor car had actually crossed the American continent – coast to coast – in sixty-five days! Closer to home, motorized taxicabs were now appearing on the streets of London and that huge city had actually set a speed limit for motor cars of an astonishing twenty miles per hour within the city limits. The world was changing more rapidly than Billy could imagine.

20

"Gone broke is what!"

"Scarpered away in the middle of the night, he did, taking whatever money he could find and the two best horses we had."

"I guess that's it for the *Wallachia y Moldavia*."

The circus folk would have been in a frenzy, but each of them had been "down" for so long that anything looked like "up" to them.

Billy's abstention from the cheap liquor and the drugs had made him seem as though he felt he was somehow superior to the rest, but during the eight months he'd been on the *Wallachia y Moldavia*, he had used his time not only to resharpen his skills to what they'd been before he'd returned from the Cape Colony, but also to learn how a circus *should* be run, and, from his observations of this show, how it should *not* be run.

He was now a sturdy and mature twenty-one. He'd learned enough from the hard times that he had no intent of repeating them. He had been about to leave the *Wallachia y Moldavia* and make another attempt to land work with a major European circus. He felt he was now good enough. It was just a matter of timing.

But looking over this woebegone group of eleven artistes – if one could still call them that – and seven roustabouts, all of whom seemed to have had the life drained from them, Billy's innate decency could not allow him to let these human beings, the flotsam and jetsam of society, become derelicts, left to starve, die of cold, or simply fade away. Thus it was that he called them all together in the sad little tent that served as the chapiteau and politely asked if they would sit and listen to him for a bit.

"Why not?" an elderly clown, close to seventy, said. "Where else do we have to go?"

There was a murmuring of assent. When they were all seated, Billy said, "Ladies, gentlemen, I'm going to start by hitting you in the pocketbook. Please don't be embarrassed. This is not the time for pride. I'd like to ask you to trust me enough to put whatever money you can possibly spare – whatever you would like to give to try to save what we can of this show – on this table. Magda, will you act as the treasurer and give each and every one of our family a written receipt?"

"'Family?' Ain't no one ever called us 'family' before," one of the crew said.

"Maybe not, but that's what we are, isn't it?" Billy asked. "We've eaten together, traveled together, gotten drunk together – by the way, I know I haven't gotten drunk with you, and I'll tell you right now it's not some conceit. I have dipsomania."

There was a collective gasp. It was the first time Billy had ever told anyone that he had been subject to a compulsive urge to drink. While there were many hardened addicts on the show, no one had ever admitted to such a problem publicly.

"I'm asking you to help any way you can."

"Including the grouch bags?" This from a middle-aged rosinback rider.

"If you feel you can," Billy said.

"Jewelry, *gazho*?" Magda, the sixty-something *rom* woman who doubled as fortune teller and ticket seller asked.

"No, only money. Whatever you can give us is entirely up to you."

Grudgingly at first, one or two of the artistes stepped up. Then, as the number of troupers stood and increased the line, there seemed to be the tiniest spark of life. The last to step up was a beefy Turkish weightlifter, who put only a few copper coins on the table. When the money, mostly coins but also a few paper bills, was counted, Billy announced, "We have enough to sustain this show for six more days before we're bust."

"Six days?" a trapeze artiste of late middle age said. "And then we're finished?"

"No," Billy said. "We are going to show for six days straight. During that time, we are going to lay on a lot of cherry pie during the off-hours."

"Getting extra work out of us for nothing? What's that going to do for us?"

"Among other things, Hans, it's going to give you some of your pride back. I've read about your history, Herr Lieblich. You were with the Donnert for two years, the Ringfedel for another three – although God knows how you stood it – the Corty-Althof, the Krone, and one or two other *real* circuses."

"But that was years ago, when I was in my twenties. You can't ask a fifty-year-old body to do what a younger man does."

"That is absolutely correct, Herr Lieblich, but you are not the tired old cripple you pretend to be. Your 'family' knows, I know, and, most important, *you* know that you are still capable of giving much more than you've given in the past."

"Why should we?" a female Joey asked. "With six days left, who'd even care?"

"Geraldina, in six days God created the world," Billy said. "All I'm asking is that in six days you try to re-create *yourself*. Even if we collapse and go bust, in those six days you will show yourself that you are capable of helping to hold up this family. I'm not saying we *will* collapse. Perhaps if we show better than we have in the past, word will go out to the jossers and there may be more of them. Ask yourself, *what do you have to lose? Six days? What do you have to gain?*" He left the question hanging in the air.

That night there was far less drinking than usual. Each trouper and crewman took only what he or she could eat, and when they did, they looked sidewise at the other members of the circus to make sure they were doing the same thing. Next morning, a high percentage of the show was awake and working much earlier than usual.

The crowd that afternoon was not *sfondone*, but neither was it a *bianca* house. The audience numbered seventy people. During the show, Billy, who'd naturally drifted into the ringmaster's role, displayed a gift of gab that made some of the artistes shake their heads. His reading of the local newspaper the night before and his talk with some of the merchants around the nondescript town had given him enough information about local administrators and local nonentities to make for spirited, timely persiflage that had the jossers rocking in their seats with laughter.

Billy stretched out his own act. Even his old plug, somehow realizing this show was different from past performances, gave an extra bit of spirit and speed that enabled his voltige to be significantly more exciting than it had been before. The same held true for the rest of the show, with the exception of Şarkioğlu, the Turkish weightlifter, who seemed, if anything, more dour than usual. The electricity of the acts transmitted itself to the audience. For the first time since he had been with the *Wallachia y Moldavia*, the flatties stood and stomped when they applauded for the acts.

That evening, Magda passed out as much camphor and liniment as she did food, but the spirit in the food tent was much different than it had been before. Halfway through dinner, Billy stood up. "Ladies and gentlemen," he announced in his loud ringmaster's voice. "We made our nut today! That means at the very least we have six *more* days! I'm not going to say how proud I am of you. Rather, each of you know how proud you should be of yourselves! Let's eat!" There was spirited applause from the circus family.

By the following day, the audience had doubled. "The word of mouth must have traveled fast," Billy said to Hans. Though feeling significantly stiffer than the day before, the troupers once again gave it everything they had, and the audience responded. By the seventh day, Billy announced they had quadrupled their money.

The final day of the *Wallachia y Moldavia's* performance brought out two hundred people – more than the circus had ever shown to before. There were hearty handshakes and gleeful remonstrances that evening. "Tomorrow morning, I will pay all of your money back," Billy said. "And, on top of that, each of you will get a full week's wage!" His next words were drowned out by a cacophony of hurrahs.

~ ∫ ~

The tober was awakened by the sound of horrified shrieks and cries. Billy ran across the pitch toward the sound. When he got to old Magda's tent, he stopped in his tracks. The old woman had been beaten about her head and arms and was clearly dead. The tent was a mangled mess. Most critical, when Billy looked in the place where the key to the bank box, the *kestel*, should have been, it was missing.

"Son of a bitch!" he mumbled to himself. Leaving three roustabouts to clean up the mess, he stalked determinedly toward the wagon where the money was kept. As he'd feared, the safe had been opened with one of the keys and was totally empty. The entire take of the circus was gone. As was Şarkioğlu.

Word flew around the tober that the "Terrible Turk," as he had been billed, truly was beneath the dregs of humanity. The breakdown that day was lackluster. There was moaning and crying beyond despair. It wasn't long before Billy was facing a once-again downtrodden group – less one evil villain – and trying to goad them into one more try.

"Even if we can hold out for three days, even if we can make it through *two* days, as great as you all have been, we can't simply throw it away, not now."

"We've got to eat," one of the crewmen said.

"Are you telling me there's never been a day in your life when you haven't eaten?" another crewman asked the first.

"Gentlemen," Billy said. "I won't tell you not to eat." He drew a thin roll of bills from his pocket. He reached into his vest and drew out his own grouch bag. "My friends, outside my horse, my ropes, and my clothes, this is all I have in the world. I have faith in all of you. I am donating this money to the *Wallachia y Moldavia*. If it gives us an extra day or two, it's better used than if I spend it on frivolous things. And if we can't start to earn it back in three days at the next town, I'll work as a janitor in a hotel if it gives us another day."

The previously downcast group looked unbelievingly at Billy Jenkins. It was almost as if they were criminals about to be hanged who had been given a reprieve at the last possible moment.

Just then there was a loud trumpeting noise. The three horses, the donkey, and the two goats left in the paddock snorted and brayed with fear. The troupers rushed to the tent's door. Standing before them were two worthies from the town where they'd just finished showing. One of them was holding a rope which was tied around the neck of a not very large, rather scruffy-looking elephant.

Billy's eyes widened. "Well … I'll … be … damned," he swore softly.

"Who is the manager of this show?"

Billy stepped forward and introduced himself.

"Sir," the man continued, "I am Lieutenant Governor, Ian Petrescu. The board of trustees of our provincial zoo has been meeting for the past month. I regret to say we can no longer afford to feed this beast."

"How much do you want for her?" Billy asked.

"*Want?* Why, nothing! We simply want someone who can take her off our hands, someone who can feed her and ensure that she will survive."

"How old is she?"

"I've no idea. I was told she was about thirty when the zoo acquired her. That was ten years ago."

"She looks older."

"She's had a hard life. Not fed regularly, not exercised, nor properly attended to, and, of course, there was no one of her own kind to keep her company. As you can see, she's rather thin for an elephant."

"Is there a cage? A ball to make sure she doesn't stray?"

"Alas, no," the dignitary said. "I suppose that means you can't take her?" he continued sadly.

"No, no, to the contrary," Billy said. "I was just asking. Does she have a name?"

"She answers to the name *Pepper*."

Shortly afterward, the two men left, beaming. But their beam was of very low wattage when compared to the smile on Billy Jenkins' face. "I'll be damned," he muttered to himself again. "Maybe there really is a God. And maybe he does look after his children at that. Now, we've only got to figure out how to feed this new mouth"

~ ∫ ~

Within three weeks Billy was delighted to find that the pachyderm, who'd been padded with a purple satin cover on which was emblazoned in yellow lettering "*Goliath – Gargantuan Giant of Golgotha*," must have been a circus performer in an earlier life, for she proved adept at a number of show tricks. Billy further extended his job to being an elephant trainer. For a few coppers and show passes, he engaged young boys to post circus paper, advertising the forthcoming show in grandiloquent language.

Shortly, the *Wallachia y Moldavia* was regularly filling its not-so-big top to its capacity audience of two hundred. For the first time, there were straw houses.

There has always been an underground telegraph in the entertainment industry. If a circus goes bust in Lisle, France, within three days troupers playing outside Istanbul will know all the details. If there is a buzz that a small mud-and-goat show playing in Iaşi, Rumania, is showing tiny but definite signs of growing, all of Circus Europe will know it within a week.

Well-established, occasionally major artistes, tired of being a footnote to a larger show, or at war with one or more of their associates, or fed up with the management, the food, the schedule, or any one of a hundred other things, may bolt and blow the stand, believing it may be better to be a giant fish in a mud puddle than a herring in the larger ocean. Nor are all of these performers cast-offs by any measure. Show people will put on a show wherever there are people to watch. Many circus folk, who want to be in on the ground floor of the next phenomenon, will often take less than half of what they were making with their previous employer, at least for the first six months of joining up with the new show in town.

Billy was astonished when two defectors from the Cirque Dumas, a major French show, appeared on his doorstep. "Ferdie? Freddie?"

"*Crikey*, it's the Rosenthal brat!" Freddie exclaimed.

"Grown up, grown handsome. Y'er Billy Jenkins, now, eh?"

"Yep, *Limeys*," he said proudly. "Why would you worthies be visiting the cesspit of Eastern Europe?"

"We'd like to set up our stand here for a bit," Ferdie said.

"Can't pay you much."

"Don't need it," Freddie said. "Got enough from the Dumas to last us for while."

"Still closer than brothers?" Billy grinned.

"Of course," said Ferdie.

"Still got your own traps?"

"That, too, *Guv'nor*." Freddie responded.

"Hey, family!" Billy shouted to his artistes and crew. "Got a couple of First of Mays I'd like you to meet!"

"Does that mean we're hired?"

"You any better than you were at *Zoltan's*?" he asked, winking at them.

By that time, a crowd had gathered to watch. Three roustabouts helped set up the Spencer Brothers' paraphernalia. Within moments they were doing their flips on the pommel-horse, and whirling through the air so fast on the parallel bars and rings that most of the artistes could not see more than colorful blurs. At the conclusion of their act, the *Wallachia y Moldavia* performers were shouting and stamping as loud as any jossers.

But Billy's greatest surprise came a week later. The *Wallachia y Moldavia* had played to a *sfondone* house, which was now the norm. A large, muscular fellow with a shaved head and a full black beard sat in the audience, about halfway back. The man appeared to be uninterested in what was going on. Billy noticed that he did not clap, stamp, or otherwise display any emotion. When the show ended and the audience had vacated the *chapiteau*, the large man continued to sit like a bored statue.

Thinking the fellow might be dissatisfied, or even a troublemaker, Billy made it a point to walk over to him. "Excuse me, Herr," he said politely, "but I noticed you didn't seem very excited by the show."

"Wasn't," the man grumbled in a gruff voice.

"Not enough action for you? Clowns not funny enough?"

"They were all right, but missing something."

"What was that?"

"No strongman," the stranger said.

"We *had* a strongman, but that's a long story."

"The Terrible *Turd*?"

"*What did you say?*" Billy gasped.

"You heard me, the Terrible *Turd*. Şarkioğlu. The one who beat Magda to death and ran off with the til."

"How could you possibly know that?"

"Been working as an inspector. Your show could use a strongman, you know. Pretty pathetic otherwise."

"Just who do you think you are to be telling me that?"

"No one important." The gruff voice was eerily familiar. "Nice to see you're not such a midget anymore." With that, the large man ripped off his full beard.

"*Sammy??? Sammy Lichtenfeld??? Oh … my … God!* What are you doing here?"

"Taking a six month leave of absence from the Slovakian Division of the Austrian-Hungarian State Police Department. I thought I'd have one last bit of fun before becoming a responsible citizen and doing grown-up stuff. Got space to put me up for awhile?"

"Depends on how much you eat," Billy said, hugging his friend, with three years' worth of emotion.

~ ∫ ~

On Billy's twenty-first birthday, the *Gran Circo Spettacoloso Wallachia y Moldavia* entered Craiova, Rumania's fifth largest city, by making parade, the first one in the history of the show. The *Wallachia y Moldavia* had made more than its nut. Surprisingly – amazingly

– the troupers had received their regular weekly pay, plus a ten percent raise, for the first time in the memory of most performers and crewmen. While the show was by no means flush, and could not rival the *Fővárosi Nagycirkusz*, the Hungarian show which defined the word "circus" in this part of the world, any resemblance between the goat show Billy had joined a little more than a year ago and the obviously up-and-coming professional circus that paraded down Craiova's main street, was purely coincidental.

In the months since the *Wallachia y Moldavia* had hit rock bottom, the troupers, under Billy's constant urgings, cajolings, and encouragement, had polished, improved, enhanced, and lengthened their acts. Five new acts had added to the show, so it was now a quite credible circus.

Craiova was the perfect place to make parade in midsummer. Nine years ago, it had become the first city in Rumania to be supplied with electric power by internal combustion engines. The *Wallachia y Moldavia* would be able to put on a day show *and* a night show.

Billy may have been a conservative gambler, but he was a gambler, and after the second *sfondone* day of performances, he contracted with a local tentmaker to produce an elongation to the tent, which added twenty feet on each side, making the chapiteau oblong rather than round. This improvement allowed the circus to nearly double its capacity to three hundred seventy-five seats. He ordered extra wooden folding chairs to be built. Within a month, the *Gran Circo Spettacoloso Wallachia y Moldavia* was playing to sellout crowds in its huge new tent.

The following month, Billy was able to acquire something he had only dreamt about since the glory days of South Africa. He made a quick trip to Germany where he spoke with the Hagenbecks. Ten days later, he reappeared in Craiova with half a dozen birds of prey. His return from where he had been the past few years was now complete.

Billy was unaware that two pairs of eyes had noted his return to Germany. Those same four eyes had unobtrusively followed him back to Rumania. The owners of those eyes would soon change Billy Jenkins' life in a way he could not have imagined.

21

While he spent the first year building up what the troupers quietly called the "Billy Jenkins' Show," the outside world Billy had known started to fray and fragment.

Port Arthur surrendered to the Japanese. Peaceful demonstrations in St. Petersburg were brutally crushed by police on what came to be known as "Bloody Sunday." While Kaiser William of Germany and Tsar Nicholas of Russia signed a treaty for mutual help in Europe, this did not aid Russia one bit in the Far East. Nicholas created the Imperial *Duma,* the first Russian parliament, to try to shore up the populace's increasing dissatisfaction with his autocratic rule. The American President Roosevelt mediated an end to the disastrous Russo-Japanese war. The Russian people became increasingly frustrated. The Tsar tried to establish further reforms, but they seemed too little and too late.

The *Wallachia y Moldavia* had been playing to sellout crowds for over a month. One evening in early August, two people, a tall, slender, blonde young woman no more than three years Billy's senior, and a shorter, rotund man in his late fifties, with hair dyed to mask its graying, approached the young circus director after an afternoon performance.

"Herr Jenkins?" the man asked.

"That's me."

He handed Billy an engraved business card of high quality.

"You are *the* James Bailey?"

"I'm sure there are lots of James Baileys," the man said, smiling. "But if you want to call me the *circus* Bailey, that's fine, too."

The attractive young woman stood in the background listening to the exchange.

"Is Jumbo the Elephant still alive?" *What a stupid, inane question,* Billy thought.

"Died twenty years ago. Phineas paid $30,000 to bring him from London to New York. He recouped his entire outlay in less than a week!"

"Thirty thousand dollars in a single week!" Billy whistled.

"Jumbo would have been a perpetual money machine." He chuckled. "Can you believe it, the poor beast was crossing the tracks three years later when he got hit by a freight train? Leave it to old Phineas to make a killing from a killing. He had the brute stuffed and continued displaying Jumbo until *he* died six years later, in 1891."

"You really were partners with him? What was he like?"

"He was a businessman first. His profession was pure entertainment."

"In Europe, we hear so much about him. Did he really say, 'There's a sucker born every minute?'"

"Never in the years I knew him, but old P.T. was a huckster to the very end.'"

"I forget my manners, Mister Bailey, and Miss … Mrs …?"

"Trautsch. Tara Trautsch," the young woman said. "And I am yet a fräulein at twenty-three, although my parents would certainly have it otherwise. You know the old German trinity, *kirche, küche, kinder.*"

"Church, cooking, children," Billy mused. "Somehow, if you'll forgive me, you don't seem like the archetype. Not that you aren't an extraordinarily attractive woman," he caught himself, embarrassed.

She laughed, a lovely, melodious trill.

"May I invite you both to dine off the tober with me?" Billy asked. "There are some quite good restaurants in Craiova."

That evening, during a repast worthy of any in central Europe, Billy asked, "Are the two of you traveling together?"

"We are," Bailey said. "We are not father and daughter, nor do we share anything other than a business relationship."

"The Governor of the Barnum and Bailey Circus. And you, *gnädige Fräulein?*"

"I am a very junior editor at Belünde Verlag. When I approached my seniors with what I felt was a very exciting idea, they turned me down flat. Last year, when I visited the United States ..."

"You visited America?"

"St. Louis, Missouri, actually, at the World's Fair. I met Herr Bailey there ..."

"Fräulein Trautsch is too modest," Bailey interrupted. "She was one of only six women – and the only German woman – who participated as a long-distance runner in the Olympic games."

Tara cleared her throat and went on. "When Herr Bailey introduced himself, I was in awe of him, just as you seemed to be this afternoon."

"She pitched her idea to me," Bailey continued. "I thought, 'Why not?' It wouldn't cost much and it might pay handsome dividends. I told Tara she need not quit her job with Belünde. Three weeks ago, I bankrolled her and we formed Werner-Verlag Deutsch, a publishing house so small no one knew or cared who the partners were."

Billy nodded at the waiter, who quietly brought another plate of petit-fours to the table. Another waiter poured more coffee for the three of them from a large carafe.

"Why would that bring you to a place so far off the beaten path there probably *is* no path anywhere nearby? More to the point, why come to a show that, with all respect, Herr Bailey, is not the hundredth part of the size of Barnum and Bailey?"

"Because of you," Bailey responded enigmatically.

"I'm listening," Billy said.

"Fräulein Trautsch – Tara's – idea was... have you read anything by Karl May, Herr Jenkins?"

"Every single book." He started to rattle off the titles and the characters.

"So I don't need to tell you of the immense popularity the American cowboy commands in Germany. But Herr May hasn't written a *Winnetou* book in three years. He's sixty-three, and his writing days seem to be behind him."

"Herr Jenkins, you know of *Buffalo Bill Cody's Wild West*?" Tara asked.

"Of course."

"And?"

"I see your point."

"The German soul loves the concept of the super-man, the noble hero," the young woman continued. "If we could somehow publish a series of books priced so low they'd be available to the average German – books whose hero would be an American cowboy who could fully understand the German mind. And if that hero would somehow be a *real* person, someone flesh and blood with whom a German audience could relate …?"

"And you're thinking …?"

"Why not, Herr Jenkins?" Bailey asked. "You've got the roping and riding skills, you're a German..."

"Forgive me my modesty, but I'm a performer in a small-time show in a European backwater most Germans don't know exists. I'm sure you could find others."

"Herr Jenkins," Trautsch said. "You're twenty-one and you've already got quite a history. Erich Rosenthal ran away from home and joined *Zoltan's Great American* before he was thirteen. He went on to become Billy Jenkins, the Prince of the Cowboys, with the Renz. Spent a year in South Africa with the Hagenbeck-Knie. Then suddenly went into almost a year in a drunken stupor."

She paused as Billy glared at her.

"That's a simple truth, and it will add to the legend. You recovered on your own, but then came the really hard part – relearning your skills and ending up with a goat show where the goat was on its last legs. It would have collapsed and died, too, but you singlehandedly pushed everyone on the show into saving it."

"How could you possibly know so much about me?"

"I'm an editor and a journalist. You're not the only one who started young."

"You're also a world-class athlete, and ..." Billy stumbled.

"And a *woman*?" she finished his sentence. "You don't have to mumble apologies, Herr Jenkins."

"I was about to say, 'And a *spy*,' Fräulein Trautsch," he said.

She ignored his tone. "Let's simply agree to treat one another as equals, and, I hope, as colleagues. In order to meet you on level footing, I felt it necessary to find out everything I could about you. I've been doing just that for the past few months."

"Before I knew anything about you?"

"Before you even knew I existed, Herr Jenkins. If we are going to be working together, I suggest you call me Tara. You needn't bother looking at me like that. We can continue with formalities and always feel slightly uncomfortable in one another's company or we can be friends. I'll play the game any way you want, but as the American cowboys used to say, I believe in laying my cards on the table."

"Rather direct, isn't she?" Bailey said, grinning. "As awed as she claims to have been when she met me, she didn't treat me any differently. To use more cowboy lingo, she's a 'straight shooter,' says what she means, and doesn't waste anyone's time."

As they walked back toward the tober later than evening, Billy asked where they were staying.

"The Grand Hotel Bucuresti," Bailey said. "Would you be interested in hearing more about what we have to offer?"

"I didn't know there was any kind of offer," Billy rejoined. "I'm rather tired tonight, but I'm open to hear what you have to say. Tomorrow's a day off for the show. Perhaps we could meet and talk then? I'll come by for you at, say, eleven in the morning. That'll give us time for a long walk in the city park."

~ ∫ ~

The following day, Billy appeared with Sammy Lichtenfeld. "My closest friend," he said, when he introduced the weightlifter to Trautsch and Bailey. "If you don't mind, I'd like him to be in on our conversation."

"No objection," Bailey said smoothly. "Frankly, I was hoping you'd have a confidant you could speak to. I'm glad you're here, Herr Lichtenfeld," he said. "That way you'll both hear what we have to say first hand, and that we have nothing to hide."

~ ∫ ~

"Let me get this straight. You're proposing a five year plan, during which time I'll move up from circus to circus, hopefully building a name for myself. What about my colleagues on the *Wallachia y Moldavia*?"

"You no doubt want your present colleagues taken care of. Very well, it is said and it is done. You have built a mud-and-goat show up to some respectability. You're entitled to be compensated for your efforts. How does ten thousand American dollars sound?"

"Ten *thousand* American dollars?"

"Or two thousand English pounds, if you prefer. Is something wrong?"

"No, Herr Bailey, it's just that I never dreamed I'd earn so much money. Two years ago, I borrowed five hundred *marks* and lived on that for seven months..."

"Eight," Tara Trautsch said casually.

Billy was silent for several moments. The foursome reached the top of a small hill, from which could see most of the new city. The six story high Grand Hotel Bucuresti was the tallest structure in sight. Billy tried to calculate everything he could do with such an astronomical sum.

Bailey continued, "We will transfer the money to your account the day after we come to an arrangement. The *Wallachia y Moldavia* will transfer ownership to a German company, Barnum and Bailey Europa, G.m.b.H. By the way, who owns the show now?"

"Why ... why ... no one," Billy stammered. "I've been acting as manager."

"You will continue to act as manager," Bailey continued. "We will offer anyone who is inclined to stay on the show a three year employment contract at ten percent over their current wages. For those who want to retire, Barnum and Bailey Europa will pay them one year's wage, which should give them time to settle down or find other work, or whatever."

"How can you afford to be so generous?" Sammy asked.

"I am not being the least bit altruistic, Herr Lichtenfeld. We anticipate we will recover our outlay many times over in a very few years. I partnered with Phineas T. Barnum, publicly one of the greatest risk takers in the entertainment industry, but privately the shrewdest businessman I ever met. He did not risk one cent he didn't think he'd get back a hundredfold."

"You said I would continue as manager?"

"Yes. At your current rate plus ten percent. Barnum and Bailey will bring in your replacement in a year or so. Herr Lichtenfeld, it is clear that Billy respects you …"

"Thank you, but no, thank you, Herr Bailey. I'm on a limited leave from the Austrian-Hungarian Police. Being on the circus has been a wonderful experience for me, but I'd rather have a steady career in one place."

Bailey turned back to Billy. "When the new manager comes, you will introduce him around and spend time showing him the ropes. By that time, we'll have made arrangements for you to move on to another circus, a bit larger than the *Wallachia y Moldavia*, well-respected, but not one of the major players on the European stage."

"What about you, Fräulein … Tara?"

"I'll continue working for my present employer. Once every few months, I'll meet with you to discuss ideas. Meanwhile, one or more writers will use those ideas and write a series of short, action-packed novels about the hero 'Billy Jenkins.' Five years from now, when you're hopefully at the height of your circus career, Werner Verlag-Deutsch, G.m.b.H. will have a catalogue of twenty or thirty titles, which we can release once every two months."

"Like Jumbo the Elephant, a 'perpetual money machine.' Clever," Billy said. "Clever but risky."

"In what way?" Bailey asked.

"How can you be certain the public will accept 'Billy Jenkins?'"

"Trust me, the Germans won't care what you're called. All they'll know is one of their own went to the United States, captured the heart of the American West, and returned to the *vaterland*. You're blond, blue-eyed, and you *look* the part. By that time, we might even create a 'Billy Jenkins Wild West Show' as an independent program."

"The books will sell the show and the show will sell the books," Tara added.

Over a substantial lunch of schnitzel, potatoes Lyonnaise, and red cabbage, washed down by an excellent Serbian wine, the four continued their discussion.

"From the time you leave the *Wallachia y Moldavia*, you'll pay ten percent of your wage back to me until I've recouped my ten thousand dollar investment," Bailey said. "The *Wallachia y Moldania* should turn a good profit for Barnum and Bailey Europa, so your only responsibility will be to remit ten percent of the take to Barnum and Bailey Europa. When you go on to the next circus, your responsibility for the Rumanian circus will end. When we start publishing, you'll receive ten percent of the gross profit from the sale of the 'Billy Jenkins' novels."

Billy looked at Sammy Lichtenfeld, who nodded approvingly.

"Done," he said.

"No negotiating?" Tara asked.

"Why should there be? Whatever it amounts to, it's more than I ever expected to earn in my life."

"He'd be a fool to turn it down," Lichtenfeld added.

That afternoon, Bailey handwrote four copies of a simple two-page agreement which he presented to them that evening at dinner. Billy, Tara, and Bailey signed the agreement, and Sammy Lichtenfeld affixed his signature as witness.

~ ʃ ~

James Bailey was every bit as good as his word. Within a week, Billy received a passbook for an account at the *Credit Suisse* in Zurich showing a balance of ten thousand American dollars. For the next eight months everything went better than any of them had anticipated. The *Wallachia y Moldavia,* energized by its newly-found funding, ventured successfully into Croatia and Hungary.

Billy met with Tara Trautsch, once in Budapest and once in Vienna. They turned out to be a wonderfully creative business team.

There were no romantic sparks between them. Billy and Tara were like the sister or brother neither of them had ever had.

By the end of March 1906, Billy wondered when the new manager would show up. The circus was due to play in Zagreb for two weeks, commencing April fifth. He knew Bailey would be ecstatic when he received *three times* as much in profit as he had projected the previous August. The next day, Billy dispatched the money to Barnum and Bailey Europa.

He was mildly surprised when he hadn't heard back from Barnum and Bailey Europa by the tenth of the month. As days went by, he became nervous about whether or not his payment to the company had been misdirected.

On April 15, Billy received a telegram at noon, two hours before the afternoon performance. As he eagerly tore open the envelope expecting hearty congratulations on a job well done, he frowned as he read, then reread, the terse message:

Regret inform u, J. Bailey died April 10, Mt. Vernon, N.Y. Need to discuss all arrangements. Chas. Ringling.

22

"We are, of course, dreadfully sorry about Mister Bailey's passing," the older of the two men, Charles Ringling, said. They were dining at Gundel's, Hungary's most prestigious restaurant. Billy had been summoned here by Charles and his brother John.

"We're presently in negotiations to buy all the Barnum and Bailey holdings in the States, but we won't be purchasing Barnum and Bailey Europa. Without further funding, that company will most likely fold."

Billy was aghast. "But Herr Bailey committed to a retirement plan for those who wanted to leave *Wallachia y Moldavia* as well as three year contracts for the artistes who elected to stay on. There was a program planned for me – one we all believed would pay great dividends. And they already have, Herr Ringling."

Although Billy was bitter at the disclosure that the Ringlings were going to abandon the Rumanian circus, even more that they were going to abandon the program Bailey had set for *him*, he realized he had no reason to be angry at the Ringling brothers. Their interests must be determined by them. After all, Billy thought, *I* intended to leave the *Wallachia y Moldavia* when my promised year was up. But what about Tara?

"We will, of course, honor the retirement plan," John Ringling said. "We are not unmindful that you have repaid Mister Bailey's confidence in you most handsomely, which is one of the reasons we asked you to come to Budapest."

Despite the disappointment he felt, Billy could not help but admire the *fin-de-siècle* grandeur of Gundel's glorious dining room, tastefully adorned with 19th-century Hungarian paintings. A ten-piece gypsy band added both sparkle and nostalgia to the place. His mood was significantly heightened when he tasted the legendary goose liver pâté and the crisp Gundel pancakes.

"Have you spoken with Fräulein Trautsch?" he asked.

"Ah, yes, that was a delicate matter. A strong girl. I have no doubt she'll eventually do what she has set out to do," Charles said.

"Eventually," Billy murmured. "What about Werner-Verlag Deutsch?"

"It never published anything, so it never lost anything. Fräulein Trautsch owes us nothing and she still has her job with Belünde."

"What about the Billy Jenkins project?"

"You own the name. Bailey financed that idea out of his personal funds, so Barnum and Bailey Europa owns no part of it. Werner-Verlag Deutsch is not a public company. It's between you and Fräulein Trautsch what you want to do with it. That's not the reason I called this meeting," Charles continued pleasantly. "I wanted to talk to you about the circus – and about your ten thousand dollar advance."

Billy reddened slightly. "I told Herr Bailey I would pay him back from my earnings and I intend to honor that promise."

"A noble thought, Herr Jenkins, but unnecessary," John said. He handed Billy a piece of paper. "As of this moment, any debt you would have owed Barnum and Bailey Europa, or, for that matter, James Bailey, is cancelled."

"I ... I don't know what to say," Billy stammered. "I am overwhelmed by your generosity."

"Barnum and Bailey Europa's generosity," Charles remarked acerbically. "Of course, that brings up a slight legal problem."

"A legal problem?"

"Yes. Barnum and Bailey Europa owns the *name Wallachia y Moldavia.* A name is only as good as the show, and without Billy Jenkins and a couple of other acts, the *name* is valueless, but it *does* belong to Barnum and Bailey Europa, even though that entity will most likely be inactivated."

"It's a profitable show, Herr Ringling. Barnum and Bailey has the right to continue to receive profits." Although Billy was not sure where this conversation was leading, his mind was weighing numerous alternatives.

"We understand that," John said. "Mister Bailey obviously thought a great deal of you because he protected your interests, even if he didn't foresee his early demise." He extracted a copy of the two-page document James Bailey had handwritten and pointed to a section for Billy to read.

Billy speared another piece of pancake with his fork, cut a bite-sized segment, and was just about to put it in his mouth, when he stopped and read the section out loud. "In the event Barnum and Bailey Europa defaults on its obligations at any time during the first three years of this agreement, then all personal property, equipment, livestock, vehicles, and all other property of every kind, other than the name and goodwill of the *Gran Circo Spettacoloso Wallachia y Moldavia,* shall revert to the present management as represented by Erich Otto Rosenthal, professionally known as Billy Jenkins."

"Which means, you now own a circus complete with tents, animals, wagons, and, should you choose to honor them, contracts. Like your friend Miss Trautsch, you are debt-free but also like her, you're substantially ahead of where you were, thanks to the soon-to-be defunct Barnum and Bailey Europa," Charles Ringling said.

~ ʃ ~

"By now, you've heard that Herr Bailey died a month ago." Billy addressed his thirty associates. "His representatives advised me that Barnum and Bailey Europa is dissolving and will no longer support the circus financially."

There was a collective groan in the chapiteau.

"Does that mean Barnum and Bailey will no longer honor our contracts." Freddie Spencer asked.

"That's correct. Further, I have other news. Barnum and Bailey Europa continues to own the name and goodwill of the *Gran Circo Spettacoloso Wallachia y Moldavia*, which means this circus as we know it will cease to exist."

The groans now turned to shocked gasps.

"You mean no more *Wallachia y Moldavia*? After all our hard work and effort to elevate it from the mud-and-goat show it was?" This from an older female clown, who burst into tears.

"That's right," Billy said enigmatically. He paused for dramatic effect, then added. "Of course, if any of you are interested, a new outfit called the *Schlamm und Bock Zeigen* will be happy to pick up your contracts, with a two percent raise in your salaries if you join up now." He grinned. "Since I will be the, ahem, proprietor of the *Schlamm und Bock*, which will own every stick and shred of our present equipment, vehicles, show stock, and everything else, I don't think you'll have to worry about any major changes. If any of you are interested in signing the contracts …"

When everyone had happily settled down, Ferdie Spencer asked, "Excuse me, boss, Governor, whatever you want to call yourself, but couldn't you have chosen a more suitable name?"

"Absolutely not, Ferdie," Billy replied. "A few moments ago, one of our number described exactly what we were – a mud-and-goat show."

"Yes, but *calling* ourselves that?" Ferdie continued, trying to mask his laughter.

"What better name to excite the jossers' curiosity? Wouldn't you go to a circus that had the nerve to call itself 'The Mud-and-Goat show?' just *once* to see if it really was as awful as its name? Can you picture the word of mouth when those same flatties learn we're a very genuine, highly professional outfit?"

"Why change the name to a German one?" a burly crew member asked.

"Because as generous as Rumania, Croatia, and Hungary, have been to us, it's still a minor league venue for a real circus. We are moving our headquarters from ... well, the *Wallachia y Moldavia* never really *had* a home base, come to think of it. Effective one month from today, we'll be headquartered in Munich. Oh, and one last thing. Just in case anyone is fooled by the name *Schlamm und Bock Zeigen*, the full name of the new circus will be the *United Schlamm und Bock Zeigen and Billy Jenkins Great American Wild West Show*."

~ ʃ ~

"So you still plan on going ahead with our idea?"

"I am, Tara. Maybe we won't get there nearly as soon as we'd hoped, but I promise you we will get there. My target date is five years from now – June 26, 1912 – my twenty-seventh birthday."

"I can't believe you're paying the same amount you'd been paying to Barnum and Bailey Europa to Werner-Verlag Deutsch."

"A loan," Billy said casually.

"An *unsecured* loan at three percent interest, payable 'when and if you can.' I'd hardly call that a well-secured investment, Herr Jenkins."

"Oh, you'll pay for it all right," he chuckled.

"Surely you don't mean …" she blushed.

"Surely I *do* mean, but not in the way you think," he rejoined. "You have a seventeen-year old niece who's *almost* as attractive as you and has graduated from the gymnasium. I'll need an assistant for my act for about a year. What better way for your niece to see Europe? I understand Abrielle is quite the horsewoman."

"Eats, sleeps, and dreams horses," Tara said. "But who would train her?"

"I have a dear old friend," Billy said. "Twice a countess, as a matter of fact. She's fifty-four and might like a month-long holiday."

~ ∫ ~

"Billy Jenkins! I thought I'd never hear from you again! You're offering me five weeks with a mud-and-goat show, at the munificent wage of five whole francs a week?"

"Ten?"

"You sure know how to charm a girl. I accept, of course! My God, what a wonderful surprise!" The telephone connection between Paris and Vienna was as clear as if Brenda Lee were standing in the next room.

"Will the Count be coming with you?"

"Henri says Wien is one of his favorite cities in the world, but his arthritis and gout have been plaguing him. He is overjoyed that I'll find something meaningful to do. When must I be there?"

"You're doing me the great favor, Countess. Whenever it suits your pleasure."

A week later, Billy met with Brenda Lee, Tara, and Tara's niece Abrielle at Sacher's. The years had been kind to the former Countess du Bourges, now Countess de Montagne. Her golden hair had wisps of a paler shade, and while she had put on a kilo or two, she was, if anything, more womanly voluptuous than he remembered.

"Why Billy Jenkins, I do declare," she said in a mock American Southern accent. "All grown up and handsomer than ever. I fear, however, your attention has been diverted by two other blonde beauties," she continued, nodding at Tara and Abrielle.

"My thoughts always stray back to the many things you taught me … about the circus." There was a noticeable pause between the words "me" and "about." Brenda Lee blushed.

"Mademoiselle Trautsch," the countess continued, "Your niece reminds me of a more beautiful version of me as I looked almost forty years ago." She sighed. "Truly, time is the greatest thief of all."

"Countess," Abrielle said, "Herr Jenkins told me you were the greatest bareback rider he'd ever seen. He told me you were the toast of Paris and they even named a color after you!"

"What a story that was!" she laughed.

"Tell me, tell me, please!" Abrielle pleaded.

How incredibly innocent she is, Brenda Lee thought. "It happened one afternoon when I was seventeen, the same age you are now."

"Before I was born?"

"Yes. One afternoon, when I was with the *old Zoltan's*, in Paris, we had a show to do. I had a pair of bright red fleshings – those spangled tights all circus females under the age of sixty seem to wear."

"I've seen them," the girl said. "They're awfully daring."

"They *appear* to show just about everything you have, but they don't really. Anyway, these fleshings – nowadays they call them léotards – were dirty and smelly with dried sweat. When I asked the wardrobe mistress for another pair, she said they'd all been sent to the laundress and weren't expected back until that evening. I told them it would not be a problem, and threw them into a bucket with warm water. I knew the moment I smelled the bleach that something was very wrong. When I pulled them out of the bucket, the water had turned red and the fleshings had faded to a ghastly pink. I swore a blue streak, I can tell you.

"I was just about to burst into tears when Zoltan himself, God rest his soul, came by. He quickly sized up the situation and said, 'Well, you really have nothing else to wear. So, my dear, wear those pink fleshings and wear them proudly. You never can tell what these Parisians will do.'"

"And that's how 'Clover Pink' came to be?" Abrielle asked, wide-eyed.

"The Parisians went wild over it, and it showed up everywhere. Not only that, that's how I came to be Countess du Bourges. I'd always dreamed of marrying a nobleman, but never really expected it to happen. Gaspar, my late husband, came to one of the shows, then to another, then to another. Next, there were flowers, huge bouquets of them, and invitations to dinner … and …Giuseppina and I …"

At that moment, Billy saw something he would never have expected of Brenda Lee. She started weeping uncontrollably.

"Giuseppina *Bozacchi*?" Tara asked.

"Y- yes, Mademoiselle Trautsch," the countess said, dabbing at her eyes with a silk handkerchief. "How could you possibly have known?"

"Fräulein Trautsch makes it her habit to know things about others they don't even know about themselves," Billy said. "When I first met her, I accused her of being a spy."

"No, no," Tara protested. "I simply consider myself a student of *people*. When Billy told me stories you had told him about your circus days, I asked him some questions. You were in Paris in 1870?"

"But how does that lead to my relationship with Giuseppina?"

"That, my dear Countess, took a little more sleuthing," Tara said. "The ballet has always been one of my great loves."

"I see," Brenda replied, her mind quickly calculating. "You knew I was appearing in Paris with *Zoltan's* during the Franco-Prussian War."

"Would you mind telling us what this is all about, Tante Tara?" Abrielle asked.

"Of course, darling. Please excuse my bad manners. You've been to the ballet with me. Remember when we saw *Coppélia*?"

"The one where the dancing doll comes to life? Of course, it's one of my favorites."

"Giuseppina Bozacchi was the *original Coppelia*-doll, Swanhilda. She was sixteen years old when she created the role. She danced Swanhilda only eighteen times before the Paris Opéra closed for the duration of the Franco-Prussian War," Tara said.

"She was as much the belle of Paris as I was," Brenda Lee said, again dabbing at her eyes. "We were both single, and we became as close as sisters to one another."

"It must have been a difficult time," Tara said gently.

"It was a *horrid* time, Mademoiselle Trautsch. Paris was under siege. People were starving. If you were wealthy enough to order filet mignon from the menu in the fancy hotel restaurants, you were likely dining on *filly* mignon. They started killing exotics from the Paris Zoo and eating them."

"How dreadful! I know the tragic story of Giuseppina Bozacchi," Tara said delicately.

"Do you?" Brenda said, her tone suddenly bitter. "*Do you really*, Mademoiselle Trautsch? No offense to you, but Giuseppina disappeared from the Grand Hotel de l'Opéra one day when I was supposed to meet her for lunch. They had the *nerve* to say she had never been a guest there. I knew damned well she had been staying in the Emperor's Suite for three months. Those arseholes, excuse me Mademoiselles, but those are the only words good enough for them."

Abrielle sat speechless, her eyes wide as saucers.

"You see, Mademoiselle Trautsch, Giuseppina Bozacchi had contracted cholera from some poorly washed cup from the hotel dining room. Of course, the Opéra would *never* admit that anything like that had happened at that *Grand* Hotel. Zoltan used every connection he had. Finally his friend Daniel Auber, that darling old man, was able to convince one of *his* friends high up in the constabulary, to do some serious investigation.

"I found her in a hôtel du charité – a charnel house – in the nineteenth arondissement. By then it was too late. She had died of starvation and cholera *two hours before I arrived – the morning of her seventeenth birthday.*"

The company sat in horrified silence. Shortly, Brenda Lee composed herself, coughed, and turning to Tara's niece said, "But enough of that long ago time. Darling Abrielle, have you plans to attend the university?"

"Oh, yes," Abrielle said vaguely. "But Tante Tara and Herr Jenkins convinced me that taking a year off to see more of the world would be more valuable to me than a year in school."

"I can't disagree with that, my dear. You may learn more than you bargained for. How long have you been riding?"

"Since I was five."

"Dressage? Haute ecôle?"

"Yes. Even some voltige," the girl said.

"Not Billy Jenkins-style voltige, I hope?" Brenda Lee said. "Well, we'll see what you mean when we get you started. I suggest we begin tomorrow morning."

23

"We do a much more graceful, but just as difficult, form of voltige than Billy does," Brenda Lee began. She looked remarkably trim in her Clover Pink fleshings. "Amazing what a good girdle can do," she laughed when she slipped it on. At Brenda Lee's direction, Abrielle was wearing tight-fitting pants and a loose blouse tucked into her trousers.

"You've already had experience with haute ecôle. Now we'll go on to *your* 'equestrian high school.' Watch me for a few moments."

Brenda Lee brought a white gelding into the training ring. At a signal from the veteran equestrienne, the horse started steadily trotting around the ring. Brenda Lee gauged the speed and gait of the gelding, then approached him from his left. Her first mount was fairly stiff, but then, like the seasoned professional she was, the countess smoothly and effortlessly, vaulted onto, then off of, the horse's back three times in succession.

"It's been seven years," Brenda Lee said, out of breath from her exertions.

The teenage apprentice simply gaped. "You make it look so easy, Gräfin."

"In the ring, I'm plain old Brenda Lee," she responded.

"Yes, Gr – Brenda Lee," Abrielle said. "Did you know that the late Empress Elisabeth of Austria did voltige riding?"

"Not only did I know that, but I knew *her*. She and I once rode voltige together. Now, young lady, we're about to start working your very nice little *toches* – your *derriere* – off. Don't look so shocked. I may say words you'd never dream of hearing a high-risen countess use, but I can promise you that during the next week you'll use every one of them and then some – that's how sore you'll be."

Brenda Lee, Countess de Montagne was correct. She was also, as Abrielle soon found out, an unrelenting taskmistress and perfectionist. By the third day, Abrielle was in tears. "I'll never be able to do even the simplest tricks," she wailed.

"Not with that attitude you won't," Brenda Lee said sternly. "No one said it was going to be easy, darling. Anything worth doing is worth doing *right*, whether it's voltige or playing with a boy."

"*Madame de Montagne!*" the girl exclaimed, shocked out of her tears.

"Yes?" Brenda Lee responded sweetly.

"Such thoughts!"

"What kind of thoughts?" Brenda continued in the same sweet voice.

"You know … uh …?"

"Sex? Losing your virginity?"

"Well... yes..."

"Honey, you think your generation invented sex? Or, for that matter, love? That's the way people have been making other people since the world began. And having fun doing it. Now, stop feeling sorry for yourself, and start working."

By the start of the second week, Abrielle was doing remarkably well, and Brenda Lee said so to Billy.

"When do I get to see the miracle you've wrought?" he asked.

"When I tell you and not before."

~ ∫ ~

"O.K., Abrielle, you've learned some tricks that were spectacular in my day. Today, they're very ordinary. People get faster, stronger, more daring every day. The *Schlamm und Bock* is anything *but* a mud-and-goat show, the name notwithstanding."

"When Herr Jenkins sees what I've learned to do, it'll 'knock him on his arse.'" She giggled. The week with Brenda Lee had wrought changes in more ways than one.

"In this next trick, we'll use two horses trotting side by side. You'll somersault from one to the other, then you'll do the same thing backwards."

"You really think I can?"

"It doesn't matter what *I* think, Abby. It's what *you* believe you can do."

Two days later, having mastered the somersaults, Abrielle moved on to the next trick: doing handstands on the horse while it was trotting, then somersaulting over to the second horse, then leaping to a standing position, with one leg on the back of each horse.

"Bravo, girl! You've learned in three weeks what it took me two *years* to master. I told you young people today are stronger, faster, more agile."

"Is there a way I can make it look more difficult, Countess?"

"The artistry lies not in making an easy trick look difficult, but in making what's difficult look easy. In America, you can get away with any cheap trick so long as it *looks* spectacular. In Europe, the commonest audience can tell the difference between real artistry and sheer toot."

Finally, when Brenda Lee felt Abrielle was absolutely secure standing on a horse while it trotted around the ring, she said, "Now

I'm going to teach you the act by which I was always remembered. The Governor's never seen it, since I never did it after Zoltan's death, but when you debut, you truly will 'knock him on his arse.'" They rehearsed the spectacle for most of the last week Brenda Lee was to be in Vienna.

"But I thought Herr Jenkins wanted me to be his assistant," Abrielle said when they'd completed the training. "I haven't learned anything that would assist him."

"That, my girl, will take ten minutes. In fact, we'll give you 'on the job training' by letting you practice with the Governor himself."

~ ∫ ~

"She's a perfect assistant. Tosses the plate perfectly, sets the six targets with great dramatic flair. Have you taught her the bullet-in-teeth trick yet?"

"I have, but I thought since it's only two days before I go back to Paris I'd like to return to the circus for one last time and do that one."

"How could I deny you anything, Brenda Lee?"

She smiled dazzlingly at him. In that moment he fell in love with her all over again. "Perhaps this evening we might not have to deny *each other* anything," she said, giving him a meaningful glance that took his breath away.

"All right, let's rehearse this trick once and see if you can still get it down right."

As he clicked back the hammer, Brenda Lee suddenly tottered, rocking back and forth. Abrielle saw the movement, but Billy was concentrating so hard on counting that he did not. On the count of five, he fired. There was a concussive *blam!* and Brenda Lee pitched face forward.

"Oh, My God! Brenda Lee!" Billy gasped and ran immediately to where she lay, not moving.

Abrielle screamed, "Countess!" at the same moment.

When they arrived at her side, it was clear that Brenda Lee, Countess de Montagne, was dead, even though there was not a mark anywhere on her head or body.

~ ∫ ~

The show cancelled its scheduled performances for two weeks. During that time, Henri, Count de Montagne, Brenda Lee's sixty-two-year-old widower, hurried to Vienna with his personal physician. Doctor Desmarché, concurred with Professor Doktor von Murtasser, the Viennese pathologist who'd conducted the autopsy.

"The woman died of an Ischemic stroke," von Murtasser told a stunned Billy. "They used to call it 'a stroke of God,' because it comes on suddenly and unexpectedly out of nowhere."

"Cryptogenic, Herr Doktor?" Desmarché asked.

"So far as I can tell, yes," von Murtasser said. "Totally unknown origin. She was in her early fifties and, so far as anyone could tell, in perfect health."

Turning to Billy, the Count said, "Young man, please, you must not hold yourself responsible for my wife's death. If anything, you provided her with a return to the time of her happiest memories. For that I bless you."

Now the tears came. They only abated after a lengthy period. Turning to Montagne, he said, "I just remembered something that might make it easier for all of us."

"What's that?" the elderly count asked.

"Eleven years ago when I first joined on the circus, Zeke Willis and I were talking one day about the founder of their circus, Zoltan. When I asked him how the old fellow had passed away, he said, 'Why Zoltan greeted his last day by coming out of his wagon, spreading his arms wide, as if to embrace the whole world. Then he just tipped over and died. They said it was a stroke.'"

~ ∫ ~

Although the Count de Montagne had made arrangements to ship Brenda Lee's remains back to Paris for a proper funeral and burial, he allowed for a brief private service in Vienna. It was a very small service indeed, for none of the *Schlamm und Bock* troupers had ever known the Countess in her glory days.

Billy attended, as did Tara, Abrielle, and the Count. Sammy Lichtenfeld had hastened to Vienna to be by his friend's side in his time of profound mourning. He stood quietly during the service and said very few words. His eyes never once left Abrielle.

In this small, quiet way, the last vestige of *Zoltan's Titanic Treasure Trove,* the once mighty circus, passed into history.

~ ∫ ~

"The Count has asked that we do him the honor of performing a single memorial show in honor of Brenda Lee," Tara told Billy. "In order to provide for her memory, he has chartered a train to take the entire troupe to Paris and bring us back to Wien."

"Of course," Billy replied without hesitation.

"It will be Abrielle's first show. Would you mind if her family came?"

"I insist they come. Although the *Schlamm und Bock* is not well-heeled, that's an expense we certainly can afford."

"What about Sammy?"

"Our esteemed police inspector has agreed to come on the circus for that one performance. That was the least he could do, since Brenda Lee was on his first show."

"It will be a private show," Tara said. "The count's family and a few others."

~ ∫ ~

"Are you nervous, Abrielle?"

"No, Tante Tara. I know I should be, but it's been two weeks since Brenda Lee passed. You know of the special surprise we've got in store for Herr Jenkins?"

"I do. I asked him as a special favor to me to let you perform your act at the very end of the show."

Unknown to Tara, Abrielle had planned a special surprise for her own family as well, one she had not shared with Billy.

~ ∫ ~

The "small, private, select group" turned out to be one hundred twenty people. Just prior to the intermission, Billy Jenkins made a special announcement.

"Messieurs, 'dames," he said. "I know this is a time of mourning, but in the midst of death, there is life. I understand one of the women in our audience is celebrating her eightieth birthday this afternoon." There was a smattering of warm applause and shouts of "Bravo!" "Congratulations!"

"This woman did not know we were going to celebrate her birthday today, but several of her friends insisted, so I'm going to ask all of you to sing "Happy Birthday" to our special birthday girl, Madame Elise Soulet!"

As the crowd sang a rousing rendition of "Happy Birthday" in French, a small, frail, doddering old woman, walking with the aid of a cane, was helped from the seats by Count Henri de Montagne himself. The count presented her with a small birthday cake. She almost expired trying to blow out the candle.

"Madame Soulet," Billy said, "our troupers would like to honor any special birthday wish you might have – anything to make your eightieth birthday a happy one."

The old lady, bent over as she was from rheumatism, couldn't hear the ringmaster. "Ehh?" she said, elevating an old-fashioned ear trumpet to hear him.

"I said, Madame Soulet," Billy repeated in a louder voice aimed directly into the old-fashioned device, a voice the entire audience could easily hear, "our troupers would like to honor any special birthday wish you have."

"You don't have to shout, you know!" the crone cackled. "I can hear you perfectly well." The crowd laughed appreciatively. "How nice of you to ask, young fellow." She toddled up to Billy and whispered something in his ear. He shook his head vigorously and decisively.

"*Non, Madame. C'est impossible!*"

"But you said …"

The audience was now very much in her corner. "Let her!" "Let's hear what she wants!" "Don't go back on your word!" echoed through the tent.

"He told me he wanted me to have a happy birthday," the old woman wailed. "Me, a good, moral widow woman! What have I left in this world?"

Now the crowd was turning surly. Billy shrugged his shoulders. "Ladies and gentlemen," he said, "we are willing to do anything *reasonably* possible to accommodate Madame Soulet, but we cannot put her life in danger. What she asks is …"

He hesitated among the shouts of, "Give her what she wants!"

"She tells me she has never ridden a horse before and she asks to be allowed to ride Thunderbolt, the wild white stallion you see yonder," he said, pointing in the direction of a snorting white horse that had been led into the ring.

"Let her! Let her!" the males in the audience roared. The women were not so eager to allow the old woman to approach the huge animal.

"I will leave it up to you," Billy finally said, in exasperation. "What do you think? Do we let this octogenarian defy death, or, at the very least, serious, life threatening injury?"

There was an overwhelming roar of approval, mostly from the men.

"Very well, then. You have cast her to her fate. The *Schlamm und Bock* absolves itself of all responsibility. Come, Madame," he said, taking the old woman by the arm. He led her to a raised platform, where two roustabouts waited to lift her onto the horse.

The beast pawed the ground nervously and whinnied in what the audience could sense was impatience. No sooner had they lifted the old woman onto the horse, then the animal started galloping wildly around the ring. Madame Soulet held on for life, and the crowd's approbation immediately turned to horrified gasps as Thunderbolt seemed clearly out of control. Suddenly, Thunderbolt reared almost straight up. Madame Soulet let out a scream that could be heard throughout the chapiteau. That scream was echoed by more than a dozen women in the audience.

Coming down, the horse now began an even more furious gallop. The old lady hung onto the horse's neck for dear life. Three crewmen shouted and waved their arms, to no effect whatever.

Just as the crowd had reached a pitch of emotion and shouts of "No!" "Stop him!" "Save her!" the old lady's shawl flew off. Then her capacious dress came off, revealing bright red bloomers. The audience did not know whether to scream or laugh at the spectacle. Suddenly the old lady's *head* seemed to come off – at least the gray hair.

Within an instant, *everything* came off, and in that moment "Madame Soulet" shook out the full tresses of her honey-golden hair, vaulted to a stand, her gorgeous body clothed in a spangled blue léotard that revealed every delicious curve, and blew kisses to the audience, which now went berserk with applause, stamping their feet so hard that the big top shook. Billy had to shout at the top of his voice, even using a large megaphone. "Ladies and gentleman, **MADEMOISELLE ABRIELLE!**"

The audience kept shouting and stamping and pounding for fully four minutes, according to Billy's treasured pocket watch. "Break for intermission after she's done!" he told the crewmen. "We can lengthen the second act, but this is the experience every circus performer dreams about."

Meanwhile, Abrielle kept doing somersaults, handstands, splits, on-and-off vaults, and a repertoire of tricks. The audience kept her going and refused to let her stop. Finally, she leapt off Thunderbolt and stood in the center of the pista, her arms raised in a giant **V**, amidst thunderous ovation from the jossers. The most animated applause of all came from Brenda Lee's widower, the Count de Montagne, and one other person.

~ ∫ ~

During intermission, Billy intercepted the young girl, who was laughing, crying, and screaming, "They liked me! They *really* liked me!"

"No, Abrielle," Billy corrected. "They *loved* you! They *adored* you! Why, if they could, they would have made you the Queen of all Europe by acclamation!"

At that moment, the Count de Montagne came up to her and said, "Brenda Lee would have been so proud of you. *I'm* so proud of you. I feel I am present at the birth of an international star!"

As Billy turned to greet the audience and graciously thank them for their patronage, the Count and Abrielle walked toward the dressing tent. "Everything's ready," he said quietly.

"Everything?"

"Oh, yes. As far as the ringmaster knows, he'll open the second act with his guns and ropes, his voltige and his birds. You'll be his trusty assistant and then you'll leave the pista until the closing spectacle – or so he thinks. My friends will force his hand."

~ ∫ ~

The audience reacted with enthusiasm when Billy did his tricks. Abrielle unobtrusively left the tent when he started his birds-of-prey act. During the remainder of the show, each artiste outdid himself or herself. Every act received a standing ovation. Just as Billy was about to announce the closing spec, there was a low undercurrent of sound, "Ab-ri-elle! Ab-ri-elle! Ab-ri-elle!"

The sound became more insistent and louder as first one, then another, josser picked up the cadence. Within a minute, the sound was a firestorm of adulation. "AB-RI-ELLE! AB-RI-ELLE!! **AB-RI-ELLE!!!**"

Billy looked around the tent and grinned. As he glanced toward the performer's entrance door, a fifteen-piece brass band entered the tent blaring the Austrian quasi-national anthem, Johann Strauss' *Blue Danube*. As Billy's gaze took in the band, there was a cascade of noise and applause coming from the opposite direction. Looking around, he saw Thunderbolt stately marching in. Seated on his back was a somewhat heavier-looking Abrielle.

The band stopped when Thunderbolt reached the pista. There was a loud snare-drum roll punctuated by a single BOOM! from the bass drum as Abrielle rose and stood firmly on the horse's back.

Thunderbolt started trotting, not around the pista, but around the entire tent. Abrielle shed her outer costume and stood attired in red, white and blue as the Count de Montagne took command of the megaphone. "The United States of America!" he bawled, as the band struck up "Yankee Doodle." The horse made two circuits of the pista before Abrielle shed her "American" outfit, and stood revealed as "Carmen" while the band launched into Bizet's *Habañera*.

Two more circuits, and Abrielle was attired in a British sailor's costume as the band played *Brittania Rules the Waves.* On and on the changes went. Abrielle became "lighter" as she shed each layer of clothing. The band dutifully played anthem after anthem from each country depicted, Germany, Turkey, and the Netherlands. At each turn, the audience roared louder, and Billy, who was a shocked as the rest of the audience, could have sworn the sound made by the jossers must have been heard all the way to the center of Paris, thirty kilometers miles away. Abrielle, dressed in green fleshings, rode Thunderbolt out of the tent.

The applause continued unabated for some period of time. Then, there was a momentous roll of the bass drum. When it stopped, there was absolute silence in the chapiteau. A flute began to softly play *Le Marseillaise,* with no accompaniment. It was joined after the first chorus by a single snare drum, then by the remainder of the band. The audience rose to its feet in respectful silence. Two horses, Thunderbolt and another matched white, walked in. Abrielle was standing, one foot on the back of each horse, wrapped in the French tricolor. One could have heard a coin drop in the big top, such was the awe that greeted her.

At that moment, a crewmember walked to the center of the pista with a large covered cage. When he opened the cage, several white doves flew out. The audience was so entranced by the birds that they hardly saw Abrielle's final "change." She unwrapped the flag, still standing astride the two horses. As the doves lit on her shoulders, every man, woman, and child in the audience gasped at the audacious beauty of Abrielle, who was clad in the carefully preserved Clover Pink léotard which the late Countess de Montagne had last worn in 1871, the day before Zoltan's death.

Was it Abrielle or was it Brenda Lee the day Billy first saw her more than eleven years ago? Billy, unable to control himself, wept unabashedly. The Count did likewise. The audience erupted in riotous acclaim as Abrielle once again dismounted and held her arms up in the classic **V** pose for a very long time.

~ ∫ ~

That evening, long after the rest had retired, Billy spoke quietly to his best friend.

"The Count told me that the garment Abrielle was wearing ... Brenda Lee last wore it more than thirty-five years ago. It's decorated with sewn-on sequins, brilliants, spangles. Each of those is a *thing* – an entity. It exists. It is a tiny thin flake of bright tinted metal. In the circus ring, under sunbeam or limelight, it reflects a sharp flicker of color. A circus audience, being not very close to the performer wearing it, sees only those coruscations of red and gold and green and blue. Which is the more real – the flake of inert metal or the vibrant glint of color – the spangle or the sparkle?"

"Ah, you've become quite a philosopher, my friend."

"Not quite, Sammy, but you'll have to admit, it was the most wondrous day since either of us joined on the circus."

"Perfect, except for one thing."

"What's that?"

"Your star, Abrielle. Wrong name."

"What? How can you say that? The audience loved her name – heck, they loved *her*. You could have called her Griselda it would not have made a bit of difference."

"I'm not talking about her first name."

"Her last name? Schönemann? It's a perfectly good German-Jewish name."

"Perhaps for now."

"You have a better, more fitting last name?"

"Yes," Sammy said. "Lichtenfeld."

24

As 1907 gave way to 1908, Abrielle's year with the *Schlamm & Bock / Billy Jenkins Great American* stretched to two. Sammy Lichtenfeld had gone back to Bratislava, where he was promoted to Inspector-Sergeant.

The *Schlamm und Bock / Billy Jenkins' Great American* had developed into a competent, reputable circus. During the preceding year, its thirty members had successfully toured several middle-sized German and Austrian towns. Tara Trautsch continued working at Belünde while waiting for Billy to move into the first rank of circus stars. They continued to meet and develop more Billy Jenkins novels, none of which had yet been published.

"You've gained a following in Braunschweig, Kiel, Erfurt, and Jena," Tara said, "but if we're going to move ahead with our plan, it's time for you to expand to a larger base, Frankfurt, Munich, Berlin, Paris …"

"You want me to go head-to-head with the Donnert?" he asked. "We'd have to expand. It would be a horrendously expensive risk."

"Risk nothing, win nothing. Look where you were three years ago. Where would you be if you hadn't taken a risk?"

"You're right, Tara. Besides, Abrielle's let me know she wants to move on. With ten artistes due to retire this year, we'll need to find new performers."

"Why not make a list of those acts you'd like to have if you could afford it?"

"Including animals?"

"Yes. The Hagenbeck's always selling exotics."

"I don't want to get a reputation of stealing from other circuses," Billy said.

"You don't have to. Every year most circuses in Europe shed some of their performers and many performers choose not to renew with their shows. You still read *The Era?*"

"Every week."

"Point made."

"All right, Tara, let's start with what we'll have left at the end of the 1908 season. Me in several roles – shootist, voltige, birds, ringmaster. Freddie and Ferdie on trap and bars, Hans, Casper, and Gerda as clowns. Mark off Gerda, she's seventy-four. Two equestriennes of serviceable age …"

She glared at him. "*Serviceable* age? As in available to be *serviced?*"

He shrugged his shoulders, put his palms up, and said, "I didn't mean it that way."

"I should hope not." Their relationship was such that neither took offense at anything the other said.

"We'll still have the elephant trainer," Billy continued, "Liesl on the high trapeze and slide-for-life, and Herrmann the Magician, that's ten. Plus the roustabouts."

"You'll need three more clowns," Tara said, quite businesslike. "What about a whiteface?"

"We'd never be able to afford …"

"Stop it right now, Billy Jenkins!" she said impatiently. "Do you want to be a major international star or not?"

"Yes, but …?"

"You're going to be playing a high-stakes game against major circuses. You can play cards without money, but you cannot play cards without *cards*. If you don't want to risk it all, I can always find another partner… " She grinned to let him know she was only teasing.

"Tara, my dear, you seem to have acquired 'champagne taste' while I'm the one putting out the money."

"Oh, Billy! One should never lower one's taste to the level of one's trouser pockets. A person who does not have a champagne palate seldom is offered champagne." With that, the tension was broken and the real planning began.

"If we're going to be a first class circus, we should be a *circus*, not a vaudeville in helter-skelter sequence," Billy said. "We should open with a flourish and close with a flourish. In between, we should be a well-considered alternation of acts that entertain and acts that thrill. Intervals of jollity relieving spells of nail biting."

"Good, good," Tara said.

"Let's start with *what* we need, not *who* we need," Billy said. Big cat trainer plus at least three cats; three more clowns; perch pole act, that's another two artistes; antipodists …"

"Antipodists?" Tara asked.

"Foot acrobats. I saw them once when I was with the Hagenbeck-Knie in South Africa, three of 'em. Strong man – be nice to have Sammy Lichtenfeld back, but he's out of the game."

"Didn't you tell me he was head-over-heels in love with Abby?"

"Yes, but he never pursued it."

"Odd. I think she might have welcomed his advances," Tara said.

"Really? I've stayed in touch with him. Maybe …?"

"Back to business, remember?"

"Two really spectacular aerialists, an equestrian director – I'm tired of handling that job. A side show …?"

"In Europe?" she asked.

"Why not?"

"Leave the freaks to the smaller shows, Billy," Tara said. "But you will need an assistant, someone to take Abrielle's place, and a gypsy fortune teller. Every European circus worth its salt has one. That's probably why so much of the *rom* language has become circus vocabulary. Do you need any other exotics?"

"As long as we're breaking the bank and dreaming impossible dreams, two more bulls would be nice. No humps, convicts, jockos, or water dogs," Billy said, using circus slang for camels, zebras, monkeys, and performing seals. "We've got three horses, one more would make the show look so much bigger. A bear, a slanging buffer act …"

"Slanging buffer?" she asked, raising her eyebrows.

"Trick dog act. Kids love them and parents love to see their children having fun."

"What about a band?"

"Six of the ten roustabouts double as musicians. If we take on four more crew members and three of them play an instrument, that'll be a nine-piece orchestra, which is as good as any circus in Europe."

"Have you totted up the number of newcomers?" Tara asked.

"Twenty humans, six exotics, a horse, and three terriers. If all goes according to plan, by 1909, we'll have thirty-six men and women, eleven big animals, and three dogs." He whistled.

"That's a good start," Tara said. "You have one year to do it. Now on to our other problem."

"Our other problem?"

"Abrielle and Samuel. She's a pretty girl, quite innocent despite her exposure to circus life. How well do you know Sam Lichtenfeld?"

"I'd trust him with my life."

"But he hasn't made a move in over a year despite what he may have told you about his feelings. That doesn't seem like the strong, confident man I met with you and Mister Bailey."

"He might be very different in his dealings with women, particularly where love is concerned."

"Well, if he's interested and she's made overtures about changing her life, I'd suggest to your friend that he do something other than sit around the state police headquarters. It's no secret to a woman that a boy chases a girl until she catches him."

"So you want me to 'encourage' him. I trust you'll play your role as well?"

"Have you ever known me to do otherwise?" she asked sweetly.

~ ∫ ~

"OK, you've summoned me to Vienna for a secret meeting. You've given me no hint of what's afoot."

"Do you by any chance remember your last circus performance?" Billy asked.

"Nearly two years ago outside Paris."

"And the star was …?"

"The incredible Abrielle Schönemann," Sam replied without hesitation.

"Do you remember some wiseacre remark you made to me about changing her name to yours?"

Sam Lichtenfeld blushed. "Yes … well … er … that is to say …"

"Did it ever occur to you that several other young men, and I include in that a number of Gräfin and Viscounts, might be interested in her as well?"

They were walking in the Prater, Vienna's world-class amusement park. Billy had just purchased a würstel for himself and one for his friend.

"I surmised you hadn't brought me here to ride the *Riesenrad*," Sam said, nodding his head in the direction of the thirty meter high ferris wheel which, in the ten years since it had been erected, had, like Johann Strauss, come to be a symbol of *fin de siecle* Vienna.

"For an inspector, you're most percipient."

"All right, best friend, how exactly do you think I should have proceeded? At the time I first saw her, I was a twenty-one year-old junior inspector, making hardly enough for one person to live on, let alone a wife. I've only recently been promoted to where I'm now earning a living wage. My God, Billy, she's a star! How am I supposed to approach someone like that?"

"You're asking *me*?" Billy said.

"Well, you *have* become like an uncle to her. She would listen to you. Here, let me treat for the next würstel and a couple of steins of beer as well."

"It's not as if you haven't found yourself in the company of beautiful women before," Billy said, more seriously.

"Yes, but Abrielle is ... different."

"You mean the old saying, 'In the dark all cats are gray' is not true?"

"In this case, not at all," Sam said miserably. "Do you think *you* might put in a good word for me?"

"For what it's worth. But *you're* going to have to move off dead center yourself."

~ ∫ ~

"I understand you told Herr Jenkins you're leaving the circus at year's end."

"Yes, Tante Tara. I felt guilty saying it because he's been so wonderful to me. Everyone in the circus has. They've protected me like I was made of Meissen porcelain."

"No men friends?"

"Yes," Abrielle replied. "More than ten at any given time – all giving me advice and warning me off anyone they consider 'the wrong kind' for me. Last month was my nineteenth birthday. Would you believe I've never even walked out with a boy?"

"Oh, stop pouting like a little girl," Tara replied. "You're a Schönemann. That means you're as independent as I am."

"Yes, and you're twenty-five and I see no man on your horizon," Abrielle remarked. "I'm sorry, Tante Tara, I didn't mean it in that way."

"I asked for that," Tara said. "I appreciate your candor."

"What about Herr Jenkins?"

"What *about* Herr Jenkins?" Tara asked.

"I always thought …?"

"Billy and me?" Tara laughed. "We're friends and business partners, but trust me there's never been more than that and never will be. I admit there's been no one to make the bells ring in my head or make me feel weak in the knees, but if that's to come, it will come, and when and if it does, I'll be ready for it."

"Funny, Aunt Tara, that *has* happened to me."

"Oh?"

"Yes. I first saw him at the Countess de Montagne's small funeral service in Vienna. The only other time was the day of my performance at the Count's home."

"Well, my dear, that leaves only eleven possibilities: the first is the Count, who is more than forty years your senior. The next nine are Herr Jenkins and his circus entourage, but you've seen *them* every day for more than a year. That narrows the field down to one. That Jewish fellow, the police inspector who performed as a weightlifter, Lichtenberg or Lichtenstein, or something like that."

"Sam Lichtenfeld," Abrielle said.

"Yes, that was his name."

"Tante Tara, can you keep a secret?"

"Of course, darling girl."

"There hasn't been a night I haven't thought about him, pictured what it would be like to be married to him ..."

"*Married?*" Tara asked, aghast. "But what about your plans for university?"

"I never had any serious thoughts about the university. Oh, I've heard you and mama and papa say what a good thing it would be, but I don't really know what I'd study. All I've ever wanted was to find a man to love me."

"You're only nineteen, for God's sake!"

"How old was mama when she married papa?"

"But you're a ..."

"A child?"

"Let's suppose for a moment that this Sam fellow ..."

"Sammy Lichtenfeld."

"Do you know anything about him, other than that he's Jewish?"

"He is – or was – with the Austrian-Hungarian State Police in Bratislava."

"So you'd know how to get in touch with him if you wanted to?"

"Yes, but young women do not initiate such contact. You and Herr Jenkins are friends. I know that he and Herr Lichtenfeld are the closest of friends. Tante Tara, do you think maybe you could approach Herr Jenkins? Please?"

~∫~

Bratislava, April 15, 1908

My Dearest One,

Are you having as much fun watching this play out as I am? Billy is trying so hard to get me to come visit the circus – he's used every excuse: "You've got to come and at least speak to Abrielle before she runs off with some nobleman." "I need someone to run the circus. I haven't had a day off in a year-and-a-half and if I don't have a week to myself, I'll go crazy."

I'm playing his game, acting appropriately tongue-tied, shy, almost desperate. My second promotion has come through, so now we can go ahead with our plans.

How silly you were, worrying that I wouldn't want you! Darling, as far as I am concerned, you could have been *Martian* and it would not have made a bit of difference. I am so thrilled your parents approve – even more that they've agreed to keep our little secret from those whose motives are so transparent. I love you so much. How does the first week in September sound to you?

All my love, my precious one, Your Sammy

~ ∫ ~

Prague, May 1, 1908

Oh, Sammy, Sammy, Sammy!

Why so long? I've been sitting here all evening writing out my new name, "Abrielle Lichtenfeld," "Frau Samuel Lichtenfeld," "Herr and Frau Samuel Lichtenfeld," "Abby Lichtenfeld." It looks so *right*. September 6 is the first Sunday of this year. Munich is lovely during that month and we can honeymoon in Hallstatt. Have you ever been there, my angel? It is truly the most beautiful place in the world!

A-

~ ∫ ~

Bratislava, May 6, 1908

But not as beautiful as you!

S.L.

~ ∫ ~

September 6 was a picture postcard sunny day. The elegant, three-story high Main Synagogue on Munich's *Lenbachplatz* had rarely, *if* ever, seen an array of characters such as presented for Abrielle's marriage to Samuel Lichtenfeld. Thirty-five circus human beings, plus – outside of course – three elephants, and four horses.

After the breaking of the ritual glass under the groom's right foot and shouts of *"Mazel Tov!"* the assembly was treated to a private performance of the *Schlamm und Bock / Billy Jenkins Great American Circus*. Billy was Sammy's best man and Tara was the maid of honor. She was escorted down the aisle by a tall, red-headed young man visiting from Chavel in far-off Lithuania, Grigori Migdalowicz.

By evening's end, the independent, secure, and established Tara Trautsch felt it must have been the wine, or the dance music, or maybe she had eaten a little too much of the delicious spread laid out by the bride's parents – it could not have been Grigori, could it? – but she was certain she heard bells ringing in her head. Was it her imagination or did she feel weak in the knees?

25

"How goes your search for new talent?" Tara asked Billy one day in late October. They'd met in Salzburg, which they both acknowledged was probably the most beautiful city in Europe. After a delicious dinner of *bauernschmaus* – mixed grilled meats – red cabbage, and *kartolfn*, potatoes, they strolled along the *Griesgasse*.

"As well as might be expected. I've convinced Allman to give us at least one season. There's our whiteface."

"Can you afford him?"

"We can't *not* afford him," Billy replied. "After he left *Zoltan's,* he became a fixture on some of the really big houses, the Donnert, the Sarrasani, the Dumas, the Busch … He'll be joining up the beginning of next year."

"That leaves …" she counted off on her fingers, "Cat trainer plus three cats."

"Hagenbeck promised me some older cats by February. I got a young elephant to keep Pepper company, and a nice show horse as well. Still trying to get a bear. Getting a cat trainer will be tougher."

"Two more clowns, a perch pole act …"

"I'm working on it"

"A strong man?"

"Got one. Bronislav Mitkof, a Bulgarian. Big as a house and gentle as a lamb. I'll have to wait until winter to see what other acts become available."

"Crew? Band?"

"That's the easiest part. How goes it with you and Grigori?" Tara blushed. "You've never looked happier or more beautiful," he continued.

"Lithuania's so damned far away!" she exclaimed. "In my cool, calm, collected way, I'm starting to get really impatient!"

"Hey, it's only been a couple of months. Don't look so downcast, my friend. If it's meant to be, it'll certainly be."

"I've never known you to be involved with anyone except Sophia and that was a lifetime ago."

"Who's got time for that? You're the one who wants me to hurry up and be a star. Ready for some dessert?"

"Why not?"

They found a small, intimate restaurant in an alley between *Griesgasse* and its adjacent large street, *Getreidegasse*. The place was emblematic of everything charming about the city – a low, open-beamed ceiling, a roaring fireplace at one side of the room, candles, and two immaculately dressed waiters. Most of the restaurant was filled with amiably happy customers when they walked in.

"*Zwei Salzburger Nockerl, Herr Ober,*" Billy said when the waiter approached.

"You didn't even look at the menu," Tara chided him.

"Why bother? The only thing I can tell you without reservation is that the prices they charge for a soufflé made of eggs, sugar and air will be higher than the nearest alp."

"Quite difficult to make and very easy to mess up. Back to business. Can I do anything to help you?"

"Find me a gypsy. The slanging buffer act shouldn't be too difficult," Billy said.

"So you've found the easy ones. Now you've got to fill the star turns?"

~ ∫ ~

Less than two weeks later, Billy wrote his erstwhile friend, Mohandas Gandhi. At the beginning of January, 1909, he received a response:

Dear Mister Jenkins,

Of course I remember you and fondly. You'll forgive me that I have not stayed in touch. How is your friend Sophia? Herr Kürtner? I haven't seen a circus performance since the Hagenbeck-Knie, but I have been busy, as no doubt you have been. Last year, when the Union of South Africa was formed, the Transvaal government passed a new Act compelling registration of the colony's Indian population. No sooner they passed the Act, I called on my fellow Indians to defy the new law and suffer the punishments for doing so, rather than resist through violent means. I fear I may be writing you my next letter from gaol.

You asked about the three foot acrobats. Although your Herr Kürtner tried to find them employment after he returned to Switzerland, he was unable to do so. They took jobs in the Durban Indian market. If you are truly interested in hiring them for your new venture, I will be glad to forward them your address. You can always reach them care of me. …

~ ∫ ~

"Hey, Rose Petal! Are you and Gertie still a pair?"

"A pair o' what? As in a pair of tits, buster?"

"No, sweetheart, a pair of beers."

"Billy? Billy Jenkins?" Rosa Davenport whooped. "Gadzooks, it's himself indeed! Hey, Gertie, I got this man on the phone doesn't call us, leaves us for dead for eight years, then drops outta' the sky and calls us on the telly-phone. Where have you been? More to the point, where are you now?"

"Geneva."

"Holy Jeezus, same place as us. How'd you find out we're here?"

"Fellow named Karl Kürtner," Billy said.

"Knie's man?" Rosa said. "We left the Greifeldomper at the end of last season to give the Knie a go. Karl was very kind, but he told us they'd just hired two aerialists off the Orfei. He asked if we'd advertised in *The Era*. That was going to be our next stop."

"Not necessary. I asked Karl if he had any acts *I* could hire."

"Ye're kiddin', boyo!"

"Meet me at the chestnut tree in an hour."

"Ye've learned the layout of this place in a hurry, Billy Jenkins."

"Not hard. It's the most famous tree in all Switzerland." A certain specific tree, known as the "herald of spring," had been a symbol of the city for ninety years.

~ ∫ ~

"Just as stunning as ever!" Billy said when the two blondes appeared. "I can't tell which of you is prettier, not that it would matter."

"What ever happened to Young Hercules?" Riane asked.

"Sammy's in the Austrian State Police. Married an exquisite equestrienne last September, and took her off the show. They've already started on their first baby."

"Goodo for him!" Rosa said. "Now, what's this about *you're* lookin'?

I heard you built up a run-down Rumanian mud-and-goat show into *The Mud and Goat Show.* Word on the circuit is you're movin' up to the front rank pretty damn fast."

"I won't deny that. I thought of you two the minute my partner and I started making a list of the acts we needed."

"Your partner?" This from Riane. "Man, woman, young, old?"

"Business partner. She's started a tiny publishing house with one helluva good idea. I'll tell you about it at lunch. And no, it's not that kind of partnership."

"Well …" Rosa said, grinning. "We might need time to think and negotiate…"

"No negotiating, girls, you're on the *Schlamm und Bock* effective tomorrow morning," he said. "Any help you can give me in finding some other artistes?"

~ ʃ ~

"He's a consummate little shit is what he is. Everyone on the Greifeldomper hated the little bastard, but he is absolutely and without any shadow of a doubt the funniest human being we've ever seen, and we've been on a lot of circuses."

"If he's such a bad actor, why would anyone keep him?"

"Simply because he *is* so damned good at what he does. He's much too bright for his own good, but he brings in the jossers and *they* love him. 'Course, they don't have to live with him."

"What's this nasty little fellow's name?"

"God knows," Riane said. "He calls himself various names. Most frequently, he's known as 'Emperor Colossus' or 'Ming the Merciless' on the circus. Behind his back, we've always called him 'That little shit.'"

"Oh, come now, you've worked with him long enough. You've got to know his real name. It's probably in his conduct book."

"No, lad," Rosa said. "He keeps three or four conduct books at any given time, all with different names."

"Where's he now?"

"Still on the Greifeldomper."

"Why would he quit that show?" Billy asked.

"Just because he *is* such a little shit."

~ ∫ ~

"Sergei Aleksandrovich Romanov," he said, bowing stiffly. "As you can plainly see, I am of the royal blood, a prince once removed from the Tsar himself, in my native Rossiya." Billy had to choke to keep from laughing out loud, even at their first meeting. The little man was one meter tall, attired in a perfectly fitting uniform of the Imperial Russian army, bemedaled and beribboned as a field marshall. He wore a moustache and goatee in a tight VanDyke cut, and carried a miniature swagger stick in his right hand and a miniature-scale rifle case in his left, which he placed at his feet.

"I am impressed, Your ... Your ..."

"Highness will do," the little man said huffily. "Now about our arrangements ..."

"Arrangements?" Billy said, raising his eyebrows. "I was not aware we had any 'arrangements' Herr Romanov. If you'll pardon my ignorance, it was my belief you were looking for employment with the *Schlamm und Bock.*"

"*I? I* should seek employment with something called the 'mud-and-goat show?'" Romanov almost screamed. "No, no, no, Herr Billyjenkins," he said, shortening the proprietor's name to one single word, as though somehow this would elevate him above the circus master, "Let us always remember it was *you* who summoned *me* to see if I might be coaxed into leaving my present employer and lowering myself so that *your* show might – and I say *might* – somehow climb to the next level."

Despite himself, Billy struggled to keep from giggling at this upstanding mouse turd. *By God, he is funny all right! By all rights, I should find him one of the most disgusting human beings on the face of the planet, and I'm struggling to keep from breaking out into fits of laughter.*

"Herr …?"

"*Prince …*"

"*Prince* Romanov," Billy said, recovering himself. "If I may be so bold as to ask, if you are such a high risen personage, why would you conceivably lower yourself to appear on a mere circus?"

"Ah, that is a long story, and a sad one," the small man said. He removed a silk handkerchief from his pocket and dabbed at his eyes.

The midget reached down, opened the gun case, and extracted a half-size violin. He commenced playing a gypsy air so sadly that Billy felt a tug at his own heartstrings.

What followed was a tale of lost love. When he was a mere child, Sergei Romanov, if that was his name, had fallen in love with a beautiful little playmate, also of the royal blood. She had red hair, green eyes, and a lightly freckled face. Alas, as time went on, she had grown to the amazing height of six feet while he had only achieved his present height. It had come to a denouement when he proposed that he could still love her, despite the disparity in their stature, by following her around with a six-foot high stepladder. Cruelly, she disabused him of this idea. Cruelly, she suggested he might consort with someone closer to his own size. All during his story, the violin swooped and cried and gave exclamation to his tale of woe.

Indeed, it might have gone much more smoothly for the *zwerg* had not Riane come flouncing into the tent where Billy was interviewing the small fellow. "Well, what have we here?" she said, feigning surprise. "What kind of blaffum are ye pealin' off now, ye little turd?"

"Ah, 'tis the tom-cunt," the man said, switching effortlessly from his "Russian" accent to cockney. "Don't tell me the Guv'nor has hired you girl-bangers on this show."

"Aye, last month, and watch yer tongue, twerp. You'd be out on your little arse peddlin' fish, 'ceptin' we told Mister Jenkins he should give your bloody little self a shot at a really *good* show."

Billy sat bemused as he watched this interchange. Hate each other in public they might, insult each other they certainly did, but it was clear they'd worked together long enough to achieve a *modus vivendi* between them.

"Now, if you'll be so kind as to have this commoner escorted out of here, Governor, we might continue our conversation."

"Have *me* escorted out of here, you little bugger?" Riane raised her voice. "I'll bite your bloody balls off first."

"Rrrrrr," Romanov said, roaring like a very small baby lion. "It wouldn't be the only head you've given lately. But enough of you, filthy boy-slut. Begone! The Governor and I have business to transact."

And that's how Sergei Aleksandrovich Romanov – or whatever his name was – came on the *Schlamm und Bock*.

~ ∫ ~

The first thing Billy thought was, *the four of 'em look pretty much alike.* Three of them were terrier-mongrel mix. The fourth was a tallish man of indeterminate early middle age who bent over in an apparent effort to lessen his height and seem more like his charges. "Tinkle, Twinkle, and Tunk," he said, as each of the terriers in turn did impossibly high athletic and amusing flips, aerial somersaults, and cavortings. On a signal from their master, two of them stood side by side, while the third leapt up and landed two feet on the back of one of dogs, and two feet on the back of the other.

"And you are?"

"Billabong, Governor, and for a mere pittance your *Schlamm und Bock* can become *Schlamm und Bock und Hintele*"

"You're an Aussie?"

"Originally from Sydney, but I've been touring Europe for so long I've forgotten what the land down under even looks like."

After Billy took a look at the Australian's conduct book and a resumé of the circuses he'd been on, the circus acquired another fourteen legs worth of performers.

~ ∫ ~

"Still no gypsy?" Tara asked.

"And still no cat trainer," Billy replied, "although I'm interviewing one next week. More important, the foot acrobats should be landing at Kiel within a fortnight."

"How are the jossers reacting?"

"Quite well. I still have trouble believing that three years ago we were playing the armpit villages of Rumania. This year it's Vienna, Salzburg, Munich, Frankfurt, and, at the beginning of June, Berlin itself ..."

"I've been meaning to talk to you about that, Billy," Tara said. "I think it's time to make our move. Can the circus do without you for two weeks?"

"In the middle of the season?"

"Yes."

"Impossible."

"What if I were to tell you Grigori and Sammy would be on the show during those two weeks to make sure nothing went amiss?"

"What do you mean? What kind of move are you talking about?"

At that moment, there was a knock on Tara's office door. When she opened it, a tall and very bulky gentleman of fifty years, in full formal dress and Homburg hat, smoking a large cigar, entered the room. "Ah, this must be the Herr Jenkins," the man said, bowing.

"Billy Jenkins, I would like you to meet Herr Alfred Rose. Herr Rose, Billy Jenkins," Tara said.

"Good afternoon, Sir," Billy said politely.

"Good afternoon, Herr Jenkins. I very much enjoyed your show yesterday afternoon. Your attendance here in Munich has been all you expected it to be?"

"Yes, Herr Rose. More."

"I'm pleased. Word of your prowess has reached Berlin, you know."

"I'm happy to hear our circus has a good reputation."

"That's not what I'm talking about, Herr Jenkins."

"Oh? What then?"

"I'm talking about *you*, Herr Jenkins. Fräulein Trautsch has done rather a superb marketing job." He held up a soft cover book with a lurid cover. Three slim American cowboys stood in front of a log cabin, each wearing a colorful shirt, jeans, bandana, ten-gallon hat, boots, and a wide belt from which hung two holsters. One of the cowboys' heads was wrapped in a blood-soaked bandage. In the background lay two other men, obviously dead, obviously outlaws, their guns lying harmlessly at the feet of the three heroes. Splashed in huge white letters at the top of the book were the words **BILLY JENKINS** At the bottom of the book in bright red letters, the title screamed **AUFRUHR IN LAREDO.**

Billy stared uncomprehendingly, first at Tara, then at Herr Rose.

"It seems, Herr Jenkins," Rose said, "that your exploits in, shall we say, an earlier time, have developed a life of their own. This book is currently the best selling novel in Berlin, probably in all of Germany. Earlier this month, it passed Karl May's *Winnetou*. Fräulein Trautsch tells me the next Billy Jenkins tale will come out in three months. Already rumors are being spread and questions are being raised whether there is a *real* Billy Jenkins ... "

"I see. Am I to trust you have some role in all of this?"

"More or less, Herr Jenkins. I am the proprietor of the Bernhard-Rose-Theater."

"The Bernhard-Rose?" Billy said, his mouth agape.

"I admit it's imposing," Rose said. "It has eight hundred seats, a café, a restaurant, and a summer garden theatre."

"'Rather imposing' is like saying the *Riesenrad* is a Ferris wheel," Tara said. "It's the largest and most spectacular theater in all Berlin, which means it's the largest and most famous theater in Germany."

Billy's head was swimming when he heard Herr Rose's next words. "Herr Jenkins, I would respectfully ask you to consider doing a solo show at the Rose Theater for the two weeks commencing on June 12 and concluding with a mammoth twenty-fourth birthday celebration for you on June 26, 1909."

"I … I don't know what to say, Herr Rose."

"You don't have to *say* anything at this moment. What you have to *do* is put a great show together in seventy-five days."

26

Although anti-Semitism was rearing its ugly head over a good part of Europe, the population of the much-maligned Jewish race had achieved staggering figures: 5,200,000 in Russia, 2,000,000 in Austria-Hungary, 1,700,000 in the United States, 600,000 in Germany, 400,000 in Turkey, 200,000 in Great Britain, and 100,000 in France.

Tara, Billy, Sammy and Grigori met in Berlin two months before the scheduled show to measure the main stage of the Rose Theater and determine how best to build a credible show. "The stage is almost as big as our entire chapiteau," Billy said. "We could probably put *two* pistas on the stage."

"Why?" Grigori asked. "This is not going to be a circus, it's going to be the Billy Jenkins solo show."

"It might be called that, but no matter how much the audience likes me, it'll be hard to perform a one-and-a-half hour show by myself. Not to say it can't be done, but it always seems shorter if there's some distraction. A liberty show would be a good come-on. One or two equestriennes would certainly add glamour." He looked at Sammy.

"Nope, sorry," his best friend said. "She'll be eight months along by then. Not only would it be dangerous, but she'd look like a circus fat lady trying to ride a horse."

"I was just wondering," Billy said. "We have three passable ladies on the show, but none as spectacular as Abby."

"How's the little *zwerg* working out?" Tara asked.

"He's every bit the *grumpelstiltschen* Rosa and Riane made him out to be – and on top of that, he's positively *weird*. His latest antic off the tober is to dress in women's clothing and paint his toenails a bright red. He might be one loathsome toad, but he is the most brilliant comic I've ever run across, which is precisely why I asked if there's enough room for *two* pistas."

"Tell us," Grigori said.

"I was making a play on words when I said he's a *grumpelstiltschen*. We've recently acquired a pony small enough to accommodate him, *Rumpelstiltschen*, and sometimes, when he's in the mood, the midget imitates my voltige act in miniature. Only it's not *quite* like my act. It's a clown knockabout of my act. It's hard to describe, you'd have to see it yourselves, but I've watched audiences come close to wetting their pants watching the act, particularly when he does it immediately *after* mine."

"Meaning," Tara said, "you have two foils for your program, beautiful women in scanty outfits, and humor."

"Yes, and we'll have *four* acts instead of one."

"Four?" Sammy asked.

"Romanov – he likes that name and it's no skin off my nose to call him whatever he wants to be called rather than what the others call him behind his back – is serious about his cross-dressing as a woman. That means he can ape *me and* he can mimic the equestriennes as well."

"A double dose of laughter, a single dose of loveliness, and the excitement of the King of the Cowboys. That sounds good to me," Tara said.

"We must remember to give the pony and the horses a stiff cathartic an hour before the show. It wouldn't seem right to have them shitting all over the Rose Theater."

~ ∫ ~

"You expect me to lower myself to doing a comic turn to make *you* look better in the Rose Theater? Worse, to demean myself twice by appearing in *public* as a woman? You must be insane, Governor. I wouldn't do it for …"

"Three times your usual salary, is that what you're saying, Romanov?"

"In cash?"

"Of course."

"It is a small man indeed who would let false scruples stand in the way of his success as a show-man, show-woman, whatever. What would you say to three-and-a-*half* times my usual salary? And two small women or maybe even a small man to keep me company after the show?"

"Whores?"

"Whatever."

"Did anyone ever tell you, you are truly disgusting, Romanov?"

"Many times, Governor. But certain parts of my anatomy need ego boosting just as much as certain parts of normal-sized people."

~ ∫ ~

Dear Erich,

I was delighted to hear that you seem to have mended yourself and will be doing a show in Berlin. My friend and I would like to attend, simply to wish you well. Perhaps we can get together after the show.

Your father."

Billy had no idea how to deal with this reminder of where he'd come from. He placed two front row tickets to the opening night's show in an envelope and asked a courier to take the envelope to his father's café. He did not include a note of any kind.

~ ∫ ~

"Herr Jenkins, we have oversold the house! Two hundred beyond our eight hundred seats. That is unheard of!"

"Could we give the audience seats at another performance?" Tara asked.

"I'm afraid the entire two week run is sold out already," Rose said, happily wringing his hands.

"Is there no way we could increase the seating?" Gregori asked.

"What do they do when a circus is oversold, Herr Jenkins?"

"A *sfondone* – a straw house … Yes, that's it! Perfect!"

"What do you mean?"

"In the old days, when they sold out a house and they didn't want to turn business away, they'd put straw on the floor all over the big top and even close to the pista, the performance ring. Could we do that?" Billy asked.

"We could try. But what if there was a fire?" Rose asked, his expression mingled with fear of such an occurrence and avarice at the thought of two hundred extra theater customers *and* two hundred extra restaurant customers *and* two hundred additional customers for beer, wine, sausages, and souvenirs. He knew that when a crowd got excited about something, saving money was the last thing on their minds.

"We could rent extra water tanks, firemen, and fire hoses," Billy said. "If they were dressed in bright colors, that would add to the festivities."

Rose did the quick mental calculations. He figured it would cost him the equivalent of twenty paying customers, but he would more than make it up on the before-show and after-show sales. He quickly decided to place thirty folding seats at the back of the auditorium, another fifty scattered throughout the large theater. The other one hundred-twenty straw-flatties would not overburden the theater.

~ ʃ ~

Promptly at eight, the lights dimmed and there was the loud roll of tympanis, which grew in volume and ended with a sudden BOOM! A loud trumpeting issued from the top of each aisle. Two elephants, each clad in red and yellow silk with the words "Billy Jenkins – King of the Cowboys!" – paraded down the aisles to the ecstatic cheers of the audience. When they reached the twin pistas, each went to one of the rings where they first established themselves on tublike platforms, then raised themselves on their forelegs, doing, in effect, a handstand. After the thunderous applause died down, they faced each other across the pistas, raised their trunks toward one another, and trumpeted once again.

Between them, Billy Jenkins, King of the Cowboys, strode out wearing tight western jeans, a spangled orange shirt, a green bandana, and boots. He looked like he had walked right off the cover of *Aufruhr In Laredo*, which was exactly what the cheering fans wanted to see.

Sidling up to the front of the stage, where he knew his voice would carry throughout the hall, he started speaking in a relaxed, casual tone. But for the fact that he was speaking fluent, accentless German, albeit in a faux-western drawl, he might have just come in from a gunfight in the American West or stepped from the pages of the book. Billy played the novel's first person narration to fine-tuned perfection.

"It happened one night about ten years ago …" he started. "It was a hot summer evening in the Texas Panhandle. There was a crescent moon that night, and it was hanging over the Pecos, all lovely and silver. The stars were piled up so thick you could've reached out and touched 'em."

While he was talking, the lights had dimmed until he was almost in darkness. The elephants were quietly led off the stage. The audience sat hypnotized, spun into Billy Jenkins' web.

"The *dogies* were pretty restless. My pardners and I had just eaten our fill of grilled steaks and western beans from the chuck wagon. We sat around a little campfire rolling cigarettes, and young Tommy, he took out his harmonica and started playing an old Confederate tune. ..."

From somewhere backstage, a harmonica hummed *Shenandoah,* while a dim electric "fire" wavered in the center of the stage.

As Billy continued his slow, drawling narrative, he picked up first one lariat, then another, doing an impressive array of rope tricks while he kept talking the whole time. Dim stage lights came up toward the rear of the stage, showing a backdrop of dry hills, saguaro cactus, a quarter-moon in a star-filled sky, and a dusty trail heading back into the hills. It was a very realistic-looking tableau out of the American West as imagined by Germany's legions of Karl May readers. The crowd was enthralled. Some women in the audience sighed audibly.

"Just as I was hunkerin' down, why bless my soul, there was a stampede," he said matter-of-factly. The lights came up quickly. Six white horses, their tails braided, tassles on their heads and forelocks, pranced around the pistas, three in each ring, in a beautiful liberty act. Without any apparent command, and with no human being in sight, they turned and pranced in the opposite direction as if on cue, then did haute-ecôle cross-over "dancing." They reared up on their hind legs, but so smoothly it looked like they were gentle statues. The already mesmerized crowd couldn't believe the spectacle they were viewing.

So it continued throughout the first half of the show. Billy alternately drawled on about his adventures. In between, the equestriennes performed what could only be described as a ballet-on-horseback; Billy performed a portion of his shootist artistry, assisted by the youngest of the riders. Then the lights went down to almost nothing and Billy returned to the dark "campfire," keeping up a running patter.

Billy, Tara, and Herr Rose had decided this was the easiest way to distract the audience's attention from the changes of scenery and acts, while at the same time keeping the show going at a goodly pace.

Just before the close of the first half, Romanov came out in a parody of a whiteface outfit. Except where the real whiteface was a disquieting combination of funny and frightening, the dwarf was simply downright hilarious. Nothing quite fit, and he managed to trip over his long clown-shoes as well as his overly lengthy pants. In between, the cunning little man regaled the audience with timely quips about overblown city fathers, whores and madonnas, and even Kaiser William himself. The audience erupted in continuous spasms of laughter.

"How does he do it?" Tara whispered in awe.

"Like all good comics everywhere. He spends a day or two in the best possible place to get good gossip."

"Certainly not the council meetings?"

"Of course not. The local hairdresser's. Even better than the saloons, because the beauty parlor is where the *real* gossip takes place. Time to finish the first half with my trick shooting."

Billy wandered to the center of the stage again. "Then there was the time I rescued a poor damsel in distress. The villains thought they'd teach me a lesson, so they said if I could shoot a single bullet so accurately that the maiden could catch it in her teeth, they'd let her go..."

The audience at the Rose theater bought into Billy's act as eagerly as any circus audience he'd known over the years. As he concluded his successful effort and the elfin girl "caught" the ball in her teeth, there was a sudden loud tattoo on a snare drum, and Romanov walked to the center of the stage, wearing a miniature cowboy outfit that precisely duplicated Billy's. In his hands, he carried a "pistol" twice the size of the one Billy had used.

The "delicate damsel" had not moved. She scratched her head, looking at the dwarf with a mixture of curiosity and incredulity. Billy put his hands on his hips and walked to the side of the stage.

Romanov grunted and sighted and aimed and repeated the moves Billy had made in the same order he had made them. Finally he nodded, aimed, and tried to hold the gun steady. His hand started shaking uncontrollably and the gun wobbled. Some people in the audience laughed, but nervously.

"Silence!" the midget roared imperiously.

He then aimed very carefully, holding the gun with one hand, bracing it with the other. On the count of three, the kettledrum gave a sharp BOOM! From the front of the gun dropped a bright red satin flag with the word "BANG!" on both sides. The bottom corner of the flag had been torn off. In a reflex action, the crowd's attention shot over to the girl. She stood the calmly, the missing piece of the flag hanging from her teeth.

With the crowd nearly apoplectic with laughter, the first act came to an end.

~ ∫ ~

Just before the second half of the show began, Tara rushed into Billy's dressing room, breathless with excitement. "We've sold five hundred autographed copies of *Aufruhr In Laredo*!" she exclaimed. "Can you imagine what this will do for us if we sell that many each night of the show?"

"How about the cowboy hats?"

"Can't tell yet," she said. "I've been too busy pushing the books to care about anything else. You're certainly the toast of Berlin tonight!"

"I just thought of another gimmick," he said. "What if I were to mingle with the audience a little bit before the second half?"

"Why not? It will certainly make you seem more approachable."

~ ∫ ~

As the audience waited expectantly for Billy to come back on stage, the lights went down and the "campfire" was lit once again. But the King of the Cowboys did not return to the stage. An uncomfortable two minutes went by. Suddenly there was a rising tide of noise from the back of the theater. Billy, clad in his show attire, was slowly walking up and down the aisles, shaking hands, uttering a greeting here and there, befriending the entire crowd. His calculated gamble paid off handsomely. Everyone reached out, trying to touch him.

Billy sensed the musky aroma of a woman who apparently had been detained and was coming down the aisle close to him, on the way to her seat. He turned slightly to let her pass. In that instant, he was blindsided as he'd not been since Brenda Lee. The woman appeared to be about thirty, tall, blonde, statuesque, an apparition of sexual invitation. Her hair hung in ringlets to her shoulders, her eyes were the largest he'd ever seen. In the entire crowded theater, his eyes saw no one but her. She seemed oblivious to his attention and said, "Excuse me. I must get to my seat to watch the rest of the show."

~ ∫ ~

After more storytelling, lariat roping, and shootist tricks, punctuated by Romanov's highjinks, and a somewhat truncated rendition of Brenda Lee's and Abrielle's "parade of nations" on horseback, Billy concluded the show with a voltige that was nothing short of amazing. He started with cowboy style, then went into the "Voltige à la Richard," where the horse was unbridled and unsaddled, then into the rough riding employed by Hungarians on the puszta. Finally he performed *tcherkesse* to ever more thunderous applause and foot-stomping and cheering.

"Always leave on a high note," Billy had been told, and indeed he did. Romanov on *Rumplestiltschen* did a fine and vigorous parody of Billy's voltige act. During a particularly violent ride, the crowd gasped as the *zwerg* fell off the little pony. Just as he was about to hit the ground, he did a hand-spring-somersault and immediately vaulted back onto the pony's back, to applause nearly as convulsive as that afforded Billy.

No sooner did Romanov complete his act, jump off the pony, and extend his arms in a **V**, then Billy started riding voltige in the adjacent pista and Romanov recommenced riding *his* version of voltige in *his* pista. Finally the two horsemen came to a stop, leapt off their horses, ran toward one another, joined hands, and alternately lifted their arms in a victory pose and bowed to the cataclysmic cheers of the audience.

After ten full curtain calls, the curtain finally came down.

"You'll excuse me if I have to leave quickly, Governor," Romanov said. "But I met an older woman in the restaurant earlier tonight, a widow, and …"

"Go ahead with my blessing, you disgusting toad!" Billy said amiably. "Just don't get lost inside her …"

"Ah, ah, ah!" the dwarf waved an accusing finger. "You're calling *me* disgusting? I've seen you for months, you old maid. At least I'm doing something more than playing the skin flute with my five fingers." He ran off before Billy could swat at him.

Billy walked out from between the folds of the curtain, where a frenzied shouting of "Bil-ly! Bil-ly! BIL-LY!" kept up a steady beat.

As he made it to the first row, he involuntarily stiffened when he saw his father standing with the rest of the crowd, neither chanting nor stamping his feet. The man nodded at him, not deferentially, but simply acknowledging his presence. Georg Rosenthal was the picture of elegance, with carefully curled moustache and goatee, a black evening coat and silk slacks, satin collar, high top hat, and patent leather shoes.

Billy noticed his father only in passing. His eyes riveted on the woman standing beside the older man. It was the dazzling blonde who had passed him in the aisle at the beginning of the second act. In a daze, he heard his father's next words, "Billy, it's good to see you. I would like to introduce you to my loving friend, Hedwig – Hedy Dietrich."

27

"Quite a performance you put on last night. You're not American, are you?"

"How did you know that, Herr …?"

"Mix, Tom Mix," the man said. He looked a little older than Billy, about the same height, and just as lean. "The way you handle the lariat is top notch, but any American wrangler would know in a minute there was something different."

"Different bad or different good?"

"Neither. Different *different*."

"How would you know that, Herr Mix?"

"'Cause I didn't start out as a cowboy either. Grew up in Pennsylvania, learned to ride horses and worked on a local ranch. I always wanted to be on the circus, but things didn't quite work out that way."

"So you actually worked on a ranch in the States?"

"Yup," Mix replied. "Most recently on the 101 Ranch in Oklahoma. They called it the 101 Ranch 'cause it covered 101,000 acres."

"But you're not a working cowboy today?"

"Correct, young feller. How old are you?"

"Twenty-four in two weeks."

"I'm twenty-nine. Pretty old to be sucking dust all day, trailing dumb-ass cattle, and taking a bath once a month, whether I need it or not. Not a helluva lot of women out on the range." Mix laughed. "You on a circus or you just do this wild west show?"

"I own a small circus. You still interested in the circus?"

"Was, but I won the National Riding and Rodeo Championship earlier this year and now I've got other plans."

The two men were sipping coffee at the Rose Theatre-Café. It was the morning after the second performance and Mix had come up and asked whether he could sit down and "jaw a bit." Billy, feeling relaxed and expansive, nodded and the two men had drifted into a natural conversation.

"What kind of plans, Herr Mix?"

"Why don't we drop the Herr this and Herr that? I'm Tom," he said, holding out his right hand.

"Billy," Jenkins said, shaking the proffered hand. "What kind of plans, Tom?"

"Motion pictures."

"Movies?"

"Uh-huh," Mix said. "Lotta' risk, but a lotta' money if you hit it big."

"*Zwei mal kaffee, bitte.*" The formally clad waiter returned moments later with a fresh pot of coffee and two clean cups. Facing Tom Mix, Billy said, "I've seen a couple of films. They run about five or ten minutes. How much money can there be in that?"

"Not much now, but remember, the motor car's not that old and the Wright Brothers flew their first few feet half a dozen years ago.

Everyone's got to start somewhere. They're shooting forty-five minute movies in Sweden. In the U.S., they're starting to shoot longer films in a place called Los Angeles."

"Where's that?"

"A little town in Southern California. They've got more than three hundred days of sunshine a year. With that much free light, some men are starting up studios there."

"How does that help you?"

"In the last coupla' nights you've seen how the Germans love anything having to do with the American West?"

"Yes."

"Audiences are even more taken with the West in the States, now that the gunslingers and the outlaws have faded into the sunset. The western shows take people back to a simpler, more exciting time. So a lot of studio owners are starting to make Western movies – 'horse operas' – and I'm there at the beginning."

Both men rose as a tall, slender blonde woman came near. "Herr Mix, this is my business partner, Tara Trautsch. Tara, I'd like you to meet Tom Mix, who tells me my roping isn't quite 'American' enough."

"I'm pleased to meet you, Mister Mix," Tara said. "I understand you're making a grand tour of Europe before going out to California to make movies."

"How would you know such a thing?"

"My friend, Grigori Migdalowicz, is a fanatic about everything having to do with motion pictures. He recognized you and pointed you out to me at the show last night."

"But I haven't made any movies yet."

"No, but as someone who's worked in the publishing industry for a while, it doesn't take much to know that as soon as someone becomes popular, people want to read anything they can get their hands on about him. There are a lot of German Jews in the publishing business. Jews tend to stick to their own and they have their own world telegraph. Just about every American movie-maker is Jewish, am I right?"

"The studio where I've been hired ...?"

"Selig Polyscope?"

"Yes, and there are others. Jewish immigrants who landed in New York and made money with nickelodeons are now headed out to Holly-wood. Laemmele, Zukor, Lasky, Mayer, Harry Cohn, the Warner Brothers, Fox, and Samuel Gelbfisch ..."

"He's changed his name," Tara said. "He thought it was 'too Jewish.' He's taken to calling himself Samuel Goldwyn."

"You are one sharp lady, Miss Trautsch."

"Just trying to keep up with the times."

"So those Billy Jenkins pulp novels were your idea?"

"I won't deny it," Tara replied.

"Smart marketing. Look, it seems we talk the same language. What if I were to give your friend Billy some lessons in *real American*-style roping and riding, and you two fill me in on some of your ideas. That way, we might both profit."

During the next week, Billy trained with Tom Mix. By week's end, his new friend had pronounced him "Pretty damned American. You could fool me." When Mix wasn't working with Billy, he spent time talking with Tara and Grigori. Migdalowicz seemed to know everything there was to know about filmmaking and filmmakers throughout Europe and the United States.

"I believe a time will come when movies will be in color as well as black and white," he said one day.

"Impossible," Mix said.

"Lumiere developed a process for color photography using a three-color screen a couple of years ago. Wouldn't it be possible to transfer that kind of technique to the movie screen?"

"Might," the American show-cowboy conceded. "You know, Migdalowicz, you might consider coming to America. Getting involved at the very beginning of the industry."

"You think so?" Grigori asked, so excited his face flushed.

"Why not?"

"I've always dreamt of going to America one day. There's so little opportunity in Lithuania."

"But you're in Germany. There are more than a thousand movie theaters here."

"Perhaps, but I'm not a German citizen, and there's a segment of Germany – even German-born Jews – who look down on us Eastern Europeans."

"Would you really consider going to America, Grigori?" Tara asked. There was an uncertain, ill-disguised worry in her voice.

"If it were offered," he said.

"But what about...?"

"Us, darling? Why, I suppose we could move there together."

"You'd expect me to give up Werner-Verlag Deutsch?"

"No, but …"

"How could I run it from America?"

"How much of your time would you need to manage it?" Grigori asked.

"Enough that I'd have to stay here. How much do you want your American dream?"

"More than anything," he said before he caught himself. "More than *almost* anything."

There was an uncomfortable silence between them.

~ ∫ ~

Billy could not tear his mind from Hedy Dietrich. The sorceress pervaded his every thought. Each night he searched the theatre to see if she'd returned. Each performance enhanced the magnetic attraction he held for Berliners, while his disappointment at not seeing her increased.

His imagination ran rampant. What would her soft skin look like without her clothes? Yet, consummate professional that he was, each night he managed to keep his drawl slow and casual, his ever-more-American style of roping cool and on target.

This was his *father's* mistress. He had no right to intrude on his father's territory. Yet what had Süssmilch been to him? Billy was nothing more than a biological accident, the consequence of the older man rutting with some other Hedy or Anna or Marlene whom he did not even recall. He owed his father nothing. Billy had repaid the grudgingly-parsed-out marks, complete with interest. There had been no contact between the two of them since that day half a lifetime ago.

Hedy Dietrich was fair game. Thoughts tumbled through his mind in the darkness of each night. In the end, he decided *damn the consequences, he must see her again.* But any move he made must be with utmost discretion. He would have to trust this woman who had given him no more encouragement than if he were a fly on the wall.

Two nights before his twenty-fourth birthday, he sent a note to the senior Rosenthal:

Father,

I am enclosing two tickets to the closing show. You and your friend might enjoy spending my birthday performance at the Rose Theatre. Perhaps we might go to a late dinner afterward.

- *Erich.*

~ ∫ ~

The final show was more than a *sfondone* house. The management had to turn away over two hundred admirers. After the performance, Tara proposed a celebratory dinner with Grigori and Tom Mix.

"I'd love to," Billy replied nervously, "but earlier I sent my father a note asking if he'd join me after the show."

"Your father?" Tara said, surprised. "I thought you and he weren't even talking."

"We aren't, but it might be fitting for me to try and make peace with him now that I can afford to do so."

"Strange," Tara said. "Perhaps your father might join us. We could serve as a foil if anything went wrong."

Billy thought rapidly. They really could provide a wall – a means by which he might somehow communicate with Hedy Dietrich.

"Well, he might be bringing his lady friend …"

"Even more of a reason for us to be with you. It would be easier if there was a crowd."

As they were speaking, the elder Rosenthal and his woman approached. Billy noted in passing that his father was attired in the same elegant outfit he had worn at opening night. Hedy was dressed in a red sheath and large hoop earrings. Billy felt a sharp stirring in his nether parts. He thought he noticed a blush in her cheeks, but of course this must have been his imagination, or his heightened desire for her.

"Erich, you wanted me to celebrate your birthday with you. I'm pleased to be here."

"Father, Fräulein Dietrich," he said noncommittally.

"These must be your friends?" Süssmilch asked.

"Yes," Billy said, turning to face them and informally introducing them. "My business partner, Fräulein Tara Trautsch, her fiancé, Grigori Migdalowicz, and my friend from America, Tom Mix. This is my father, Georg Rosenthal and his friend, Fräulein … Greta …?"

"Hedy," she said huskily.

"I'm sorry, *Hedy* Dietrich," Billy said, nodding politely and lifting her hand to his lips. He was immediately overwhelmed by the same musky scent he remembered from two weeks before.

"Where do you suggest we go, Erich?" the elder Rosenthal asked.

"The *Vier Jahreszeiten* has an elegant restaurant-bar. Since this is my birthday, please permit me to treat each of you," he continued expansively.

Dinner was wonderful. The party was lubricated by several bottles of *hock* and sparkling wine. Conversation centered on the entertainment business, how well Süssmilch had done in his café venture, the successful publishing venture, and Tom Mix's planned return to America, where he'd commence working in California.

Billy had difficulty concentrating on any of this conversation. His answers were automatic and monosyllabic. Throughout dinner, his eyes kept darting toward Hedy. She appeared to maintain her cool demeanor, focusing her attention on his father. Halfway through the evening, Billy excused himself to go to the men's room. While there, he scribbled out a message on a small card, then returned to the table.

Once, when Billy actually caught her eye, he thought he saw Hedy smile uncertainly. This brought on a rush of desire so intense he almost felt faint. By the time the group left the restaurant, it was close to midnight. While they were making their goodbyes, unseen by the others, Billy casually slipped the note into Hedy's hand.

Later that night, after returning to his hotel room, Billy felt a mixture of excitement and fear. He had never done something as underhanded as this. He had no idea how Hedy would receive what he had to say. He wanted this woman as desperately as he had wanted anything in his life. It was as though there were unseen wires drawing them closer. He had passed her the note in a moment of insane bravado, not knowing what effect it might have.

In her toilette in Georg Rosenthal's spacious residence later than night, Hedy removed the note from her pocket and read, "You are the most beautiful and desirable woman I have ever seen. I would be very much honored to see you again – alone. I pray this note does not offend you and that you will treat it in confidence. I am staying at the Kempinski. I will be in the lobby all morning and all afternoon tomorrow. - Billy Jenkins."

~ ∫ ~

The following morning, Hedy said, "Süssmilch, if you don't mind, I'd like to prowl the city on my own today."

"That's not a bad idea." Even though she was as attractive as any woman he'd been with, he had to admit that in the harsh light of day she would not attract the stares she did when they went out on the town.

As she took a roundabout way toward the Kempinski, her thoughts tumbled one after the other. Georg Rosenthal was a sweet, generous man, by no means an exciting lover, but certainly prominent. She'd always eschewed young men closer to her own age. It seemed they only wanted one thing, and the ones she had known before Süssmilch were not only clumsy, but possessive to the point of annoyance.

Still, a secret rendezvous held its own excitement. Who knew what young Billy Jenkins, né Erich Rosenthal might be like? He was passably good-looking in a rugged way. He was, at that moment, the most popular man in Berlin, one who, if he so wanted, could have had his pick of nubile Berlin beauties. Hedy Dietrich was not unmindful of her own appeal. She stood five-feet eight inches tall. Her blonde hair, which hung to her shoulders, framed a gorgeous face. Long lashes, sultry brown eyes, full, sensual lips, an extraordinary bust...

Hedy had by no means been a virgin before Rosenthal, but she was selective. In earlier days, she would have been called a courtesan. As she was fond of saying, she would marry when she found a man rich enough and handsome enough, but how could she pick one flower unless she'd sampled the entire field? The attention of Berlin's "King of the Cowboys" was only fitting.

Still, Süssmilch had been her only man for the past eight months and she felt a tingle of forbidden excitement as she crossed Unter den Linden and approached the grand Kempinski Hotel. As she entered the lobby and looked around, she didn't see him, but she sensed a presence just behind her. "How long have you been waiting for me?" she asked, without turning her head.

"Since you started ambling down the other side of the street."

"You're pretty sure of yourself, aren't you?"

"You must have felt it, too, or you wouldn't have come. Would you like to go for a walk first?"

"That sounds wonderful."

"You are even more beautiful in the morning sun," he said. "Your face and your body were in my eyes and in my dreams all night."

It surprised her that his direct confidence in what they both knew would happen did not offend her in the least.

"How old are you, Herr Jenkins?"

"Billy, please. As if you've already forgotten last night. I'm twenty-four."

"Ah, yes, your birthday celebration. You seem somehow older. I'm thirty. Does it disturb you that you're with an 'older woman'?"

"Not if it doesn't bother you," he replied.

"Are you originally from Berlin?" she asked.

"Magdeburg."

"You've been to the United States?"

"Unfortunately no. South Africa, though."

"And I'm sure many places in between. As they say about sailors, 'A girl in every port?'" She smiled flirtatiously.

"Not really," he said seriously. "Too busy building a show."

They continued walking along Unter den Linden, neither concentrating on where they were walking. They talked of many things, mostly nothing things, as each felt the heat of the other work its way into and through their bodies.

She waited for what she anticipated would be a brotherly kiss on the cheek, but when they were close to the hotel, he surprised her by kissing her full on the mouth. Soon, she found herself kissing him back. Hedy felt Billy's hardness against her, and smiled inwardly. There was no attempt at sophistication, no attempt to hide what was quite obvious. She pulled his face down to hers and kissed him again, this time much more passionately.

"Hedy…?"

They'd hardly gotten in the door of his room when they resumed where they'd left off. Soon, Hedy knew that kissing would not be enough. She heard a slight scratching at the door and looked at him questioningly.

"It's nothing. Probably the maid wondering if we need room service."

Soon, Billy's hand was under her sweater. His touch was alternately tender, then masculinely strong. … She sighed as he led her toward the bed. …

Afterward, they lay still for several minutes. She thought she heard the scratching sound at the door once again. Probably her imagination. They reached over toward one another, alternately stroking and holding each other and she soon drifted into sleep.

~ ∫ ~

Billy glanced at the clock ticking away on the end table. Four in the afternoon. He looked over at Hedy, quietly sleeping beside him. Gently he lifted the covers and gazed at her lovely, shapely body.

Hedy moved slightly. She wrapped her long legs around his and nuzzled closer. She opened her eyes, shut them, opened them again, and smiled at him.

"We have half an hour before I have to leave," she said. "Shall we see if it's as good the second time?"

It was even better.

Later, Hedy brushed out her hair, using Billy's comb, straightened out her clothing, which had been casually tossed onto a nearby chair, and sauntered out to Unter den Linden, where she caught a taxicab back to Georg Rosenthal's residence. Unknown to Hedy, a pair of eyes were watching her as she left the area of the Kempinski.

~ ∫ ~

When she unlocked the door to the flat, Georg was standing there polishing a decorative sword and a pistol, an inscrutable look on his face.

"Well, my love, did you have a nice day in the city?"

"I did," Hedy said, smiling serenely. "I feel rather sticky after my day's activities. Have we got an hour so I can just soak in a hot bath before we go to dinner?"

"Of course, my dear. But I'd like to talk with you for a few moments first."

"Can't it wait, darling?"

"I'm afraid not," he said. He finished polishing the gun, pointed it in her direction, and said, "It seems you've been a bad girl, today, Hedy. A very bad girl indeed..."

28

The concussive reverberation of the gunshot tore through her eardrums. She instinctively thrust her hands in front of her face. When the sound died down, there was a ringing in her ears. Remarkably, she was still alive.

"I could have killed you. A centimeter to the right and you would have been dead." He spoke calmly, rationally, but there was no mistaking his intent.

"I ... I ..."

"You need not try to explain," Georg continued in the same deadly calm voice. "You felt you needed to screw your brains out with a younger man – with my *son*, for God's sake. Why, Hedy? Haven't I given you more than you've ever had?"

"Y ... yes," she stammered.

"I could understand your motive if you'd been forced into a compromising position. Billy could no doubt have threatened you with some deep, dark secret of your past. He could easily have taken advantage of your innocent nature to foment his own carnal lusts. I could forgive you for that."

"Yes, yes, that's it. You know I would never willingly betray you," she said, reaching out her arms to embrace him.

"Of course, slut," he said, pushing her roughly away. "And I'm sure you could make a police report of the rape. Coming this late, they might not accept it, but it would protect my reputation, not to mention your life."

"What happens then?"

"Well," he said, rearing back and punching her below both eyes with a closed fist, "first we make it look more realistic. Then, after you make your tearful report, we wait and see, my dear. We simply wait and see."

~ ∫ ~

"The lady's accused you of forcible rape, Herr Jenkins. Come with us, please. Don't make it harder on yourself."

"But I …"

"You'll get a chance to tell your story to the judge. You may be the biggest name in Berlin, but it takes a slimy excuse for a human being to beat a woman up like that."

"I swear I didn't …"

"As I said," the policeman said. "You can tell it to the judge."

~ ∫ ~

He'd been in Bielefeld jail for two days when he was assaulted in the prison yard by three toughs. As two of them stood shielding him from the sight of the guards, the third punched him hard enough in the stomach to double him over. "That's for fucking Süssmilch's woman," he said.

"But I didn't …"

"Bullshit!" the second man said, kicking him in the groin. "Süssmilch doesn't lie."

As Billy lay writhing on the ground in agony, the third man said, "Not that I really blame you. Helluva good looking woman. You understand, of course, that we mean you no harm."

~ ∫ ~

Chief Inspector Rolf Gottleib felt something did not ring true. Twenty-five years on the Berlin Police Force and more than a thousand successful investigations had given him a second sense about these things. His lieutenant agreed.

"It's a high-profile case, that's for sure, but it smells like a set-up. How many of these have you seen?"

"Hundreds, Gerhard. They're all different. Her face was beaten up pretty badly. Two black eyes, but not a mark on her arms and legs."

"Do you want to talk to Jenkins?"

"Why should he want to speak to me? Odd, he's been in jail three days, he himself was battered yesterday afternoon, and he still hasn't called a lawyer. For a man in his position, that's very strange."

~ ∫ ~

The two men sat across from one another in the visiting room of the jail. Billy's face was mottled from the beating he'd taken and his left wrist was broken.

"Herr Jenkins? I'm Inspector-Sergeant Rolf Gottleib, Berlin Police."

"I apologize for my appearance Sergeant."

"I'm surprised you haven't asked to see a *rechtsanwalt*."

"Why should I? The whole thing simply doesn't make sense."

"What doesn't make sense?"

"Hedy, of all people."

"May I ask you a few preliminary questions, Herr Jenkins?"

"Of course, Sergeant. I have nothing to hide."

"Man to man, Herr Jenkins … have you been, ummm, intimate with her?"

"Yes, Sergeant." This without hesitation or embarrassment.

"Recently?"

"Four days ago. In my room at the Kempinski."

"On the one hand, I'm afraid that's not the answer I'd hoped you would give, but it appears to be an honest one, Herr Jenkins. It matches exactly what Fräulein Dietrich said. She accused you of forcible rape."

"You wanted an honest statement. I have nothing to hide, Sergeant."

"Perhaps if I took you under my custody we could visit the scene of the alleged crime?"

"Can you do that? Get me out, I mean?"

"You haven't been charged with anything yet."

"My room is paid up for an entire month. I'm sure they haven't rented it out … that is unless they know about this."

~ ∫ ~

The inspector could not betray his amazement at the opulence of the suite. Silk curtains hung from valences in the windows facing Unter den Linden. Two matching sofas faced one another in the smoking area, and the room conveyed an atmosphere of old walnut and rich marble.

"Do you know of my reputation, Sergeant?"

"I do, Herr Jenkins. I was privileged to attend one of your shows at the Rose Theatre. At this moment you are probably the most eligible bachelor in the city. Unquestionably, Fräulein Dietrich is a beautiful and desirable woman, but she is not the only beauty."

"True," Billy said thoughtfully. He was searching for a motive for Hedy accuse him. Unless she was the world's greatest actress, it was impossible to believe she would voluntarily lodge such a complaint. She'd not only climaxed twice when they'd been together, but it was she who had proposed additional clandestine meetings between them to continue what she'd called "our loving friendship."

"Herr Jenkins, please understand I am only an inspector. I cannot make a decision whether or not to prosecute you. But I have been on the force for a long time. Perhaps you could think of a motive. Did she have money? A jealous lover? Could you have threatened her with anything? Fräulein Dietrich says you induced her to go to bed with you because you'd threatened to disclose private information about her."

"I only met her twice. Once on the night of the first performance and once on the last night, my twenty-fourth birthday. Both times she was accompanied by my father, Georg Rosenthal – Süssmilch."

"The café-cabaret owner?"

"Correct."

"What was your relationship with him?"

"Nonexistent for the past several years. I had a rather brief period when I was dipsomanic, Inspector. I stayed in his home and borrowed five hundred marks from him, which I paid back with interest. I'm sure you can check this out with the bank from which I withdrew the funds to pay him."

"Could you have threatened to disclose any of *his* secrets?"

"If I knew them, Inspector. He went from one woman's bed to another, which he hardly kept secret. We've not spoken for years."

"Yet he came to your show twice?"

"I invited him. I no longer felt I had to prove myself to him."

"You sent him *two* tickets?"

"Also quite natural, Sergeant. My father has been a philanderer all his life. It would be naïve of me to think he did not have a companion."

"Other than her beaten face, Fräulein Dietrich is a rather attractive woman."

"Ravishing, Inspector. I sent him the two tickets to the final show because I was hoping she'd be with him. I wanted her from the moment I first saw her. She undoubtedly told you I secretly passed her a note when she, my father, and I dined together after the last show."

"No, she didn't," the inspector said. He extracted a small notebook from his breast pocket and scribbled a few entries in pencil.

"Would you mind giving me a formal statement, Herr Jenkins?"

"Of course not, Inspector Gottleib. You've got your job to do, just like I have mine. I have nothing to hide and you may ask me anything you wish. Shall we do it here or do you want me to go to the jail with you?"

Just as the inspector was about to answer there was a sharp knock on the door.

"*Wer ist das?*" Billy asked through the door.

"Romanov."

"Sergei, can it wait? I'm with someone important right now, and ..."

"Oh?" the voice said from the other side of the door. "Screwing your daddy's girlfriend again?" As Billy opened the door to shove the little man out of the way, Romanov pushed his way through and came face-to-face with Inspector-Sergeant Gottleib. "What's this, Billy Jenkins? Man, you look like you've been through a meat grinder. Your daddy probably caught on to the fact you were playing hide the salami with his lady friend. I see you've traded a luscious woman for an older *man.* And not such a good-looking one at that. Are you taking after those two toms on the show?"

"Are you out of your mind?" Billy snarled. He looked shamefacedly at the bemused inspector.

Romanov continued, "If you want to play around with the man, then introduce the woman to me. She's two feet taller than me, but in bed they're all the same height. I'm sure I can make her sing like you did the other day ..."

"How could you possibly know that, you, you …?"

"Please. You may call me by my proper name, Prince Romanov."

"*Prince?*" This from the inspector, who, by this time, was stifling a most unprofessional giggle.

"Yes, and might I ask who you are?" the dwarf said, addressing Gottleib.

"Chief Inspector-Sergeant Rolf Gottleib, Berlin Police."

"Am I supposed to be impressed? What are you inspecting? The bedsheets where the young woman was probably thrashing about? Did someone make a complaint about the noise she was making a few days ago? My God, you could hear her all over the hotel! Some old biddy who hadn't gotten anything like that for thirty years probably complained."

"Inspector Gottleib," Billy said. "I must apologize for this man's behavior."

"*My* behavior?" Romanov screeched. "*My* behavior! Lieutenant …?"

"Sergeant."

"This man comes up to his hotel room with his father's lady friend," the dwarf continued. "A pair of bosoms like you wouldn't believe and looking at him all googley-eyed like a bitch in heat. They don't see me, because I'm coming around a corner hoping maybe I can filch one of those fancy cigars the hotel gives the Guv'nor here. He's a big shot, you know, so they're trying to kiss his arse any way they can. *I*, on the other hand, have to stay at the *Blinde Huhn…* "

"The Belinda Horne," Billy supplied.

"*Blind hen* is more like it. I'd be surprised if they gave it a half-star. What a dive! And me, a prince of the royal blood."

The two taller men stood silently as the little fellow, who commanded the floor, went on. "Well, he and big tits went into this room, they shut the door, latched the lock, and I figured 'No cigar this afternoon except what she might take in *her* mouth' …"

"Romanov, you are positively disgusting!" Billy exclaimed. He realized that the *zwerg* was absolutely credible because no one could *possibly* have made all this up. Besides, there was no way Romanov could have known the reason for Inspector Gottleib's visit, let alone who he was.

"Now, Herr Romanov…" Gottleib ventured.

"*Prince* Romanov."

"Yes, ahem, *Prince* Romanov. You say you knew this woman?"

"Only by sight. The night of his birthday, Jenkins was going to go to dinner with his business partner and her fiancé and that *real* American cowboy who was in town, Herr Mixed, or something like that …"

"Tom Mix," Billy supplied.

"Yes, him. Anyway, up comes Herr Jenkins' old man and this lady friend. The next thing I know, the six of them go waltzing off to some fancy place for dinner, not that they invited me, of course. I could see how the lady was looking at him. Kind of like a starving cat looks at a big, fat arthritic mouse, if you get my drift."

"Did you see her again?"

"For an inspector, Herr Gottleib, you're pretty dense. Didn't you hear me just say I saw them come up to this love nest, or sex den, or whatever you want to call it?"

"I suppose you saw them *in pari delicto*?" Gottleib said sardonically.

"Of course," Romanov said, with equal disdain. "I immediately ran out and hired a dozen workmen and a crane to lift me up to the fifth floor bedroom window so I could peek in. No, Inspector, *you* might have been able to 'inspect' such goings on, but no one had the courtesy to leave me a key to the room. I told you I *heard* what went on. She may as well have had a megaphone."

Inspector Gottleib realized he was fighting a losing battle to keep a straight face. This arrogant runt was providing him with more entertainment than he'd had on any case in the past dozen years. Romanov, who had not *seen* much of anything was giving him a voyeur's tour. If he was to be believed, there was no question of who was seducing whom.

"I suppose you remained outside the room for an extended period of time, Prince Romanov?"

"No, Inspector. I had better things to do with my time than eavesdrop on two rutting animals. I scratched on the front door once or twice, hoping against hope they would cease their obscene mewlings, but that never eventuated. When I came back three hours later, it was just in time to see this woman staggering out of Herr Jenkins' suite."

"Anything unusual about her face, Prince Romanov?" Gottleib asked.

"Yes, Inspector."

At that, Gottleib's antennae went up. "And that was?"

"She had this glassy-eyed look. I hoped for her sake she'd wipe that idiot smile off her face before she went home to daddy."

"No other marks?"

"Do you truly think she'd let me see where there might be other marks?"

"She claims Herr Jenkins raped her."

"Oh, she does, does she?" the dwarf replied. "I saw you were writing notes, so you obviously have a pencil, Inspector. Would you, by any chance, have a piece of string?"

"Why do you ask?" Gottleib inquired.

"I'd like to provide a simple demonstration to you."

"I just remembered, the hotel tries to provide for every emergency. Buttons always come off jackets or shirtsleeves," Billy said. He walked over to a desk at the far end of the sitting room and brought forth a needle and a spool of thread. "Will this do?"

"Perfect," the midget said.

"Herr *Miniatur* ..."

"*Prince*," Romanov repeated, without missing a beat.

"Herr *Prince*," Gottleib continued. "What is this foolishness?"

"It's not foolishness," the small man said. While he was talking, he had bitten off a piece of the thread and tied it into a loop about as large as his fist. "This game is very simple. All you need to do is take your pencil and stick it through this loop."

"What kind of idiocy ...?" Gottleib reached out his pencil to jab it through the much larger ring of thread. Just as he was about to complete the task, the midget quickly raised the hand holding the loop. The inspector's pencil missed the thread by three centimeters.

"Try it again, Inspector," Romanov said. "More carefully this time."

Gottleib tried. Once again, the *zwerg* raised the loop at the last moment and the inspector missed again. After three more unsuccessful attempts, Gottleib growled, "Just what the hell are you trying to prove?"

Calmly, the dwarf replied, "Herr Jenkins is accused of *raping* this woman, right?"

"Yes."

"In order to do that, he would have to ... you know ... somehow get inside her."

"Correct."

"The little game we've just played easily proves this could never happen. A woman with her dress up can always run faster than a man with his pants down."

"Very funny, Romanov. Is there anything else you wish to say?"

"Yes, Inspector. Could you possibly ask Herr Jenkins to give me one of those cigars? Make that two, please."

~ ∫ ~

"Fräulein Dietrich, I hate to bother you again, but perhaps you could give me some additional details?"

"Why, Chief Inspector Gottleib?" Georg Rosenthal asked. "You should have concluded your investigation by now. My friend's dreadfully abused face, the obvious pain she is suffering every day. Why can't you simply bring this predator to justice?"

"He is your son, is he not?" Gottleib asked politely.

"In a manner of speaking. But what *son* would rape his father's …?"

"Yes, there is that," the inspector murmured. "Now then, Fräulein Dietrich, if I may, I have just a few more questions and we can hopefully conclude this. Did Herr Jenkins ever pass a note of any kind to you?"

"Why would he do that?"

Gottleib noticed that Hedy refused to look at him directly.

"Sometimes an extortionist will betray his intentions by a writing of some sort."

"N – no, there was no writing."

"When did he communicate his threat to you?" Gottleib avoided asking her the specifics of what the threat might have been.

"Just as I told you, the day he had his way with me."

"Morning? Afternoon?"

"Late morning, Inspector."

"Where did this communication take place?"

"In the lobby of the Kempinski."

"What were you doing there?"

"Nothing in particular. I had been walking in Unter den Linden and thought I'd stop at the hotel restaurant for a cup of tea."

"No previous arrangements?"

"None."

"You had met him before?"

"Yes, Inspector Gottleib, on two occasions, both times when I was with Georg."

"Did he ever give any indication that he was, umm, interested in you?"

"None," the woman said. "That's why I was so surprised by his behavior."

"You didn't encourage him in any way?"

"Of course not," Georg Rosenthal replied.

"Was she a virgin when you met her, Herr Rosenthal?" Gottleib said laconically.

"What kind of idiotic question is that?" Rosenthal exploded. "Such impertinence! Why, Sir, I suppose you would take offense were I to take this up with your superior?"

"Not really," Gottleib responded. "My retirement is secure. I doubt if I'm going any higher in the force. But if you or the young lady are offended by the question, I'll move on. Now, Fräulein Dietrich," he continued, scrupulously polite to the point of deference, "you say he came up to you in the middle of the Kempinski lobby and made this proposition to you."

"That's so."

"Did anyone witness this?"

"How should I know, Inspector? I was so upset when he propositioned me that I didn't notice if anyone else was around."

"Did he physically grab you, force you to his quarters?"

"Not at that time. He told me to think about what he had proposed, and if I agreed, I should come to his room in half an hour."

"He left you alone?"

"Y- yes, I guess so."

"Couldn't you have simply gone home?"

"I suppose I could have," she said uncertainly. "I never gave it much thought."

The inspector glanced around Rosenthal's residence. Strong, masculine. What had Jenkins said, "He was a philanderer?" The furniture seemed to emphasize that comment. Paintings of scantily-clad, overly voluptuous women graced the walls of the living room. Gottleib was certain he would find similar, perhaps more graphic, paintings on the bedroom wall. The man probably had installed mirrors all about the bedroom.

"Why didn't you return to Herr Rosenthal's flat?"

"I wasn't thinking at that moment. I was so shaken up by what Billy – Herr Jenkins – had proposed."

"So you went to his room on your own?"

"I did."

"Alone?"

"Yes."

The inspector hesitated. The woman did not seem stupid. She had to have known how flagrantly unbelievable her story sounded, yet she did not budge from it.

"Just another couple of questions, Fräulein Dietrich. Did anyone come by – did you hear any strange sounds during your time in Herr Jenkins' room?"

Hedy looked thoughtful for a few moments, as if deliberating whether there was a secret message in the detective's questions. "Now that you mention it, I remember hearing what sounded like scratching on the front door to the room. It happened twice. I was of two minds. First, I was frightened, but I also thought that if I could make it to the door, whoever was there might be able to help me. When I started toward the door, Herr Jenkins roughly threw me back on the bed. Here, you can see the bruise on my arm."

As she displayed the mark, it was obvious to Gottleib that the bruise had been inflicted earlier that morning.

"So the little *zwerg* was telling the truth," Gottleib muttered to himself.

His investigation complete, Gottleib now had his own suspicions confirmed as to what had really happened.

~ ∫ ~

"Herr Jenkins, please call this man," he said, handing Billy the card of a well-known criminal lawyer. "I shouldn't be telling you this, but I believe Fräulein Dietrich's life is in danger. I'm certain your father was the one who inflicted the bruises. We could arrest him and bluff our way through, but usually the woman is so afraid of the man that she refuses to testify. As soon as the police are gone, he takes his anger out on her."

"Do you have any suggestions, Inspector Gottleib?"

"I will deny under oath that I said this to you, but in circumstances such as this, it would be best if you'd seek help for Fräulein Dietrich – that is if you're interested in helping her – "

"Which I am – "

"From what we covertly call the 'alternative police force.'"

"Thugs and hoodlums?" Billy said, arching his eyebrows.

"You could call them that. They're far more organized than they appear."

"What makes you think my father hasn't enlisted them?"

"I'm almost certain he has. You've already met three of them. However, those fellows need *us* more than they need Rosenthal. They want to maintain a safe relationship with us. There is one thing, however, which is a bit more sensitive."

"What's that, Inspector?"

"They're not particularly tolerant of Jews."

~ ∫ ~

"Hedy, I must speak with you."

"Billy? How dare you call me here? You're fortunate Süssmilch is out."

"I know he is."

"You know?"

"Yes, Hedy. He won't be coming back for awhile. It will give you a chance to clear out."

"But if he finds I'm gone he'll … he'll hunt me down and …"

"Is that why you …?"

"Yes. Oh, Billy, I'm so sorry."

"Not important, Hedy. How many possessions do you have at the house?"

"One or two trunks full of clothes. Nothing else important."

"I'll be there with an assistant in half an hour."

"But …?"

"I'll explain everything then."

~ ∫ ~

"He'd obviously been spying on us. When he pointed the gun at me …"

"Do you have family in Berlin?"

"Frankfurt-am-Main. Two brothers. He'll find me, you know."

"I don't think he'll be interested, Hedy. Not after what I've told you."

"Will they …?"

"Rough him up? Probably a little, but they won't do any serious damage except to his pride. The most they'll do is frighten him a bit, and that's a good thing. A bully is nothing more than a coward trying to cover up his own fears."

"Where can I go?"

"For the immediate future, I'll find you a place on the outskirts of Berlin. Inspector Gottleib said he'd see to it that you had protection."

"I'd feel safer if you were with me, Billy." His stomach lurched and he felt the same weak feeling that had overcome him when he first saw her. "I promise I won't interfere with your life – unless you want me to."

"Hedy, a week ago I would have killed someone to hear you say that. Why don't we just see where our paths take us?"

"I know exactly where they'll take us tonight," she said softly.

PART TWO

1914-1932

29

October 15, 1914, Berlin

Dear Tara and Greg,

When you left for the United States two years ago, I was crushed, but I wished you only the best. I can't say you "left me in the lurch," because you'd converted Werner-Verlag to a publicly-held company. With *Billy Jenkins* books selling carloads each month, our stake in the company is worth a fortune.

I'm pleased that Grigori found *his* fortune in the States. Changing his name from Grigori Migdalowicz to the more American-sounding "Greg Migdale" was a stroke of genius. Tara, are you really an assistant director? At least you had the good grace to get married in Berlin so we could all attend. Can you believe Arpad has turned five and Imi will be four in a couple of months. Sam and Abby claim they'll stop at two kids.

Sam confided in me he's thinking seriously of leaving the police force and starting his own body-building academy which he intends to call – what else? – Young Hercules. I don't blame him. Even though he made captain, he thinks that soon there won't be any Austria-Hungary Police to be captain *of.*

Here I am, an old man of twenty-nine spouting philosophy, but it's what everyone in Europe seems to be doing nowadays. Sarajevo can only bode ill for the Continent.

Sarrasani's, Greifeldompfer, and even Donnert have approached me about selling the "Mud and Goat Show." None of them have discussed money yet, but what an incredible feeling to know you're being courted by shows of their caliber! Did *you* pressure Tom into asking me to do a movie with him or was that his idea?

I don't know how he did it, but Romanov impregnated, then married an extraordinarily lovely, very classy, normal-sized woman. She's such a wonderful musician that I hired her as music supervisor for the show. As Rosa and Riane told me years ago, he may be the ultimate little *scheiss*, but he *is* the funniest human being I've ever met. He and the soon-to-be-mother of his little "prince" or "princess" have set up housekeeping together. If I sell out to one of the larger circuses, I'll try to convince Romanov to come with me to the Wild West Show. Whatever I pay him – and it's quite a lot – he's more than worth it.

Hedy moved back to Frankfurt. When we're in the same town, we see one another, but I've never broached the question of marriage to her. Still, I wonder … This letter is starting to ramble, but I wanted to let you know what was going on here. Please write when you can. Fondly, Billy

~ ʃ ~

"What in God's name is that monstrosity?" Billy exclaimed. The entire structure appeared to be lumpy, melting, congealed oatmeal mush.

"It is exactly that, Señores," their guide responded equably. "It is being built for the glory of *God's* name. *Sagrada Familia,* the Holy Family."

"It's a godawful holy mess," Billy persisted.

"Ah, that may be," the middle-aged guide continued, not the least bit insulted. "But when it is finished it will be a symbol of the centuries. Pilgrims will flock to Barcelona as they now gather at the Alhambra in Granada."

"When it is finished …?" Dieter took up Billy's question. "When will that be?"

The guide shrugged his shoulders. "I have no idea, Señores. The Master has been working on it for thirty-two years. The Señor Gaudi must not be rushed. This is to be his crowning masterpiece."

"You mean he's done more than this?" Billy asked.

"Oh, yes. Fine parks, fine buildings … Indeed, the entire neighborhood calls itself The *Eixample.* Why, he designed the *Casa Vicens, Palau Güell,* the *Church of Colònia Güell,* the *Park Güell …*" the ebullient Catalan continued.

"Seems like an awful lot of stuff named Guell," Billy remarked sardonically.

"But of course. Señor Eusebi Güell, the great industrialist, sponsors all his works. The *Casa Calvet,* the *Casa Batilló …*"

"Another monstrosity," Billy said, under his breath. "You've been very helpful, Señor," he added, paying the guide and giving him a generous tip. Turning to his circus manager, he continued, "I suggest we take a hansom cab down the *Ramblas* to the harbor."

"Why? You don't get many sunny days like this in January, even in Barcelona. I say we take the cab as far as *Plaça de Catalunya* and walk down the Ramblas."

"Sounds fine to me."

As the two men strolled down the Ramblas toward the Joan Brossa Gardens, where the circus had pitched its tober, they purchased *tapas* from open-air merchants along their path. "If you've got to play somewhere in winter during a war, thank God there's a warm Mediterranean city in a neutral place like Spain," Dieter said.

"So far, we've managed to escape the war by playing neutral countries – Scandinavia, Italy, Spain, Portugal, and Switzerland – but the war has been going on for more than six months. It looks more neutrals will be drawn in by this year or next."

"Not to mention, we're essentially a *German* circus."

"True, Dieter, but a circus has as many nationalities as it has performers. We don't dabble in politics, we entertain. We've got Englishmen and women, an Aussie slanging buffer, Italian and French acrobats, Indian antipodists…"

"Yes, but to the Germans we appear to harbor 'enemy alien' elements, and to the Entente countries we're a *German* show, the target for anti-*Boche* sentiments from the local populace. Any word on negotiations for the sale of the show?" He was neither surprised nor upset that Billy wanted to sell out. Forty-five year-old Dieter Hoffman was a veteran ringmaster who'd successfully survived numerous mergers and acquisitions and had always been in demand wherever he went. Despite his German name, he was from Fribourg, in the French-speaking canton in Switzerland.

"More interest than ever," Billy said as they wandered through the bird market. Numerous parents and their young offspring congregated in this portion of the *Ramblas*. The chirruping, singing caged birds competed with the earnest entreaties of children that mama or papa buy them at least one canary, parakeet, or other colorful bird to take home as a pet. "Mostly Donnert and Sarrasani. The problem is, each of them wants to pay in German currency. I'm holding out for Swiss francs or greenbacks."

"My bet is you'll sell by the end of the year. Frankly, I think you should, Billy. War usually boosts economies and people need to get their mind off war."

"That's for certain, Dieter. Our receipts were up forty percent over last year's. Seventy percent of that increase came about after the war started."

When Billy and his manager arrived at the tober, they came into a furious maelstrom of shouting, mostly from Romanov. Although his wife was neither cowering nor shrinking from the argument, she was in tears.

"Insulting bitch!" the little man screamed. "How *dare* you allow such ... such *dreck* to be played!"

"*Dreck* it is not!" she hurled back at him. "It is by no less than the Maestro Grieg. If you had an ounce of knowledge in that oversized head of yours, you'd know it was a marvelous composition, maybe even on par with *Peer Gynt*!"

"I refuse to abide that trash as my entrance music!"

"Whoa!" Billy said, in his best peacemaker tone. "What is this all about, Greta, Sergei?"

"That *witch* is what it is about," the little man shouted, pointing an accusing finger at his heavily pregnant wife. "She expects me to enter the *pista* to the accompaniment of ... of ... I won't even say the name of that piece of drivel!"

"I did not know he was so sensitive, Herr Jenkins," the woman replied. "I thought he'd be proud to march in to ... Come, let me play it on the Victrola for you."

Inside their wagon, Greta Romanov lifted the handle on her proudest possession, an HMV Gramophone, and cranked it up to full power. She placed the handle on the rotating disk. Billy and Dieter listened as a bouncy march issued out of the machine. "It's by Grieg," she said.

Turning to the small man, Billy said, "Sergei, this is a perfectly good march. I'm pleased Greta has taken the time to modernize and freshen our musical repertoire. Why would you have any problem with it?"

Growling, the midget whipped the handle off the disk, grabbed the disk off the gramophone, and thrust it into Jenkins' face. "Read the label, Herr Jenkins."

"*Zug der Zwerge*," Billy read. "I still can't see why …?" Suddenly, he coughed.

"There is nothing funny about it!" Romanov stormed. "Nothing at all! I suppose you'd be happy with a song called 'March of the Cowboys,' but I, for one, refuse to be accompanied by something so stupidly named as '*March of the Dwarfs*.'"

"Prince Romanov," Dieter Hoffman said diplomatically, "I fear you are insulted by the German translation. In its original Norwegian, the name of the piece translates as 'March of the *Trolls*.'"

"Is there a difference?" the little man blurted.

"Of course," Hoffman continued smoothly. "A dwarf is, well, a *dwarf*, a little person. But a *troll*, ah, that is something entirely different. Small, yes, but powerful, fearsome, frightening, very clever, and even a bit evil."

"Really? You don't say … Well, perhaps I *might* reconsider my position."

"Indeed, Prince Romanov," Dieter said. "You, being such a *bon vivant*, are no doubt aware of the metamorphosis of music," deliberately elevating his choice of vocabulary to make the small man feel important. "Take the universally recognized theme song of every circus in Europe, in the entire world, for all I know …"

"Of course," Romanov said, humming the first several bars.

"The very one," Hoffman smiled. "Most people don't even know its original name is *Vjezd gladiátorů* – the Entrance of the Gladiators – or that it was written by Julius Fučik, the Bohemian Sousa."

"My wife," he said, patting the woman's behind possessively, "was instrumental in bringing that song to the *Schlamm und Bock*."

"In the circus, they call it *Thunder and Blazes*," Greta added. "Fučik wrote over three hundred marches, polks, and waltzes, yet he is known for only that one piece. Worse yet, I can't think of one person who, when they hear that music, even knows he wrote it. Sort of like Pachelbel's *Canon* – one hugely well-known song and that's your contribution to immortality."

~ ∫ ~

"Did you ever think what you'd do if – when – I sell the circus, Dieter? I'd love to have you manage the Wild West show."

"I appreciate that, Billy. I'll certainly consider it when the time comes, but I'm circus to the bone, just like you. I live every day for that day alone. Have you ever been to Colmar?"

Billy's mind raced back to the last time he'd been to that lovely Alsatian town. *And to Brenda Lee.* "Once, briefly," he replied. "Can't go there now. It's in a war zone."

"Pretty close," Hoffman replied. "It's German territory. Even though it's west of the Rhine, it's still east of the Vosges."

"Why do you ask? We're wintering in Spain, which is warm and safe."

"A friend wrote me about a new act a few weeks ago. Two young fellows, never been more than ten miles outside their town. He saw an exhibition they put on at the municipal swimming pool." Hoffman poured himself a other glass of sherry.

"An exhibition at a swimming pool?"

"A diving act."

"A diving act," Billy repeated. "And you expect us to go to the western edge of Germany, look at this diving act, purchase an entire municipal swimming pool, and drag it along with us wherever we go?"

"Trust me," Dieter replied. "It's not like that."

"Why do you even bring it up?"

"I just thought, when we're in Frankfurt in a few months … Well, Frankfurt's not that far from the Alsace."

~ ∫ ~

Spring and the *Schlamm und Bock* circus arrived in Frankfurt concurrently in mid-April 1915. Although they were long familiar with each other's bodies, Hedy and Billy's afternoon bout of lovemaking in an elegant suite at the Frankfurter Hof was passionate and delicious. He never ceased to marvel at her wonderfully shapely breasts and the phenomenal things she could do to bring him overwhelming pleasure.

"Shall I order dinner in our room?" he suggested.

"Please. By the way, this may be our last time together." He felt a mild wave of disappointment. "I've become … close … with a nice young man, a Danish engineer working for I.G. Farben."

"That's wonderful, Hedy," he replied, not sure if he was being entirely truthful. "I'm pleased for you."

"Yes," she said wistfully. "At thirty-five I'm halfway to grandmotherhood. A shame I've never had a child of my own. I once thought you and I …"

"'If only' are the saddest two words in any language," Billy said. "But you might still have a baby with your future husband. When's the date?"

"Oh, Billy," she said, stroking his chest gently. "He hasn't even asked. He's a sweet man, though. I think you'd approve of him."

After dinner that night, he wished Hedy a fond adieu. As he left the hotel the next morning, he was half-regretful and half-relieved.

~ ∫ ~

The two men could have passed for identical twins. Carl Metz and Karl Larrainceau looked to be in their late teens, each stood five-foot-seven inches tall, and their bodies appeared to have been cast from the same mold. Dieter had preceded Billy by two days, so he'd seen the show before. Billy estimated that about one hundred spectators had plunked down their few marks or francs to sit in the bleachers watching the event, many for the twentieth or thirtieth time.

The two men climbed the ten meters to the diving platform. They wore identical black bathing outfits and black rubber caps. They walked in lockstep to the edge of the platform, mouthed an inaudible *un, deux, trois*, and executed a graceful swan dive. What seemed like a split second later, but must have been longer, Billy watched as one man entered the water with a barely noticeable splash. So far, there was nothing exceptional about the entry.

But where was the second man? Had he mysteriously remained on the diving platform? Or disappeared altogether? Billy's eyes returned from the high board to the pool. He rubbed his eyes in disbelief as *both* men emerged from the water.

"*C'est impossible!*" issued from the stands. "*Gott im himmel!*" responded other onlookers.

Meanwhile, the two divers had exited the pool and were smoothly climbing the steps to the platform. The second dive was far more spectacular than the first, a double somersault. Again, there was barely a splash when the divers entered the water. This time, Billy knew in advance that both men would be diving, and he carefully trained his eyes on both of them. But again, he would have bet a hundred marks that only one man executed the dive and only one man entered the water. Still, *two* men emerged from the water.

The show lasted just short of an hour. So fascinating was the performance that it seemed to Billy to take only a quarter of that time. Carl and Karl executed dives seemingly impossible for one man – triple somersaults, triple *backward* somersaults, twists, turns, aerial cartwheels; yet they were virtually indistinguishable.

"It's called 'synchronized diving,'" Hoffman said when Metz and Larrainceau were climbing to the top of the platform. Billy had taken a small notepad from his pocket and was scribbling on it with a mason's pencil. Hoffman smiled knowingly. "Their manager has already figured precisely how large and how deep the pool has to be, exactly what is needed for a portable diving platform, how high it must be from the ground …"

"How much will it cost me to hire them?" Billy asked.

"Far less than you think. They're willing to talk with you about arrangements."

~ ∫ ~

Billy decided to spend the afternoon in Eguisheim, a few kilometers south of Colmar. The village looked like something out of a fairy tale: steep-pitched, half-timbered roofs and flower boxes everywhere. It was hard to believe a war was going on anywhere nearby. Enjoying a quiet hour in the village, he murmured "If only every place could be as peaceful as this one."

One of the shopkeepers suggested he circle back toward Colmar on a lovely trail west of town which led into the foothills of the Vosges Mountains.

"Is it safe?"

"Of course," the man chided. "The fighting was up north, far from here. You'll most likely find you're the only soul on the trail."

Halfway between Eguisheim and Colmar, he came to a lovely meadow, one of the most beautiful places he'd ever seen. It was filled with spring wildflowers. Billy felt compelled to wander through the middle of it.

He'd gotten a hundred meters into the field when the land mine exploded under his feet. Billy saw a brilliant flash before everything went dark.

30

The operation on Billy's shattered leg lasted ten hours. The burn specialists concluded there'd be no need for skin transplants. The medical team would depend on zinc compounds, constant moisturizing coolants, time, and nature to heal their patient's burns. The fractured femur was something else. Efforts to regenerate the nerves would be highly speculative at best. The orthopedic surgeon located most of the bone fragments. Centimeter by arduous centimeter, he achieved a reasonably good fit. Pins and metallic devices would be necessary to hold the delicate mechanism together. Fortunately, gangrene had not set in, but there were ugly indications the infection had spread and, unless brought under control swiftly, could easily become gangrenous. When they emerged from the theater, the eight doctors and their nurses were exhausted.

~ ʃ ~

"The first operation took ten hours. Since then, they've done two others to clean you up, or whatever it is doctors do."

"I itch dreadfully."

"You should. You had serious burns over more than half your body. The doctors tell me you're healing nicely and that the worst of the itching is over. Now that you're back in our world, the doctors are looking forward to beginning the real work."

"Tara?"

"Of course. You don't think I'd let my partner and breadwinner become 'late' so soon in life."

"*Damn God and damn this war!*"

"You have every right to damn God, but try to remember He didn't start the war."

"I need a drink."

She poured him a cup of cool water from a pitcher. He glared at her. "Resorting to wine or *schnapps* is something you don't need, my friend."

~ ʃ ~

Billy was still in the hospital on Christmas Day, 1915. Tara hugged Billy tightly and handed him a gift wrapped in red tissue. "This is from Tom Mix, who sent his regrets he couldn't come." Billy unwrapped the paper carefully. It was a silver-plated six shooter.

"I've brought you an even greater gift," Romanov said, handing Billy a package carefully wrapped in gold foil. When Billy opened it, he beheld a star-shaped badge that said, "Honorary Texas Ranger."

"Now I've got a surprise for all of you," Billy said.

He rose slowly from the bed, pulled himself up until he was propped by the bed railing, and said, "Remember when they said I might never walk again?"

He put his cane aside and took one cautious step forward. Then another. The assembly buzzed excitedly as he reached out to take his third step. The spasm came like a thunderbolt, and he collapsed in a heap at their feet, screaming in pain.

~ ʃ ~

"Go away. I don't want to see anybody." His voice was muffled, the covers pulled over his head. He'd turned toward the wall.

"Don't you think you're acting childish, Billy? Sooner or later you'll have to face me or suffocate," the dwarf insisted.

"Maybe that's the best thing," he mumbled.

"Running away from the problem's not going to make it any better. Besides, it's awfully hard to run when you haven't even tried to use your legs. You sat in a wheelchair, then you walked with a cane. Then, when you thought you were ready, you stumbled and fell. And after all that work, just because you fell once, you simply gave up."

"That's a low, cheap thing to say! You of all people know what it's like...."

"Oh I do, do I?" he blazed back. "What do you mean, Billy Jenkins? What *exactly* do you mean? Do you mean I know because I've been a midget all my life? Because I've been taunted because of my size? Because I grew up so poor our family of six survived on two potatoes a day? Just *which* indignity do you think's the greatest, mine or yours? I can't do anything about my size – and, yes, for your information, I *did* suffer rejection by a girl I loved – not a princess of the royal Russian blood, but a peasant wench no better off than me, who screwed her brains out and got pregnant at fourteen by some brawny pig who kicked the living shit out of me when I tried to protect her 'honor'? You *can* do something about you condition – the doctors have told you that over and over – but you *won't! What have you suffered that's so great you have any right to tell me what I can or cannot say?*"

Billy was so shocked at what was spewing from the normally hilarious little man that he could not answer. Finally, he mumbled, "Nothing in life happens without consequence."

Romanov was thoughtful for several moments. When he spoke, his tone was uncharacteristically quiet. "What sin could I have committed before my birth which led to my deformity? If there's nothing any of us can do about what happens, why bother to have doctors or teachers or scientists? Some things can't be changed. I've come to grips with my size. I can't change. Long ago, I forgave God for the way I was born. My soul remains my own. Put what happened behind you, my friend. I have."

As Billy turned to face Romanov, the dwarf continued. "When there's something I *can* change and I don't *try, then* I invite God's retribution. When there's something you *can* change and *you* don't try, I cannot forgive you that. There's nothing wrong with your legs. You've convinced yourself you'll never walk again. I can forgive you almost anything. But if you let me down and cause me to have wasted the two United States dollars on the gift I got you, I will never forgive you!"

For the first time in weeks, Billy smiled. Then, uncontrollably, he started to weep, the emotions of months finally leaching out of his soul.

Next day, Billy redoubled his efforts. If the physical therapist wanted him to work for an hour, he worked for two. Within three months after Christmas Day, less than a year after his injury, Billy walked with only a slight limp. Other than that slight limp, no one would ever have known that the incident near Colmar had happened.

31

The clear, warm Adriatic brushed lightly against the rocks a hundred feet below where they stood. To the right, a hundred yards away, a secluded beach was filled with picnickers of all ages. Children splashed happily in the shallows, while young men wearing scandalously brief outfits – pants so short they barely covered the knees and bathing shirts so tight they revealed every rippling muscle in their torsos – took turns doing death-defying leaps and dives off high rocks into deeper waters.

"September's always lovely in Dalmatia," the tallest of the four men, the American Clark Michaels, said. "A month ago, it was forty degrees centigrade in the afternoon."

"Seems the war is a thousand miles away," one of his two companions, a redbeard of forty, Patrick O'Shea, said. "Except when you go up to Trieste. You should see how many ships flying the Union Jack use it as a port of call."

The fourth man in the group, Jürg Knie, nodded. The group moved closer to the ruined stone walls surrounding the highest point on the island.

"I'd love to work with the Knies again. It 's been fourteen years. Before I got injured I received offers from German, French, and English circuses. Now a consortium of Swiss, Irish, and Americans are interested in making a deal."

"Your previous suitors, the Donnert, Sarrasani, Cirque d'Été, Orfei, and Smart's each have a small percentage of what we're trying to put together."

"The Orfei?" Billy asked, surprised.

"Uh-huh," Michaels replied. "The sun will be down in about an hour. Why don't we walk into town and discuss this over dinner?"

Over the next few hours, lubricated by generous draughts of local wine and an assortment of appetizers, roasted veal haunch, stuffed calamari, and dumplings, they put together the outline of a deal that would benefit them all.

"How is this going to be structured?" Billy asked.

"The consortium will own sixty percent of both shows. Donnert and the rest will own twenty and you'll keep the other twenty percent. All you'll need to do is perform. Dieter Hoffman stays. The two of you and the dwarf each get raises in salary …"

"Very generous," Billy replied.

"Then there's the capper," Knie said. "You get three hundred thousand U.S. dollars outright for your eighty percent interest, plus generous bonuses for each of your artistes and the roustabouts."

Billy whistled. "How can you afford that?"

"We have very deep pockets," Michaels said. "We're confident that when word spreads about the acquisition, we'll attract enough star artistes to generate a very good return on our investment. *Prosit!*"

~ ∫ ~

Although it was eleven at night, the narrow streets and alleyways of Murter Village were festooned with hanging lights. There was a carnival atmosphere throughout the small town. Street vendors sold every kind of sweetmeat and comestible. Thrown-together bands of musicians played Greek, Croatian, Serbian, and Italian songs. People of every age strolled everywhere.

"My God!" Billy exclaimed. "I have never in my life seen so many beautiful women and handsome men!"

"Yes," Knie said. "I've been to Croatia half a dozen times. I never cease to marvel at what a wonderfully attractive people they are. What are you gaping at, Billy?"

"Look yonder," he replied, pointing about half a block away. "That young woman. She is absolutely the most exquisite girl I've ever seen in my life – *and she must be at least six-and-a-half feet tall!*"

The object of Billy's attention was, in fact, very close to that great height. Not only was her face astonishing, but her body, as tall as she was, was in perfect proportion.

"Ah, I see your showman's intuition is already hard at work," Paddy said.

"I don't know if she has any talent, but she wouldn't need any. Can you possibly imagine what our audiences would think when they saw her? Particularly what the *men* would think?"

Michaels, ever the practical American, said, "How would you dare approach her? I'm certain her parents keep their treasure tightly guarded. You'd probably risk a riot by even uttering a word to her."

"Perhaps," Billy said, wistfully. "But one will never be invited into someone's house unless he knocks at the door. What have I got to lose?"

"Your virginity?" Paddy said.

Billy glared at him, then said, "Let's follow her at a discreet distance."

They did. Everything about the girl seemed provocatively attractive – her swaying walk, the way she flipped her long, dark hair, her multicolored peasant blouse. Young men nodded deferentially, but none seemed to make any advances. As was the custom in the town, girls danced with girls and boys with boys. The young woman's movements were lithe and graceful.

By midnight, no parents or chaperones had appeared. Billy got up his nerve and approached her. Calculating that if she spoke any foreign tongue, it would most likely be German, he said, "Excuse me, Fräulein, I've been watching you for the last hour, and …"

"Following me, you mean," the woman responded. "You and your companions weren't very subtle. Of course, from my height, how could I miss anything that went on in the village?" She seemed matter-of-fact. Her tone did not indicate she'd taken offense. "I suppose it was my stature that initially impressed you?"

"As long as you are being so direct, Fräulein, may I be as well?"

"I'm listening."

"Very well. You are, quite simply, the most beautiful creature, man or woman, I've ever seen. Is that direct enough? I note you're not blushing."

"Herr whatever-your-name is, it's not the first time a man has said such a thing to me. Unfortunately, that's usually as far as he gets. It seems I put men off by my …"

"Your height? My name is not 'whatever-your-name is,' by the way. It's Billy Jenkins."

"That's a strange name," she said, laughing infectiously. "It's not German. The Germans who holiday here are usually named Dieter, Rolf, Karl, or something equally military-sounding."

"It's an American name."

"But you're not American."

"I'm German. I adopted the name for my act."

"You are an actor?"

"More or less. Would you allow me to treat you to a sweet roll and a drink of punch? If you are offended …?"

"Not at all Herr Jenkins. I'm Ksenija Krasnovic. You are the first man who has invited me anywhere in a long time. You're not put off by how tall I am? Not ashamed to be seen with me?"

"You must be joking, Ksenija. Any man who would not consider it a great privilege to be seen within five meters of you is blind or crazy, and I don't consider myself to be either."

After he'd purchased sweet rolls and punch for them both, they walked in comfortable silence for several minutes. Billy had lost sight of Knie, Michaels, and O'Shea. He was sure they'd catch up with him eventually, and equally certain they'd have plenty to say when they did.

"Have you lived on Murter Island all your life?" he asked casually.

"No. I was raised in Ljubljana. Last year I attended the university in Zagreb. I'll probably return as a sophomore at the beginning of next year. My parents suggested I might want to take respite from the war, and ..."

"You're involved in the war?"

"My father and mother are both physicians. I became a nurse at an early age. It's terrible to see so many young men cut down or grotesquely disfigured in the prime of their lives, simply because politicians insist on proving their manhood through waging war and sending the young to the front as their surrogates."

"You've traveled beyond Croatia?"

"Well beyond. Gallipoli. That proved the idiocy of war more than anyplace I've seen in my life. Nine months long, half a million young boys killed, and at the end not one meter of land changed hands."

"How old are you, twenty?"

"Twenty-three."

They walked farther on. Soon, they'd left most of the lights, noise, and tumult of the town behind. The main road doubled back on itself as it climbed steadily. Halfway to the top of the rise, Ksenija said,

"Herr Jenkins, I've a friend I must meet – a girlfriend – tomorrow morning for breakfast. I'm afraid I lost track of the time. It's only a block to my flat. I thank you for a wonderful evening."

"Might I see you again, Ksenija?"

"I'd like that."

"Where?"

"How about at the top of the highest hill on the island? Tomorrow afternoon, say one-thirty?"

"I'll be there."

~ ∫ ~

Ksenija looked even lovelier in the bright sunlight than she had the night before. She wore a bright yellow and green sundress, which accentuated her dark hair and clear skin. She wore no makeup. A light fragrance of orange blossoms surrounded her.

As they talked about everything and nothing, the afternoon raced by, one of the shortest in his life. The evening seemed even shorter, although it was past midnight when he walked her back to her lodgings.

Ksenija and Billy saw one another each day and every evening for the next week. During that time, Ksenija told him how she'd been a normal child in every way until she was about nine, when she realized she was much taller than her classmates. Her mother and father loved her unconditionally and had impressed upon her that it didn't matter what one looked like on the outside – it was what was in one's heart that counted for everything. Thus, Ksenija had grown up proudly, without false modesty and without feeling remorse or shame at her stature.

One evening, they chose not to go into the village and instead climbed to the top of "their" hill. A gibbous moon hung in the sky as they reached the top of the rise. He reached out and took her hand in his. For a while they looked out over the sea, watching the moon cast a silver reflection on the water.

"No boy has ever tried to make advances to me," she said, sighing. "That's such a shame, because every girl needs to feel desirable enough to be wanted, or even pursued. I've never even been kissed, except on the cheek at family gatherings. Even then I have to bend down and that must embarrass the boys."

"Ksenija?"

"How old are you, Billy Jenkins?" she asked.

"Thirty-one," he replied.

"An old man," she said mischievously.

"Just a minute!" he retorted.

"I didn't mean in that way. I'll bet you're not a virgin."

Billy felt himself reddening, blushing furiously. He said nothing.

"I am," she continued softly. "A virgin, I mean. Oh, God, why am I saying such a thing to you? You must think I'm scandalously forward."

"Are you? Scandalously forward, I mean?"

"No, Billy, I'm not. I feel I'll be a lonely old maid simply because every boy I've ever met seems so afraid of me," she said.

"I'm not afraid of you, Ksenija."

"Would you kiss me then?"

"Only if we sit, so you don't feel you have to bend down."

They found a stone bench overlooking the sea. Billy kissed the tall, lovely woman more tenderly than he'd ever kissed anyone in his life. Then he kissed her again. His arms went out of their own accord and he held her gently, not daring to move beyond that.

When she looked at him, her eyes were bright.

Later that night, in her room, to the shock of both of them, but more likely as naturally as if it had been preordained, they made love, he for the first time in a year, she for the first time ever. It was a fulfillment, a validation of the value each held for the other, and a celebration of life. For both of them.

~ ∫ ~

During the next several days, Billy found that Ksenija possessed many talents which would make her a valuable addition to his show. She knew a wide variety of folk songs, which she sang mischievously or hauntingly as the mood dictated. She was an adept and graceful dancer. Most appealing to Billy was her sly wit and her intuitive sense of how far one could go and still be genuinely *funny* without stepping over the line of hurtfulness or bad taste. Ksenija, like the *zwerg* Romanov, could effortlessly propel him into gales of laughter.

He told her of the events that had led him to Murter Island. He soon realized that he desperately wanted this woman to be with him. Not that he loved her exactly, it was far too early for that, but he could not picture a day without her companionship.

"Ksenija, you mentioned you'd go back to the university next year."

"If nothing better presents," she replied.

"Have you ever given any thought to being an entertainer?"

"My only memory of such a thing was hurtful. When I was thirteen and almost my present height, a man from a circus came through and suggested to my father that I might earn a good living in a sideshow. My father almost strangled the man."

Billy blanched. He knew such scouts were common throughout Europe, even more so in America. These agents meant no deliberate malice, they were simply searching for oddities as attractions which "normal" people would pay to see.

"I'm sorry my question offended you."

"Oh, Billy, I'm sure you meant no harm. Was there some reason you asked?"

"We've been entirely honest with one another since the night we met. I won't change now. We've been together a week. It's been the happiest time since … it's been the happiest time in my life."

She looked at him oddly, tilting her head sideways as if she did not know what he was going to say next.

"Ksenija, there's so little I know about you, so much I *want* to know about you. It will take me a lifetime to find out and this week is coming to an end and I have to go back to Germany to start to earn the vast amount my benefactors are showering on me, and …" The words were coming out in such a torrent he hardly knew what he was saying. Above all, he did not want to frighten her off by his impetuous babbling.

"Surely you're not asking…?"

"I would not insult you by such a suggestion," he said. "But Ksenija, we'll never know what could happen if we lose each other after such a brief time, if we don't at least try to make more time for us to know one another."

"What do you suggest?" she asked.

"Put off your return to the university. It's almost nineteen-seventeen. The war can't last forever. Come and be part of my show, not the circus part, the cowboy part. That way we can be together every day."

"And every night?"

"If you prefer, you can have separate quarters. We'd never even touch each other. Just so long as you'd be part of my life."

"Billy Jenkins," she said, mock sternly. "Until a week ago, no man had so much as come near me. I had no idea what it would feel like. And now you're asking me to give that up?"

"Uh …"

Then she smiled, and the universe lit up for him.

"You asked me if I'd ever thought to be an entertainer. Does that mean you expect me to work for my keep?"

"Only if you want to," he said, stunned at her acceptance of his proposal.

"Doing what?"

"My God, woman, in addition to being so beautiful, you can do so many things so well. I suggest we live from day to day and find out what aspect pleases you most."

The tall, exquisite woman crossed her arms over her chest. Her expression was inscrutable. Finally, she said, "Well, Herr Billy Jenkins, it looks like you have just hired your newest employee."

32

By February 1917, it was clear that the gamble placed by the consortium would pay off handsomely. So eager were the top circus acts in Europe to join out with *Billy Jenkins' Circus of Circuses* at the end of their contracts that it became necessary for the circus to place *two* separate shows on tour in different European arenas, the first time in history this had ever been done.

As if this were not enough, plans were afoot to make the *Billy Jenkins Wild West Show* the star in the crown of the conglomerate's show business empire. That show deliberately showed in smaller, out-of-the-way venues where, if it were successful, word would spread to the major centers of Western Europe.

"Billy," Ksenija asked one day, "have you ever thought of marrying Europe to America?"

"What do you mean?"

"Europe is totally taken with the American West. What if we were to create a sequence between the first and second half of the show where we provide European culture – Strauss waltzes, Gypsy music, operettas, folk music, dancers?"

"How would an audience who expected to see one thing react to something entirely different?"

"We won't know 'til we try, will we?" she said.

"It could be an expensive risk."

"I don't think it will be much of a risk at all."

It wasn't. By May 1917, the *inter'acte* was nearly as popular as the main show. Ksenija and Romanov had devised a program in which the orchestra and chorus were made up of young, attractive instrumentalists and singers. The *danseurs* wore impeccable *faux* military uniforms that were so bright, beribboned, and adorned in colors that they brought the comic opera of an earlier day to audiences starved for diversion. Many a young girl's heart fluttered at the sight of slim, handsome young men who were in such shortage because of the war. And many a man of any age felt stirrings in other places, for the young women in the show were clad in such low-cut outfits that it was clear to all but the blind that every single turn and curve was most generously displayed.

Ksenija had chosen the orchestra leader with scrupulous attention to charming the greatest number of people attending the show. Andre van Damm, a Dutchman from Maastricht, was well into his fifties, but seemed ageless. He wore shoulder-length blond hair, which he shook vigorously and theatrically throughout every performance. Instead of leading the orchestra with a baton, he played solo violin while standing in front of the musicians. When the need arose, he used his violin as a baton.

Van Damm's appeal lay in his ability to speak, joke in, and charm the ladies in whatever language the country or the occasion demanded. "How many languages do you speak, Andre?" Billy asked when it became clear that the orchestra leader might seriously rival Billy Jenkins' own popularity.

"Fluently, Dutch, French, German, and English."

"That's pretty common for most Europeans over the age of twelve."

"Ah, yes," the man said, winking slyly. "There are many more I speak only slightly, but enough to get by in."

"Surely you couldn't have attended that many courses?"

"*Mais non*," van Damm replied. "Most of the languages I've learned from my many, umm, wives."

"How many times have you been married?"

"Never," van Damm replied.

"But how can ...?" Billy caught the drift of what Andre van Damm was saying.

"Some for as little as a night, some longer. I know bawdy stories and expressions in almost every European language, and some of the most obscene *Rom* and *Rus* and *Ungarn* words you've ever heard in your life – Hungarian gypsies can be the most fiery and exciting – and *downright dangerous* – women in the world."

By June 1917, the consortium decided to move the Wild West Show to the largest and most profitable locales. "Your thirty-second birthday would be a fitting date, would it not?" Michaels suggested.

"You're the financial barons. I'm merely the hired help."

"How about the Rose Theatre?"

"A natural homecoming. How long would we play the Rose?"

"Two weeks, same as your first performance."

"Let's do it," Billy replied quietly.

~ ʃ ~

Within the week, Romanov and Ksenija privately approached Jürg Knie to solicit his blessing on an idea they'd conceived. "Billy would never have suggested such a thing for the sheer embarrassment of it. But his lady friend and I are both comfortable enough in our skins that we're not ashamed to try it."

When he heard what they had to say, Knie grinned broadly. "Brilliant. But wouldn't it be better if it came as a complete surprise to Billy?"

"Of course," the dwarf said. "Can you arrange for the equipment within such a short time?"

"Money always talks, Herr Romanov," Knie said, "and on what the *Circus of Circuses* has achieved even in this short time, we can do a lot of talking."

~ ∫ ~

"In three weeks we'll be opening the largest show Germany has ever seen. Each of us needs time away, Billy," Ksenija said.

"I can spare the 'prince,' but how do you expect me to survive without you?"

"Even the happiest of married couples sometimes needs time away from one another. Two weeks is not forever. Why don't you go visit your friend Lichtenfeld and his wife and kids?"

"Not a bad idea. Where will you be, Romanov?" Billy asked.

"In my native Russia," Romanov said, stretching to his full, but minuscule, height. "Visiting my royal relatives, of course." Billy raised his eyebrows archly. "Well, maybe Vilna would be a nice place to visit in the spring. God knows it's probably the *only* time one could call it a nice place to visit."

"Ksenija?"

"I saw Mama and Papa for only three days while we were in Zagreb. Every girl needs the love of her family."

~ ∫ ~

Because of the very anonymity of Geneva, Jürg's private hall, adjacent to his palatial mansion ten kilometers outside of the city, was ideal for Ksenija, Romanov, and van Damm to work up the act. Romanov had given Knie the precise specifications he needed. Knie's engineers had quickly perfected the technical requirements. By the second week the dwarf and the giantess had exactly what they needed.

When he visited the practice arena, Michaels said, "Andre, I am thrilled at what you've done with the band. Would you mind terribly if, just for the first performance, you shared the baton with another conductor?"

"Whom did you have in mind?"

"An American. An older fellow, sixty-three, but still hale and hearty." When he mentioned the name of the conductor he had in mind, Andre actually blushed. "You think he would condescend to be on the same stage with me?"

"Trust me, he's very gracious."

"Is he willing to come to Europe?"

"To the land of his forebears? Of course. Like most Americans, he's a European mongrel. His parents were of Portuguese, Spanish and Bavarian descent. His grandparents were Portuguese."

"How long has it been since he's conducted in Europe?"

"Seventeen years, when he and his band marched through the streets of Paris, up the Champs-Élysées and through the Arc de Triomphe."

"I would be supremely honored," van Damm said.

~ ∫ ~

When word got out that Billy Jenkins was making his first appearance in years at the Rose Theater, tickets to the newly-expanded twenty-five hundred seat auditorium, plus an additional three thousand folding seats on the outdoor lawn for a matinee performance, were sold out within twenty-four hours. Within two days after that, professional scalpers and those ordinary mortals who were simply willing to roll the dice that lady fortune would favor them, were getting five times the price they had paid for admission to both of the opening performances.

Werner-Verlag rushed ten thousand copies each of *Der Goldene Sattel, Texasfieber, Aufruhr in Laredo, Der Letzte Schuss,* and *Der Neue Land* into print. After four days of personally signing every copy, Billy's hand ached, but the pain was assuaged by the knowledge that he would be realizing a hearty commission from each book sold.

Ksenija reappeared in Berlin two days before the performance. Billy put her parents, the Doctors Krasnovic, up at the *Vier Jahreszeiten,* where he, himself, was staying.

Neither Alain Krasnovic nor his wife Maria were anywhere near as tall as their daughter. They were a remarkably handsome couple. He'd met them only briefly when he'd gone to Zagreb to explain what he'd proposed for Ksenija, and earned their respect and their gratitude when he actually had asked for their consent to take her to central Europe.

A day later, keeping up his pretense of returning from "the East," Romanov appeared. Simultaneously, Andre van Damm, who'd conveniently taken a week off "to visit his ailing mother in Maastricht," also met Billy and Ksenija at the Four Seasons.

Michaels, O'Shea, and Knie had arranged a private dinner for Billy, Ksenija, Romanov, van Damm, and the Krasnovics. During the evening, there were several toasts to the success of the forthcoming opening. At precisely nine o'clock, the dinner was interrupted when the tall, bald maitre d', who must have been close to eighty and who sported a magnificent all-white full beard, surreptitiously handed a card to Jürg Knie. The Swiss magnate nodded and quietly left the room. A few minutes later, he reappeared. Billy's eyes widened in delight.

"Gregori? Tara?" he beamed. "How did you – ? *Tom*? Tom Mix? I'm ... I'm ..." He was tongue-tied, but he actually yelped with joy when four other people appeared. "Sammy? Abrielle? Arpad and Imi? My God, how the boys have grown!"

"And all of us expect you will give a performance worthy of us *worthies*," Lichtenfeld said. Billy noticed his oldest friend had filled out a bit and was now wearing a stylish moustache. Abrielle, still an eye catcher, had become slightly plump. Billy felt it would only be a matter of a few years before she became matronly.

"I'm so … so very glad you could all come," he said, lifting a cup of wine to toast them. He noticed that his hand was trembling from the emotion of the moment.

It was the dwarf who afforded the appropriate comic relief. "I suggest if our benefactors are going to be able to afford this evening, you may as well stop drinking. I can just see you shooting the bullet into the teeth of Abrielle's replacement. If your hand shakes like it's doing now, she will be the loveliest pincushion in the Rose Theatre. There's no need to waste good wine," he said, grabbing the glass out of Billy's hand and finishing it off in one gulp. "Now that everyone is all gathered together and we've said our hellos, we may as well say our *auf wiedersehens* as well." With that, he yawned theatrically and left the room.

~ ∫ ~

An hour before the outdoor matinee was to start, the company was startled to hear the sound of melodious thunder. Turning to where the sound was coming from, Billy saw bass and snare drums, brass horns, trumpets, and clarinets of every size and timbre coming down the street. Every few bars they were momentarily drowned out by a deep-throated bass sound like nothing Billy had ever heard before.

"What in the …?"

"It's called a sousaphone," van Damm said, grinning. "Named after …"

"*Gott im himmel!*" Billy exclaimed. "It's ... it's ... *him*! *Himself!*"

And it was. Striding in front and leading the fifty-piece marching band, his outsize grin as glorious as the bright Berlin sun, was America's march king, John Philip Sousa. The band was blaring and tootling and booming out the *Washington Post March*. Like the fabled Pied Piper of Hamelin, the band was flanked on both sides and in back by swarms of children – Billy guessed there must have been over three hundred boys and girls – and half again as many men and women – clapping and marching in time. They went into paroxysms of joy when the Maestro, having led his charges onto the bandstand, stepped up to the podium and welcomed the cheering crowd in both English and German.

For the next half hour, the band kept a steady tattoo of thirty years' worth of the Sousa marches that had captivated America. When the paying audience arrived, the throng obediently cleared the seats, but refused to leave the area. They spread out onto the lawns and into the streets surrounding the Rose Theatre. *Billy Jenkins* novels flew out of the booksellers' hands as fast as they could be produced, and the salesmen returned to the storage facility over and over again to secure more cartons.

When the audience was seated, the band stopped. Then Sousa launched into *The Lion Tamer* March, and in strode the star of the show. Billy started out spinning yarns. But where before, he had worn a simple and traditional "cowboy" outfit, today his chaps, Stetson hat, even his vest and belt buckle were studded in rhinestones and spangles.

The "bullet-into-the-teeth" trick had a new, ingenious twist. "Now, ladies and gentlemen," he began, "I will shoot a single bullet straight into the mouth of yonder midget."

Romanov, unlike the Brenda Lee of old or the more recent Abrielle, shivered and shook and pranced about the target area. When he turned his back on the audience, the laughter pealed out in gales, for someone had painted a bright, multicolored circular target on the back of his tight black pants. "This is not funny!" he screamed, as he turned to face the audience. "If you do not keep still, I will have the Herr Direktor invite *you* to take my place." The audience laughed uproariously.

As Billy took aim, the laughter turned to shrieks as the jossers saw that Billy was aiming deliberately high. Then the shrieks became screams of horror as an extraordinarily tall, attractive young woman, dressed in the same western wear as Billy, walked by just behind Romanov. With a concussive *BLAMM!* the gun went off. At that moment, Romanov tripped and fell on his face. When the audience, many of whom had closed their eyes in anticipation of a horrid scene, looked toward the middle of the stage, they saw the woman strolling toward Billy, extracting a spent bullet from her teeth.

"Excuse me, Herr Cowboy, did you lose something?" she asked casually, holding the shell between her fingers. The audience erupted in startled, relieved gales of laughter.

During the intermission, Ksenija led her dance troupe in an explosive barrage of Russian, Hungarian, and Kazakh dances, while Billy strolled through the audience, shaking hands and standing patiently while the paying customers stroked his chamois and buckskin boots, chaps, and shirt.

The second half of the show was even more exciting, but what ultimately brought the crowd roaring to its feet was the closing spectacle when the troupers marched off the stage while Maestro Sousa segued into his signature *Stars and Stripes Forever.*

~ ∫ ~

The matinee was to have concluded at four-thirty, but the audience kept the performers onstage for more than an hour thereafter. Finally, after his twelfth curtain call, the King of the Cowboys announced, "*Herren und Damen*, we must do another show tonight, but I invite each of you, as guests of the *Billy Jenkins Wild West Show* to attend the Odeon Cinema any time during the next two weeks at *half price* when you present your ticket from this show – and here is the star of the movie you'll see playing there, my good friend, the *American* movie cowboy hero, Tom Mix!"

~ ∫ ~

That the audience at the evening gala dressed in fancy, expensive clothing did not alter their excitement. Even before the show, the evening papers carried banner headlines that Billy Jenkins was back, and he was more spectacular than ever. Midway through the second half of the program, four large, well-muscled men, led by none other than Sammy Lichtenfeld, now the "not-so-young Hercules," came on stage and gently manhandled Billy to an old-style bentwood rocking chair.

"Our hero has entertained for six hours straight," Lichtenfeld called out. "Now we will present a special entertainment for him!"

"What?" Billy intoned, surprised.

"Just sit," Lichtenfeld whispered.

As Billy reclined, the limelight cut away from him. At the roll of tympani, two electric arc spotlights converged toward center stage right. Part of the stage seemed to fall away as a cloud of fog engulfed the area, rising toward the ceiling. In the midst of the fog, a round platform, eight feet in diameter rose slowly to stage level. Standing on the table was a tiny man attired in a Spanish flamenco dancer's costume. After sharp strumming by a pair of Spanish guitars, the fellow stamped and clapped and struck heroic poses in miniature. The cheering crowd fell silent at another roll of the kettledrum.

A platform of similar size *descended* from the ceiling above the stage. Standing atop this table was the largest woman most of the audience had ever seen, made even taller by the three-inch high-heeled shoes she was wearing. As her table stopped in mid-air, the woman did precisely the same flamenco dance as the little man had done a few moments before. The audience exploded with applause, cheers, and laughter, which increased as the odd couple reprised the dance, each mirroring the other's every move.

The table on which Ksenija stood lowered some more. Simultaneously, the platform on which Romanov stood ascended until it was even with his partner's platform. Ksenija bent down as if to embrace him. Romanov stood on tiptoe trying to embrace her, but he was able to embrace no higher than her knees, while she was grasping nothing more than thin air.

"Higher!" some of the audience shouted.

"Lower!" came the response from another segment of the crowd.

Romanov's platform raised and Ksenija's lowered so they were eye to eye. The audience roared, for rather than even their height, the disparity of the tables only emphasized the difference in their sizes.

"My dear," Ksenija wailed, "Whatever will we do? I fear we are no different than a little boy Dachshund trying to make love to a little girl Saint Bernard."

"No problem at all, my dear," replied Romanov, hauling out a huge Cuban cigar and tapping it with his finger. "When we are horizontal, we'll each be as tall as the other."

Women tittered. Men guffawed.

After a few minutes more of distinctly double entendre badinage, Romanov and Ksenija put their heads together and commenced singing an Italian love aria – which they sang remarkably well, their voices blending beautifully. The audience, stunned by this sudden shift in the show, applauded wildly, urging the couple on to three encores.

To the utter amazement not only of the audience, but of Billy as well, the two platforms were respectively raised and lowered until they were even. Then Ksenija, with the agility of a much smaller person, lightly somersaulted onto Romanov's platform while Romanov somersaulted onto Ksenija platform. The table she was on disappeared *below* stage, while Romanov's new "home" rose up beyond the ceiling. *Schuplattler* folk-dancers, the girls clad in low-cut *dirndls* and dashing young men in loose-fitting black trousers, each wearing a bright red, yellow, green, or blue satin shirt rushed onto the stage to the accompaniment of Dvorak's *Furiant Slavonic Dance.*

"Now you can get up and finish the show," Lichtenfeld said, smiling. "Surprise!"

The audience stomped and cheered and demanded several encores, while Billy, flanked by the small man and the tall, beautiful woman, simply smiled and bowed. Maestro Sousa brought the evening to a spectacularly fitting climax when he closed the show with *Stars and Stripes Forever*, but then swung into the most popular march ever written in German-speaking lands, Johann Strauss *Vater's Radetzky March.* The audience stood clapping in rhythm, as audiences had done for the past seventy-five years at New Years' galas throughout Berlin and Vienna. Fittingly, while the audience was still on its feet, the Maestro conducted the *Star Spangled Banner,* followed by *Deutschland Deutschland Über Alles.*

That evening marked Billy Jenkins' triumphant return to Berlin and signaled that his star was to rise yet higher in the firmament of the most popular entertainers in Europe.

33

While Billy recalled the year between the summer of 1917 and August of 1918 as the happiest, and certainly the most financially remunerative, time of his life, Europe continued to crumble as the war dragged into its fourth year. In August 1918, the Allies opened an offensive on western front. For the first time in hundreds of years, enemies threatened to invade German soil. When it became apparent that the war would be lost, Germany and Austria agreed to retreat to their own territory. The great German hero, Ludendorff, was dismissed. On November 11, the victorious Allies convened a conference at Versailles. Left with no alternative, Germany submitted to the most punitive peace terms in modern times. What was now being called "The War to End All Wars," had finally come to an end. The peace envisioned by the Allies was to last less than twenty years.

34

Billy and Ksenija had spent the last three weeks alternating between Zagreb and Murter Island, with side visits to Šibenik, the nearest town on the Croatian mainland, and farther south, to Split and the wondrous medieval town of Dubrovnik.

"What a year it's been!" Billy crowed.

"Meaning?"

"The books, the circus and the Wild West show put two hundred *thousand* U.S. dollars into my account in Geneva – and that's *after* all the expenses."

They had spent most of the morning in *Stari Grad*, with its marble-paved squares, steep cobblestone streets, tall houses, convents, churches, palaces, fountains and museums, all cut from the same light-colored stone. After they'd climbed to the top of Dubrovnik's fourteenth century city walls, they drank in the vista of the Adriatic Sea, the dry, limestone mountains to the east, and the old city sandwiched between. The noontime sun was brilliant. The few puffy clouds in the otherwise blue sky emphasized how spectacular winter could be in this southeastern corner of Europe. Billy's gaze shifted from the glorious sights of the town, to the even more magnetic sight of the exquisite woman beside him. Her lustrous dark hair hung below her shoulders and the white peasant blouse she wore was anything but modest.

"I'm not surprised, Billy," she said, squeezing his arm possessively. "Nor can I thank you enough. I've made more in the past two years than most people earn in their lives. The only shame is that you haven't had anyone to leave all that money to."

"What are you talking about woman? I'm barely thirty-three and you'd have me in the grave? I'll have you know I'm hale, healthy, and hearty, and you, of all people should know that. Or have you forgotten how wonderful it was last night?"

"Oh, I've not forgotten," she said. "In fact, you'd probably be the first to admit I give as good as I get." She grinned mischievously. "Many, many times, in fact. So many times that it seems you soon *will* have someone to leave your money to."

"What do you mean?" Suddenly the back of his hand flew to his mouth as he grasped what she was saying. "My God, you're not telling me - ?"

"*We're – .*"

Although he knew he'd strain himself trying to lift the very tall woman, he did the next best thing. He grabbed her around the waist and gently patted her tummy. "How long have you known?"

"It's been a week since I missed my second – . Oh, Billy, I didn't know what you'd think when I told you! I worried you'd be upset if I had to leave the show. Then I thought I could dress as an Indian squaw with a papoose on my back. The baby could be with us during the shows, and …"

"Wait a minute, woman! You expect *my* son or daughter to *work* from the time he or she is born? In a cowboy show? Are you mad?"

"Not as mad as you, my dear," she said, amused at his befuddlement. "You're obviously so taken by the news that you're blithering."

"You're right," he responded. "It's just that I'm so … so confused and so *happy* I don't know what to say. You realize we must marry immediately. We'll post the banns, do whatever they do – what *do* they do in Croatia? And what last name will we call the child? Jenkins? Rosenthal? Krasnovic?"

"Why not Romanov?" she asked, mock-coyly.

~ ∫ ~

"We could wait 'til spring."

"No, darling. By that time you'd surely be a *bulging* bride rather than a blushing one. I wonder who I should ask to be my best man."

"Sammy, of course," Ksenija replied without hesitation. "He's certainly your oldest and best friend."

"Yes, but the dwarf's been such a good companion over the years. And …"

"Why not have *two* best men?"

"And Tara Migdale?"

"I'd hardly call her a best *man*."

"True. Oh, Billy, I'm so happy." She suddenly started weeping.

"That's a unique way of showing your happiness," he said, not knowing what else to say.

"I'm truly the happiest woman that ever lived."

"And I'm not?" he said, holding her gently.

"No, you are certainly not the happiest *woman* who ever lived, my dear."

~ ∫ ~

In the end, they opted for a small, private wedding on Murter Island, at the top of the highest hill, where it had all started for them.

Tara and Abrielle served as Ksenija's matrons of honor. Samuel Lichtenfeld and Romanov served as co-best men. Arpad and Imi Lichtenfeld were the flower *boys*, but just to give the wedding some semblance of tradition, one of Ksenija's distant cousins, a beautiful tyke of three, was the flower *girl*.

While Billy waited nervously for his bride to come stately down the aisle, he kept looking at his pocket watch. Ksenija was late – dammit, she was *never* late to *anything*. For an instant, he had a dreaded premonition that his bride to be had backed out at the last moment. Doctor Krasnovic, who was to give the bride away, fidgeted uncomfortably in his chair. Five minutes went by. Ten. Suddenly he heard the blare of horns and a wild gypsy tune that sounded like anything *but* the appropriate wedding march. As he looked up, he saw Ksenija *dancing* down the aisle, accompanied by five bandsmen. A sixth, beating a big bass drum, followed. During the ceremony, it was Billy who broke down in tears of joy.

~ ∫ ~

San Sebastian, which its Basque inhabitants called Donostia, on Spain's northwest coast, was exquisitely beautiful. Colorful Mediterranean flowers bedecked its main street. Its bay was a perfect crescent, with a high hill on each side and an island in the middle. People seemed to occupy ever square meter of gorgeous beach. The Grand Promenade, which skirted numerous hotels, reminded Billy of Barcelona's Las Ramblas. It was the perfect honeymoon locale.

There was only one thing rather strange about the place. Ksenija mentioned it their second day, as they walked the boardwalk from one side to the other. "Perhaps it is a Basque affectation," she said, "but have you noticed how many people on the beach are wearing white masks?"

"I wondered about that myself. Covers their noses and mouths, but not their eyes."

During dinner at the *Palacio de Miramar*, which had been built by Queen Maria Cristina, they noticed that everyone from the Maitre' d'hotel to the elegantly clothed and coiffed nobles also wore similar masks. When Billy asked the headwaiter about his strange attire, the man put his finger to his lips and said, "Masks, Señor? What masks?"

They got the same enigmatic response in the marketplace the following day. Normally loquacious peddlers turned strangely silent and standoffish when they were asked, and hastily changed the subject.

"Billy, something's wrong here. No one wants to admit it. It's a little frightening."

"No, darling, it's a *lot* frightening," Billy responded. "There's something eerie going on. We'll leave for France, which is only ten miles away, tomorrow morning."

They did, and were surprised to find the population of those French towns wearing the same kinds of masks and acting with the same cautious, frightened restraint in Saint-Jean-de-Luz, Biarritz, and Bayonne.

When she awoke on the fifth day of their honeymoon, Ksenija complained of tightness in her chest and diarrhea. "I'm sure it's just that so many things have happened so fast, darling: my pregnancy, the wedding, and all the rest. It's probably just my body telling me to relax and rest for a bit. Would you mind if I stayed in this morning?"

"Of course not. I'll stop at the boulangerie for some hard rolls to settle your stomach, and perhaps some tea with milk."

"Well … " she said. "I thought I'd be famished, but I'm really not hungry. Perhaps after I take a little nap I'll feel better."

But things did not get better. By that afternoon, Ksenija's face had a blue tint. Within the hour, she complained she could not breathe. By evening, she had started coughing up blood. Billy bundled her up and hired a cab to rush her to the *Soeurs de Charité Hôpital*. When they arrived there, Billy had a sickening, sinking feeling, for he saw no less than a hundred people crowding the emergency room, every one of them complaining of the same symptoms exhibited by Ksenija. The doctor who saw them looked as though he'd not slept in two days.

"It's the influenza," he said sadly, hopelessly to Billy, pulling him aside once he had examined Ksenija. "I cannot lie to you, M'sieu. The mortality rate is almost one hundred percent."

"*One hundred percent?*" Billy shouted. He didn't care who heard him. "But you are a doctor! This is the twentieth century! You act like it's the Black Plague!"

The physician only shrugged. "It's worse," he said.

"Worse? How can that be? The Plague killed ten *million* people!"

"And this pandemic has killed *twenty-five million* in its first five months!"

"But ... but ... we were married less than two weeks ago ... and my wife ... she ... is with child," he sobbed miserably.

"Would you prefer I lied to you?" the physician asked gently.

Billy started babbling uncontrollably. "H-how long?" he finally stammered.

"If God is kind, it may be tonight. For her sake, pray that it is."

"Is there anything ... anything at all you can do, Doctor? If it's a question of money ...?"

"No, M'sieu. All the money in the world cannot keep this angel of death at bay. It doesn't matter if you are the Prime Minister of the Union of South Africa or Bufallo Bill's daughter. Very few escape the call."

"That's why the masks ..." Billy said, the horrid secret sinking in.

"For all the good it does," the doctor replied.

"Can you at least ease her suffering, Doctor?"

"Yes, M'sieu. I will tell *madame* I am giving her a mild sedative. It will, of course, be quite strong and she will feel nothing. Go and be with her. Hold her, comfort her. But if you must say goodbye, only do so from your heart, not your lips."

Thus it was that Ksenija Krasnovic Rosenthal, the woman Billy Jenkins had truly loved most in the world, and the child she was carrying, passed as silently and gently as a shadow that night.

~ ∫ ~

By the time the virus had mutated and the human body had accommodated to the disease, between fifty and one hundred million people had been killed worldwide – more than double the number of combatants killed in World War I.

These figures were meaningless to Billy Jenkins. Only one death mattered. His life had been shattered. But Billy's tragedy was not yet over.

A week later, when he returned to Berlin, he was met at the station by a skeletal Andre van Damm and Greta Romanov, who looked like she'd been weeping for days.

"Oh, Herr Billy," she blurted, "I am so sorry – so very sorry – to hear about Ksenija and the … the baby."

"There's more bad news," van Damm said simply. "I survived. Sergei did not."

"Sergei? Who's …? Oh, my God. *Romanov?*"

As if to underscore his words, Greta broke into loud, hacking sobs.

35

"You don't have to lecture me. I know everything you're going to say."

Jürg Knie said nothing. O'Shea and Michaels sat in the room looking at their star attraction, now coming off his fifth – or was it his tenth? – bender since Ksenija's death.

"Drugs or alcohol?" the Swiss finally asked.

"Does it make a difference?" Jenkins said, his voice a raw rictus.

"Not really," Paddy said. "No matter how much you go at it, lad, it's not going to bring the lady or the midget back. They say we Irish are the worst of all – we drink when we celebrate, we drink when we mourn, hell, we don't even need a reason to load up on the poteen. Ye haven't thought going back to work would help?"

"There *isn't* any show to go back to," Billy said dully.

"Not the way is was, anyway," said Michaels. "Your friend Lichtenfeld said he'd help cobble together something. Van Damm's still on board. Circus artistes from all over the Continent are clamoring to show you how willing they are to lend a hand."

"That's wonderful," Billy said listlessly. "But a show can't survive without its heart, and that heart doesn't beat anymore."

"Let's set the record straight," Michaels continued. "You can drink yourself into oblivion every waking hour of every day. You still won't run through a hundredth part of the money you've made before you kill yourself. It's not going to bring Ksenija back. You don't need to scowl at me, Billy, it doesn't work. The last time you went into such a rut was when, what was her name, Sophia? ... and that didn't bring *her* back either. People live, people die. You don't get the right to play God and say when they're going to die.

"But this goes beyond – "

"Beyond what?" Paddy asked, more gently. "One out of every three people in Europe are gone. *One out of every three.* If someone had said to you a year ago, 'Look to your left, look to your right – one of you isn't going to be here next year – would you have believed it? Have you spoken with the Krasnovics?"

"What could I possibly say to them?"

"They're *doctors*, for God's sake. You think they don't know what's going on around the world? Do you honestly think they hold you accountable for Ksenija's death?"

"I never thought about it."

"Think about it, my friend," O'Shea concluded. "While you're at it, think about something else. *You* survived. You dishonor Ksenija's memory if you don't do something to relieve that small part of the world's suffering over which you have some control. If you go back to the show, you can help someone else. If you can bring a long-forgotten smile or thrill to someone else who's died the same death you've died, even if it's for five minutes, wouldn't that perpetuate her memory better than drowning yourself in liquor or putting a mask over your suffering by cocaine?"

"Perhaps a few days away from this city?" Knie suggested. "Maybe Munich or Salzburg?"

~ ʃ ~

The shabbily-dressed man approached Billy as the showman left Munich's Hauptbahnhof and strolled desultorily up Bayerische Strasse. Although the stranger was woefully unkempt, he radiated an indefinable force. "Excuse me, Herr, are you, perchance, the cowboy Billy Jenkins?"

"I might be."

"I was sorry to hear of your tragedy. I attended one of your shows in Munich. I'd been seriously wounded on the French front. For awhile I thought I'd never see again. Your performance gave me great pleasure. It came at a very bad time in my life, when I never thought I'd be interested in anything again."

"Are you from rhese parts?"

"No, I moved here recently. Would you mind if we chatted a bit?"

"I have nothing better to do with my time."

"Thank you for not calling my attention to my appearance. I'm a bit down on my fortune at the moment."

The two men turned right onto Sonnenstrasse and walked several blocks to the Sendlinger Tor before turning into Sendlinger Strasse and the fashionable shopping district. "Grossman's Department Store," the man pointed out. "Schönemann's Haute Couture, Perlstein and Sons." Billy noticed a distinct bitterness in the man's tone.

"Would you permit me to treat you to a meal?"

"I would appreciate that, Herr Jenkins. I know of a cheap *bräuhaus* nearby."

The place was noisy and crowded with working class men. Although Billy had sworn he'd never so much as look at another woman after Ksenija's death, his eyes betrayed him as numerous buxom waitresses busily served patrons their steins of beer or their *backhun* dinners. The roast chicken was delicious, if a tad salty for his taste.

"They cook it that way so you'll become thirsty and drink more beer. That's how they make their profit," Billy's companion said.

"I notice you only nibbled at your chicken."

"I've developed a taste for vegetables – cabbage, potatoes, beets. Quite healthy, I'm told. I've had problems with my digestion since the war."

Later, out on the street, Billy ventured, "I notice each time you pointed out a large department store or other successful business, you seemed displeased."

"Correction, Herr Jenkins. Every time I pointed out a large *Jewish*-owned business I seemed disgusted. And I am. They and the socialists started the war, they profited from the war, and now that it's over they're the only ones in the Fatherland who seem to have endless amounts of money to throw around. I don't blame *you,* of course. You made your money through honest, *wholesome* entertainment. Not like those filthy Jew-owned *cabarets* and smut clubs."

Billy listened to the man's angry rantings. Now was not the time to bring up that his father was Jewish. Billy had never given his father's proclaimed heritage much thought. He'd never practiced Judaism nor had be become a *Bar Mitzvah*. With the exception of Sammy and Abrielle Lichtenfeld and Gregory Migdale, he could not number one Jewish friend.

As they passed a newsstand, Billy's companion pointed out two of the largest newspapers. "Jew-owned, of course. They've always controlled the media. Now, every major cinema studio owner in the United States is Jewish. Money, money, money, that's their *real* religion. They attract money like a magnet attracts iron."

"Surely there are people other than Jews in positions of power?"

"Only when the *Yids* allow a select few into their charmed circle. Rothschild, Lehmann, Goldman-Sachs, the bankers, the stock market manipulators. The ones who forced an unjust war on the Fatherland, who stabbed us in the back at Versailles, and who now gleefully jump up and down on the bones of Germany."

"Tell me," Billy said, changing the subject as they rounded a corner and came into the Marienplatz. "If you were in power, how would you make Germany a better place?"

"First, I would increase security measures. There's no respect for law. No morality. Our crime has increased fourfold. The city doesn't have the money to hire proper law enforcement agents. Even if there was money, its value loses close to fifty percent every *day*."

"That's true. It costs a million marks to buy a loaf of bread."

"Next week it will be *two* million for that same loaf. If things don't get better, people will soon be taking wheelbarrows to the bakery with them. Not to carry the *bread* home but to carry the amount of money they'll need to buy the bread."

"How could Germany slow down the inflation?" Billy asked. This conversation seemed an interesting game for him.

"Mortgage our steel production and our chemical production by government-backed loans to Aryan industry. Let GAF or AGFA-Gevaert sell their product to the Jewish moviemakers. Insist that our countrymen buy *only* goods manufactured in Germany. Promote austerity at home. Aggressively market what we can abroad."

Billy noticed that the man's right hand betrayed a slight tremor. Before Billy could get in a word, his new acquaintance launched into further bluster.

"Take you, Herr Jenkins. You could bring hundreds of thousands of every European currency into the Fatherland, simply by touring your show to countries outside of Germany. People don't know or care that you're German. They want to see *you*, they want to be entertained by the King of the Cowboys. If one hundred Germans could do the same thing – I don't just mean entertain, I mean sell goods – even cuckoo clocks," he said, chortling, "This would bring hard currency into the Republic"

"Shouldn't I be allowed to keep some of the money I earned?"

"Of course. It would be idiotic to tax anyone out of existence. But you could find it your patriotic joy, if not your duty, to pay ordinary taxes on your foreign earnings."

"Would it offend you greatly if I told you I have Jewish blood?"

"That may be so, but you're not Jewish. Herr Jenkins, let me be frank. I am neither blind nor deaf to the fact that you are as famous and beloved in Germany as Strauss was in Vienna. I believe in time you might be useful to me, so I am prepared to deal with the, umm, accident of your birth. Jews only consider someone to be one of their own if their *mother* was Jewish. I know your father, Süssmilch the Clown, claims to be Jewish. But your mother, Anna Fischer, was a pureblood Aryan."

"You've spoken with her?"

"No, Herr Jenkins. We only know that she took up with Rosenthal for a time, long enough to give birth to you. Other than that we know very little."

"We?"

"Friends."

"So you'd consider me …?"

"A *mischling*, a mixed race person, not a Jew. Not to me anyway."

"How would you know of such things?"

"Because I am a student of the human condition, Herr Jenkins. I am slowly making a few like-minded friends in this city. Mark my words, when things become intolerable there will be a revolution from the bottom, the 'have-nots.' The Jews know this. They led the Bolshevik Revolution in Russia."

"I've never thought of Bolshevism as *Jewish*." Billy started to light a cigarette, thought the better of it, and put the pack back into his shirt pocket.

"Thank you for respecting my sensitivities," the man said. "If you need something to put in your mouth, may I suggest herbal tea?"

Billy and his new acquaintance stopped at a *konditorei*, where the showman bought the down-and-outer a cup of tea and a Danish pastry and purchased a cinnamon roll and a cup of coffee for himself.

Somewhat eager to continue this odd conversation, since it was the first time anyone had said anything to him outside of condolences, Billy said, "You said Bolshevism was Jewish?"

"Trotsky's one of its beloved leaders. The Communist Manifesto was written by the Jew, Karl Marx. You've heard of the *Protocols of the Elders of Zion*?"

"No."

"You must read it, my friend. Perhaps then you'll see why I feel the way I do."

The shabby-looking man glanced at a cheap steel wristwatch he was wearing. "I fear I have detained you too long, Herr Jenkins. I have a meeting I must attend and I am late. It has been my great pleasure meeting you." With that, the man took his leave.

It was only later that night, when he thought about what the man had said, that he realized he'd never even bothered to ask the fellow's name.

But the man had said something that reflected what Paddy O'Shea had said. As poverty-stricken as he seemed to be, he had remembered that at a low point in his life, Billy had brought him momentary joy. If he could bring such happiness to others, for no matter how infinitesimal a period, perhaps it would help him confront his own demons.

Thus it was that in early 1920 Billy Jenkins returned to the stage with a new Wild West Show. Although he might never know true happiness again, he could at least strive for contentment. And perhaps that would be enough.

36

Billy now lavished his greatest love, time, and attention on his birds of prey. He acquired everything from golden hawks to peregrine falcons, from the world's most silent hunter, the owl, to the symbol of America, the bald eagle. Billy tirelessly trained them to perform previously unheard of acts. "These are not 'tricks,'" he told the press. "These are learned behaviors. In their own way, these birds are brighter than most human being I've met, and quite loyal besides. After all, they are the ultimate survivors."

Andre van Damm proved to be as adept at the humorous turn of the phrase as Romanov had been. Beautiful, scantily-clad women served as Billy's "assistants" – they came and went every few months. While Billy occasionally bedded one or another of them, he never once uttered the word love. Still, he was astute enough to know that a well-turned leg and an expanse of breast promising hidden delights was a *sine qua non* of any show, whether circus, wild west show, or opera.

By the fall of 1923, when Billy was thirty-eight, his star remained firmly at its zenith, while Germany had sunk to a postwar nadir and was close to anarchy. Billy learned in passing that Adolf Hitler had become the leader of a small political party, one of hundreds in the Weimar Republic. Hitler's party had recently been renamed the *Nationalsozialistische Deutsche Arbeiterpartei* – the National Socialist German Workers Party. Every now and again, Billy would receive an invitation to attend a meeting of the NSDAP or a pamphlet announcing the party's platform, which he still found confusing and a bit repugnant. He had no idea why he'd been singled out for their attention. As far as he knew, he'd never met a single Nazi.

Occasionally, he'd read an NSDAP pamphlet when he had nothing better to do. On paper, the party's promises sounded rational once he'd divorced himself from its strident anti-Semitism. It favored a strong active government, where the rule of law would be respected, where law-abiding citizens would be safe from foreign influences.

One evening, while Billy was performing in Munich, one of his several short-term female relationships canceled a date because she'd come down with a bad cold. On the spur of the moment, he decided to visit a NSDAP meeting at a nearby bräuhaus, first because it offered free food, although he did not concern himself with that minor expense, and second because *any* companionship was better than none.

The man the Nazis had been promoting, the one called Hitler, was to be the featured speaker – not hard to predict, since he'd assumed the position of Führer, leader of the party.

When he walked into the cavernous room, Billy gaped in shocked surprise. Adolf Hitler was the same down-and-out fellow he'd met three years before, the one he'd treated to a meal, a stein of beer, and later a cup of herbal tea. As soon as the "Führer" saw Billy, his eyes lit up with sheer delight. Pushing a cowlick of hair back from his forehead, he approached the showman, smiled broadly, and seemed consumed by this happy happenstance.

"Herr Jenkins! I cannot tell you how pleased and how privileged I feel that you have come! Gentlemen!" he called out to his cronies,

"Do you not see who is here tonight? The world-renowned *Koenig der Cowboys*, Billy Jenkins himself!"

As Hitler's intimates gathered round, the Führer introduced Billy to them. Billy was most impressed by a large, strikingly handsome man named Hermann Göring, whom Hitler told him had been a great war hero and a flying ace with eighteen confirmed kills to his credit.

As he continued to introduce Billy, the cowboy showman nodded politely, acknowledging each of Hitler's associates by name.

"You'd be surprised how quickly our movement is growing Herr Jenkins! We never claim we are fighting a lost cause. We support causes that have not yet won. We've even made friends with General Ludendorff, the hero of the late war."

After generous platters of roast chicken, wurst, and sauerbraten, and even more generous tankards of beer had been passed around, devoured, and quaffed, Hitler stood to address his party. Billy counted twenty-seven men in the room, himself included. The Führer's address was a mixture of reason and bombast designed to cater to society's lowest rung, the revolutionaries, the *unterklass*. As Hitler spoke, he attacked those who were higher on the social scale, sometimes only the next rung up from his listeners: social democrats, communists, and labor leaders. Although he lumped the Jews in with all these evil movements, he also made sure his audience knew that many Jews also constituted the capitalist class that was bleeding the republic dry. "They use your strong backs to climb over you and push you farther down!" he shouted.

Against his better nature, Billy found himself magnetically attracted to Hitler's astonishing and theatrical oratorical skills. Time and again, the Führer's speech was interrupted by loud cheers, standing ovations, and the pounding of beer steins.

After the speech, Hitler walked over to Billy, and asked, "What did the great Herr Jenkins think of my modest talk?"

"I found your rhetoric hypnotic."

"Ah, you liked it, then?"

"I was impressed, Herr Hitler."

"You did not find my allusion to the Jews disgusting or shameful?"

"You told me some years ago you didn't consider me a Jew."

"True."

"Then why would you think I'd find what you said offensive?"

"Because your father – "

"I'd as soon kill him as speak with him. I view him as a contributor of sperm, little more."

"Delicate toes, Herr Jenkins?" another voice asked.

"Indeed, Captain Röhm. I see no reason to ruin an otherwise pleasant enough evening by bringing his name up."

"Would you consider visiting us again sometime soon?" Göring, the pilot-hero, with whom Billy felt an instant affinity, asked.

"If time permits, Captain … Colonel …?"

"Herrmann will do just fine. Odd where our footsteps lead us, isn't it Herr Jenkins. I must say, I am pleased to be in the company of America's greatest gift to the *Vaterland*, even if that gift is German through and through. Might I ask a small favor of you?"

"Certainly."

"I've always been a great fan of yours, of course, but I would so like to meet the Herr Tom Mix if that could be arranged."

"I see no reason why it couldn't. He's coming to visit next month and bringing a friend with him, a fellow named Will Rogers."

~ ʃ ~

"I'd stay away from Hitler if I were you," Sammy said when they next met in Bratislava. "He's crazy and he's dangerous."

"You say that because you're Jewish," Billy replied, his tone cooler than he'd thought it would be.

"I'm not part of his preferred scapegoats," Sammy said. "Right now he's content to shout and scream about the German Jews. God help them if a man like that were ever to come to serious power."

"You have to admit he makes some good points," Billy persisted. "The Communists are pulling us one way, the capitalists and millionaires another, and the poor *Volk* are, as always, like a fish between two cats."

"You think so?"

"Isn't it always that way?"

"Billy, you're an intelligent man and a good one. I'm surprised you've let this kind of vomitous drivel actually get to you. I'd have expected to you to examine what he's saying more carefully, to see if he's really attacking *issues* or simply using *people* as his whipping boys."

As the two best and oldest friends parted company the following day, each felt for the first time the beginnings of an estrangement that had never been there before.

~ ∫ ~

"You're an Indian?"

"Half Cherokee." The man was forty-five, six years Billy's senior. "Not because my mother was Indian and my father a white man, or vice versa. Each of them was half Indian. Heck, my dad was a Confederate soldier."

Two weeks had passed since Billy had attended the NSDAP meeting in Munich. The three of them were seated in Billy's commodious penthouse apartment off the Ku'dam in Berlin's fashionable east side. Billy found Tom's friend to be extremely likeable with a wide smile and a charmingly humorous manner.

"So your ancestors didn't come over on the Mayflower?" Tom Mix quipped.

"Nope," Will Rogers said. "They met the boat when it came."

Billy didn't catch the joke, but he smiled politely. "Is this you first trip to Europe Herr Rogers?"

"It is. Berlin's quite impressive, all these green parks and lakes, fancy buildings, rivers, and stuff. More bridges than I've ever seen in any city. Back in Oklahoma. there's nothing but wind and dust and a few scraggly trees."

"Do you have any pictures of Oklahoma, Herr Rogers?"

"Not with me, Mister Jenkins, but I suppose I could send you some. Why?"

"I'd like to build a house for myself someday, not that I have anyone I'd want to live with me in it, and I'd like it to have a real western look to it, so if anyone comes to visit …."

"If you want a genuine western *Oklahoma* house the way they were forty or fifty years ago, you might just as well order a custom-made teepee," Rogers chuckled. "Where would you build the house?"

"Reinickendorf, on the outskirts of northern Berlin. Lots of cheap land there."

There was a sharp rap on the door. "*Wer ist das?*" Billy called.

"Göring."

Billy opened the door to greet the large pilot. Göring seemed visibly unnerved when he saw Jenkins' two visitors, then said, "Excuse me, Herr Jenkins. I was unaware you had company. Herr Mix, I presume?"

"Yes."

"I am most privileged to make your acquaintance. My name is Hermann Göring, late a pilot in the Luftwaffe."

Billy introduced Will Rogers to Göring as well.

Ever urbane, but nervously, Captain Göring said, "I regret that I must imposition your friends, Herr Jenkins, but I'm sure they will read about it in the papers tomorrow. Our Führer is in hiding. The police are seeking to arrest him on charges of high treason."

~ ʃ ~

"Case Number 89317, The Republic of Germany versus Adolf Hitler, Ludendorff, Röhm, Frick ..." the voice of the bailiff droned on. February 24, 1924, was a typical late winter's day in Munich. The courtroom was large enough to accommodate over one hundred spectators, including Billy Jenkins. Billy had succumbed to Göring's plea that he attend at least part of the trial. Although he considered himself neither a friend nor a confidant of the Führer, he could not deny his fascination with the man.

After the prosecutor's opening statement, Hitler, who did not use a lawyer despite the seriousness of the charges against him, commenced his own opening argument.

"My Lord Justices: The perpetrators of the Kapp Putsch all pleaded innocent. Every man raised his hand to swear he had known nothing. None of them had the courage to stand before the Court and say, 'Yes, this is what we did. We wanted to overthrow the state.' I confess to what happened on November 8, but I do *not* confess to the crime of high treason. How can there be a question of treason in an action which aims to undo the betrayal of this country in 1918? And if I *were* committing treason, where are those who had the same aims I did, Kahr, Lossow, and Seiser? Why aren't *they* sitting beside me now? I reject the charge of high treason until I am joined by those gentlemen who wanted the same action as I did, who discussed it with us and helped prepare it down to the smallest details. I do not consider myself a traitor. Even though I was born in the Östmark, I have always considered myself first and always a German, who desires only what is best for his people."

Stormy applause erupted from the audience, many of whom were NSDAP sympathizers. Billy noticed that the Presiding Judge seemed not to be in any hurry to gavel the courtroom to silence.

"The Führer knows you're here and he told me to convey his personal thanks," Göring whispered. " He said something about *The Lion and the Mouse*, Aesop's fable."

"Herrmann, he's turned this courtroom into his own stage."

"That he has, my friend. Not that it'll do him any good in the short term. The result, even the sentence, is pre-ordained."

The trial lasted two weeks. Billy was once again in Court when Hitler delivered his final impassioned oration. "I stand accused of wanting to be a minister. I consider it unworthy of a great man to go down in history as a 'minister.' No, what I wanted from the first is to destroy Marxism. I shall carry through this task, and when I do the title of minister will be utterly ridiculous.

"When I first stood at Wagner's grave, my heart overflowed with pride. Here was a man who had forbidden his family to write anything on his stone but his name. I was proud that this man was content to transmit his *name,* not his string of petty accomplishments, to posterity."

There was the sound of muffled coughing in the courtroom. The Presiding Judge glanced at the lay judges on either side of him.

"Our army is growing every day," Hitler continued. "The hour will come when the small bands will form into battalions, the battalions into regiments, regiments into divisions. The old banners will wave proudly. The eternal judgment will come from none but God and history. I already know what verdict Your Honors will hand down. But that other Court will not ask us 'Did you or did you not commit high treason?' That Court will judge us as Germans who wanted the best for their people and their Fatherland, who were willing to fight and to die. You may declare us guilty a thousand times: the goddess of the Eternal Court will smile and gently tear in two the State Prosecutor's brief and the verdict of this court; for she acquits us."

~ ∫ ~

The day after the verdict, the *Münchener Rundschau* carried the banner headline:

WILL THE COURT'S VERDICT BE HISTORY'S VERDICT AS WELL?
Hitler convicted, imprisoned at Landsberg. Ludendorff not guilty

"National Socialist leader Adolf Hitler was convicted yesterday of attempting to overthrow the government. The decision was clearly a compromise and was an embarrassment for the State Prosecutor. The three lay judges were initially opposed to passing any guilty verdict at all. They revealed to the press that they had voted to do so only after they had been assured that Hitler would be pardoned before serving his full sentence.

"The verdict stressed the 'pure patriotic motives and honorable intentions' of the defendant. In imposing the sentence, the Presiding Judge emphasized that Herr Hitler would become eligible for parole in six months. The audience, which filled the courtroom to overflowing, applauded wildly when the court announced it was waiving the mandatory deportation order in the defendant's case because 'Herr Hitler thinks and feels in such German terms.' General Ludendorff, a co-defendant, was acquitted. ..."

37

"Isn't he supposed to be a prisoner?"

"So they tell me, Billy," Göring replied, laughing. "He's got more power than the prison warden. I'll bet if he asked them, they'd command you to do a Billy Jenkins Wild West Show at Landsberg."

They'd just returned to downtown Munich. "He gets special meals," Göring continued. "He's allowed to sit at the head of the table under a swastika in the common room. He doesn't have to report for any work detail. Other prisoners are assigned to clean and tidy up *his* room every day. He wears any kind of clothes he wants…"

"I wonder if they'd let me wear *my* western regalia if I were convicted of treason."

"Probably not. What do you think of his new friend, the 'doctor?'" Göring asked.

"He seems bright enough and the Führer's obviously taken with him, but I could tell the man didn't like me. Nothing I can put my finger on, but I feel uncomfortable around him. I suppose I should feel sorry for him, crippled from the war and all."

Göring gave Billy a curious look. "Injured in the war? The man never served a day in the army."

"But I thought … his limp …"

"Club foot. During the war, he studied at Heidelberg, earning his doctorate in Eighteenth century romantic drama. Maybe he thinks your brand of entertainment is beneath his dignity."

"That might explain why he acted like he did. I've heard the Führer's writing a book?"

"That he is. He's been dictating it to Rudolf Hess. He calls it *Four Years of Struggle against Lies, Stupidity, and Cowardice.*"

"That's quite a mouthful."

"So the party thinks. You can't tell the Führer anything he doesn't want to hear."

"Couldn't he just shorten it?"

"Would *you* want to tell him?"

"Doesn't matter to me. I'm not NSDAP and you've said he trusts me."

~ ∫ ~

"It is good of you to visit, Herr Jenkins. This marks the third time. I know you don't agree with many of my ideas, so that makes it especially gracious."

"My pleasure, Herr Hitler."

"I also appreciate that you don't toady to me like the rest of my associates."

"I'm a leader in what I do, you're a leader in what you do. Mutual respect."

"I agree. Göring said you'd talked to him about my book."

"Just the title."

"What do you think?"

"Speaking as a marketing man, the publisher's going to have to put a lot of words on the cover. The more words, the smaller the typeface."

"I was thinking that myself. What would you think if I changed the title to two words, *My Struggle?*"

"*Mein Kampf?* Much better. By the way, I completely approve of your new style of dress. A lot different than when we first met."

Hitler chuckled. "We've both come a long way since that first day, Billy Jenkins."

~ ∫ ~

"He got out in less than a year. I've never asked what you think of Hitler, Dieter."

"I'd call him a dangerous crackpot except I've learned through the years that today's 'crazy' may be tomorrow's head of government."

"Andre told me the same thing. What is it with you, Dieter?"

"Billy, if I may talk frankly, without you getting riled up …?"

"I feel a morality talk coming on."

"I've been your friend for more than a decade. It almost seems as if you've sworn off women and you're using Hitler as a substitute."

"That's insane! Just because I went to a few meetings, visited him in prison a couple of times …"

"If you don't want to hear what I have to say, it's OK with me. I'm just the hired help."

"Why would you even think such a thing?"

"How're the plans going for Reinickendorf?"

Billy was polishing his six shooter for the evening's performance. Summer had come to northern Germany and it was glorious. Kiel in July was a wonderful place to be.

"It'd be better if I could get the land cheaper. Wassermann wants top *reichsmark* for the real estate."

"So now you've got two reasons to cozy up to the Nazis," Hoffman said.

"I've no idea what you're talking about Dieter."

"Reason number one, you hate your father."

"That's nothing new."

"When you took up with Hedy Dietrich, you were one-upping your father in the most intimate way possible. Taking his lady away from him. The Nazis detest all Jews and they know your father's Jewish. If they ever come to power, well, I don't need to say anything more."

"They know I'm half-Jewish," Billy said stonily.

"As long as the Nazis need you for their purposes – you're still the most popular entertainer in Germany – they don't care if you're a *schwartze* or Mohammedan."

"You said there are two reasons."

"You've probably never given it a conscious thought. Wassermann's a Jew. Wassermann has something you want – something that could take Hedy's or Ksenija's place. But he doesn't want to give it to you at the price you want to pay and maybe not at all. So you might need the Nazis in power for *your* purposes. A marriage of convenience you might say."

"You sound as bad as you say *they* are. Shaping their agenda to fit your anti-NSDAP sentiments."

"I didn't know I had any agenda, Billy. Don't forget, I'm Swiss. We're neutral."

~ ∫ ~

The two men sat across from one another at Hitler's retreat overlooking the resort town of Berchtesgaden, a thin thorn of land punching into Austrian alps.

"So you're the famous Billy Jenkins? The Führer speaks highly of you. Odd we've never met."

"Actually we did, Doctor Goebbels. Three years ago, when Hitler was at Landsberg. I'm glad to hear you and he have reconciled after the Strasser matter." Billy knew he'd trod on sensitive toes and didn't seem to care.

"A small bump in the road, Herr Rosenthal. Different political philosophies often adjust to the times. I'm surprised he's friendly with a Jew," Goebbels said coolly.

The dislike between them was palpable, but each knew he'd been invited to Berchtesgaden because Hitler could use them both.

"The name's Jenkins," Billy replied. "You're bright enough to know that the blood passes through the mother. Besides, I've never practiced the religion."

"Who said anything about *religion*. You're part of a *race,* just as much as if you'd been born with black skin. Excuse me, the Führer wants to see me about something."

"Looks like the dislike is certainly mutual," Göring, who'd heard the last part of the conversation, said.

"Slimy bastard," Billy said under his breath.

"You'll find a lot of those types kissing the Führer's behind. Our leader's quite adept at playing one against the other. Everyone, myself included, wants to be close to where they think the power and the money will be. Still, it's a wise idea to watch your own backside."

"Berchtesgaden's a long way from the slums of Munich, Herrmann."

"Yes, and the *Billy Jenkins' Wild West Show's* a long way from the *Gran Circo Spettacoloso Wallachia y Moldavia.* You've both come a long way."

"What about you, Herrmann? You could have succeeded anywhere."

Göring looked thoughtfully south toward the Bavarian Alps, the most dramatic and beautiful part of the country, took a canapé proffered by one of the beautiful, dirndl-clad waitresses, then stared back at Billy. "I suppose I could have. We're moths drawn to a flame, my friend. And wherever the flame leads us, we're bound to follow."

~ ʃ ~

September 15, 1931

Berlin

Dear Erich:

You and I have never been close. Let's admit, for the past several years we have hated each other – you as much as I. We would have been content to see the other one wiped off the earth. No one can take back the hurt inflicted or the words said or not said.

You are the *Koenig der Cowboys*, the most successful entertainer in German history. I don't begrudge you that. My life, good or bad – and I've had more good times than bad – is shortly coming to an end. The doctors say it's lung cancer. They've given me less than a year to live.

Am I writing to make peace with you? We've tried that more than once and it has not worked. I doubt it would work now.

I am writing you as a warning. I am aware that you have cozied up to the Nazis; that you have turned your back on your birth religion, and that you are spouting the same vile, racist, antisemitic remarks as your new friends have done since they were a trashy little party in Munich.

I've no doubt that when I am gone, you will do everything in your power to dissociate yourself from everything I was and everything I stood for. For all I know, you might even get a patch of skin sewn on so you will be uncircumcised. That is your choice and you will have to live with it.

But whether you like it or not, the Nazis view Jews as a *race*, not a religion. You have fifty percent Jewish blood in your veins. The Nazis will accept you as a *Mischling* – for now. But Erich, as Hitler and his gang blame the Jews for everything, isolate Jews, pass laws against them, humiliate them, put them in concentration camps, or even murder them, one thing stands out: the Nazis *need* the Jews as scapegoats. If every Jew were disposed of, who could the Nazis blame for Germany's troubles?

So as the Jews start disappearing off the face of the German map, the Nazis will tighten the laws on who is a Jew. Today it will be if you have fifty-one percent Jewish blood, you are a Jew. In a few years, if you have twenty percent Jewish blood, you are a Jew. *Und so veiter* until it's less than one percent.

You may fool the world and perhaps even yourself by claiming you are so famous they cannot touch you – and that you are a friend of their self-styled "Führer" himself. But you will be wrong, Erich. You will be what you now are for only so long as they can use you – and when they don't need you anymore, they will spit you out like a well-chewed chicken bone, or they will eliminate you as surely as they eliminate waste from their bodies each day. And when that day comes, you will learn that I was right.

Get out of Germany – get out of *Europe* – while you can. There are lots of places that will now accept Jews – America, South Africa, Turkey, even Palestine – especially Palestine. Do not turn your back on Judaism, lest God – the jealous God of the Jews – turns His back on you.

Süssmilch

~ ʃ ~

On February 27, 1932, Georg Rosenthal died. Billy did not attend the funeral, nor did he so much as send flowers or a note lamenting the passing of his father.

Within a month, with Göring's assistance, Billy officially changed his name from Rosenthal to Fischer, his Aryan mother's last name. He received official identity cards with his new name and Erich "Billy Jenkins" Fischer was enrolled as a member of the National Socialist Party. To all intents and purposes, Erich Rosenthal no longer existed.

~ ∫ ~

Though Hitler had left Austria in 1913, he still had not acquired German citizenship and hence could not run for public office. The state government of Brunswick appointed him to a minor administrative post and also made him a citizen of Brunswick, which, in turn, made Hitler a German citizen and thus eligible to run for president.

For the first time in German history, the candidate campaigned by aircraft, which allowed him to speak in two cities in one day, practically unheard of at the time. Hitler came in second, with more than thirty-five percent of the vote. Although he lost to Hindenburg, the election established him as a realistic alternative in German politics.

In May 1932, Hindenburg appointed Franz von Papen as Chancellor. Von Papen immediately called for new elections in July. The Nazis achieved their biggest success yet and won two hundred thirty seats, becoming the largest party in the Reichstag.

Papen tried to persuade Hitler to become Vice-Chancellor, but Hitler refused to settle for anything less than the chancellorship. The aging, weakening Hindenburg refused to appoint the "Bohemian lance corporal" to the chancellorship.

After a vote of no-confidence in the Papen government, the Reichstag was dissolved. New elections were called in November. This time, the Nazis lost some seats but still remained the largest party in the Reichstag.

In January, 1933, General Kurt von Schleicher, the acting chancellor, asked Hindenburg for emergency powers along with postponement of elections. The president responded by dismissing Schleicher.

Now, every shade of the political spectrum tried to form a coalition to prop up the tottering Republic. Even though a combination of the Social Democrats and the Christian Democrats had the necessary votes to form a majority coalition, they continued to bicker until ultimately, all the conniving and back-door deal-making collapsed.

On the morning of 30 January 1933, in a brief and simple ceremony in Hindenburg's office, Adolf Hitler was sworn in as Chancellor of Germany. Although he could not claim a majority, he had been elected by a plurality in a democratic vote.

Thus it was that the Weimar Republic passed into history and the thousand-year Third Reich was born.

PART THREE

1933 - 1954

38

Even before sunset, replicas of American Indian teepees stood next to a row of lights adjacent to the half-circular driveway in front of the Foreign Ministry. As Mercedes, Bugattis, and Daimlers arrived, lean, leathery-skinned cowboys, outfitted in Texas Ranger garb, presented each alighting passenger with a souvenir of the "American West," a ten gallon hat for each man, a cowgirl vest decorated with rhinestones for his lady. Formally dressed guests murmured appreciatively as they were escorted over a sawdust-covered floor into the cavernous ballroom. A white canvas tent, representing an Indian meeting Hogan, draped the entire room. A huge ball, with hundreds of mirrored glass squares embedded in its surface, hung from the ceiling. Spotlights on either side of the room were aimed at the ball. As the huge fixture rotated, a thousand bursts of light created an ever-changing kaleidoscope of artificial stars.

Three hundred guests sat on hard wooden benches at long tables, "Western" style. Women in scandalously short skirts and outrageously tight western blouses wafted by the tables, leaving behind a mild scent of incense and spices. In each corner of the room a grizzled old "cowpoke" stood by a chuck wagon, yelling, "Come and git it!" The cowgirl-waitresses approached each of the cooks, carrying large platters. The cooks placed huge barbecued T-bone steaks or giant slabs of beef ribs for the men and smaller filet mignon steaks for the women, on the platter, after which the waitresses served the guests.

At each table, there were monstrous tubs of chili beans, potato salad, green salads consisting of iceberg lettuce, beefsteak tomatoes, onions, and green peppers, trenchers of garlic-buttered Western bread, tankards of beer and endless cups of hot, black coffee.

Billy's mouth was agape, such was the unparalleled feast. He looked in vain for someone he might know. He heard two American-accented voices behind him.

"What I see going on, even in the few days I've been here, upsets me. Everyone toadies up to the Führer as though he's the next Christ, but beneath it all, there's fear. In America, everyone speaks his mind, sometimes too much so. Here, in this 'civilized' land, there's terror just below the glittering surface. People are so cautious when they speak," the first man said.

"You're right, John," the second man replied. "In medieval times, scholars argued for hours about how many angels could dance on the head of a pin. These fools are those very angels, dancing on the edge of the abyss. Amazing how few of them see that. Even more amazing how many Americans admire the Führer and what he's done for Germany."

As the two men drifted apart Billy approached the second speaker and found himself looking into the clear, brown eyes of a man in his thirties, with thinning hair and thick spectacles. "Excuse me, might I join you?" he asked.

"Of course." The man smiled. "You're the famous German King of the Cowboys, Billy Jenkins, aren't you?

"Yes, but how would you know?"

"It's part of my job," he said, shaking Billy's hand. "I'm Ed Baumueller, *New York World*. I happened to be in Berlin when the foreign minister kindly invited me to fill a vacant space."

"Mr. Baumueller – of *the* Baumuellers? The ones who founded the *World*?"

"Don't tell anyone," he said in a stage whisper. "We're a Jewish-owned outfit. That wouldn't go down well with His Holiness, the next Frederick Barbarossa."

They'd been talking for five minutes, when a white-haired, distinguished-looking man approached and greeted the American in heavily-accented English. "Herr Baumueller, I was asked by an old friend, Paul Gottlober, to convey his greetings."

"Gottlober? His father and mine went to school together, many years ago."

"So he told me. I am Bernhard Schönemann. Twenty years ago, I traveled to New York and observed how Jews have done so well in your country. Macy, Gimbel, Levi Strauss, and, of course, your own family."

"What do you do, Herr Schönemann?"

"I took a lesson from you American Jews. I started my own dry goods store. I was lucky – the Yiddish word is '*Mazeldicke*' – and it prospered. Then I built another, and another. So now I am fortunate. The name 'Schönemann' is known from Berlin to Vienna."

"Schönemann's Department Stores. Of course!" Billy said, brightening. "I saw the three-story building in Unter den Linden. Please don't think me forward, Herr Schönemann, but haven't I seen you somewhere before?"

"Yes, Herr Jenkins. You were the best man at my great niece's wedding."

"Abrielle?"

"Correct. She married that fellow from Bratislava, Sam Lichtenfeld."

"My best friend for several years," Billy mused, suddenly feeling a cold stab of guilt. After a few minutes of pleasantries, Billy asked, "Herr Schönemann, what's your candid opinion about what will happen to the Jews with the Führer in power?"

"Frankly, I believe his anti-Jewish talk will blow over. Storm clouds have always hovered over the house of Israel. We Jews have kept the mercantile life of Germany going since the Middle Ages. Where would the universities, the law courts, the great orchestras be without us? The Führer may rant and rave about *Juden* this and *Juden* that, and how Jews have polluted the master race. That's only to obtain votes. I myself donated several thousand *Reichshmarks* to his campaign – as I have to the campaigns of all the major candidates. In the end, these politicians know where their bread is buttered and who pays for their tirades."

"You don't think all this anti-Semitic talk will last?" Baumueller asked.

"Hardly. The brown shirts will carry on for a while. The *Reichskanzler* may let them throw a few stones at our poorer *landsmen.* Give Hitler a couple years and he'll be like all the rest. Fat, content with what he has, squirreling away as much as he can in a numbered Swiss bank account for the day he leaves office."

"My uncle talks a brave game. I disagree. Hitler's is a dangerous madman. Anyone who attempts to predict what he'll do is a fool." Billy found himself staring into the largest, deepest eyes he'd ever seen, green with pale yellow flecks. The woman's oval-shaped, freckled face was framed by shoulder-length auburn hair. Billy felt an electric shock.

"Gentlemen, I don't know how outspoken women are in your countries, but it's certainly not Jewish tradition to silence our relatives. Frieda, may I introduce you to Herr Edwin Baumueller of the New York *World* and Herr Billy Jenkins. Gentlemen, my niece, Frieda Schönemann."

"I'm pleased to meet you both. I'm sorry I missed my cousin's wedding, Herr Jenkins. She's always spoken very highly of you." Her voice was warm. She was about five feet five inches tall, slender, and most attractive. She wore the new Chanel look, which accentuated her slight but definite feminine curves. Frieda Schönemann wore no scent. Billy noticed a clean, light aroma when he stood near her. Although he'd sworn off all serious romantic entanglements after Ksenija's death, he found himself wondering what she would look like beneath the dress. Would her whole body be as freckled as her face? He felt a hot flush suffuse his neck. The woman appeared not to notice.

"Do you find Berlin much different since the Nazis came to power, Herr Jenkins?"

"It's a little early to make a judgment, Fräulein … Frau …?"

"Either is fine. I was widowed three years ago."

"I'm sorry," he replied, feeling not the least bit sorry. He tried to hide the trip-hammer pounding he felt in his chest. "The parks seem neater and greener. The shops are filled with much more nowadays."

"Yes," she murmured. "The Germans have always been very meticulous. They work together like cogs in a well-oiled machine. Why shouldn't they? They are the sons and daughters of the gods." Billy said nothing. Frieda Schönemann continued, "They give minute attention to detail. Every rose in our municipal gardens must be perfect. Every tree must be just so. They say the Führer wishes to purify the German race along the same lines."

"You appear to be a well-informed German citizen."

"You are wrong, Herr Jenkins. I understand you're classified as a *mischling* and have special papers to protect you. I'm a full-blooded *Jewish* German citizen. That makes a rather significant difference."

"Darling, sshhh," her uncle interjected. "You never know who might be listening."

She continued, caustically mimicking her uncle. "Sssh. You never know who might be listening. It doesn't matter who hears, Uncle Bernhard. We are doomed if we stay in Germany. And it won't only be us. There are gypsies and Catholics, Communists, Slavs,..." Billy looked directly at this beautiful, sophisticated woman. "You heard me correctly, Herr Jenkins. Turks, Russians, Frenchmen, it doesn't really matter. Have you ever been an outsider? I mean a *real* outsider? Do you have any sense of what it means to be an outcast simply because of an accident of birth? Have you ever known what it is to foresee your future in a cracked mirror, knowing you are tied to that future because you haven't the courage to make the right decision?"

"Frau Schönemann, Herr Schönemann, Herr Baumueller, I would very much like to continue this conversation in a more private setting." He looked at his wristwatch. "But, much as I would like to do so now, Herr Göring has signaled that I must prepare to be on stage in twenty minutes."

"I understand," Frieda said. "Your leader commands and you obey." She looked at him strangely. "Perhaps our paths may cross again."

~ ∫ ~

"Ladies and gentlemen, *Herren und Damen*," Göring said in a firm voice. "We are privileged to have with us tonight a member of the Party, a source of immense pride to the Reich, and my personal friend, *Der Koenig der Cowboys* – our very own international star of stars, Billy Jenkins!"

The technicians had set Billy's stage, an elevated wooden platform, in the center of the room. A huge, blood-red Nazi flag hung suspended from the rafters above his head. Because of the limited space and the proximity of the crowd, his act was limited to his yarns – accompanied by guitars, a harmonica, and a quartet of male vocalists clad in cowboy outfits with swastikas on their shirts – and his roping act. Thinking about Frieda Schönemann, he felt guiltily conscious of the fact that his Stetson hat and the sheriff's badge he wore were also emblazoned with swastikas. At the conclusion of his act, the singers and musicians segued into the *Horst Wesel Song*, followed by *Deutschland Deutschland Über Alles*, which brought the assembled crowd to its feet.

As he left the stage, Billy was assaulted by a series of uncomfortable and conflicting feelings: a bold stab of lust for Frieda Schönemann combined with a need to hold her, comfort her, assure her that everything would be all right. But he was uncertain if things *would* work out for this Jewess, who, he knew, was indeed an outsider. Billy was troubled. Deeply troubled.

~ ∫ ~

A few nights later, Billy received an invitation to dine at Bernhard Schönemann's home. When he arrived at the elegant estate in a chauffeured Mercedes, he was surprised to see a pair of uniformed officers wearing Swastika arm bands, standing just outside the electric gate.

"It's a good thing I'm not in my own car," Billy remarked to his driver, feeling the guards' sinister look. "I'm certain they've marked our arrival."

Once inside the gates, there was no hint of anything amiss. The large sedan crunched over the circular driveway. As it stopped in front of the entryway to the two-story, classic structure with its pseudo-Greek columns, a footman promptly opened the car's door. Billy did not miss the tiny red, white and black Nazi flag pinned to his lapel.

As Billy entered the heavy oak double doors, he found himself in a rich, tastefully furnished hallway. A butler led them to the formal dining room, where a teakwood table was set with Bohemian crystal, English bone china, and German silverware, all in the best of taste. A crystal chandelier, which matched the glassware, hung suspended from a high marble ceiling.

"Good evening Herr Jenkins. I'm so pleased you could come on such short notice." Bernhard Schönemann was dressed in an elegant black tuxedo with maroon bow tie and matching cummerbund.

"It is indeed my pleasure," Billy answered, nodding his head formally. "It's my first night out since the command performance at the ministry the other night."

"My niece will be down momentarily," Schönemann continued. "Since the night of the Reichstag fire, the Führer's decided to post sentries about the homes of Berlin's wealthier Jews. Frieda's quite nervous about it, although I've tried to convince her it's simply another ploy to show the extent of the Reich Chancellor's control."

"I can well understand her fear, Herr Schönemann. The proximity of such guards would concern me as well."

"As I'm certain it's meant to do, Herr Jenkins. The display of power has always been a German characteristic."

"And we women are expected to sit by and watch as our brave men play their cat-and-mouse games." Frieda Schonemann entered the room, looking exquisite in a pale peach evening gown. Her words jarred Billy.

"Enough," their host said genially. "We've invited our new friend for a pleasant social evening. I refuse to spoil it just because a couple of ruffians want to brave the chill night air outside our gates."

The servant who'd greeted them in the entry hall, held out Frieda's chair. He was a dignified old man, bewhiskered in the courtly manner of the old Germany.

"Ludwig's been a family retainer for... how long?" Bernhard asked, glancing up.

"Forty-one years, Herr Schönemann. Before that, I served your father, Sir."

"Tell me, Ludwig, what do you think of all this National Socialist buildup?"

"I'm not political, Sir. I'm surprised that von Hindenburg entered into an alliance with them."

"The old man's senile, Ludwig."

"Still, Herr Schönemann, he does have a following in Germany."

"There, Uncle Bernhard," Frieda interrupted. "Does that show you these people are serious?" Her smile was bleak. Billy felt the tension in the room.

"Achh, it's nothing," her uncle said. "A consolidation of power, nothing more."

The servant turned and discreetly left the room. Immediately Frieda became more composed. "I'm sorry if I've upset you," she said, turning her gaze to Billy, "but I felt you should get an objective view of what's going on."

"Herr Schönemann," Billy spoke up. "I don't for a moment doubt you, but just in case there's some validity to what your niece says, have you arranged for any options?"

"There's no need for them," the merchant said smoothly, signaling a servant to bring some white wine. "Even if the Chancellor should extend his Jew-baiting games, the German people would never go along with it. They know we're all loyal Germans and that the loss of the merchant class would cripple their already weak economy."

"But what if things truly did get worse? What if Hitler closed the borders?"

Frieda was looking directly at him. He felt an alliance between them, but more than that, he felt a renewal of the lightning jolt he'd felt the night of the ministry party. Her eyes were dazzling, but it was her presence that moved him most.

"Close the borders, Herr Jenkins? I should think he'd open them and help the Jews be on their way if he truly wanted to dispose of them," Schönemann said.

"Would you leave the Reich, Uncle?" Frieda asked. "You have half a dozen department stores. How easily could you give up the stores, this estate, our naïvely spoiled way of life?"

Schönemann sat in silence for awhile, chewing a bit of the perfectly prepared roast brisket. He did not seem the least bit upset by his niece's outburst. When he spoke, his tone was quiet, thoughtful. "I would find it very hard to leave such a life, Frieda. Praise God it will never happen during our lifetimes."

"I don't mean to be impolite, Uncle, but we women have a stronger intuition than you might realize. Nothing good can come of this."

"That's not necessarily so, Frieda. Our unemployment lines shrink each day. There's food and money in circulation. Even I have to admit that things seem better now than they did a few months ago. There's a sense of dedication."

"But dedication to what, Uncle? And at whose expense? It seems this economy is fueled on terror, on compliant silence. We're no longer free to say what we please. There's no telling when we might need a safe harbor."

"Perhaps one day we shall look for one, Herr Jenkins," Bernhard Schönemann said. "But for the present, I am too taken up with our businesses. We've just introduced the spring line. In another month it'll be time to consider our autumn selection of ladies' apparel."

After dinner, Bernhard invited his guests to sit on the veranda and enjoy a bracing Berlin spring evening. They'd been outside a quarter of an hour when the sky clouded over. A swift thunderstorm drove them inside, but within the hour it cleared and a bright crescent moon appeared. "A good omen," Bernhard remarked. "Just as the storm has passed us by leaving the beautiful silver light of the moon, so will the problems we discussed earlier pass as well."

~ ʃ ~

A few nights later, Billy was walking in the Unter den Linden after attending *Grand Hotel*, one of the few American films being shown in Germany these days. As he approached the intersection of Unter den Linden and Museumstrasse, he was attracted by a large crowd outside Schönemann's Department Store. Fifty brown-shirted SA troops had cordoned off the area around the store. They bore signs that read *"Deutsche! Wehrt Gut! Kauft nicht bei Juden!"* Several other toughs were plastering garishly colored signs all over the front walls, printed in German, which exhorted, "Germans! Arm yourselves against Jewish atrocity propaganda! Buy only at German shops!" The doors to the department store were locked. Iron bars covered the windows. Half a dozen brown shirts smashed at the protective coverings with sledge hammers. Billy shuddered.

"Could I be wrong? Could Frieda be right?" he murmured to himself. "I must ask Herrmann about this." Then, feeling not a little like a coward and a fool, he turned the corner and walked quickly away from what he'd seen.

39

"I can't believe it, Herrmann. The Party's *giving* me seventeen hectares in Reinickendorf?"

"Happy fiftieth birthday, my friend. You've been a loyal National Socialist. We take care of our own."

"But this is prime hectarage. Wasn't this part of the Wassermann holdings?"

"It might have been, Billy. Herr Wassermann is no longer involved."

Billy looked over the rolling hills adjacent to the *Tegel See*, the largest lake in northwestern Berlin. He could not understand how such a plum had fallen in his lap. He'd been trying to get a lesser piece of land for half a dozen years, but Wassermann had wanted a king's ransom for the ten hectares Billy had been interested in buying. Still, survival in the Reich meant not looking too far beneath the surface of what presented.

"Far enough from Greenwich Promenade that you can have your privacy, close enough to go into town if you need to."

"It's perfect, Herrmann. How can I possibly thank the Party?"

"By continuing to do what you do so well, and by building your dream house as soon as possible. We must have it finished by spring of next year. The Government will help defray the cost of construction."

"Why such generosity?"

"It's not generosity, my friend. The Reich intends get back every Reichsmark we spend within six months after it's built."

The two men ambled along the *Tegel See*. "How's Emmy? I hope she's not upset that I couldn't come to the wedding."

"She knew you were doing your patriotic duty, Billy, performing in Switzerland and bringing hard currency back to the Reich. You didn't ask how we're going to get the money back."

"I gather it has something to do with next year's Olympics."

"Correct. We thought you'd get it built – with our help, of course – live in it for a couple of months, and let us borrow it for private events during the Olympiad."

"Done," Billy said, grinning. "I understand the Führer's quite a talented architect. Perhaps he and Speer could help me design it?"

"I think that would give them both the greatest pleasure."

~ ʃ ~

"You don't mind Herr Lindbergh passing on the plans?" Speer asked.

"Lucky Lindy, a *genuine* American hero? I should say not!"

They were seated in Albert Speer's huge suite in the Department of Engineering and Architecture, adjacent to the monumental public buildings in downtown Berlin. The day was crisp and cold, heralding the approaching north German winter, but the first snows had not yet fallen.

"Good. He's a great friend of Germany. We need as many positive spokesmen we can get."

As Lindbergh looked over the plans, he marveled at the accuracy of the re-creation of a miniature frontier town straight out of the Old West. "How big is the ranch house?" he asked Speer.

"Seven hundred square meters."

Lindbergh whistled. "About the size of eight ordinary houses in the States."

"Five bedrooms, four baths, a ballroom big enough to hold a hundred people."

"Your design, Albert?"

"A lot of hands, German and American."

Just then, the Führer came into the room, dressed casually and looking relaxed.

"Heil Hitler!" Billy said, snapping to attention and giving the Nazi salute.

"Relax, Herr Jenkins, you need not jump to your feet. This is not a Party rally. How do you like the ranch house?"

"Brilliant, my Führer. Utterly brilliant."

"I hoped you'd like it. What do you think of the layout?"

"That's the best thing of all. Plenty of room for privacy, and wonderful facilities for entertaining."

"I thought that myself," Hitler said proudly. "Do you think it looks like the *real* American West, Herr Lindbergh?"

"Pretty damned close, Chancellor. When do you plan to start construction?"

Hitler looked at Speer. "I'd say within the month, my Führer," Speer replied.

~ ∫ ~

Billy was amazed at the speed at which the work progressed. Although he'd never been involved in the construction trades, over the years he'd heard stories of innumerable delays, one tradesman blaming another, deadlines missed, slipshod quality, and projects where there'd be weeks without a worker on site.

Not so on Billy's ranch. No less than sixty workers showed up every day, all dressed exactly alike in gray slacks and gray work shirts. Each worker shambled or shuffled when he walked, and seemed frightened, as if there were evil spirits lurking at his back. Had Billy been more attentive, he might have noticed that no workman spent more than a week at the project and thereafter was never seen again. The laborers worked from sunrise to an hour after sunset, seven days a week.

On one occasion, Billy saw someone he thought looked vaguely familiar. As he came closer, he saw with a shock that it was the man who had formerly owned every plot of developable land in Reinickendorf. "Wassermann?" he asked.

"Used to be," the derelict-looking man answered. "Now just number 1596269," he continued, showing his right forearm to the German celebrity.

"How …?"

But Wassermann had disappeared among the rest of the workers, a gray shadow, nothing more.

~ ∫ ~

By April 1936, the work was completed. Hitler, Göring, and Speer accompanied Billy on horseback around the perimeter, which took the better part of two hours. During the ride, Billy noted with amusement how uncomfortable and downright silly each of these powerful men seemed in the saddle. He said nothing.

The ranch spread over seventeen hectares – forty American acres. As they rode, Billy pointed out the ten-horse stable, riding arena, riding trails, and fields of Saguaro cactus, mesquite, dust, and rocks – a transplanted piece of west Texas wasteland – in the midst of copious forests and bountiful lakes, less than fifteen kilometers northwest of the center of Berlin. There were a dozen wooden "Indian teepees," each large enough to comfortably house six people.

Billy noticed that Propaganda Minister Goebbels was not present, even though he had sent one reporter each from *Der Angriff* and the even larger *Völkischer Beobachter*.

"How many cowboys and cowgirls will be tour guides during the Games?" *Reichsmarschall* Göring asked the majordomo in charge of publicity.

"Thirty on each four-hour shift. Trained to rope and ride like American natives. At least five will speak *American* idiomatic English. The rest will speak whatever languages they need to speak, as long as they're Western European."

"And Indians?" Hitler asked.

"Three or four on a shift, my Führer. They're actually Turks, who are dark-skinned enough, and you can find them anywhere. They don't need to do anything but mumble, wear headdresses, and jump around like they're doing some sort of dance."

"Good, good. Well, Herr Jenkins, what do you think?"

"It's more authentic than I believed possible, Führer. When does the State take possession?"

"Next month, if it's convenient with you."

"It is."

~ ∫ ~

Two weeks before the opening ceremonies, the Nazi Party held a grand opening gala at Billy's ranch house. Although there was a huge American-style feast, the center of attention was neither the spacious house nor the plenipotentiaries in attendance. Rather, all eyes seemed to focus on a twelve-inch screen on which flickering black-and-white images appeared. "It's a television set," a spokesman explained to the guests. "Our Olympic games will be the first in history to have live television coverage. The Post Office will broadcast coverage to special viewing rooms throughout Berlin."

As Billy wandered through the great room, shaking hands and mingling with the select crowd, he picked up snatches of conversation.

"Has Leni Riefenstahl really been commissioned to film the games?"

"Yes. The Führer's approved funds for the production of *Olympia*. It'll be second only to *Triumph of the Will.*"

After an hour of meandering, Billy announced, "Ladies, gentlemen, if you don't mind, I think I'll mosey outside for a breath of this wonderful spring air." As he ambled toward the nearest fabricated wigwam, two voices called out to him from behind a group of trees. "Guv'nor? Guv'nor? Over here."

When Billy walked in the direction of the voices, he saw two frail, elderly men. The moon illuminated their sickly pallor and the noticeable limp of one of them. An odor of cheap wine emanated from the other. "Who are …? Freddie? Ferdie? My God, what happened to you?"

"You don't want to hear about it, Guv'nor."

"Last I heard, you were on the Donnert. I thought you'd be with them forever."

"We tried to make it on the Dumas," Ferdie said. "They promised we could start in June. Too late."

"What do you mean?"

"Two months ago, they rounded up a group of us. Homosexuals, gypsies, those they believed to be mentally retarded," Freddie said.

"We weren't given a chance to protest. Not even to see a lawyer," Ferdie continued. He broke down and started crying. "Sent us to Dachau."

"Concentration camp?"

"They said we'd been brought there to check out our health in the infirmary – to make sure we hadn't contracted any diseases because of … because of the way we were."

"Check us out, my arse!" Freddie said. "Bloody bastards said they were going to put us under for an hour. Next thing we know, they'd … they'd castrated us."

Half a year ago, Billy had seen with his own eyes the Nazi excesses perpetrated on Schönemann's Department Store and other Jewish-owned businesses. Earlier in the month, he'd seen the once wealthy Wassermann reduced to a common laborer. Now, this. Billy was starting to wonder in earnest whether he'd made a deal with the devil.

"Couldn't the Donnert protect you?"

"Guv'nor, *no one* could protect us. No one even raised a voice to complain. When it comes to protection here, it's each man for himself," Freddie said, bitterly.

"So now our lives are over," Ferdie added.

"You can stay here as long as you want. I'll make sure you have jobs …"

"No, Guv'nor," Ferdie said sadly. "We can stay here only as long as *they* want. For God's sake, Billy Jenkins, open your eyes before it's too late."

~ ∫ ~

"Your performance at the opening was appreciated," Goebbels said with no hint of emotion. Electric fans kept the *Reichminister's* offices tolerably cool, despite the sizzling early August temperature in Berlin.

"Thank you, Herr Minister," Billy replied neutrally He harbored no illusions about their mutual dislike of one another.

"I trust you heard my opening remarks, Herr Jenkins?"

"I did. And the Führer's as well. I was most impressed by his speech."

"I wrote that, of course," Goebbels said. "He delivered the words quite well. He always does. We must promote the Reich to friends and enemies alike. Show our friends we can be powerful allies. Convince our enemies, like Spain, that it would not be in their best interests to further alienate us."

"Spain, *Reichsminister?*"

"Not the *Spanish*, Jenkins. Their Bolsheviki government. Can you imagine, when they lost out on their bid to have the Olympic Games, they boycotted our Olympics and organized their own so-called 'People's Olympiad' in Barcelona. Fortunately, forty-nine nations are here. The Communists and Jew-lovers in the United States were unable to convince Herr Brundage that America should withdraw from the *real* Olympics."

"I see that all of the anti-Jewish signs have been taken down."

"For the duration, Herr Jenkins," Goebbels said coolly. "We don't need to upset our guests unnecessarily."

"Is there a reason you asked me to come over this morning?"

"Yes, Herr Jenkins. I've just received word that a Civil War has broken out in Spain. It started one day before their *ersatz* Olympiad was to commence."

~ ∫ ~

"So the Reich is supporting the Nationalist Rebels?"

"We prefer to call them the legitimate government. Of course, the Soviet Union is backing the so-called 'Loyalist Republicans,'" Goebbels replied.

"May I ask what this has to do with me?"

"You're an internationally prominent figure, Herr Jenkins. The Führer feels a man of your stature would be a most powerful goodwill ambassador."

"You've talked with him about this?"

"He agrees entirely with my idea."

"And Reichsmarschall Göring?"

"I don't see where it's any of his concern."

Billy considered the implications of what the propaganda chief was saying. On the one hand, Billy's popularity throughout Europe would enhance the Reich's reputation and his own. On the other hand, what Goebbels suggested would get Billy out of the way and into a backwater of Europe. Billy was known to be close with the Reichsmarschall. Equally well known, Göring and Goebbels were each competing with the other for the Führer's favor.

"I think I'd like to get the Reichsmarschall's views on your proposal," Billy said.

"What?" Goebbels exploded. "You *dare* question the Führer's orders?"

"I don't recall hearing an order from Herr Hitler," Billy rejoined, by no means afraid of Goebbels.

As quickly as he had erupted, the propaganda minister cooled down. "All right. Let's say you talk with Herr Göring and he approves?"

"That would be fine. I wouldn't need to trouble the Führer with such things. I'm sure he has more important concerns than a circus performer. Assuming I go along with this, when would you expect me to go?"

"December. That will allow you to finish your regular schedule in time to go south while we have to shiver in the winter cold. Of course, we'd expect you to take your circus with you."

"Of course. How long would you – would the State – want me to stay?"

"Not beyond the end of May."

~ ∫ ~

"I'd recommend you do it, Billy," the Reichsmarschall said. "In the military, you get promoted faster when you serve on the front lines.

The Führer intends to use the Spanish Civil War to show Germany's emerging military might. If you're there supporting our troops, it can only enhance your own career, not that you need it. What do you have to lose?"

"Half a year's worth of popularity in the Reich."

"I very much doubt that. There's got to be something else."

"Yes, Herrmann, there is. Ksenija …."

"That was a long time ago, my friend. And life goes on. Perhaps you could give Spain a chance to make it up to you."

~ ∫ ~

The loyalist Republicans, supported by the Soviet Union and Mexico, were concentrated in the places closest to Billy's heart, Catalunya and the Basque Country, where he and Ksenija had so happily started their tragic honeymoon.

When Billy and his entourage entrained for Genoa, Göring himself came to the station to give Billy and his lieutenants a briefing on what to expect. "The loyalists hold Madrid, Valencia, a good part of the south, and a piece of the Basque country. Our allies, the rebels, control most of northern and northwestern Spain and the southern part of Andalusia including Seville."

"Reichsmarschall, do we actually have troops in Spain?" Billy asked.

"Two thousand advisors, mostly stationed in Portugal. Salazar's friendly to the Reich."

Billy glanced at the schedule which had been carefully orchestrated by the Propaganda Ministry, and the map showing where the show would appear. "Once we get out of Barcelona, it looks like we'll be playing in the Nationalist strongholds. As his fingers traced the map, he hesitated in one spot and looked at Göring. "San Sebastian? I thought we discussed …"

"Actually not in San Sebastian itself, Billy. I appreciate how sensitive you are to that. We believe that by the time you get to that area, it will be under Rebel control. You'll actually be playing in a small market town of no consequence outside of San Sebastian. It's so inconsequential I don't know of anyone who's ever even heard of it. It's called Guernica."

40

In mid-December 1936, the troupers arrived in Genoa, where they boarded the Hapag-Lloyd ship bound for Barcelona. Although the city, was nominally in Republican hands, it considered itself to be independent of Spain altogether. It was, after all, Catalunya, not Castille. While Barcelona had expanded dramatically in the years since Billy and Dieter Hoffman had last been there, the *Sagrada Familia* did not look like anything had been done to it since the last time they'd seen it.

"Alas, the Maestro came to an unfortunate end ten years ago," Dieter said. "For the last forty years of his life, he refused to walk in the street because he had an overwhelming dread that he'd be killed in a traffic accident."

"How *did* the man die?" Billy asked.

"His friends ultimately convinced him his fears were silly, so he finally left the *Sagrada Familia*. While he was crossing the street, he was hit by a tram. He might have survived, but he was dressed so shabbily that taxicab drivers refused to pick him up and take him to the hospital. They didn't think he'd have been able to afford the fare."

The circus encountered no problems in Barcelona, nor in the next cities where they played, Tarragona, Castellón and Valencia. The warmth along Spain's Mediterranean coast was matched by the exuberance of the audiences who came to cheer the "American" King of the Cowboys and his entourage. Every show was filled to capacity. Germany happily accepted the money, even if it came from those areas at war with the Nationalist rebels.

"We've had a great time, eh, Billy?" Dieter said one day in late February when the circus train chugged leisurely north toward Madrid.

"Thank goodness we haven't seen anything resembling war."

"We aren't in the war zone yet," André van Damm said. "We're still in the Republican area. I imagine we'll start to see more action once we're northwest of the capital. They say there are nineteen thousand German troops in Spain, fighting on the *other* side."

"*Wehrmacht?*"

"Officially, several thousand *volunteers.*"

"Unofficially?"

"Sixteen squadrons of *Luftwaffe.*"

"Over one hundred aircraft," Dieter said, whistling.

"Actually one hundred thirty-six," a voice said. They'd been joined by a young German lieutenant dressed in an Air Force uniform, who'd boarded the train at Albacete. "Might I please to join you?"

"Of course," Billy replied. "We're happy to have you. I'm Billy Jenkins," he said, reaching out to shake the young man's hand.

"The famous cowboy? I am honored. Leutnant Heinrich Trettner."

Dieter Hoffman passed out German cigarettes and soon the four men were discussing the circumstances that had brought them to this southwest corner of Europe. "This is the first time in a week I've been able to wear the German uniform," Trettner said. "Our Command sent me down to reconnoiter the Republican territory."

"If you're meant to be a spy, *Leutnant*, you don't look the part," Billy said. "You hardly fit the picture of the native Spaniard."

"So I'm told, but since I'm one of the few volunteers who's fluent in Spanish, they made do with what they had."

"Surely there are Spanish Nationalists …?"

"Yes, but Commander von Richthofen wanted first-hand information from a German. He doesn't trust our allies that much. They're still Spaniards, you know."

"Von Richtofen?" Dieter broke in, his eyes widening. "The Red Baron?"

"That was Manfred von Richthofen, who was shot down and killed almost nineteen years ago. This one's Wolfram Freiherr von Richthofen, a distant cousin. He's commander of my unit at Burgos."

"Should you be telling us these things, *Leutnant*?" Andre van Damm asked. "Aren't they military secrets?"

"What military? We're all *volunteers*. The three of you are obviously supporters. I first learned your circus was in Spain when Commander von Richthofen mentioned you'd be up near Bilbao in April. He said he was going to ask Colonel Sperrle if you could put on a show for the Condor Legion at Burgos."

~ ʃ ~

From the outskirts of Madrid, which was in Rebel hands and where they played for two weeks, the troupers learned that the fighting had become so vicious on both sides that trains no longer ran between the areas controlled by each of the warring factions. The German volunteers provided three heavy trucks, which bore German license plates and traveled under the protection of the Reich Foreign Ministry.

After a week in Toledo – "It's an El Greco painting come to life," van Damm marveled – they entered Nationalist territory as they came into Salamanca Province.

A surprisingly large number of Germans, Italians, and Portuguese attended the Billy Jenkins Combined Circus show in the beautiful city situated on a mountain several hundred feet above the Tormes River. After their one week stay in Salamanca, the circus next played for two weeks in Valladolid, an industrial center more than twice as populous as the city they'd just left. Where Salamanca had always been a Christian city, Valladolid had originally been Moorish. The Billy Jenkins Show pitched its tober in the Plaza Mayor, adjacent to City Hall.

While Valladolid was by no means as stunningly located as Salamanca, Billy, Dieter Hoffman, and André van Damm found tremendous satisfaction in the local cuisine.

Whenever a place offered seafood in its various forms, Van Damm made it a point to seek out as many restaurants and purveyors of fish and shellfish as he could.

"I'm sorry to say you won't find much here to satisfy you," Dieter said.

"That's where you're wrong, *Schweizer*," the Dutchman replied convivially. "They bring red bream and hake from the Cantabrian Sea. Like the Portuguese, they conjure up a hundred different ways to cook fish. Plus, they've got all kinds of wild mushrooms, asparagus, pine nuts, *pata de mulo.*"

"Mule's leg?" Billy arched his eyebrows.

"A wonderfully sharp local cheese," van Damm said. "I could eat a different dish at each meal for a month."

"And you'd weigh one hundred fifty kilos by the time we left Valladolid. I'd be happy to eat their *lechazo* every day of my life."

"I agree," Dieter said. "Roast lamb has always been one of my favorites. Looks like we're going to see more than Germans in Burgos," he said, changing the subject.

"Trettner told us the Condor Legion was stationed there and he was trying to get us rerouted to the Air Force Base, but he neglected to tell us it's Generalissimo Franco's Nationalist capital. Add another week to the schedule." Billy sighed dramatically.

~ ∫ ~

On April 20, the circus arrived in Burgos. Leutnant Trettner met Billy at the train.

"I can't tell you how pleased I am that your show is here, Herr Jenkins. The Commandant has authorized me to give you a special tour of the Condor Air Base."

~ ∫ ~

"Right now, we have three groups at Burgos stationed," Leutnant Trettner said, as he and the King of the Cowboys walked down row after row of aircraft. "Everything from these old Heinkel 51 fighters," he said, patting the side of a vintage wooden biplane, "to the one I fly."

"Which is?"

"They're parked in their own hangars in a special section just beyond the line of aircraft ahead. I'll let you see for yourself."

As the two men had traversed the tarmac, Trettner pointed out the Junkers-52 *Behelfsbombers,* converted Deutsche Lufthansa airliners; the strange looking Dornier-17 flying pencil; and the much larger Heinkel-111 bombers. Soon they arrived at a series of hangars at the far end of the line. When Billy entered the first of the hangars, his eyes widened and his jaws hung slack. "My God, that looks like it's flying and it's just *sitting* there!"

"That's what I thought when I first saw it. I've never flown anything like it, and I'll wager very few other pilots have." Trettner said proudly. "I can truthfully say this is the best fighter anyone will ever build!"

The aluminum bird looked stunning, with its large three-bladed propeller, low body, and rounded tail. Trettner continued, "It can fly over six hundred kilometers per hour."

"Twice as fast as an airliner!" Billy exclaimed.

"That's the Messerschmitt Bf-109."

Billy said nothing, but thought to himself, *Why would Germany need such a monster unless it intends to become involved in a serious war? But why would Germany be interested in war? Didn't it learn its lesson less than twenty years ago?*

~ ∫ ~

Members of the Condor Legion and their supporting 'volunteers' stood and stamped and clapped wildly throughout the show. Like young men far away from home, the audience was homesick. The Billy Jenkins show was a most welcome taste of the way things were back in the *Vaterland,* and, for the older ones, a poignant reminder of a more peaceful time not so long ago.

~ ∫ ~

On Saturday afternoon, April 24, 1937, Billy and his combined show departed Burgos for Guernica. For the first time since they'd left Madrid more than a month before, the troupers entered Republican territory. Franco's Nationalist troops had eaten into the area controlled by the Republican Government. The Basque Government, which supported the Republicans, sought to defend the remaining Loyalist enclave, particularly the large city of Bilbao, with its own Basque army.

Neither side had any military presence in the small market town of Guernica, the show's next scheduled stop. This civilian enclave wanted nothing to do with the war. Neither its population nor Billy Jenkins and his troupe had the remotest idea that Guernica stood between the Nationalists and the capture of Bilbao, which the Nationalists saw as the key to bringing the war to a conclusion in northern Spain. Guernica was also the path of retreat for the Republicans from the northeast.

The three trucks bearing the Billy Jenkins show arrived in Guernica twenty-four hours after leaving Burgos. "Billy," the orchestra leader addressed him, "we're not scheduled to play until Tuesday matinee. The crew can easily set up tomorrow without you. I thought maybe – "

"I know what you're going to say André. I've thought the same myself. I can't keep running away from the memory, can I?"

"San Sebastian's not that far. You could easily be back by Tuesday noon."

"Maybe you're right. God, it's hard to believe it's been almost twenty years. Where did the time go?"

"I don't know, my friend. But when you get past seventy, like me, it goes mighty quickly."

~ ∫ ~

By Sunday evening, Billy had had more than enough of the idyllic town where he and Ksenija had started their all-too-brief honeymoon. He decided to take the early morning train back to Guernica the following day.

~ ∫ ~

"*Today?* You've got this planned for *today, Oberstleutnant*t?"

"Don't worry, Heinrich. The Messerschmitts will only fly over in the last wave."

"But Herr Jenkins and his friends are there right now. "I've got to warn them …"

"I'm sorry, *Leutnant,* our orders are *no* communications – *none at all* – until it's over. And those are *your* orders as well."

"But …?"

"That's all, Leutnant Trettner. Be prepared to go at 1530 hours."

"*Jawohl,* Herr Commandant."

~ ∫ ~

"Billy? What are you doing back so soon?"

"André, you can't imagine how lonely San Sebastian can be, especially when it's filled with so many memories. Ksenija was everywhere, but when I opened my eyes she was nowhere."

"I suppose if you had to come back, this was as good a time as any to return. Monday's market day in Guernica. The whole town – so far as I can tell the whole countryside – will mill around market square until just after sundown. We may as well get lost among the crowd. No sense in going until we've pitched the tober, though. Shouldn't take more than a couple of hours."

~ ∫ ~

At 4:30 that afternoon, Billy, Dieter Hoffman, and André van Damm were nibbling on sweet pastries they'd just purchased when they heard whistling sounds, followed by a series of concussive explosions. Moments later, a Dornier light bomber passed over the town square from south to north, some two thousand feet above them.

"Looks like we may finally see a piece of the war," Hoffman remarked.

"Who'd want to drop bombs on a small civilian town that's not even involved?" This from vanDamm. "What the h---?"

His voice was drowned out as three more planes, Italian from the insignia on their tails, zoomed over the town from the opposite direction. Moments later, they heard the noise of *many* bombs exploding and saw a man run into the square shouting, "They've destroyed the bridge and the road east!"

"The Church, the Church!" a woman screamed. "It's been hit!"

Things had just started to quiet down when two giant He-111 bombers escorted by five Italian fighters dropped a far heavier load of bombs, destroying most of the town, killing and injuring hundreds of civilians who'd done nothing but come to the market.

"The circus tent!" Billy shouted to everyone within hearing. "The Germans will know it's our show and they won't bomb it! We'll set up a hospital there!"

He, vanDamm, and Hoffman managed to organize a hundred locals who'd not been hit. These men and women looked around for carts or whatever else they could find to follow Billy's instructions. The able-bodied were just starting south toward the pennants flying over the big top when the fourth wave, eighteen tri-motor Ju-52 bombers, rained further death and destruction on the town.

"*Andre!*" Dieter screamed, rushing toward the elderly musician.

Billy dropped the small cart he'd been hauling and ran to the side of his fatally injured comrade. "Andre - ?" Then Billy saw the gaping hole from the man's neck to his stomach. What had been his friend's intestines were already starting to spill out. Van Damm, unable to breathe, drowned in his own blood.

Billy howled in agony and frustration, but his voice was cut off when a fifth wave, fifteen German bombers, escorted by Messerschmitt Bf-109 fighters pounded the town into rubble. He barely heard Dieter Hoffman's muffled "I'm hit! I'm hit! Oh,. Christ! Mama! Mama!" before a truck that had been bombed, rolled over on him. The king of the cowboys fell unconscious, both his legs shattered.

If the aerial attacks had stopped at that moment, the town would have suffered a totally disproportionate and insufferable punishment. However, the biggest part of *Operation Rugen* was yet to come. Within a quarter hour, three squadrons of the Condor Legion – one hundred thirty-six planes plus another dozen Italian escort fighters – attacked the defenseless civilian town, three bombers abreast — an attack front 150 meters across. At the same time, and continuing for twenty minutes after the bombing wave, Bf 109Bs and Heinkel He 51 biplanes strafed the roads leading out of town, adding to civilian casualties.

The screams grew fewer and turned to desperate moans as more perished in what later became known as the first carpet bombing of a totally undefended civilian town in history. By sundown, three quarters of the city's buildings were destroyed. All but four sustained major damage. Of forty-five hundred inhabitants, seventeen hundred had been killed and another nine hundred seriously wounded. Lovely, peaceful Guernica, which played absolutely no part in the vicious civil war, had, to all intents and purposes, ceased to exist.

Within two days, the Nationalist forces claimed they had played no part in the death of Guernica – that the destruction had been caused by Republicans burning the town as they fled, and that only twelve people had died.

When he heard that, something snapped inside Billy Jenkins, who'd barely survived and who'd been evacuated to the Condor Legion hospital at Burgos. He felt unmitigated anger toward the government that had sent him here. As he lay mending in his comfortable hospital bed, he thought: *How could anyone with a shred of decency tolerate the premeditated murder of so many innocent civilians whose only "crime" was that they had come to market expecting to live quiet, peaceful, ordinary lives?*

For the first time, he felt with certainty that he had hitched his star to a cause that was wrong – and worse, that was rotten. But he had cast his lot with these villains, and he saw no way he could escape the prison of his successful existence.

41

Billy, who was now walking with the aid of a cane, returned to performing, albeit to significantly reduced audiences. By the time his fifty-third birthday rolled around, he was in constant pain from the fractures and from the onset of arthritis. While he was no longer capable of voltige riding, he remained an adept marksman, thanks to show trickery, as well as a superb bird trainer. He found it harder and harder to ignore that the venues where he performed, and the number of people who came to see and cheer him on, were becoming progressively smaller.

By December 1938, Billy was happy to accept employment at a party being held at the Turkish Embassy in Vienna. That evening, Billy was surprised to notice the Schönemanns, uncle and niece, on the periphery of the small crowd. They appeared desperately to be signaling him. Bernhard Schönemann was almost unrecognizable. He'd lost twenty-five kilos. His eyes were sunken, red-rimmed. He had a haunted, hopeless look.

"I gather you know what's happened to us," he began. "We've lost almost everything. I fear we'll shortly be receiving documents advising us that we're being `resettled.' Herr Jenkins, I beg you, if you can't help me, can you at least help Frieda?"

Billy winced. He'd heard of these "resettlement" camps. The tales were veiled but sinister. He looked sympathetically at these people. Frieda was thinner than he'd remembered. "Have you any contacts in Turkey? Anyone who would sponsor you? It's a neutral country. If you could make it to Istanbul …"

"The *khakham*, the Jewish spiritual leader … "

"So you could be safe in Istanbul within the month."

"If we can survive that long."

"I'll see what I can do …"

The following day, Billy returned to Berlin via Deutsche Lufthansa's workhorse Ju-52 airliner. He was able to secure an immediate appointment with his old friend, Reichsmarschall Göring, who looked like he'd gained the twenty-five kilos Schönemann had lost in the six months since Billy had last seen him.

"I'll try to help," Göring said absently, somewhat coolly.

Still, Göring did expedite all necessary papers and exit visas, which one of his underlings personally brought to Billy's ranch house. Within three weeks of the morning he'd left Vienna, Billy returned to that *gemütlichkeit* city of Strauss and *Sachertorte*. When he knocked on the door at the address Schönemann had given him, he was greeted by a heavyset, sad-eyed woman. "I'm so sorry," she responded. "The Schönemanns have been resettled. I'm afraid I don't have a forwarding address for them."

~ ∫ ~

"Tom, it was so good of you to come."

"It wasn't that easy, Billy. FDR doesn't care much for your Führer, and I'm sure the feeling's returned. Anyone going in this direction is kinda' suspect nowadays."

"You wrote me you hadn't made a movie since *The Miracle Rider* in 'thirty-five."

"That's how it is when you get to be our age. I hear you got beat up pretty bad in Spain."

"They almost lost me. It's not easy getting old, is it?" The two friends were riding slowly around Billy's forty acres. "Hell, I could no more think of cantering through the fields than I could of flying to the moon. How goes it with that circus you bought?"

"It sure ain't Ringling, but the choice gigs just aren't out there anymore. Lucky for me that feed company wanted to produce the *Tom Mix Ralston Straight Shooters* radio series. They pay me chicken feed compared to what I was making in the movies, but at fifty-nine you take what you can get."

"Don't I know it? This may be the last roundup on this spread for me."

"That bad?"

"That bad, Tom. I always believed I'd never have to worry about money again, but I just can't afford the upkeep on this place. When I looked into what I've got in savings, it was pretty grim."

"You had a big Swiss bank account as I recall."

"*Had.* I bought into Hitler's patriotic talk, took out the money and put it in Reichsmarks and some industries that promised the moon but folded soon after."

Billy and Tom Mix rode to a far corner of the property. When Jenkins had satisfied himself that he was beyond the listening range of anyone, he said softly, "Tom, I've become disgusted with the whole mess …"

"The Führer, the Nazis, the whole Reich thing?"

"Uh-huh. You wouldn't believe what I saw in Spain, and, to tell you the truth, what I've seen going on here. Like everyone else, I turned my back on it. Now it's too late to fight it and I'm scared shitless."

Mix looked at his old friend with sympathy, but said nothing. "D'you think I'd have any kind of chance in the States?"

There was a profound silence.

"You don't have to answer that, my friend," he said sadly. "I can see by your look there's nothing there."

"Shit, Billy. If there was any way I could help … but … aw, hell, I can't find work for *myself* anymore. Ten years ago I was making twenty grand a *week*. Tom Mix, the greatest American cowboy that ever lived. Bullshit. Ten years ago I was a pallbearer at Wyatt Earp's funeral. Now *there* was a *real* cowboy."

The atmosphere on Billy's ranch was one of quiet desperation. Two old men, no longer in their prime, trying to pretend the next break was just around the corner.

"How's your friend Will Rogers?"

"Died four years ago, trying to fly around the world with Wiley Post."

"So the two of us are the only ones left. Neither Dieter nor André survived Guernica. Jürg Knie's gone. Seems I've got no one but my birds to talk to. Let's go into the house," Billy said, dismounting.

When they entered the living room off the kitchen, Billy asked, "Cognac?"

"No coffee?"

Billy looked embarrassed. "I'm trying to keep expenses down. The coffee we get in Germany's mostly chicory and it's expensive. More so than this rot they call cognac, which is guaranteed to be three weeks old."

"You hitting the bottle again, Billy?"

"No. Well … maybe two or three shots a night, but that's just to keep the loneliness at bay."

"I thought you were the darling of the Nazi higher-ups."

"Used to be. Goebbels never liked me. I remind Adolf too much of where he came from. Even Göring's gotten too busy to see me."

"I'd be happy to do anything I can."

"But there's not much you can do, eh, Tom? I don't think I'd be high on the list to get an American visa. I'm afraid I'm married to Germany's little neighborhood, which means Poland, Czechoslovakia, Austria, and Italy."

"Not bad places."

"Not if you're working steadily or have the money to live in the style I was used to living."

Tom Mix spent the night with his old friend. The following morning, after Tom left, Billy found he had left five hundred U.S. dollars on his bed. Billy wept silently.

~ ∫ ~

On March 16, 1939, Billy awoke to hear the *Deutsche Rundfunk* announcer proclaiming, "Last night, the *Wehrmacht* marched into Prague amid reports of savage attacks on German citizens. Thousands of delirious men, women, and children lined the streets of *Stare Mesto, Mala Strana,* and Wenceslas Square as the Führer announced from the Palace Grounds that effective immediately Bohemia and Moravia were becoming protectorates of the Reich ..."

Later that morning, Billy approached the Reichsmarschall's opulent offices. He'd managed to wangle a thirty-minute segment of time in Göring's busy day. He'd used their long friendship to get that appointment. The Air Force leader listened sympathetically to his friend's tale of woe.

"Herrmann, I simply can't afford to keep the place any longer. I appreciate everything you've done, more than I can say, but I have to get out from under."

"Times are tough, Billy. I know that better than anyone. The British will start screaming that the Führer's actions are a betrayal of the so-called Munich Pact. Our Leader is convinced we'll be at war with most of Europe within the year. It must be awfully embarrassing for you to have to come to me."

"It is, but I've got to eat and I've got to keep a roof over my head, and keeping the ranch is eating *me* up. I feel like I'm dangling at the end of a rope."

"The market around Reinickendorf's not good right now. There used to be a lot of Jews up there, but they're all gone now. The social climbers want to be closer to the city. I'll see what I can do."

"What if I were to just turn the place over to the Reich in exchange for some kind of support for the rest of my life?"

"That would be a good deal for both sides. What kind of money are you looking at?"

"I hadn't given it much thought, Herrmann."

"Perhaps we can work something out. If – and I say *if* – we go to war, the troops will always need entertainment. Perhaps we could get you commissioned as an *Oberstleutnant*, a Lieutenant Colonel, as a troop morale officer."

"I'm almost fifty-four. Isn't that kind of old to join the *Wehrmacht*?"

"Not that much older than me, my friend."

~ʃ~

"Date: 15 May 1939

To: Erich Fischer, Professionally known as Billy Jenkins

From: JDFP / H. Stadtmann, Oberst, Commanding

NOTICE OF ORDERS

GREETING: By Order of the Office of Defense, you are hereby appointed *Brevet Oberstleutnant* in the *Heimwehr* for the Districts of Brandenburg and Saxony-Anhalt. Your duties are to arrange for and participate in programs designed to entertain the German *Wehrmacht, Kriegsmarine* and *Luftwaffe* Personnel under the Reich Joint Defense Ministry, and to do and perform such other duties as shall properly be assigned. Your *brevet* rank is confidential and not a matter of public record. You will not wear uniform, insignia, or other manifestations of military office, nor will you be required to engage in active combat should the need arise. Your commission is effective 1 June 1939. You are to report to *Hauptmann* Ernst Warlimont at the Headquarters address listed below. Your pay and allowances will be as set forth in the accompanying schedule ..."

~ ∫ ~

Hauptmann Warlimont, twenty years Billy's junior, was a beefy young man with ruddy complexion. A large map of Germany, Czechoslovakia, Austria, and Italy occupied the wall to the left of his desk. The captain's office was on the third floor of a bauhaus-style, square building adjacent to the Ministry of Armaments in central Berlin.

"Thank you for coming so promptly, *Oberstleutnant*," Warlimont said, snapping his heels together. Billy noticed Warlimont did not salute, most likely because the circus showman was dressed in civilian attire.

"It's my pleasure, Captain," Billy said. "Are you, by any chance, related to General Warlimont?"

"My uncle. That's the first thing everyone seems to ask me. Would you like some coffee, tea?"

"Tea, please."

Warlimont lifted a telephone receiver on his desk and dialed a single number. Within moments, a livery-clad waiter brought in a silver tray with tea service, china cups, and milk biscuits.

"Have a seat, Herr ... do you prefer Fischer or Jenkins?"

"I've been called Billy Jenkins for as long as I can remember."

As Billy sat in an overstuffed chair, Captain Warlimont approached the map with a pointer. "The pins on the map represent military bases. Red is for the *Wehrmacht*, blue for the *Luftwaffe*, yellow for the *Kriegsmarine*."

"None in Czechoslovakia?"

"Not yet."

"And the black pins? I see they're located near Dachau, Terezin in the Bohemian Protectorate, in the southeast of Germany …"

"Well … umm …" Warlimont hesitated, clearly uncomfortable. "I haven't been advised what military units they represent. I think we should work on a schedule of your performances, Colonel Jenkins."

"What size show did you have in mind, *Hauptmann*?"

"Something quite small, really. Yourself, a couple of assistants, tumblers, a couple of clowns, that should do it. You'll be traveling quite a bit. Many of the bases are connected by our new *Autobahnen*, the Führer's military roads."

"I've seen them. Very impressive."

"Our planning department believes you can pack everything into three trucks, and use a small bus for your performers."

"What about roustabouts, *Hauptmann* Warlimont?"

"There'll be more than sufficient men at each base to help you set up."

"No animals?"

"The big cats are far too large and dangerous for so much handling. We can allow for a horse or two. You have a voltige rider?"

"It used to be me. I think the troops would appreciate a couple of pretty young girls much more. Particularly since we won't have a trapeze act. What about my birds?"

"Won't they get nervous traveling every day in strange surroundings?"

"No, they're well trained. They don't take up much room."

"I can't see where they'd be a problem. Let's try them out for a month and see how they work out."

Within half an hour, they'd plotted a circuit through Germany and its allied lands that seemed quite manageable. Billy had only a few more questions.

"Some of these bases are fairly close to cities. Could we play a stand for three days or more, so we could boost the civilians' morale and bring in some extra Reichsmarks for the State?"

"I'd have to clear it with my superiors," Warlimont said. "But until you travel to farther places …"

"Farther places?"

"A slip of the tongue, Herr Jenkins," Warlimont said, embarrassed. "One always hopes we'll have more allies, and if our boys are sent to defend those places, they'll want a taste of home."

~ ∫ ~

"You're sure you want to do this, Billy?"

"It cost me nothing to buy it. I've been away more than I've been here. It's an awfully big and lonely place without someone to warm your bed at night. Heck, at my age, it's more important to have someone to *talk* to at night."

"You know there'll always be a place here for you. If not the ranch house …"

"I think the back of the property would be more useful if it were made into a city park, a place where parents can watch their kids come and play."

"Is there nothing you want to take with you?"

"Not really. As big and beautiful as this place is, the woman I'd hoped to share it with never lived to see it."

"You're a good man, Billy, and a generous one."

"Actually, *Reichsmarschall*, it's you and the State that are generous in taking it off my hands and providing me with insurance for the time I can no longer earn my keep."

42

By July, Billy had settled into a comfortable routine. He ate steadily and well. While his lieutenant colonel's salary was not munificent, neither did he have to worry about the feast or famine elation and frustration of owning and running his own business. If his performances lacked the luster of years past, the compact, appreciative audiences did not seem to notice. The shows were workmanlike and professional, and that's all that seemed to matter.

One afternoon, he chanced to be in Bratislava and wondered what ever had become of his oldest friend, Sammy Lichtenfeld. It had been years since he'd seen Lichtenfeld, and they'd parted on strained terms. He had mixed feelings as he approached the still peaceful neighborhood. Why shouldn't it be quiet? Bratislava was part of the Protectorate. But what would it be like for Jews?

Approaching a certain door, he knocked gingerly. At first there was no response. He knocked louder. "Moment, *bitte.*" He did not recognize the voice. Shortly, the door was opened by a man of twenty-five. His face was neither hostile nor friendly. "Yes?"

"I'm looking for Samuel Lichtenfeld?"

"He does not live here."

The young man looked vaguely familiar. A younger version of Sammy.

"Do you know where he went?"

"I do not. May I ask why you'd want that information?"

"I'm … I'm an old friend of Herr Lichtenfeld and his wife."

"Name?"

"Abrielle. Abrielle Schönemann Lichtenfeld."

"Not *her* name. Yours."

"Erich … Erich … Rosenthal. Billy Jenkins?"

"Uncle Billy?" the young man's face broke into a wide smile. "But you look so much … different."

"So much older? Is that what you're trying to say?"

The man colored slightly. "Well, yes."

"We all get older, and each year goes by more quickly than the last. Arpad?"

"No, Imi. Come in, Uncle Billy. I'm sorry I seemed so suspicious. Things are not easy here. I assume it's worse in the Reich?" As Billy entered, he saw that the furnishings in the house were sparse. "Scotch whisky?"

"No, thank you, Imi. I swore off it some time ago. I'll take a beer if you have one."

"Good. That's all I have." He went into the kitchen and returned with two bottles of warm bock.

"You say things are not easy here, Imi?"

"Not for Jews. Not for anyone. Word's spread that Hitler intends to attack Poland any minute. If that happens, it won't be much of a battle," Imi said cynically. "Messerschmitts and modern tanks against farmers armed with pitchforks and cavalry right out of the eighteenth century. Exactly how long do you think they can hold out?"

"I haven't heard of any such plans."

Imre drank a long draught of beer. "How's the circus business?"

"I don't have one anymore. I'm the hired help, going from base to base providing entertainment for the troops."

"*German* troops, no doubt?."

"Yes – and Austrian, Italian, Czechoslovak ..."

"No Czech or Slovak would willingly fight for the Reich."

"Sudeten Germans, then. If things are so bad for the Jews, why do you stay here?"

"I notice you used the term '*the* Jews,' rather than 'us Jews.'"

"Your father knows I've never practiced Judaism."

"When I last spoke with my father he said he hadn't seen you in seven years."

An uncomfortable silence pervaded the room.

"Would you like me to leave?"

"Suit yourself. I don't mind if you stay."

"The house seems emptier than I remember."

"We used most of the wooden furniture for firewood during the past couple of years. What we didn't use, we gave away to those less fortunate than us. They probably used it as firewood as well."

"Are you always so bitter?"

"You'd be if you'd lived here during the last few years. We've managed to survive by wit and by fist."

"Are you the only one here?"

"Yes."

"Is your father still alive?"

"Yes."

"What about your mother?"

"Aunt Tara arranged for her to visit America for awhile. I haven't heard from her in two months."

"Arpad?"

"In Budapest. Thank God and Admiral Horthy that Hungary's still safe."

"Where's your father?"

"It's a pleasant evening, Uncle Billy. Why don't we go for a walk?"

"If you don't mind, I'd just as soon stay here."

"Yes, but it's such a warm evening. I'll bet you haven't seen the changes to our National Theatre. Bratislava's grown so much since you were last here you'd hardly recognize it." Imre cocked his head toward the neighboring house and put his fingers to his lips.

"Perhaps you're right, Imi. I could use a good walk."

~ ∫ ~

"The neighbors are spies for the Germans. I've seen them watching our home at odd hours. Once a week a visitor arrives in a Mercedes. There are very few Mercedes cars in Bratislava. You get my drift?"

Despite the early hour, the streets were practically deserted. Here and there a shadow appeared and Imre would nod. "We've set up our own network," he said, answering Billy's questioning look.

As he spoke, one of the shadows passed close to him and surreptitiously handed him something. Imre stuck whatever it was in his jacket pocket without acknowledging he had received anything and kept walking.

"Would you mind telling me where your father is?"

"Over the border." Billy said nothing. Imre continued. "In the high Tatras."

"Poland?"

"Or Slovakia. More than that I can't tell you."

"Can't or won't?"

"Both. You're his friend, but you work for *them*. Not all Jews let themselves be led to the slaughter like meek little lambs. The mountains of southern Poland are thick with forests. And thick with partisans."

"How come you chose to stay here?"

"I didn't. I was assigned to Bratislava."

"You're a partisan, then?"

"For the time being."

Another shadowy figure, small, lithe, and feminine, passed within a foot of them. Imre reached into his other jacket pocket and passed something to the figure.

"For the time being?"

"Uh-huh."

"You intend to join your comrades in Poland?"

"Maybe, maybe not. They say life is much better for Jews if you can make it to Palestine."

Just then a policeman stopped them. "You're out late tonight, *yid*."

"I'm sorry, officer," Imi responded. "I must have lost track of the time."

"May I see your papers?" he said, raising his truncheon.

"Of course, Sir," the young man responded respectfully. "He reached into his jacket pocket, the one where he'd put whatever had been given to him, and handed something to the officer."

"Do *you* have papers, Herr?" the officer asked Billy.

Billy dutifully handed the man his identification papers. The policeman looked at them cursorily and handed them back. "You are a German citizen?"

"I am."

"Very good. It might be wise to be careful with whom you associate. And *yid*, you should know better than to be out on the streets at night. Heil Hitler!" he said, raising his arm in the Nazi salute. He tipped his hat and took his leave.

Billy noticed that the policeman had not handed Imre's papers back. He looked questioningly at his old friend's son. Imre said nothing until they'd walked another block.

"One of ours," Imre said.

"But ...?"

"Uniforms are not hard to come by if you have a contract to do their laundry."

"The papers you handed him?"

"As I said, the mountains are thick with forests and thick with partisans. Although many are Orthodox Jews, our means of communication are highly *un*orthodox."

Shortly afterward, they stopped at an apartment building. Imre signaled Billy to follow him to the basement of the building, where they entered a tiny coffee shop that had four small tables with two chairs at each table. Once they were seated, a small, potbellied man of fifty brought them each a cup of tea without being asked.

"Would you mind if we talked for awhile, Uncle Billy?"

"I thought that's why we left the house."

"I don't mean that kind of talk."

"Go ahead."

"Why did you do it?" Imre's tone was not accusatory, but Billy sensed the talk would not be pleasant.

"Am I supposed to say 'do what?'"

"I think you know what I'm talking about."

"I told you I'd never practiced Judaism."

"Many Jews don't. We don't all wear earlocks and kaftans and funny hats. And we don't all bow and scrape and let ourselves be pushed around by the *goyim*. It doesn't bother me and it didn't bother my father. What neither of us could understand is why you cozied up to the Nazis."

"I had to make a living. Under the Party it became a very good living."

"You made a very good living *before* that, Uncle Billy. You played all over Europe. You could have been a star anywhere you wanted."

Billy did not like the way this conversation was going.

"I've never had anything in common with Jews," he said, somewhat weakly.

"I see," Imre said, his voice expressionless. "My father was your best and oldest friend?"

"That's so."

"Your business partner, my aunt? Her husband, who I understand has sent you money during the past year?"

"Yes."

"My mother?"

"Where is this conversation going?"

"Who knows? I'll take the voyage if you will."

"Go on."

"Are you aware that the midget was Jewish?"

"Romanov? Impossible!"

"Why is it impossible? Did you ever ask him?"

"No."

"Perhaps you should have."

Billy sipped uncomfortably at his tea, which was now tepid. "You seem to know all the answers."

"Could you have done it to get back at your father?"

"How dare you say that?"

"I dare," Imi said. He waited a beat, then continued, "He's dead. How much can you hurt him now?"

~ ʃ ~

"You've never gone to church either?"

They'd returned to the street and were now walking toward Lichtenfeld's house.

"I haven't."

"So where has it all gotten you? Fancy home, king of his domain, so long as you bowed down to the higher power with the Charlie Chaplin moustache. When was the last time you could even afford to do what you wanted? Travel where *you* wanted to go?"

Each question stung like a slap in the face, a punch to his jaw. Billy looked at his wristwatch. "And your point is?"

"I'm just asking you to *think*, Uncle Billy. There's still time …"

"You talk like a preacher."

"I thought you said you never attended church. You mean like your Führer?"

"Why do I need to hear this from a twenty-year-old …?"

"Twenty-five."

"I'm more than twice your age. I've been and done more than you've ever – "

"Yes, Uncle Billy. You've *been* and *done*. But that was yesterday. Many yesterdays. And we're living in *today*."

"I think I'd like to go now."

"That's fine with me. Do you want me to walk you back to your quarters? You might need protection. I understand my father protected you once, long ago."

"No, thank you. I can take care of myself," Billy said frostily.

"Can you?" He said nothing more and they parted.

43

"*ATROCITIES AGAINST GERMAN WOMEN AND CHILDREN!*" "*HUNDREDS OF INNOCENT GERMANS RAPED AND KILLED!*" "*FÜHRER VOWS THEY DID NOT DIE IN VAIN!*" screamed *Der Angriff* and the *Volkischer Beobachter*.

Crowds lined the main streets of Berlin, thirsty for blood – Polish blood – as they cheered the hundreds of jackbooted, black-uniformed troops goose-stepping proudly, marching east. The skies overhead were filled with Reich fighters and bombers. Anti-Polish feeling had always been strong in the German army. The nearly cloudless first-of-September morning heralded a fine day for invasion as Nazi troops gathered just short of the frontier, awaiting orders to cross the border.

As Imre Lichtenfeld had predicted, the Polish armed forces' resistance to the German invasion was hopeless. Poland was surrounded on three sides by German territories. The newly formed Slovak State attacked Poland from the south. Polish forces were blockaded on the Baltic Coast by German and Soviet warships. Nazi Panzer divisions rapidly advanced into the hapless Polish state. Dive bombers broke up troop concentrations. Aerial bombing of undefended cities sapped civilian morale. As Imi had said, it was the most modern armed force in the world fighting farmers with pitchforks.

The *Wehrmacht* threw 1.6 million men, 250,000 trucks, 67,000 artillery pieces, 4,000 tanks, and a cavalry division into the fray. The *Luftwaffe* pounded the dying nation with twelve hundred Messerschmitt Bf-09s, three hundred Junkers 87 Stuka dive bombers, three hundred Heinkel He-111 bombers, and two hundred naval aircraft.

Aligned against this murderous force, the Polish nation mustered 800,000 men, thirty thousand artillery pieces, a thousand tanks, and four hundred obsolete aircraft.

Seventeen days after the invasion had started, the Soviet Union, which had just signed the Molotov-Ribbentrop Pact with Germany, attacked Poland from the East. After four weeks of fighting, it was all over. The Polish army had lost seventy thousand troops, the Germans a fifth that number. Eighty percent of the Polish air force was obliterated, while two hundred eighty-five of the two thousand German aircraft were destroyed. Within a month, independent Poland had been wiped off the face of the earth.

The prominent Reich attorney, Hans Frank, was appointed Governor-General of the occupied territories on October 26, 1939. Frank oversaw the segregation of the Jews into ghettos in the larger cities, particularly Warsaw, and the use of Polish civilians as forced and compulsory labor in German war industries.

~ ∫ ~

In May 1940, Billy was summoned to Headquarters, where Warlimont, who'd been promoted to Major, greeted him. Once ensconced in the Major's office, Warlimont told Billy, "Looks like the Führer was prescient. Even though England and France declared war on the Reich, they turned out to be paper tigers."

"The newspapers called it the *sitzkrieg*. Congratulations on your promotion."

"Thank you *Oberstleutnant*." He lit a cigarette, offered one to Billy, who declined, then continued. "So much for treaties of eternal friendship between the Frogs, the Limeys, and the Pollacks. I'm sure they thought twice about tangling with us and our new friend, the Russian bear."

"I trust this isn't a social call, Ernst?"

"Correct. Among other things, it's time to work out your schedule for next year."

"Among other things?"

"Yes. The Reichsmarschall wanted me to talk to you in private. Friend to friend."

"Herrmann and I have been friends for more than fifteen years. He knows how to get hold of me."

"That's true, but it's not … politically expedient … for him to be seen with you right now."

"What do you mean?" Billy's face and hands suddenly felt cold and clammy. "Is it …?"

"That you're classified as a *Mischling*? No, that's not it … oh, maybe it's part of it, but not the major part."

"How does that concern me?"

"Recently America's become a problem. There are plenty of reasonable voices in the United States – Gerald L.K. Smith, the German Bund, even your friend Lindbergh. But lately their president, the *verkrüppled* Roosevelt – they say his *real* name is *Rosen*feld and he's got Jewish blood – has started making unfriendly noises about Germany and threatening to protect England if anything were to happen."

"How should that affect me, Ernst?"

"Have you heard anything about *Fall Gelb* or *Fall Rot*?"

"Case Yellow? Case Red? No."

"Then you did not hear what I am about to tell you. The days of the phony war are over. The Führer intends to invade France and the Low Countries within the month."

Billy whistled softly. "And England would be next?"

"That would be the logical step."

"How come you're telling me this?"

"Because the Reichsmarschall wants you to be on your guard. He's no friend of Doctor Goebbels and he's told me Goebbels is no friend of yours."

"It's no secret in Party circles that they've been competing for the Führer's affection for years."

"If Göring knows what's planned for England, and America says they'll come to England's defense, that means Goebbels has been ordered to engage in a 'truth campaign' to reveal the United States for what she 'really' is."

"To inflame the German public against America," Billy said.

"I didn't say that," Ernst Warlimont said, putting the back of his right hand to his lips. "For thirty years Billy Jenkins has represented the epitome of the *American* cowboy – of all good American things – throughout Europe. Göring wanted you to know you'd make an ideal target for Goebbels' propaganda machine. The Reichsminister doesn't like you and he doesn't like the Reichsmarschall. If America is seen as the 'bad guy,' he kills two birds with one stone."

"I see," Billy said. He steepled his hands and rested his chin in the cup formed by his thumbs, his nose resting against the raised fingers.

"Goebbels has managed to get all the Billy Jenkins novels banned."

"Does Herrmann have any suggestions?"

"He says you should become invisible for awhile."

"What does that mean?"

"There are plenty of cities and towns in *Reichsgau Wartheland, Reichsgau Danzig-Westpreussen, Ciechanów,* and *Katowice.*"

"Poland."

"It used to be called that. They're now Reich administrative districts. The Reichsmarschall suggested there are more troops in the East than there are in Germany. They need entertainment and they don't care what you are as long as you've got legitimate papers showing you're a German citizen."

"So I'd drop through the cracks, drop out of existence?"

"Yes."

"Same pay?"

"Certainly. Same work. You might have a problem trying to enlist the young German girls to go with you. It would probably be easier to attract local women."

~ ∫ ~

On May 10, 1940, Germany invaded France. Thirty-five days later, Paris fell to the Germans for the second time in less than a century. The humiliation of Versailles was erased. Swastika flags lined the Champs-Elysée. The City of Light was plunged into darkness. Ten days later, the French Republic capitulated. The Reich divided France into a German occupation zone in the north and west, an Italian occupation zone in the southeast, and a collaborationist rump state in the south, Vichy France.

On June 18, Prime Minister Winston Churchill addressed the House of Commons, saying "The Battle of France is over. I expect the Battle of Britain is about to begin."

~ ∫ ~

The *Luftschlacht um England* began on July 10, 1940. By the end of October, England, which had started the Battle of Britain with less than half the number of aircraft thrown into the fight by the Luftwaffe, had broken the top secret German code and somehow survived. The stunned, heretofore invincible German Air Force had lost two thousand, five hundred men and eighteen hundred aircraft. The Führer, seething with frustration and resentment, suspended his plan for Operation Sea Lion, the planned amphibious invasion of England, indefinitely, and turned his eyes East.

~ ∫ ~

Billy's show was performing in Łódź, which the Reich had renamed Litzmannstadt, in May, 1941, when he observed something he thought very strange. He remarked on this to one of the clowns while the circus was packing to move on to their next stop, Thorn in northwest Poland. "Did you notice how many German troops were headed East?"

"Might be troubles in Warsaw," the fellow replied.

"No more than usual. The Poles are resentful of their liberators, but I haven't seen anything like this since the *Reichswehr* invaded Poland in 1939. This looks like a much larger operation."

When he got to Thorn, two days later, large masses of troops were still headed East, but now they were joined by countless trucks, tanks and armored personnel carriers. He checked in with the military commandant of the area, *Oberst* Otto Hünchen, who seemed much more open and friendly than most administrators he'd met during his year "between the cracks." Hünchen was not particularly meticulous when he checked Billy's papers. He seemed more interested in talking with someone "from home," and invited the circus showman to his residence.

"Looks like us two old-timers are necessary cogs in the Reich's wheel, Herr Jenkins," Hünchen began. "*Schnapps?*"

"Please."

He poured Billy a draught and one for himself. "Would you mind doing me a favor, Herr Jenkins?"

"If it's in my power, *Oberst*."

"Otto."

"Billy. What kind of favor?"

"My family and I attended one of your shows in Berlin back when it was the biggest show in Europe. I've kept the program from that show for more than ten years. Could you ... could you autograph a copy of it for me?"

"Absolutely," Billy said, nonplussed that he was still remembered and appreciated after so many years.

When Hünchen returned from the back of his quarters with a faded program, Billy not only signed it with a flowing encomium to the Colonel and his family, but also asked for separate pieces of paper which he subscribed separately to each member of the administrator's family and to Hünchen's subordinate commanders.

For the next hour, the two men talked about old times in "another" Germany.

"You're not a member of the Party, Otto?"

"No. I've never gone along with some of their ideas. I suppose that's why I am where I am. Before it became *verboten*, some of my closest friends were Jews. Good people. That's why I've remained a Colonel since 1930. They can't get rid of me unless they shoot me, so they did the next best thing. They exiled me to the armpit of the Reich, an 'elephant's graveyard.'"

"Should you be telling me this?"

"Who're you going to tell?"

"No one."

"So I figured. More *schnapps*?"

"I won't say no. Tell me, Otto, have you noticed anything unusual in the last several days?"

"As in millions of troops headed East?"

"Yes. Why is that necessary? Aren't we friends and allies with the Soviets?"

In response, Colonel Hünchen said, "Aside from the Jews, who were the Führer's favorite targets?"

"The Bolsheviks."

"Give the man a cigar," Hünchen said expansively.

"You think the *Wehrmacht's* going to attack Russia?"

"I do."

There was a companionable silence between the two men.

"Maybe I will have a cigar if you're offering me one, Otto."

The corpulent, now nearly tipsy colonel responded by opening a nearby box of Cubaños and handing it to his guest.

"So what happens now?" Billy asked.

"We go on living as best we can. We wait for the hammer – and sickle – to fall."

~ ∫ ~

At 3:15 am on Sunday, June 22, 1941, four-and-a-half million Axis troops invaded the Soviet Union along an eighteen hundred mile front. Hitler believed Russia was a country of backward Slavic *untermenschen*. History was to show how badly he had underestimated both the capacity and the resolve of his former Pact allies.

44

On October 2, 1941, the *Wehrmacht* commenced Operation Typhoon, the drive to Moscow. The first blow took the Soviets completely by surprise as the Second Panzer Army took Orel. Three days later the Panzers pushed on to Bryansk while the Second Army attacked from the west. To the north, the Third and Fourth Panzer Armies attacked Vyazma, trapping another five Soviet armies. Moscow's first line of defense had been shattered. The Soviets had only ninety thousand men and 150 tanks left to defend Moscow.

Eleven days later, the Third Panzer Army penetrated to within ninety miles of the Soviet capital. The weather started to deteriorate. Temperatures fell while continued rainfall turned the roads into mud and slowed the German advance on Moscow to as little as two miles a day. The supply situation rapidly worsened. On October 31, the German Army High Command ordered a halt to *Operation Typhoon* while the armies were reorganized. The pause gave the Soviets time to reinforce. By mid-November, the Soviets had organized eleven new armies, including thirty divisions of Siberian troops, a thousand tanks, and another thousand aircraft.

Meanwhile, the Germans were nearing exhaustion. With the ground hardening due to the cold weather, the Germans once again began their attack on Moscow. Although the troops were now able to advance again, the supply situation became increasingly grim. The Germans now faced six well-stocked Soviet armies who were fighting to protect their own land. In two weeks of desperate fighting, without sufficient fuel and ammunition, the Germans slowly crept towards Moscow. By December 2, the Fourth Panzer Army had penetrated to within fifteen miles of Moscow. But then the first blizzards of the winter struck.

The Wehrmacht was not equipped for winter warfare. Frostbite and disease caused more casualties than combat. The dead and wounded reached 155,000 in three weeks. Some divisions were now at fifty percent strength. The bitter cold caused severe problems for the German guns and equipment. The weather grounded the Luftwaffe.

Newly built-up Soviet units near Moscow now numbered over half a million men. On December 5, the Red Army launched a massive counterattack which pushed the Germans back over two hundred miles.

~ ∫ ~

By January 5, 1942, Billy had finished his Christmas shows in Eastern Upper Silesia, which had formerly been in the southwest edge of Poland. He'd been away from Germany for a year-and-a-half and found he didn't miss it nearly as much as he'd thought he would. His pay in Reichsmarks went much farther in Poland than in Berlin, and he found he was able to put by extra money each month.

The afternoon was a typical winter one in Breslau, two degrees centigrade, but there was no wind, and walking in the city was a pleasant experience. As was his custom whenever he was in that city, he gravitated toward the town square and Breslau's garish Gothic town hall, a cacophony of towers, turrets, carvings, and color. He found it to be one of the most astonishing landmarks in all of Eastern Europe.

Despite the chill, the town square was filled with people celebrating the last days of the Michaelmas holiday. Gaily festooned pine trees lined the streets of the square, their electric lights winking gaily, day and night. Breslau was one of the few places in Silesia where the war remained far away. Refugees from the rest of Poland, as well as from Czechoslovakia and the Ukraine, had swelled the city's population to almost a million.

Billy felt a gentle tug on his coat, which he mistook for a nearby branch. He shook it off, only to feel a second, more insistent tug. When he looked around, he saw a woman slightly shorter than he. By her ravaged face and the shapeless, tattered clothing she wore, he would have guessed her age at somewhere between fifty and sixty. He reached in his greatcoat pocket to hand her a *kopeck* or two.

"I don't want your money," she said, her voice ragged. "You are Billy Jenkins?"

He looked more closely at this derelict. Then, he recoiled in shock. "Frieda?"

"Yes."

"Oh, my God."

"There is no God. Not here," she rasped.

"Is there a place we can talk? Someplace warm?"

"There's a cheap café on Cathedral Island. The owner lets me sit there from time to time and even gives me a free cup of hot water every now and then."

When they arrived, Billy asked if the proprietor had any pastries to go with the tea he'd ordered for both of them. "But of course," the man replied. Moments later, he brought them a platter of sweetmeats. Frieda's eyes devoured the unaccustomed rolls, but ever the lady, even in her present state, she nibbled daintily at them. Billy did not know what to think. She'd entered his mind several times during the past year, but he'd had no hope he'd ever see her again. Now she'd appeared, like a shadowy apparition, no longer youthful, not even pretty, but alive.

"Bernhard?" he started.

"Dead, I assume. Last time I saw him was the week after we saw you in Vienna. He was sent to Theresienstadt. I was sent east." Billy contemplated the haggard face, which still gave faint hint that she'd once been a very attractive woman. Frieda continued. "We traveled for two days in a barred cattle car. No windows, no food, no water, no bathroom, one hundred-fifty in a car. We urinated, we defecated, we stank. It didn't matter. The second night the Russians or the Poles, I don't know which, attacked the train. I didn't bother to take notes," she said bitterly. "Someone opened the car door. I was pushed out. There was gunfire. I was too exhausted to pay attention to what happened. I heard the door of the cattle car slam shut. The train was on its way again, but I wasn't on it. The Germans left me for dead. My attackers looked more carefully. I was still relatively young, pretty enough for their purposes. I was a woman, I had the right equipment. That's all they cared about."

"Are you sure you want to share this with me?"

"Why not?" she replied in a monotone. "Four days later they'd had their fill of me. They were filthy. I don't know who they were. I know they weren't Jewish. They'd not been circumcised." Her eyes had a rheumy, faraway look. Billy could tell she did not see him at all. "Then I heard shooting from a nearby forest. One of their messengers said troops were combing the area and they'd have to move. I was left behind. I hid in the forest for the next few months, eating berries, leaves, whatever it took to stay alive.

"One night, I heard men speaking Yiddish nearby. I followed them at a distance and found they'd camped near where I was hiding. I didn't reveal myself for more than a week. Finally, when I couldn't stand the loneliness any longer, I came out of the brush in broad daylight. My hair was a greasy, rotted tangle. What clothes I had were in tatters. I'm sure I stank worse than they. I hadn't had a bath since Vienna."

Billy said nothing, but sat in stupefied amazement, listening to the season in hell, which had been Frieda's life since the last time he'd seen her. "For the next year, I `serviced' most of the men from time to time. It's not as if I were a whore. We were a small unit at war. Everyone, man or woman, did what they had to do. I ran weapons to the outskirts of Warsaw. Occasionally they sent me to visit one of their Polish or Russian informants. If they wanted me to spread my legs for a bit of information, I spread them. What difference did it make? My life had no value to me. The Germans had already destroyed it. If I could repay them by lying on my back, so much the better."

Billy shuddered. He was horrified at the thought of what had once been a lovely woman, who'd captivated him with her shoulder-length auburn hair and stylish black sheath dress, pinned beneath sweating brutes. "How did you get here?" he asked.

"Three months ago, I learned you were touring Poland. By then I felt I had done more than my part for the cause. I heard you'd tried to help us before ..."

"I came directly to the house, Frieda."

"You don't have to explain. You may not be Jewish in your own mind, but you're the last connection to my previous life. Can you help me in any way? I'd do anything you want. Cook, clean your clothes ..."

Her pathetic words touched him more deeply than he would have thought possible.

"I can always use an assistant on the show."

"I have no papers. If they caught me your life would be in jeopardy."

"Your contacts in the partisans use forgers?"

"I'm afraid I've burned my bridges behind me, at least for the time being."

"I may have a friend who can help us."

~ ∫ ~

"Otto, I need a favor, a rather large one I'm afraid."

Billy had taken the express train from Breslau to Bromberg, then hitchhiked the thirty miles to Torun by flashing his identity papers to the leader of a truck convoy. From there, it had been an easy trek to Hünchen's headquarters.

"Name it, my friend."

"I wish to hire a new assistant. She seems to have lost her papers."

"Jewish?"

"Yes."

"I see. A love interest at your age?" he grinned.

"The niece of an old friend."

"What name do you want on the papers?"

"Frieda Schönemann."

"Why not simply call her 'Sarah Jew?' You've got to come up with a better name."

"What do you suggest?"

"Maria Fischer?"

"We're not married."

"Fischer's a common German name. You wouldn't want her to have a Polish name if she were to go back to Germany. She is German, I trust?"

"A Berliner."

"Schönemann? As in Schönemann's Department Stores?"

"Her late uncle."

"Late?"

"Theresienstadt. Then, who knows?"

"How quickly do you need it?"

"As soon as possible."

"A week?"

"Wonderful. And if I haven't said it before, a million thanks, Herr Oberst."

~ ∫ ~

Billy remained in Thorn for the time Colonel Hünchen had proposed. Frieda had left him a postbox number in Breslau where he could leave a message for her. A week went by. No word from Hünchen. Two weeks. By the beginning of the third week, Billy was concerned that something was not right.

That Tuesday, he went to Thorn administrative headquarters. He was surprised to see that the name on the sign outside the building, "*Oberst* Otto Hünchen, Commandant," was missing. Probably being cleaned and replaced, he thought. Spring was just around the corner and the Germans were meticulous about things looking fresh and pristine.

He opened the door to the office, closed it behind him, and advanced to Otto's office door. "Herr Oberst? Otto?" he called out.

"Enter." Billy didn't recognize the voice.

When he went into the office, he came face to face with a smallish, balding man wearing thick, rimless glasses, ten years younger than his friend. The man's expression was that of an exasperated civil servant.

"Excuse me, Herr … *Major*," Billy said, looking at the man's insignia. "I'm looking for Oberst Hünchen."

"No longer here," the civil servant replied. His voice was high-pitched, petulant.

"But he was here only last week."

"You saw him?"

Billy answered cautiously. "No. I came on business two weeks ago."

"Then you haven't heard?"

"Heard what?"

"Hünchen's been arrested and sent back to Berlin for General Court-Martial. It seems he's been consorting with various undesirables. Bribery, graft, black marketeering, selling false papers ..."

Billy hoped the bespectacled accountant type didn't see the nervous twitch in his cheek. The man looked up from his desk work. "You are?"

"*Oberstleutnant* Erich Fischer, Herr *Major*. Heil Hitler!" he said, crisply extending his arm in the Nazi salute.

"Oh, Billy Jenkins, the showman," the Major responded. "I am Hans Verkaufner of the General Accounting Office." He extended his hand. Billy grasped it and found it to be limp. *An undertaker's handshake*, he thought.

"So you're the new Commandant, Major Verkaufner?"

"Hardly. I'm an auditor sent here to review what records we could find. I got here this morning. The records are an absolute mess. Hünchen kept his records in an unlocked file cabinet. He obviously felt no one was ever going to invade his sanctum."

"Have you found anything of interest in the files?"

"About thirty new sets of identity papers. I haven't read or even catalogued them yet. Too busy working on the receipts and disbursements ledger. It'll be easy to snag Hünchen's collaborators when they come looking for their papers. That's why those papers are the lowest priority. I've got more important things to do. Why are you here, Herr Fischer?"

"Planning and scheduling, Major Verkaufner," Billy said smoothly. "My season opens in April. I normally make it a point to visit the Commanders of most facilities to clear their calendars."

"I see. Well, Oberstleutnant, there'll probably be a new commandant here within the next ten days or so. I imagine you'll be leaving Thorn before then?"

"Yes, Sir. My next stop is Bromberg."

"Do you plan on coming back to Thorn in the next month?"

"Only for the show."

"Godspeed, then."

When Billy left, he had the unshakable feeling that someone was watching him. He couldn't put his finger on it, but he didn't want to act suspiciously in any way, so he kept walking purposefully until he'd reached his hotel. Once in his room, his breath started coming in uncomfortable gasps. He barely made it to the bathroom before he started retching in the toilet. Afterward, he took a mild sedative and lay down on the bed, where he remained until half past three that afternoon.

~ ∫ ~

Half an hour later, Billy quietly reentered the headquarters building. Knowing that the commandant's suite of offices was to the left of the entryway, he turned right and went to the reception desk.

"May I help you, Herr Jenkins?" The elderly sergeant, Rudolf Erdbacher, who was a few years older than Billy, had always been cordial during the time the showman had been coming to the base. The sergeant had done nothing to improve his slothful appearance and looked as though he'd been born in the grease-stained uniform he'd worn every time Billy has seen him.

"Rudi, the times must be changing. It's …" he looked at his watch, "ten past four and you're still here. I thought the *Schnapps* hour started at four."

"Gotta' look good for the accountant from Berlin," the sergeant said sourly. "I suppose you heard Otto's been cashiered?"

"There was some talk about that in town. You know, Rudi, in all the time I've been coming here, I've never had to go to the toilet. That's the only reason I came into this building. I've got no idea where it is."

"Down the hall to the left, just after the Ladies' room."

"The *Ladies'* room?"

"Another German habit. They may not have one woman on the post, but they build a Ladies' room in every headquarters building. Hell, *Oberstleutnant*, use whichever one you want. The other men stationed here do." The sergeant looked at his own wristwatch. "Four-fifteen. You know, I think I will take your advice and go down to the Club for a *Schnapps*. Nothing else to do here. You got any other business here?"

"Nope."

"I'd appreciate it if you don't say anything to the guy in the big room if he asks."

"Wouldn't know him if I saw him. I'll only be a couple of minutes."

"I don't care if you're there all night. I'm gone. G'night Herr Jenkins."

"G'night Sergeant Erdbacher."

~ ∫ ~

As soon as Billy entered the ladies' room, he locked the door behind him. A few minutes later, he heard the rattling of the door followed by Verkaufner's voice.

"Odd, this one's locked and the other one's open."

Billy quietly entered one of the three cubicles and pulled the latch to the locked position. Then he heard Verkaufner's voice again. "Oh, well, since there isn't a woman within a hundred meters of this building, that slob of a sergeant probably keeps it locked to make sure it's sanitary," He heard the accountant's footsteps moving back down the hall and breathed a sign of relief.

Billy remained in the ladies' room for forty-five minutes. At half after five, there was still enough daylight so Billy could make his way to the commandant's office. But now a new thought assailed him. What if Verkaufner had locked the door? Unfortunately, the door leading to the commandant's office was securely bolted. The only other way into the suite was a window at the back of the building. At Billy's age and given his physical condition he was not equipped to play cat burglar. There might be another way.

There was. Billy vaguely remembered that Sergeant Erdbacher kept an extra set of keys in the bottom right hand drawer of his desk. Old habits die hard. Billy silently uttered a hope that the keys were there and the drawer was unlocked. Fortune smiled on him. Shortly afterward, he tried each of the dozen keys attached to a large ring. The sixth one worked. Before he entered the commandant's office, he carefully put the key ring back where he'd found it.

As Verkaufner had said, Hünchen's file cabinet was open and filled with a number of files. There were thirty of them. One marked, "Fischer, Maria," was halfway toward the back of the cabinet. If Verkaufner had indexed the files, he would certainly note if one of them was missing. Frieda's file was relatively slim. He extracted the papers from that file. He quickly read through the first sheet, then recoiled in shock. He riffled through each of the remaining documents in Maria Fischer's file. Each one related to a "Helga Gottlober."

"Damn!" he swore quietly. "Someone's been here and changed the files!"

At the moment, he heard a distinct click as the door to the front office opened. He heard footsteps approaching the file room where he was now trapped. He looked desperately around the room for a mean of escape. None. A place to hide? Also none. The fear of being arrested, and much worse, gripped him. Perhaps he might somehow bully his way through, but not with someone like Verkaufner. The footsteps came closer.

"No business here other than to go to the toilet, *Oberstleutnant*?"

Billy raised his eyes and found himself looking into the open face of Sergeant Rudolf Erdbacher.

"Uh … what am I supposed to say, Sergeant?"

"I suppose you might say 'thank you,' Herr Jenkins."

"What do you mean?"

"You were so eager to find my keys in the bottom drawer that you neglected to look in the *second* drawer. Are these what you're looking for?" He handed Billy a neat sheaf of perfectly official identification papers, duly stamped, in the name Maria Fischer.

"How did you know…?"

"Otto was my good friend for the two years he was here, much closer than commandant and subordinate. He somehow realized what might happen sooner or later. He asked me to keep a very few files in my desk for 'special handling.' Your Frau Schönemann was one of those special cases."

"But there was a Maria Fischer file and papers in them."

"Of course. *Alles in ordnung.* The German mind being what it is, we index and cross-index everything. If there is a file with papers, we assume it is in proper form. If there is an empty file, we get suspicious."

"Helga Gottlober?"

"Who knows? We just took a few papers out of one of the thicker files and inserted it in Maria Fischer's file. By the time anyone checked carefully to see what was inside the file …"

"Rudi, you've probably saved the life of a brave and deserving woman. If there's anything I can ever do for you …"

"As a matter of fact, there is. My grandchildren would never believe I knew the real Billy Jenkins. They think their grandpa is simply an old gasbag. I wonder if I could have a friend of mine take a photograph of us together at the Club?"

~ ∫ ~

"They caught Hünchen. I'm almost certain they suspect my involvement."

"That's to be expected," Frieda said. Through a series of signals, she'd managed to come to Rózewo, ten miles southwest of Deutsch Krone. The place was so small the Germans hadn't even bothered to change its Polish name. She and Billy had met at the old Mennonite cemetery.

"So what do we do now?"

"I managed to get these for you."

She gasped and stared in wide-eyed amazement at what appeared to be genuine German identification papers, even down to a recent photograph and the proper stamps.

"How did you …?"

"A long story, Frieda. The important thing is they're here."

"What do we do now?"

"We start feeding you, getting a little meat back on your bones, clothing you, and training you as a circus performer."

~ ∫ ~

"Colonel Warlimont's been transferred to the Western Front."

The man who greeted Billy couldn't have been more than twenty-eight, tall, blond, and Aryan-handsome. The placard in his desk read, "Major Springer."

"So you're the new Director of Entertainment for the Administrative Sector?"

"I am. That's one of the reasons I asked you to come this morning. Do you by any chance know a woman named Maria Fischer?"

"No, Sir, I do not," Billy said. *Why would he have asked such a question?*

"She has the same last name as you. I thought she might be a relative."

"I doubt it, Major. My mother's name was Anna Fischer. I was an only child and if I have any Fischer relatives I never met them. You've probably gone through my records and found my original name was Rosenthal."

"Jewish?"

"My father was Jewish. I've been a member of the Party since 1932 and was granted special exemption as a *Mischling*." Billy thought it best not to ask any questions. His face remained passive.

"Frau or Fräulein Fischer's name showed up in Otto Hünchen's personal records. The auditor found thirty-six files that matched these personal records, but the thirty-seventh file, Maria Fischer's, had papers for a Helga Gottlober, who died in 1935."

"You are, of course, aware that I played many shows in Thorn. I had many occasions to meet with Colonel Hünchen."

"We know. That's why I asked you whether you had any information. It's not just you, Herr Fischer. We're questioning anyone who associated with Hünchen. Anyway, we have more important things to discuss."

"Such as?"

"The Reich's war effort is going well, but the Defense Ministry's budget for entertainment has been cut severely due to more pressing expenses."

"Yes?"

"The Ministry has decided to put the entertainment contract for the Polish territories out for bid. While your show has been very successful, we have decided to consolidate our operations. The Zirkus Busch has proposed to take over the entertainment for both the East and the West."

"I see. But I am a Lieutenant Colonel, Major Springer. The Reich doesn't have to pay extra for me."

"Correction, Herr Fischer," Springer said, a bit stiffly. "You are a *brevet* Lieutenant Colonel, a *temporary* assignment, revocable at the pleasure of the Defense Ministry. The Ministry has decided your salary and benefits are an unnecessary expense. Unless, of course, you would like to transfer to a combat unit."

"Are you not aware, Major Springer," Billy said, with equal disdain, "that I obtained my appointment through Reichsmarschall Göring himself? That this was part of a contract where I gave my ranch to the State in exchange for a promise of lifetime income?"

"A written contract, Herr Fischer?"

"Of course not. Herrmann Göring and I have been friends for nearly twenty years. I've always taken him at his word."

"Yes … well, Herr Fischer, the Reichsmarschall has many larger concerns at the moment. But the Ministry is not without a heart. We recognize you have given service to the Reich, so we're prepared to be charitable. It's now August. Your show and your commission will come to an end at the end of December. That should give you more than enough time for you to get your affairs in order."

As angry as Billy was, he'd been around long enough to know that arguing with this mid-level bureaucrat would get him nowhere. The German State operated just so and he *was* serving at the pleasure of the Ministry.

"*Jawohl, Major. Heil Hitler!*" he said, raising his arm in the stiff-arm salute.

"Heil Hitler!" Springer responded. "Oh, and one more thing, Herr Jenkins?"

"Yes?"

"I suggest this Maria Fischer person, whom you do not know and have never met, leaves your show at the earliest moment."

~ ʃ ~

"We couldn't have expected more from those bastards," Frieda said. "We've had four months together and it's given me a new beginning I thought I'd never have."

They'd become lovers a month ago. Their relationship was based on the mutual loneliness they'd experienced. Still, their feelings ran deep.

"Well, now the old cowboy's really been 'put out to pasture,'" Billy said morosely. "But there's not much grass in the pasture. No home, no job at the end of the year, no prospects, and very little money in savings. And what money's left is in Reichsmarks. If they're as dependable as my 'friends' …"

"Billy, you can always go back to doing small shows, playing with smaller circuses. You *are* still a famous name …"

"Yes, but where? Face it, Frieda, no one's heard of Billy Jenkins in the past few years. As far as the world's concerned, I may as well be dead like my friend, Tom Mix. At least he died in style. He was driving his Cord Phaeton when he drove into a gully where a bridge had been washed out by a flash flood."

"He's dead. You're not," Frieda said thoughtfully.

"There's something to be said for that. And as long as there's life, there's tomorrow. Enough of feeling sorry for myself. We'll be in Litzmannstadt in a little while and I can't stick the jossers with my problems."

~ ∫ ~

At the end of the show, Billy was approached by a middle-aged man dressed nattily in a seersucker suit, white shirt, bright red tie, and spats, the latter an affectation he'd not seen in years.

"Herr Jenkins?" the man asked.

"Yes."

He handed Billy a card. *Anton Busch, Zirkus Busch, München.*

"My successor, I presume?"

."That's true. However, I wanted to tell you how much I enjoyed your trained raptor show. The Busch has contracted with the Reich to play all over the territories during the coming year. I wonder if you'd be interested in joining on for our French tour."

"You know I'll be unemployed at the end of the year."

"So I've been told. We have a mutual friend, Herr Jenkins, and he asked if I would consider your act. Now that I've seen it, I believe you'd make a worthy addition."

"There's a woman …"

"Very few of our artistes travel alone, Herr Jenkins. She's welcome to come with you, although we'll only pay for one. Shall we meet after tomorrow evening's show?"

"Splendid. And many, many thanks."

45

The August evening was balmy in Litzmannstadt, which diehard Poles continued to call Łódź. Poland's second largest city was only eighty-four miles southwest of Warsaw. For the past two hundred years, this great agricultural center had seesawed between Russian and German hegemony, only briefly becoming a part of battered and often dismembered Poland. Billy, feeling expansive after his talk with Anton Busch, was dining at Bamberger on Piotrkowska Street with his lover.

"I feel guilty about this," Frieda said. "Gorging myself on sauerbraten while two hundred thousand Jews are crammed into the few square blocks of the Ghetto, knowing it's only a matter of time before ..." She shuddered.

"It *is* wrong. But what can we do about it? You yourself said only yesterday we must somehow survive. Thanks to Busch, we may just do that."

"You're not the least bit suspicious? I mean, here he is, a favorite of the Reich, offering you work when the State is well aware that I'm with you"

"Maria Fischer is with me," Billy replied. "A Lutheran."

"You think they don't *know*? Those people know everything."

"Perhaps not everything, Frieda. They've gobbled up more territory than any country can comfortably digest. They have to keep the lid on the simmering pot of hatred in ten occupied countries. Sooner or later they'll run out of money, manpower, or both."

They were interrupted by the *whoo-ee, who-ee, who-ee* whine of sirens coming from the direction of their tober.

"What the …?"

One the roustabouts suddenly materialized. "Herr Jenkins! Come quickly! One of the circus trucks is on fire!"

~ ʃ ~

As he rushed to show area, Billy saw the truck housing his menagerie suffused in an eerie, copper-colored light. "God, no!" he screamed. "My birds are in there! They can't get out!" He ran toward the car to do what he could to help. Heedless of his own safety, he grabbed a nearby axe and chopped through the door. His nostrils were immediately assaulted with the odor of gasoline fumes mingled with something that smelled like roasting chickens. As it happened, there was precious little he could do to save his charges.

As the inferno spread to a second truck, a large number of malcontents, having no power to do anything *but* make trouble, started other fires throughout the city. The fire brigade nearest the trucks discovered to its horror that the district's fire hoses had been cut. Within a quarter hour, flames had engulfed all three of the show's trucks and had spread to the tent, driving those who could flee to run as though they were escaping from hell.

Not Billy Jenkins. He had only one objective. He must save his birds at all cost.

Outside the fire cordon, Frieda ran to anyone in a uniform she could find, crying, begging, entreating them to help. Bewildered artistes huddled in the streets.

Meanwhile, Billy leapt into the burning car where his birds were being systematically broiled. He was totally oblivious that the metal inside the car had heated to several hundred degrees. As he reached for the cage handles, he never felt the cinders dropping from the car's wooden ceilings, nor did he hear the loud crack as support timbers shattered and fell. Even as the flames ignited his hair and his clothing, his only thought was to save those trusting winged friends who'd depended on him all their lives.

Within an hour, the fire died down.

Only one body was found in the twisted, charred wreckage. Although the Germans blamed the "subhuman *yids*," the Poles, the gypsies, the Bolshevik revolutionaries, and the anti-Nazi partisans, no one ever found out how the blaze first started.

~ ∫ ~

Two days later, the *Volkischer Beobachter* ran a small story on the bottom right-hand corner of page five.

CIRCUS PERFORMER DIES IN FREAK FIRE

Litzmannstadt. August 18. Erich Fischer, 57, professionally known as Billy Jenkins, a well-known circus performer in the 1920's and early 1930's, was burned to death in a fire of unknown origin late Wednesday evening while tending to his birds of prey. Fischer had been touring the administrative territories on behalf of the Reich. A long-time member of NSDAP, he was a Lieutenant Colonel working for the Ministry of Defense and entertaining our gallant troops. His remains were charred to the degree that they were unrecognizable, but witnesses confirm he was the only one in the area of the truck at the time of the fire. He was a native of Magdeburg.

~ ∫ ~

"Where am I?"

"You don't need to know."

"Why can't I see?"

"Your face is covered in bandages. So is the rest of your body."

"How long have I been here?"

"Since you were 'burned to death.'"

Billy lost consciousness again.

~ ∫ ~

"My feet are freezing."

"That's good."

"Good?"

"We're changing the dressing. It's the first time you've been conscious when we've done that. It won't take long."

~ ∫ ~

"Three months?"

"A little less."

"At least I can see shadows. Are you a doctor?"

"I was one, once. Do you remember anything?"

"No."

"Perhaps that's best."

~ ∫ ~

In late November 1942, Billy became conscious for the first time that he was in a bed of some kind and was being fed a warm, thin broth. Surprisingly, he was not in much pain, but he itched horribly and the need to scratch was maddening. He looked around at his surroundings – a small, dark, half-timbered room, lit by three candles. A weak fire burned in a fireplace in the far corner of the room. Beside a man of his own age, whose voice he seemed to recognize, he saw Frieda soaking rags in a washbasin and wringing them out. A third man, dark-haired, twenty years younger, kept steady watch on the door.

Billy's hands, arms, and feet were swathed in bandages. He was covered by a heavy, dark blue woolen blanket. "Where am I?" he asked.

"Alive," the older man answered.

"You said you were a doctor … once."

"You've a good memory Herr Fischer. I said that a month ago. Beryl Halevi."

"A Jew?"

"A Jew."

"You saved my life?"

"God saved your life. But if you want to stay alive, you're going to have to help Him. That's going to take some time."

"I remember a fire in Littzmannstadt … and trying to save my birds."

"Neither God nor you could do that. One of your Polish crewmen tried to save you. He didn't make it. I think you should sleep now."

~ ∫ ~

By mid-December, Billy was able to walk, take food, and even perform his necessary ablutions on his own. He was startled when he first saw his skin, more so when he saw the haggard old man staring back at him from the mirror. His body was mottled and discolored everywhere he could see. He could only raise his arms to the level of his chest before the skin seized up. What hair he had left was thin, wispy, a pale gray-white. For the first time in his life, he was possessed of a full beard.

"Put a *kaftan* on me and I'd look like a rabbi in his dotage," he remarked, trying weakly to inject some humor into the conversation.

"Try studying the Torah and you might just look like one at that," Halevi said.

"Or you might look like me," the younger man said. "I really was a *yeshiva bocher* before the troubles."

"Where's Frieda?"

"She'll return before nightfall."

~ ∫ ~

Day by day, Billy regained strength. Through conversations with Frieda and the two men, he was able to piece together what had happened.

"When you went into the flaming truck, I thought everything was lost," Frieda said. "When the partisans found you, you were unconscious and burned over most of your body. I don't know how they were able to get into and out of the Ghetto after dark or how they even knew who you were. When the *boches* came to investigate, they found the body of a Polish roustabout. They had me identify 'your' remains."

"We're nowhere near Littzmannstadt?"

"We're in the Žabia Valley, a no man's land between Poland and Slovakia, two kilometers from Mengusovské lake. Safe."

"Halevi said he was a doctor once."

"He was senior professor and chief of the burn unit at the University of Vienna Hospital for twenty years. He got out in '37, just before the *Anschluss.* Einstein had gotten him an exit visa and he had a job waiting at Princeton, but he chose to stay here and join the partisans instead."

"Who's the other fellow?"

"Mischa Albov, rabbinical student, lawyer, businessman. He's our link to dealing with the devil."

"The Nazis?"

"Uh-huh. The angels, too."

"The angels?"

"The underground railroad. From Poland south. Ukraine, Romania, Bulgaria, all the way to Turkey and then to Palestine."

"Frieda, when I first saw you in Breslau, you told me you'd moved around a lot. Why didn't *you* go south?"

"That was going to be the next place I went. But I saw you in Breslau. It's just like life. We're always told it's better on the other side, but no one really wants to let go of *this* life to see what it's like."

"So it wasn't just love for me?" His face crinkled into a rather ugly smile.

"Who knows?" she replied. "As Halevi says, 'That's a matter you have to take up with God.'"

~ ∫ ~

"Have you ever been a member of *any* church, Herr …?"

"Take your pick, Professor," Billy said. "Rosenthal, Jenkins, Fischer, it really doesn't matter. Why don't you call me Billy. That's the name I've gone by since I was thirteen. And the answer to your question is no. I can't remember ever going into a church or synagogue except for my friend Sam Lichtenfeld's wedding."

"So you never studied anything about religion?"

"No, Doctor Halevi. As far as I'm concerned, it's all a matter of do this, do that, forgive me Father, I have sinned. I don't need to be told I'm a sinner," Billy said sardonically. "I know that on my own."

Halevi puffed contentedly on a pipe. Its cherrywood aroma smelled so natural in the cottage.

"Isn't that what religion's all about?" Jenkins continued.

"I never gave it much thought, Billy. Not that I'm a great scholar or even a student of Torah. I spent all my life as a secular Jew.

"I appreciate your saving my life. I'm not a religious man and I probably never will be. But assuming I was even remotely interested in learning about Judaism, how long would it take me to learn enough about it to qualify as a Jew?"

"Twenty seconds," Halevi said.

Billy was intrigued. "O.K., Doctor, you've got your twenty seconds."

"It's not 'my' twenty seconds, Billy. Two thousand years ago, a nonbeliever told the great Rabbi Hillel, 'If you can teach me all there is to know about your religion while I'm standing on one leg, I'll convert to Judaism. Without batting an eye, Hillel said, 'Do not do unto others what you would not have them do unto you. Everything else is commentary.'"

~ ∫ ~

"I can't read Hebrew, Mischa."

"Wouldn't matter if you could. We don't even have a prayer book around here."

"So assuming … supposing I'd want to learn more about being Jewish than Hillel's quick answer, how would I go about it?"

"Just by talking."

"Talking about what?"

"Whatever comes into your head, or, better yet, whatever comes into your heart."

"All right, tell me the difference between Judaism and Christianity."

"I can't *tell* you anything. You have to come to your own conclusion."

"What do *you* think is the difference?"

"My opinion? If you're a Christian and you have absolute *faith* – faith in the Resurrection, faith that Jesus of Nazareth is the Son of God, unquestioning belief in the Christ – that's enough to get you into 'Heaven.' But Judaism teaches that's not enough. Faith alone without good works, without responsibility for what you do – or don't do – doesn't guarantee you anything."

"Isn't that taking over God's job?"

"You might think so. A lot of people do. I'm just telling you what I believe."

"No 'official' Jewish line?"

"Not hardly. We're probably the most opinionated and intellectually combative people on earth. They say if you get two Jews together you're bound to have *three* opinions. Why do you think so many Jews become lawyers?" Albov chuckled. "What say we go for a walk? In another few weeks, spring will come to the Tatras. You've been laying around like a sack of potatoes long enough. Time you started earning your keep."

~ ∫ ~

Two months passed. Billy cut wood and harvested what winter vegetables grew on the plot of land surrounding the house. By the last week of March, his body was lean and sinewy. His hands had become calloused, roughened. He found he was in better physical condition than he'd been at any time during the past decade. The mountain sunshine and crisp air acted like a healing balm. His face displayed a more natural coloring. He no longer looked like the ancient who'd stared back at him from the mirror that first day he'd taken time to look at himself. Because of long walks and talks with Halevi and Albov, he'd also taken time to look at himself through a different mirror – one from the inside.

Frieda was frequently gone. Whenever she returned, he found an air of excitement to their lovemaking. He and Doctor Halevi often played chess with the doctor's old ivory set. They talked politics. Halevi never once inquired into his past. What really mattered was the future. With a makeshift shortwave radio, they listened to the BBC every night. They learned the words and music to "There'll be Blue Birds Over the White Cliffs of Dover," as well as code words directed to the underground. Slowly, Billy found himself reaching out for his Jewish roots.

During the last week of March, several men appeared at the cottage. They were uniformly between twenty-five and thirty, bearded, and dressed in rough garb. They bore half a dozen wooden crates. They spoke in hushed whispers with Albov and Frieda, even though the cottage was miles from any habitation Billy could see. Within two days they and the crates were gone. When Billy asked Frieda what this was all about, she answered in one word. "Warsaw."

46

"The Jews in the Warsaw ghetto have finally decided enough is enough.," Doctor Halevi said.

"You know about Auschwitz-Birkenau of course." This from Mischa.

The four of them were sitting around the only table in the cottage. Albov had warmed a pot of tea over the fireplace stove and poured a mug for each of them.

"Doesn't everyone?" Billy rejoined. "It's a resettlement camp near Krakow. The commandants at some of the military bases where we've played have shown me postcards they've received from Jews who've been moved there. Actually, it looks like quite a healthy place – outdoor work, a vigorous life ..."

Halevi looked at him strangely. "So that's what you've been told?" he murmured.

"Have you heard any different?"

"Billy, we haven't only heard, we've *seen*," Frieda said. "Less than a dozen people have escaped in the year it's been in operation."

What followed was a lesson for Erich "Billy Jenkins" Rosenthal-Fischer in the depths to which man's inhumanity to man could fall. During the next hour, he was escorted through the hell of the grim truth: *Arbeit* did *not "Macht Frei."* After traveling for three days in cattle cars, each packed with one hundred-fifty men, women, and children with no food, with a single bucket of water used for drinking or defecating, the vast majority of those who'd survived the journey made it as far as the "delousing showers," where they were instantly gassed with I.G. Farben's *Zyklon-B* gas.

"I never knew," Billy said, white-faced. He tightened and loosened his fists several times to take the edge off the tension and revulsion he felt.

"Those Jewish men who'd somehow avoided the scimitar wielded by the featureless Aryan who pointed 'left' or 'right,' got the great privilege of piling dirt over the mass graves of those who'd been shot instead of cremated," Mischa said.

"It was worse for the women who'd been spared," Halevi continued quietly. "Because they were young enough or pretty enough; those who weren't the playthings of every man from the commandant down to the lowest brute laborer were subjected to 'medical experiments,' where they were impregnated with pig's fetuses or subjected to freezing cold and scalding heat when they were in a state of shameful nakedness."

Billy horror had now turned to anger. He stood up and thrust two large logs into the fire with a force that showed he would like to have done the same to a prison guard.

"Those who were assigned to work details came 'home' each night to bunks packed eight to a single bed. Each day, they had a single meal of slimy broth with rotted potatoes. The usual lifespan of such a survivor was between three and six months," Mischa added.

"Warsaw's a hundred of miles from Krakow," Billy croaked.

"Yes," Halevi said. "Four hundred thousand Jews were packed into the central area of the city, the Warsaw Ghetto, in October 1939.

During a two month period last year, three-quarters of them were liquidated at Treblinka extermination camp. Those left in the Ghetto knew it was only a matter of time before their turn came …"

Frieda extracted a packet of documents from a drawer at the bottom of the closet. In response to Billy's questioning look, she replied, "Your official papers. 'Erich "Billy Jenkins" Fischer, *Oberstleutnant* Reich Defense Ministry.' I've kept them in my private papers since you gave me my 'birth certificate.' I figured you never could tell when they might do you some good."

Billy rose, walked over to the fireplace, and turned his backside to the now-roaring fire. By his shivering, it was obvious that the heat did not relieve the cold chill he felt.

Has my whole life since that day I met Hitler in Munich been a string of lies, one piled atop the other? Has the God of the Jews somehow dictated that I would achieve my greatest material wishes on the broken backs of innocent human beings?

He shuddered as he thought back to how he had suddenly been given the munificent ranch house and the Germanic dude ranch on the forty acres behind it. How he'd turned his back on Wasserman. How he'd turned his back on the Spencer brothers, who had been his friends for more than thirty years.

"I need to walk outside for awhile," he told his three associates. "Alone if you don't mind." No one said anything as he left the cottage.

Spring had come to the High Tatras with a vengeance. Everywhere he looked, he saw verdant fields of mountain flowers, jagged, snow-covered Alpine peaks, peaceful meadows planted with the promise of bountiful crops, the lake swollen with the runoff from the mountain snows. All of God's beauty in the midst of all of man's cruelty, heartbreak and misery.

As Billy walked along the lakeshore, his thoughts swung from the secular world in which he'd lived for so many years – and in which he'd obviously and publicly been so successful – to that darker, Jewish side of his soul that had always been there, just waiting on the periphery of his life. He'd turned his back on his Judaism – his father – while his oldest and closest friends he'd embraced had been Jewish: Sammy, of course, and Abrielle and Grigori, Frieda – and Romanov. He'd still never come to grips with the very idea that the midget who'd played a larger-than-life role in his existence was a Jew. And a small group of Jews he didn't even know, who had saved his life when they knew he was working for the Nazis.

The Nazis had given him the title *Mischling*. Sort of like being an "honorary" Aryan. But how much honor could there be in being an "honorary" part of a race whose members thought themselves so superior they could kill those whom *they* considered lesser subhumans simply because they *weren't* Aryan.

He recalled the ironic joke that Romanov – yes, Romanov – had told one day. "An Aryan approached a Jew and said, 'You know, everything would be just fine and there would be no problems if only you Jews were Christians,' to which the beak-nosed, bewhiskered whitebeard replied, 'Yes, but perhaps things would be even better if you *Christians* were Christians.'"

"More than a million went to their death as meekly as sheep," he muttered. "And Christ said 'The meek shall inherit the earth.' *These* sheep only inherited gas chambers and mass graves where they'd be an anonymous heap of bones and rotted flesh."

When he returned, each of the cottage's inhabitants were busily gathering what goods they could find – tins of food, woolen blankets, two old underhand rifles. In response to his questioning look, Frieda said, "Winter's over. We won't be needing these for awhile. The Jews of Warsaw need everything they can get."

"I'd like to visit Bratislava. I heard Sam was part of the resistance."

"Too late, Billy."

"Is he dead?"

"No, gone."

"The camps?"

"No, a much happier place. Six months ago Sam, Abrielle, Arpad, and Imi made it through the net to Palestine. The partisans helped the family escape. They made it on a fifty-year-old coal scow, but they made it. And for a change there've been arms coming back *our* way instead of steadily pouring out."

"How do you know all these things?"

"I'm a Schönemann, remember?"

"What are they doing in Palestine?"

"Living instead of surviving. Farming, helping others run the blockades. Abrielle wrote me that Imi's developed a new means of hand-to-hand self-defense, *Krav Maga*. Don't even ask me what it means."

"So there'd be no sense in my going to Bratislava?"

"Probably not." Halevi had entered the room. "But if you want to do *something* useful, the resistance could sure use volunteers to go *into* Warsaw, particularly at a time when any Jew who's got a connection anywhere wants to get as far away from that place as possible."

"An invitation to get killed – and for what?" Billy asked cynically.

"There's another old Jewish proverb: He who saves a single life, it is as though he has saved the universe."

~ ∫ ~

Crazy Herschel wandered through the spectral crowd, crying, "Please … a piece of bread … a little water." He picked his way carefully, allowing passage for Miriam, his imaginary goat. He led her on a slack rope, trailing several feet behind him. Around his neck a small metal pan hung on a cotton strip strung through its handle. As he walked along, his gaunt frame trembling, the pan tapped softly against his chest, marking cadence. "Please ... a piece of bread for a pan of milk."

It was past curfew. The unlit street was full of Jews awaiting deportation. Families sat huddled together, singing quietly or whispering. The more resourceful made last minute preparations, sewing money into their clothing. Some boiled tea or scraps of food over an open fire. A few discussed the morning, voicing hope or utter pessimism. Others prayed.

Occasionally someone looked up as Crazy Herschel went by, searching his face for a glimmer of the person they had known before the war. But there was no sign in his eyes – once so bright and expressive – now lying shrunken and recessed – of a life beyond Miriam.

Among those gathered in the night, Avram Blutstein, sixteen, did not need a sign of what had been. He still remembered Uncle Herschel as the handsome, jovial man who had told him enchanting stories and spun the Chanukah *dreidel* on its thin stem with fingers that could crush the hardest walnuts. On Passover he gave them each an extra glass of wine and saved them from bed with his sonorous rendition of the Exodus. It was longer than it needed to have been, and not entirely accurate, but he had been teaching them history and their parents could not protest. After all, Uncle Herschel was a rabbi.

This was not to say he was an ordinary rabbi. Sometimes he had played lively songs on the harmonica, then drew forth a handkerchief and blew his nose as loudly as a trumpet. The children imitated him, shouting "Gabriel's horn!" and honked like a gaggle of geese. That had been Herschel's cue to bring the barnyard to life. He made animal sounds and comic faces and rolled his eyes. Naturally, his performance had always delighted the children.

Even before his Bar Mitzvah, Avram had heard of gruesome experiences of those who had been "relocated" before them. His father had refused to discuss these tales with him. But Avi believed them. There had been almost half a million Jews sealed behind the ghetto walls three years ago. Now there were fewer, far fewer. Most were now dead of hunger or illness or they had been beaten or shot to death or dragged from their rooms during wild raids and shoved into trucks and trains chartered for unannounced terminals. Once gone, there would be no word from them.

The first raids had been unpredictable, but recently the madness had taken a calculated turn. People were given a time and a place to report for "selection" and a reason to believe, if they wished, that they were being "relocated" for constructive purposes.

Even if Avram's suspicions were false, they were vivid enough that he was concerned with nothing but survival. Avram had parted from his father spiritually the morning he had found Uncle Herschel on the stairs, insensible and grotesquely disfigured as the result of a Nazi "interrogation." It disgusted him that his father, Uncle Herschel's own brother, had refused to allow Herschel's body into the house, stubbornly insisting that to do so would mark their whole family for similar treatment.

Avram and his friend Yakov had carried Herschel to Dr. Adler's house. Every day they went there to help care for him. But no amount of effort could restore him. First his synagogue had been closed down, the building ransacked and the congregation dispersed. Then the Nazis had tortured him. Finally his own brother had barred his door to him. It was more than any man could bear.

And so it was that Rabbi Herschel Blutstein had become a ghetto legend – living on the by-products of an imaginary goat.

A distant sound caused Avram to turn in the direction of the bleating. "Please … a piece of bread for a little milk."

His mind had not yet discerned the words, but immediately Avram knew that Uncle Herschel was in the vicinity. He had developed a special sense for his presence. His father had tried to force him to ignore Herschel, to deny his existence altogether. A year earlier, his father had even stopped Avram from going over to Herschel when they encountered him on the street. More than once, Avram had sneaked out, with his mother's blessing, to bring Herschel food or clothing. When his father found out, the man had maniacally beaten him until earlier this year when, at six-foot-one, the fully-formed Avram had returned the trouncing his father had regularly given him, and moved into an abandoned flat on Jabotinsky Street.

Avram thought back bitterly. If only his father had been home the afternoon the Gestapo had called. *He* might have been taken away and murdered. At the least, *he* would have been tortured.

~ ʃ ~

The Gestapo had come for Menachem Blutstein, his father, on the suspicion that he was an agent of an underground resistance publication. When they arrived, they found only Avram, his mother Leah, and Herschel. His father was out delivering papers. The officer in charge demanded to know where he was. No one could tell him.

"All right," the officer had said brusquely, "the boy comes with us. He will not be harmed. But Menachem Blutstein, thirty-five, must present himself at headquarters before sundown tomorrow. There will be no extensions."

One of the officer's henchmen had grabbed Avram by the scruff of the neck and began shoving him out the door. Leah rushed forward, throwing herself at the man who held Avram. "You can't …!" she shrieked, and found herself slammed to the floor. The Jewish policeman, who had been forced to accompany the Germans, pulled a short truncheon, and with several rapid whacks to the head beat her into unconsciousness.

Avram was being pushed down the stairs.

"Wait," Herschel had implored. "You're making a mistake."

His calm rabbinical manner had detained the chief officer, who was still at the door. He eyed Herschel quizzically.

"What is it, *rabbi*? he asked sardonically. "Have you just remembered where your brother is?"

"No," Herschel had said. "But the boy is innocent. You mustn't take him."

"I said no harm would come to him," the officer said. "Do you doubt my word?"

"No."

"Then what is it?" the officer insisted, "I have no more time to waste with you."

"There is something I should tell you," Herschel said. "Something about my brother."

"You're not as religious as I thought," the officer sneered. Herschel had looked down at the floor where Leah lay, her hair matted with blood. "Well?" said the officer.

"Not here," said Herschel. He dampened a rag and held it to Leah's scalp. "Bring the boy back and take me instead. Then I'll tell you what I can."

Avram would never forget the love and fright in Herschel's gaze as they'd passed each other on the stairs.

~ ʃ ~

Herschel had stopped at a fire around which sat Billy, Avram Blutstein, Yakov Horovitz, and one or two others.

"Good evening," Herschel said. "It's a nice night for sitting in the street."

"Yes," said one of the men. His voice lacked hostility.

"Thank you," said Herschel. "Very kind of you …" He asked Yakov to hold his rope and leaned gingerly toward the fire. "It feels good," he said, rubbing his hands together over the flame and warming his face with his palms. "Ah," he purred, his frail, bony hands trembling with pleasure. "Very good."

When Herschel had comforted himself sufficiently, he removed the pan from his neck, nudged Miriam into position for milking, hunkered down beside her flank, and in an elaborate pantomime, filled the pan to the brim.

"A little milk?" he said, offering the pan to the man who had spoken to him.

"Thanks, no," said the man. "We've eaten." The man dug into a sack and brought out a piece of potato. He skewered it with a stiff wire and singed it in the fire.

"Here," he said, pointing the heated potato toward Herschel.

"Won't anyone have some milk?" Herschel entreated. He turned to each man, offering the pan. No one took it.

"Come on," said the man, waving the potato. "It's getting cold."

Gratefully, Herschel put the pan down and pulled the potato off the wire, gripped the potato in both hands and attacked it with mottled gums.

47

A line had formed some time before the bakery was due to open.

It was going to be a sultry day. Already, dark puffs of factory smoke gushed out of the stacks like billows of thick, black paint. The street was wet, although it had not rained, and a foul odor hung in the dampness, as if a large quantity of garbage had been scattered everywhere in the moisture.

Billy glanced at his wrist and then at the back of the man in front of him. He'd left his watch with Frieda ten days ago, when he'd come to this miserable and forlorn place, but he'd looked at his watch every day since he could remember, and that habit persisted. Now he looked upward into the haze. Both the sun and the moon were in place.

"Five-thirty," he said to himself.

The man in front of him turned sideways in response to Billy's voice. His face was caved in, his features tangled. Billy dared not ask how that had come about. Gathering that Billy had not been addressing him, he turned his head forward again. The back of his skull and his thin neck suggested an ostrich.

Five-thirty, Billy thought, this time to himself. Little by little he was getting better at guessing when it was five-thirty in the morning, when it was five-thirty in the evening, when it had been five-thirty and when it would be five-thirty again.

Billy was eighteenth in line. In front of him he counted four men, nine women, and four bodies of indeterminate gender. There were more than twice as many people behind him. He was, by all indications, the healthiest person in line. After a week, his posture sagged a bit, and he'd started leaning on his cane more dependently, but he remained fairly upright and had not yet lost his muscle tone. As he had let his beard grow, his general appearance had increased in likeness to those around him.

His stomach gurgled and contracted. He worked up a ball of saliva and swallowed it. His hunger pangs were coming earlier each day. Potatoes. Garlic. Eggs. Greens. Onions. Salami.

He had thought he appreciated them properly when they had been in his possession, but now he saw that it was not so. After the food in the south, potatoes and onions were nothing special. He'd considered them interim staples, so he had not conserved them, and they had run out all too quickly.

Each word was a picture. The dried, hard, brownish-red salami, speckled with white veins of fat, the round end casing tied in a knot, the sliced end smooth and oily, with a spicy odor. The potatoes, brown skinned, with dark, muddy eyes. The eggs, lovely white enamel shells faintly tinged with pink, each oval pearly white and bright warm yellow inside, capable of reproducing the miracle of life.

Salami. Potatoes. Eggs. Garlic. Greens. Onions.

The bakery had still not opened. As the line grew longer, Billy's hunger grew. If only he had those provisions back, he could make do for a month on what he had eaten in a few days. But he had not come to the bakery to think about food.

"Excuse me," he said to the back of the ostrich-headed man in front of him.

The head did not move.

"Excuse me," Billy repeated.

Again there was no response. He tapped the man on the shoulder weakly, then more firmly. Finally the head moved, ever so slightly, tightening the skin on the neck.

"Could I ask you something?" Billy said, leaning toward the man's ear and tapping him.

With exaggerated slowness, the man turned sideways, sliding his feet in tiny increments without lifting them off the ground, until he was facing Billy. His collapsed profile was even less pleasant head-on. He seemed to be regarding Billy with his entire face rather than just with his eyes.

"I'm looking for someone," Billy said. "Perhaps you know him. Marek Edelman?"

Billy's voice came out louder than he'd intended. The man held his impassive pose for a moment, as if trying to digest what Billy had said. Then his body began to move, almost imperceptibly, rotating in his slow motion, leaving Billy once more viewing the back of his ostrich neck.

Billy angled to catch a glimpse of the man behind him. As he did so, he felt that he was being watched. He turned to face the man fully. "I don't mean to bother you," he said, "but I'm looking for someone. Marek Edelman?"

The man, who was younger and whose face was still a face, looked at Billy as if he would bore holes in his forehead.

"Excuse me," Billy said, turning around.

Wherever he had been, he had gotten the same blank stare. No one had heard of Marek Edelman. Billy's stomach gurgled loudly. He pulled in his abdominal muscles to cut off the noise, but the gnawing persisted. It was, for the hungry moment, a happy coincidence that his search had brought him to the bakery.

"Open up!" someone shouted from the back of the line. His voice sent a wave of complaint through the line.

"Open up!" said another voice, weakly echoing the first.

"It's torture standing in one place!"

"We've been waiting since dark!"

"Please."

"It's almost supper time."

"My wife is dying."

The voices were low, indistinct, as if each were addressed to itself.

"I'm hungry," Billy heard himself say. He could feel the stones pushing unyieldingly against the arches of his feet.

At last the door opened. The line came to life, tightening up and surging forward. A table was placed in front of the door and a large cauldron of piping hot soup was placed upon it. A woman brought out a stack of soup plates and a man followed with an armload of cups. The man, who had a long, narrow face, said something that Billy could not hear. The line began to move. Billy watched the man ladle the steaming soup into the first bowl and hand it to the person at the front of the line, who took it and stepped aside. The second person received his bowl. He, too, moved off to the side, but did not walk away.

"There's no bread," Billy heard someone say. The words did not register.

Instead of remaining straight and growing shorter, the line was forming a knob around the table.

"No more bread."

"No bread."

"Nothing to eat."

The message had passed Billy and was making its way to the back of the line before he grasped the situation. The bakery had been late to open because of a problem. They were not serving any bread. Just soup. Swallowing their disappointment, the first people in line finally moved away from the table and found spots to drink their soup, leaning against the building or sitting down on the ground. Three places in front of him, a woman slumped and toppled onto the street. The woman behind her walked over her, as did the man in front of Billy. No one as much as looked down. Billy hesitated and considered kneeling to see what was the matter, but he stepped over her feet. He did not want to call attention to himself and his stomach was starting to spasm.

When the man who was serving the soup saw that the fallen woman was not moving, he called inside for help. A large, muscular fellow who couldn't have been more than thirty appeared. Billy recognized him as having helped bring out the table and the cauldron. The young giant had dark, closely-cropped hair, a broad forehead, wide cheekbones, a thick neck, square shoulders, and strong hands which, like his neck, were prominently veined. Billy saw him gently turn the woman over on her back, feel her pulse, and press his ear against her chest. Then he lifted her off the street and carried her onto the sidewalk.

"I need a piece of paper," he said, laying her body parallel to the curb.

The woman who had set out the plates brought some paper. The muscular young man laid it over the dead woman's face. Billy's nostrils twitched. The soup had a light yellow color. He could see right through it as the man with the narrow face, whose name he had learned was Melech, filled the ostrich-necked man's bowl.

"There'll be seconds today because there's no bread," the man said to ostrich-neck. The recipient's hands were so unsteady that the soup splashed out of his bowl as he walked away. *He won't have anything left by the time he finds a place to drink it,* Billy thought.

"Excuse me," Billy said, clearing his throat as his soup was being poured. "Perhaps you could help me. I'm looking for an old friend, Marek Edelman. I thought someone here might know of him?"

The narrow-faced man. handed Billy his bowl. "Step aside," he said, plunging the ladle into the cauldron and filling a bowl for the next man in line. Billy moved to one side of the table. A few drops of soup jumped out of his bowl and scalded his thumb. His hands had been perfectly steady before, but holding the soup they were trembling almost as much as ostrich-neck's. He leaned against the wall to steady himself.

The dead woman lay unceremoniously under a sheet of paper. Billy wondered what the strong man who had tended to her was doing inside the bakery. Something about him struck a curious chord.

"Now who is it you're after?" Melech asked over his shoulder.

"Edelman. Marek Edelman."

"Doesn't ring a bell."

"Before the war he worked in a slaughterhouse. Someone who was leaving the ghetto entrusted me with something to give to him. I promised I would."

"What is it?"

"It's personal," Billy said.

"Can you describe him?" Melech asked.

"I understand he was muscular," Billy said. "About thirty, dark hair."

"You said he was an old friend?"

"Of my uncle's. I've never met him personally. He was close with my uncle, Doctor Halevi of Vienna?"

"I'm afraid I can't help you," Melech said. "I'll remember the name though. You can check back if you want."

"Much obliged," Billy said. By now, his hands had grown accustomed to the heat of his bowl. Holding it as steadily as he could, he moved away from the table and found a spot on the sidewalk facing away from the serving table.

The soup was disappointingly tasteless. It had no fat, no bubbles, no film, no trace of skin or marrow, no carrots, no hint of salt, pepper, or paprika. He wondered how long it would have sustained the dead woman had she been able to reach the table. Thirstily, he polished off his bowl and assumed a new place at the back of the line.

No one seemed to pay attention as the black wagon approached. The line moved forward slowly, steadily. The steaming yellow water filled bowl after bowl. Billy watched the skinny, swaybacked horse that was drawing the wagon come to a halt without any signal from the old man who was holding the reins. Beside him sat what appeared to be an unsightly beggar; next to him, a young boy with brown hair and a smooth, earnest face. "Hello there," the old man called down from the wagon.

"Hello," Melech said.

The large, muscular man emerged from the bakery and took over the ladle.

"If it isn't Samson," the old man said.

"Might be. You're certainly not Delilah," the big man said, grinning.

"Miserable day," the old man said, mopping his brow with his shirt sleeve.

"It could be worse," said narrow-faced Melech, coming over to the wagon.

"Not for her," the old man said, referring to the woman on the sidewalk.

"She fell out of line when she heard there was no bread."

"Can't blame her," the old man said.

"Good morning," Herschel, the "beggar" who was sitting on the wagon said. "A fine day, isn't it?"

"Ready to come down, Herschel?"

"If you please."

Holding the boy's hand, Herschel stood and edged over to the side of the bench. The old man reached up and grabbed him under the armpits.

"Down we go," he said, lifting him up and swinging him onto the ground. The boy handed the old man Herschel's rope.

"Here," the old man said, placing the rope in Herschel's palm.

"Thank you." He turned toward the looped end of the rope and groped in the air for Miriam's head. "We're at the bakery, my love," he said, stroking her mane. The end of the rope was very near the dead woman's feet.

"Come," Melech said, taking Herschel by the elbow and leading him over to where Billy had downed his bowl of soup.

The old driver stooped over the dead woman, scooped her off the sidewalk, and flung her up to the boy, who had gone over the bench onto the platform.

"Sorry there's nothing for you today," narrow-face said to the old man.

"We'll survive," the old man said, climbing back onto the bench.

"You'd better. Someone has to keep the streets clean."

"The horse knows the route as well as I do," the old man said. "She could do it alone if only the passengers would get on without help."

"If they could, they wouldn't want to."

The old man smiled. "Giy-yap!" he said, picking up the rein.

The wagon pulled away. Billy heard the steady clip-clop, clip-clop, clip-clop as it turned the corner at the end of the street and disappeared.

48

"You wanted to see me?"

"Marek Edelman?"

"I might be. Depends on who's asking."

"Billy Jenkins."

"The Nazi cowboy who died last year? Sure, and I'm Father Christmas."

They were seated in the basement of the bakery. Billy was not surprised to find himself facing the young man who'd been called "Samson." The hatchet-faced man, Melech, had passed him a note yesterday morning when he'd returned for a bowl of tasteless soup, this time accompanied by a single crust of bread that had tasted very like he imagined sawdust would taste. The note had said simply, "After dark tonight. Door open. Go downstairs."

"Have it your way," Billy said. He reached into an inside pocket of his thin, worn coat and took out a single sheet of paper.

The young man's eyes widened almost imperceptibly. "You could have gotten this off the body."

"The body was totally charred, in case you don't remember."

"Where, then?"

"Does the name Frieda Schönemann mean anything to you?"

"No."

"Mischa Albov?"

"Maybe," the young man said noncommittally.

"How goes it?"

"What kind of bullshit question is that? You've been here eleven days. You know things are terrible and they're getting worse. We have exactly two rifles, six handguns, and less than a day's worth of ammunition left."

"So you are Marek Edelman?"

"If you say so, *Oberstleutnant*. I'm sorry I've not offered you anything. We seem to be temporarily out of filet mignon. Come to think of it, we do have some tepid water, some yellow food coloring …"

Billy stood up and paced the small room. "Here," he said, offering his host a small chunk of salami he'd brought with him from the outside. He watched as the young man attacked it voraciously. He nodded his thanks, but otherwise said nothing.

"So if you're not here to arrest me, why *are* you here in this hellhole?"

"You said you needed arms and ammunition."

"And you're a magician who's about to turn out his shabby coat and show me everything we need to win this war?"

"Not quite. But this might keep you going for another day or so." He reached into the other side of his coat and brought out a hundred rounds of ammunition.

"Go on, I'm listening," Edelman said, his voice still betraying no emotion.

"I'll be leaving the ghetto later tonight. The death wagon comes by the bakery each morning at six. Tomorrow there'll be two barrels of flour but nothing for bread. Make sure you have someone who'll exchange these barrels for the empty ones in your storeroom. The day after that there'll be another exchange."

"In the end it won't make any difference you know."

"It may give you another day or two to hold out. I understand *Bystry* and *Chwacki* have mined the ghetto walls."

"So? The Germans have committed two thousand well-armed *Waffen-SS Panzergrenadier* troops and three hundred-fifty Polish Blues to cordon off the walls of the Ghetto and go house-to-house. It'll be a matter of days at the most."

"Perhaps," Billy said sadly. "We can always pray."

"To whom?" Edelman remarked sourly. "There is no God. At least not in this place. And with Passover coming in three nights we're supposed to be happy and celebrate our freedom."

~ ∫ ~

Seven of them attended the morning meeting: Mordechai Anielewicz, Marek Edelman, Billy, Avram Blutstein, Henryk "Bystry" Iwański and Józef "Chwacki" Pszenny from the *Armia Krajowa*, the Polish Home Army, and a man from the Polish Communist *Gwardia Ludowa*. The bakery's two ovens kept the large room warm, but not oppressively hot.

"Thanks to our friends in the Resistance," Marek said, nodding to Billy, "we've increased our rifles by a factor of twenty. Not nearly enough, but it's a start."

"A shame they couldn't send ten thousand *men*," Chwacki said dryly. "Like in your Bible – 'I will create an army out of dry bones.'" He snorted. "You'll need that and more. Frankenegg's supposed to launch an action tonight."

The fact that SS-Oberführer Ferdinand von Sammern-Frankenegg, the widely feared and equally despised commander of the entire cadre of *Schutzstaffel* and police forces in Warsaw was personally taking control of this *Aktion* meant the Germans were taking the uprising seriously.

"Where?" Anielewicz asked. He was the head of the United Jewish Military, the ZZW, for the entire ghetto.

"Muranowski Square."

"Marek, you'll be in charge of alerting the troops," Anielewicz continued, nodding at his deputy. "Blutstein?"

"I know," Avram answered. "Yakov will be with me."

"No matter what happens, if you can bring this off, they'll talk about you for years."

Avram swelled with pride.

Each of the commanders gave a brief report. Then Anielewicz wished each of them godspeed and dismissed the meeting.

~ ∫ ~

"God will understand if we have to celebrate *Pesach* early."

"You still believe in God, Avram?"

"Of course, Herr Jenkins. Whether or not He chooses to forget *us* for whatever His reason, we simply cannot abandon *Him*."

"Even in this place?"

"Herr Jenkins, you don't understand," the teenager said, as if he were addressing a young child. "As long as there is one Jew left alive in the world, it is our obligation, indeed our privilege, to worship and pray to *Adonai* and to trust that His plan is greater than we can comprehend. Please, Herr Jenkins, would you do me the honor of joining us for our *Seder* just after one this afternoon?"

"I wouldn't know what to say or do, Avram," Billy responded. During the past week, he'd come to feel an incredible closeness to the strapping younger man. It amazed Billy how quickly relationships developed in times like these. Of course, he thought, one had to make close friendships rapidly. You never could tell whether these relationships would last a lifetime or only a few hours.

"It doesn't matter. Just follow what I do. It'll be a short service. It's supposed to be a day for family happiness, but that assumes you have a family. I don't have anyone except my mama, who may drop by, and Uncle Herschel … There are three others with whom I share an apartment. It's in the only building on the block that hasn't been bombed out yet."

Yet. Another word indicating the fluid nature of life in the ghetto.

~ ∫ ~

That afternoon the service was brief, but especially meaningful. Edelman, whose regular job was in the bakery, had somehow managed to bake eight pieces of *matzo* and distribute them to Avram. After gratefully accepting Avram's invitation, Billy went into the Aryan sector of the city, his *Oberstleutnant* papers in hand, and cadged two bottles of wine, not Kosher, but real wine, and God would have to understand. At the end of the *Seder*, the tiny makeshift "family" deferred to Crazy Herschel, who somehow remembered the words of the *Kaddish*, the memorial prayer for the dead, and led them in prayer as beautifully as though he still were a real Rabbi.

~ ∫ ~

At five o'clock that afternoon, an hour before the sun went down, an excited buzz spread through the ghetto. An hour later, Warsaw's entire downtown could see for themselves that what had, at first, only been whispered, was indeed true.

"I saw it with my own eyes! Two boys climbed up on the roof of the Jewish army headquarters on Muranowski Square and raised two flags: the red-and-white Polish flag and the blue-and-white ŻZW pennant!"

"That'll drive the *Boches* nuts!"

"Look at 'em wave! Higher than any Swastika in the city!"

"God keep 'em flying!"

By sundown, there were bonfires in the ghetto. These were replicated all over Warsaw and the news continued to spread. Within the hour, SS-Brigadeführer Jürgen Stroop had received an angry call from Berlin. He trembled as he heard the voice of none other than Himmler, who started out rationally enough. "Brigadeführer, those flags are of incalculable political and moral importance. It gets them all worked up and unifies the subhuman scum Jews, and also the Poles. You understand, Stroop, that flags and national colors are just as important a means of combat as rapid-fire weapons." By now the Reichsführer had worked himself up to a frenzy and he bellowed into the phone: "Stroop, you must at all costs bring down those two flags, immediately, do you understand?"

"Yes, my Reichsführer! Immediately! Even as we speak, SS-Oberführer von Sammern-Frankenegg has initiated action!"

"What the hell does that mean?"

"He's entered the ghetto and his forces are taking control."

"Never mind 'taking control' Stroop. I want that whole fucking rathole liquidated. Obliterated. Wiped off the face of the earth. And get those damned flags down by midnight tonight, is that clear? Midnight tonight!"

"Yes, my – " But the line had gone dead.

~ ∫ ~

Next morning, the flags were still proudly flying above ZZW headquarters. The radiotelephone between Warsaw headquarters and the field command crackled.

"Frankenegg, what the hell is happening?"

"Someone must have leaked our *Aktion* plan, Brigadeführer. We came into the ghetto with three thousand forces expecting a rapid action. We'd planned to do a quick mop-up during the next two days."

"Clearly that's not happening, Ferdinand."

"The *yids* obviously knew what was coming. We've suffered unexpectedly heavy losses. They ambushed us from alleyways, sewers, windows, bombed-out buildings … Molotov cocktails, hand grenades … and they've got snipers all over the quarter. For the moment it seems our advance has been halted."

"*Halted? Oberführer* von Sammern-Frankenegg, we are the SS – the *Schutzstaffel!* The word *halted* does not *exist,* do you understand?" Stroop said, his voice tight. He noticed that his hand was shaking with an unaccustomed palsy.

"*Brigadeführer,*" Frankenegg responded evenly. "If you think you can do a better job, I respectfully ask that you come down here and see exactly what is going on. Perhaps you could redirect bomber aircraft from Krakow?"

"I might just do that, Frankenegg," Stroop hissed. "You have two hours – *two hours* – to haul those *verdammte* flags down."

~ ∫ ~

Three days later, the flags were still flying over Muranowski Square. Frankenegg had been cashiered, replaced by *SS-Brigadeführer* Jürgen Stroop. Throughout the day on April 24, recorded bullhorns issuing from Mercedes armored vehicles bellowed the same message throughout the ghetto: "Jews of Warsaw! Lay down your arms immediately! You have absolutely no chance of surviving if you continue in your lost cause! If you surrender unconditionally right now, you may survive! This is not *Masada*! Mass suicide is idiotic! Lay down your arms immediately!"

In response, snipers shot out the vehicles' tires and the bullhorns atop the roofs of the vehicles. Billy Jenkins took out two vehicles, surprised at his skill as a rifleman.

That evening, the Nazis resorted to systematically burning houses block by block with flamethrowers and blowing up basements and sewers. By noon of April 25, German machine guns had destroyed the stanchions from which the flags flew, and the banners lay listlessly atop the roof of the ZZW headquarters.

At midnight, six of the seven men who had attended the meeting the morning before Passover convened at midnight.

"Yakov is dead," Avram remarked matter-of-factly."

"A shame," Edelman said. "Better a hero's death than a number at Treblinka."

"Do you have more flags, Blutstein."

"I do."

"Is there any other high ground?"

"Mila 18."

All the men except Billy nodded. When Edelman advanced his idea, Billy said quietly, "I would like to go with Avram."

"I beg your pardon?" Edelman said.

"Let me be the other one who goes."

"You, *Oberstleutnant*? Forgive my saying so, but this is not your battle. You're not Jewish."

For the first time in his life, Billy felt as though Judaism had rejected *him* rather than the other way around. Although stung, he reacted calmly but forcefully. "Marek, *God* says who's a Jew and who's not. Perhaps I turned my back on my heritage during my life, but no more. I'm going."

"Cane and all?"

He noticed that Edelman's voice was not condescending. More concerned.

"Cane and all."

Edelman looked at young Blutstein, who nodded.

"You'll take care of him?"

Billy suffered his second shock in as many moments. A younger man had been asked to care of *him*. As if he were an old man on a bus and someone had stood up to give him a seat. *My God, do they consider me that old?* he thought.

Remarkably mature and sensitive to Billy's feelings, Avram replied, "We'll take care of one another, Marek."

~ ∫ ~

Three hours later it was nearly dawn.

"Ready?" Avram asked.

"Yes."

"Scared?"

"Of course."

"Me, too. Helps you stay alive, though. Can you climb a rope?"

"If I can't, I'd better learn PDQ."

"PDQ, Herr Jenkins"

"Pretty damned quick. An American phrase I picked up before you were born, Avi."

"The rope's tied to one of the flagpoles. The poles are rusty. I hope they'll hold.

They did. Avram Blutstein and Billy Jenkins completed their assignment within half an hour.

~ ∫ ~

"What the fuck?"

"I have no explanation, my Reichsführer," Stroop bleated.

"I don't want any fucking explanation, Stroop. Two new flags are flying above the ŻOB command post at Mila 18 Street. Now there are ZZW and Polish banners in the windows of every building in the ghetto," Himmler screamed. "If those flags aren't gone by noon today you will be!"

The Nazis, whose forces outnumbered the defenders ten-to-one, continued slowly and methodically to sweep through the quarter. A sea of flames flooded houses and courtyards. There was no air, only black, choking smoke and heavy burning heat radiating from the red-hot walls and from the glowing stone stairs. The banners, pennants and flags were destroyed one by one, building by building, brick by brick. On the evening of April 28, 1943 Mordechai Anielewicz convened the final meeting of what was left of his organization in the same bakery where the men had met ten days before.

"My friends," he began heavily. "The battle is lost. We've no more guns, no more ammunition, and no more soldiers to throw into the war. You have all been heroes. Of fifty thousand ghetto inhabitants, more than twelve thousand have been killed during the past two weeks. We have not been defeated by the Germans. We have been defeated by smoke and fire and by the world ignoring us. But we have won. We will never willingly be led like lambs to the slaughter again. God has seen that. One day, God will give His own justice. Let us recite the *Kaddish* for all of our fallen comrades."

~ ∫ ~

"Herr Jenkins?"

"Call me Billy, Avram."

"I have nowhere to go. My mother and my father were killed. I have no one left."

"You have me. You have your life ahead of you. Come with me, Avram. Tomorrow at dawn we'll join others. By tomorrow evening, we'll be in the Michalin Forest where we'll meet up with my friends."

~ ∫ ~

The remaining Jews, civilians and surviving fighters took cover in bunker dugouts which were carefully hidden among the largely burned-out ruins of the ghetto. The German troops used dogs to discover the hideouts, using smoke grenades, tear gas, and even poison gas to force Jews out. In many instances, the Jews came out of their hiding places firing at the Germans, while a number of female fighters lobbed hidden grenades or fired concealed handguns after they had surrendered. Small groups of Jewish insurgents engaged German patrols in night-time skirmishes. However, German losses were minimal following the first ten days of the uprising.

On May 8, 1943, the Germans destroyed the ŻOB's main command post at Mila 18 Street. Most of its leadership and dozens of remaining fighters were killed. Others committed mass suicide by ingesting cyanide. The dead included the organization's commander, Mordechaj Anielewicz. His deputy, Edelman, escaped through the sewers on May 10 with a handful of comrades.

On May 13, 1943, the newly-promoted SS-*Gruppenführer* Jürgen Stroop wrote to Reichsführer Himmler:

"The former Jewish quarter of Warsaw is no longer in existence. The large-scale action was terminated at 20:15 hours by blowing up the Warsaw Synagogue. Total number of Jews dealt with: 56,065, including both Jews caught and Jews whose extermination can be proved. Apart from 8 buildings (police barracks, hospital, and accommodations for housing working-parties) the former Ghetto is completely destroyed. Only the dividing walls are left standing where no explosions were carried out.

"Our best available records show that the Reich's forces suffered 16 killed in action and 86 wounded, including over 60 members of Waffen-SS. This does not include the Jewish collaborators. The real number of losses, however, may well be higher ..."

49

"This must be one of the most beautiful places in the world," Avram remarked.

"That's what I said when I first woke up in the Žabia Valley. I never asked you, Avram. Are you originally from Poland? Blutstein is a German name."

"If I were a dog, you'd call me a mutt, Herr Billy. The family's got roots in Germany, Russia, Poland, Lithuania ... wandering Jews. May I ask you something?"

"Of course."

They'd come to the northern edge of *Mengusovské* lake. Billy never ceased to marvel at the variety of birds and animals that frequented the area or the green countryside that displayed so much life, even in the high summer.

"On our way down from Warsaw, you told me you'd turned your back on Judaism because of your father. Was he really such a bad man?"

Billy though several moments before he answered. "I certainly thought so."

"Yet you liked Herr Hitler?"

"When I met him, he was down and out. Not like today."

"I hated my father after what he did to Uncle Herschel," Avram said. "But I couldn't hate a whole people because of one man. I always wished Uncle Herschel would have been my real father. He was kind and funny and loving. I despised one man and idolized the other. They were both Jews."

They walked a while further in silence. Billy was not uncomfortable with their discussion. His father had died eleven years ago and his memory was that of a distant shadow. Given different circumstances, Avram Blutstein might have been the son Billy'd never had. They'd spent the last month moving from one partisan center to another, living like animals in forest redoubts, spending a night here, two there, carrying messages, and fleeing from the baying hounds which the Germans had set loose in their periodic sweeps through pockets of Jewish resistance.

A week ago, they'd finally made it to the cottage in the Žabia Valley. Last night, after Avram had gone to sleep, Halevi and Albov had told him that partisans had spotted a platoon of German soldiers ten kilometers to the northeast. The safety of their hideout might be compromised any day.

"You're saying I shouldn't measure all Jews by my father?"

"I didn't."

"You didn't know my father."

The two of them broke into uncontrollable fits of laughter, the kind that diffuses what could be among life's most uncomfortable moments. Spoken in a vacuum, Billy's statement might not have been remotely funny, but after the harrowing escape from Warsaw and the troubles of the last few weeks, each needed the emotional relief of that instant.

When they'd recovered, Avram choked out, "You didn't know mine either. But to use what I *think* is a Biblical phrase, should either of us visit the sins of the father on the sons?"

"I hope not. You know, Avram, during the past few months I've taken quite a dose of Jewish medicine. First Doctor Halevi, then Mischa, now you."

"And Frau Frieda?"

"She never talks about her Judaism one way or the other except to show anger at how everyone else treats the Jews."

"A 'salami, *lachs* and herring Jew?'"

"Now you're losing me."

"Back when he was rational, Uncle Herschel used to tell us about people who were Jewish by birth, but who never once set foot inside a synagogue except during the High Holy Days, never celebrated *Shabbos* at home, never sent their children to *cheder*. They dressed in the latest Western fashion, they were lawyers, actors, engineers, and they lived in Berlin, Paris, Vienna, even New York. They always thought of us as backward cousins. They were ashamed of us. Yet, if anyone asked them what *religion* they were, they immediately snapped, 'I'm Jewish to the core.'"

"So you're accusing me of being one of those?"

"Not even." Avram smiled. "At least you never pretended you were Jewish."

"So why in the devil did I come to the Warsaw ghetto?"

"That's something you have to ask yourself, Herr Billy. I try to remember what Uncle Herschel told me. Not all Germans are bad people. Most of them are very good people who are just trapped with their current government."

"And you'd put me in that category?"

"No, Herr Billy, I think you're just a Jew who hasn't discovered it yet."

They'd started back to the cottage when Billy said, "I'm sorry Herschel was killed during the Uprising."

"I'm not. He'd been a walking dead man ever since …"

"But as crazy as he seemed to be, he never stopped living."

"We Jews are like that."

~ ∫ ~

"Dammit, Avram, this is hard work!"

"If you think you're too old to learn Hebrew …"

"Watch it, youngster! Have some respect for your elders." He grinned.

"I do, Uncle Billy. I don't know if I'd have the courage to try to become a Jew at your age."

"I'll have you know I'm not *that* old. Why, I won't even be sixty for another couple years, and …"

He caught the sudden look on the young man's face and quickly said, "I'm sorry, Avram. I shouldn't have mentioned that."

"Not your fault. I'll have to learn to live with it. Uncle Herschel would have been forty-two next birthday. My father would have been forty."

"So you have to go on living for them both."

"I guess so."

A little while later, the young man started humming a hauntingly fierce marching song. Tears came to his eyes, but he refused to weep as he started singing in Yiddish.

> *Zog nit keyn mol az du geyst dem letsten veg,*
> *Khotsh himlen blayene farshtelen bloye teg.*
> *Kumen vet nokh undzer oysgebenkte sha'ah,*
> *S'vet a poyk ton undzer trot mir zaynen do!*
> *Kumen vet nokh undzer oysgebenkte sha'ah,*
> *S'vet a poyk ton undzer trot mir zaynen do!*

Billy sat transfixed. When Halevi, Albov, and Frieda heard the partisan hymn, which those in the Warsaw ghetto had never lived to hear, but which had become the very symbol of what they'd stood for, they stopped what they were doing, came into the room, and joined young Avram in the song.

> *Fun grinem palmenland biz vaysen land fun shney,*
> *Mir kumen on mit undzer payn, mit undzer vey.*
> *Un vu gefalen s'iz a shpritz fun undzer blut,*
> *Shprotzen vet dort undzer gevurah, undzer mut...*

That night, after dinner, Billy and Frieda walked to the lake. He'd carried a blanket with him and they'd made tender love under the stars. Afterward, Billy, who'd not understood a word of what they'd sung that afternoon, but who had been captivated by the melody and the force with which his four companions had sung it, asked Frieda what the words meant. She translated for him:

> *"Never say that you must walk your final road,*
> *Though leaden skies above conceal the days of blue.*
> *The hour that we have longed for will appear,*
> *Our steps will beat a thousand drums 'cause we are here!*

> *"From green lands of palms to lands all white with snow,*
> *Here we come with our all pain and all our woe.*
> *Where our drops of blood has fallen like the dew,*
> *There our might and courage then will sprout anew.*

> *"The morning sun will come and shine on us one day,*
> *Our enemy will vanish and will fade away.*

> *"But if the sun and dawn for us will come too late,*
> *The generations teach us to forgive, not hate.*

> *"This song is written in blood and not in pencil-lead.*
> *It is not sung by free-flying birds o'erhead.*

But a people stood among collapsing walls,
And now they sing this song in heaven's glorious halls."

~ ∫ ~

"We must leave right now, this morning."

"How far away are they, Mischa?"

"Half an hour. An hour at most"

"So we've been betrayed?"

"I doubt it, Billy. There's no one within twenty kilometers of here. Probably just random luck. Theirs' good, ours bad."

"Raze the cottage?"

"No," Doctor Halevi said. "It would lead them here faster. I suggest the five of us carry what we can, money, papers, rifles, and scatter in two different directions."

"Wouldn't it be safer if we all traveled together?" Avram asked.

"It's risky either way," Billy said. "Five people are certainly more visible than two or three. Where should we meet?"

"Budapest." This from Halevi. "Mischa and I will go west, Billy. You, Frieda, and Avram travel east. We'll meet at the Pest end of the Elisabeth Bridge at five in the afternoon, ten days from now."

~ ∫ ~

They'd been waiting at the bridge since four o'clock. Billy looked at his wristwatch. Five-thirty. Their comrades were half an hour late. "Frieda, d'you think one of us should walk up *Vaci Utca* and see if there's any sign of them?"

"Halevi said five at the foot of *Elsbet Ter.* I trust his word."

Just then, a motley-looking beggar shambled up to them. "A *forint* my lords, lady?" he asked.

Avram reached into his pocket, but the beggar put his hand on the young man's arm. "It's me, Avram. Mischa."

"Where's Doctor Halevi?"

"Shot three days ago, just as we were coming out of the Slovakian Mountains. For what it's worth. I took out his two killers. I've been hiding out in Buda for the past two days, just in case their associates might have followed my trail."

"Where are you staying?" Billy asked.

"At the home of friends. I've made arrangements for you to stay there as well. Taxi!" he hailed a cab that had just let two passengers off at the bridge.

Within twenty minutes, they'd arrived at a large, upper middle class home in the Buda hills. That evening they enjoyed the best meal they'd had in months. A handsome, plump Hungarian woman served Billy, Frieda, Avram, Mischa, and five others.

The first course was Drunkard's Soup, a tasty, tart dish of pickled cabbage. Next came Robber's Meat, chunks of lamb, onions, mushrooms, tomatoes and green peppers alternated on a skewer and cooked over an open fire.

"That's perhaps the only decent thing the ancient Huns brought to Hungary," their host, a middle-aged man named Ferenc, said.

The Robber's Meat was accompanied by little pinched dumplings and potatoes served in a red pepper sauce. The company shared two large jugs of Hungary's wines, a straw-yellow Tokaji and the dark red Bull's Blood.

"So you are wondering where to go next?" Ferenc asked his guests.

"We are," Mischa replied. "Budapest is charming and beautiful, but not home."

"Where in Europe is for Jews?" a small, dark-haired woman, whose name was Rachel, asked rhetorically.

"Nowhere," Ferenc replied. "Mark my words, Hungary will fall into Germany's lap any day. Rumania will be the next to go. Bulgaria's already a Nazi ally, but at least they've stood up for their Jews."

"That leaves Turkey and points south," Billy said. "Palestine."

"That's the *only* place," Mischa responded.

"From green lands of palms ..." Avram murmured softly.

"Ah, *palatschinken!*" their host exclaimed, breaking their somber mood as the servant brought a tray heaped with paper-thin crepes stuffed with apricot jam, strawberry jam, or cream cheese.

While they were plunging into their dessert with relish, the servant reappeared and started pouring a steamy, aromatic beverage into their mugs.

"My God, *real* coffee!" Billy exclaimed. "It's been four years since I've had a real cup of coffee. No thank you, Mademoiselle, I like mine American style, black."

~ ∫ ~

Later that evening, the four surviving friends discussed their immediate future.

"No question Avi should migrate to Palestine at the earliest possible moment."

"That's possible," Mischa said. "Ferenc has a direct link to the underground in Cluj. It's just over the frontier from Rumania, which, as of now, is still independent, but we don't know how long it will stay that way. The Reich's got Rumania surrounded on three sides and they want the Ploesti oil fields."

"If they can get him to Constantia, it's not that far to Kilyos," Frieda added.

The boy's eyes lit up with the idea of going to what those in the Warsaw ghetto had lovingly called *Eretz Israel*.

"Who'd come with me? All of you, I hope," Avram asked.

"Mischa?"

"Strange as it may sound, I belong here in eastern Europe."

"Uncle Billy?"

Billy looked uncomfortable. He and Frieda had discussed this very possibility. To leave Avram, who was not even seventeen, on his own to emigrate to a new land would be an immense cruelty. Or would it? Avram had seen more injustice and experienced more scars than anyone deserves in a lifetime. Yet he'd survived, and he was the future.

"I think maybe Avram and I should talk alone for a little while."

~ ∫ ~

"I can't understand why you'd want to go back to *Germany* of all places."

"Avram, it's hard for *me* to know. I guess Frieda and I are like a pair of salmon. The salmon is born in a mountain lake. As soon as he's able, he swims down to the sea, where he spends almost his whole life. Then one day, he is pulled by a certain urge he can't resist. He'll go for days, even weeks, without eating, as he fights his way to the lake where he was born. I guess you could say it's one of God's true miracles, but that salmon will somehow find the exact lake or stream where he started his life. Once he gets there, he will breed, his mate will lay her eggs and bring forth new life, and then they quietly die."

"But you're a man, not a fish."

"Avram, I can only hope you'll understand and forgive me when you get older. I was born and grew up in Germany. Frieda grew up in Germany and married there. Both of our memories and most of our lives are tied to Germany. Neither Frieda nor I are young anymore. It's time to go home, to live out our lives in our homeland."

"But the Reich can't be the Germany you remember. The Nazis are systematically destroying Jews, the gypsies, and God knows who else."

"True, Avram, but I've known the *Germans* for years. I'm convinced that sooner or later the thousand-year Reich will come crashing down.

I believe in my heart, despite everything that's happened, that the Germans are, on the whole, a good and moral people, neither better nor worse than any others. I also believe that one day they will try to make amends for what they've done. And if we don't learn from this ghastly experience and forgive them, and welcome them back into the family of nations, then it's *we* who are the lesser human beings."

"But you'd have a safe home, a wonderful home, in Palestine when it becomes *Eretz Israel* once again."

"No, Avram. As much as I might like to be part of what may happen, *Eretz Israel* is a brand new country, a country for the young. You remember the story of Moses?"

"What does that have to do with you and Frieda and me?"

"What happened at the end?"

"He wandered in the desert for forty years, which I've always thought odd, because it's less than a forty *day* walk from Egypt to Palestine. At the end, he was allowed to see Israel in the distance, but never to enter the Promised Land."

"Why do you think he wasn't, Avi?"

"The Bible tells us it was because the Almighty told him to touch the rock with his staff so it would gush water, and he disobeyed God and struck it instead."

"You really think that's why God punished him?" Billy arched his eyebrows.

"Who are we to question God's ways?" From the room where they sat, they could hear gentle snoring coming from nearby bedrooms.

"Back in Warsaw, you said no matter what happened you believed God had a Plan," Billy continued.

"I did and I do."

"I don't know God's mind anymore than you. But suppose, just suppose, God caused the ancient Israelites to wander in the desert for forty years, when, as we both know, it would take no more than forty *days* to get from Pharaoh's capital to the Holy Land. Suppose He did that because He wanted the old generation, the generation that had known slavery under Pharaoh, to completely die out, so that whoever entered the Promised Land would be someone who'd been born and grown up in freedom. As for Moses, as great as he'd been, why would God want that dour old man around to remind the Israelites where they'd come from?"

The two sat silently, each thinking his own thoughts, each filled with love for the other. At the end of that time, Avram was weeping softly.

"You know, Uncle Billy, for someone who's never practiced any religion you certainly seem to know what Judaism is all about better than the wisest Rabbis I've met."

"Like Hillel said, Judaism in half a minute," Billy said, smiling. "Do you think you'll be able to make the journey alone?"

"Mischa said a group of us would meet in Turkey and travel to Palestine together from there. My biggest fear is that when I get there I won't know anyone, no relatives and now no friends."

"That describes most of Palestine, Avram. Just about every Jew there started out someplace else. That's what a new country's all about. But just to make sure you needn't be concerned about *that* fear, I think I could help you."

"How? Unless you know people who're already there."

"As a matter of fact, I do. But it's now past midnight and this old man is very tired. Tomorrow morning, I'll tell you about a weightlifter named 'Young Hercules' and one of the world's most astonishingly beautiful young women, Abrielle, and their two sons, Arpad and Imi … But that's for tomorrow morning."

50

The old man's white hair was trimmed so short it seemed almost military. He walked with the aid of a cane from Nuremberg's Berlinerstrasse to Hochstrasse and back twice a day, precisely at seven o'clock each morning and three o'clock every afternoon. He did not look out of place. He did not wear the yellow star outlined in black and embroidered with the word *Jude* on his chest. If anyone had asked, he would have shown them his papers proving he was an *Oberstleutnant*. But no one asked. No one cared. Those few men and women on the streets at the same time as Billy were more concerned with their own lives than with inquiring who he was and from whence he'd come.

The war had taken a decided turn against the Germans. The British Eighth Army had routed Rommel's forces in Egypt. Stalingrad was by no means a critical city on the way to the Caucasus' oilfields, but the conquest of that place had become Hitler's obsession. Russian troops had fought the German Sixth Army for every block and rubble pile. Then, a year ago, the Russian troops had begun a counteroffensive to the west of Stalingrad, designed to cut off the Sixth Army. By year's end, hundreds of thousands of German troops had either been killed or captured. An even larger group of survivors had been left to wonder bitterly over a leadership so fanatical it would not permit its troops to give up one foot of conquered ground, regardless of the cost in human suffering.

To add to this horrendous news, there were startling rumors that the Americans had mounted an assault on Germany's axis partner, Italy, that was so massive that the *Duce's* command was dissolving. Even German soldiers were said to be deserting. German civilians found their faith in their country's ultimate victory shaken.

Now, nearing the end of 1943, the infallible Führer no longer held monster rallies in Nuremberg. He rarely appeared in public at all anymore. The Germans left in the large cities wondered with more than a little trepidation what would happen when … But no one dared mention *that* possibility in public.

Within a week of their arrival, the word of mouth spread by those few Jews who dared to live in the eye of the storm, those very few who had not been "resettled," broadcast that two new people in town might be Jews. A few days after that, Billy, who was living with Frieda in a small, drab apartment on the western outskirts of the city, answered a knock on their door one afternoon, just after he had returned from his walk. The man who stood there was in his mid-thirties, tall, and handsome in an Aryan way.

"Herr Fischer?" the younger man asked. In answer to Billy's cautious gaze, he continued. "Mischa Albov suggested I introduce myself and welcome you to the land of the Hun. I am Fritz Berger."

Billy's suspicions were not allayed. "Describe him."

Fritz did, even down to the wart on the left side of Mischa's nose.

"Mischa consorts with both the good and the evil ones. Which one are you?"

"Whichever you'd like," Berger responded. "I don't blame you for being cynical. I've lived underground in Berlin for the past year-and-a-half. The only reason I risked coming to Nuremberg was that the Partisans asked me to make sure you were all right." He extracted several Reichsmark notes from his pocket and held them out to Billy. "To help you pay your next month's rent," he said.

"Thank you. And thank the partisans. I trust you're aware that we used most of our remaining savings to pay for the first month's rent."

"Billy, who is it?" a female voice came from the back room.

"A man who claims his name's Fritz Berger."

Frieda gave an unaccustomed whoop and came rushing to the door. Billy watched as her normally closed face opened into a wide smile. "Fritz? Willy Berger's son?"

"In the flesh, Frieda. I must say you're certainly as lovely as ever."

"You're a liar, but charming as always. Is Marlene with you?"

"For the week. She's pining to get back to Berlin 'cause Lena's staying with a righteous gentile woman in Wilmersdorf."

In response to Billy's questioning look, Frieda explained. "I first met Fritz when he was, what, fifteen years old?"

"About that," the younger man replied.

"His father was the most successful merchant in Deutsch-Krone, a hundred eighty kilometers northeast of Berlin. Willy and my Uncle Bernhard became great friends, since they were both in the same line of business. Come in, Fritzi," she said. "You'll forgive our surroundings. The least I can do is offer you hot tea. No lemon or milk, of course, but it's better than nothing."

"It's about three times as large as where we're living now," Fritz said, as he entered their front room. "Ah, a real fire," he continued, backing up to the fireplace and sighing with pleasure as it warmed his backside.

While Frieda was off in the tiny kitchen brewing tea for the men, Fritz explained soberly to Billy, "I grew up the richest, most spoiled brat in Deutsch-Krone, which is like saying the biggest fish in a mud puddle. I had a Fiat limousine at my disposal when I wasn't driving my BMW motorcycle all over the northeast. One time I made it from Deutsch-Krone to Berlin in under three hours!"

"Sorry, Fritz," Frieda said, re-entering the room. "No cookies."

"Tea'll be fine, Frieda. Your Uncle Bernhard?" She looked down at the floor. "I'm so sorry," he said.

"What about your father?" she asked.

"Deported east."

"How many Jews are left in Berlin?"

"According to our sources in the Gestapo, although the government will never admit it, some four thousand."

"Oh, my God!" she said. "There were a hundred sixty thousand ten years ago."

"Goebbels decided to make the capital *Judenfrei*. He's just about done it."

"You're living in Berlin, Herr Berger?"

"Fritz, please, Herr …?"

"Billy's fine."

"Yes, I live there. My wife, our three-year-old daughter, and I. If you can call it living. At most, we stay in one place two or three months. We survivors call ourselves 'U-boats.' Like submarines, we only come up for air only occasionally."

"Why do you stay there?"

"Because I'm a German, Billy. No one is going to drive me out of Berlin. Not Hitler, not the cripple, and not the *verkackte* Gestapo. I'm part of this country. Besides, we really have no choice. Marlene and I thought we'd be in Palestine by now."

"Why aren't you, Fritzi?"

"It's a long story, Frieda."

She poured him a mug of tea. "Our social calendar has a rather large hole in it for the foreseeable future. We've got a lot of time to listen. You're better than the shortwave."

"Back in 1938, Marlene and I went to the *Aliyah* office and filed our applications. For the next months, one of us would go there several times a week to see how our visas were coming. Finally, they were approved. By that time, I'd already deposited several thousand U.S. dollars in a bank in Amsterdam. We packed our clothes, the motorcycle, and half our furniture and shipped them to Palestine.

"On March 20, 1939, we got word to be at the depot that evening to take the train to Marseilles, where we'd board an illegal transport. Two hours later, we got another call telling us there was no room on the transport and we'd receive word of a new passage within a few days. By that time, we were broke and very upset. We went back to the Palestine office every day. Each time we went, we were told come back the next day. Finally, I told them we had no more money. Instead of putting us at the head of the line, they refunded our passage money and told us we were off the list. Just like that. Can't say I had a wonderful experience with my *landsman*," he finished bitterly.

As Billy and Frieda warmed to Fritz Berger, they traded stories with him about the travails they'd shared during the past two years.

"Eight million Jews, eight million stories," Billy concluded.

"I don't think so," Fritz said sadly. "Three quarters of them ended up in the camps. Their stories died untold. We're the last remnant, and any day we could be next to die. You had your chance to go to Palestine. Why didn't you?"

"Same reason as you," Frieda said. "It's been ingrained in us for years that we're Germans first. And we're older, not exactly cut out to lead a hard pioneering life."

"Sometimes I think anything's better than this." He stood up. "I've been gone an hour. We're only here for a week. Marlene believes the Gestapo's got eyes everywhere, that they know exactly who and where we are."

"Where are you staying?"

In response he handed Billy a small handwritten card. *Frau H. Plötzl, 56 Selmannstrasse.* "Perhaps you might join us for dinner tonight?"

"Only if I can bring something," Frieda said.

"We'd be thankful," Fritz said. "This is no time to rely on pride."

~ ∫ ~

"What's Marlene like?" Billy asked Frieda on their way over to Frau Plötzl's that evening.

"All I can say is you'll be surprised. But I assure you she's an Orthodox Jew."

Billy was more than surprised. Marlene was a stunning young woman of thirty, with blonde hair, blue eyes, and coloring and facial structure that the Nazis extolled in their propaganda. He could only try to imagine what their offspring must look like.

Frau Plötzl was in her mid-fifties and wore her salt-and-pepper hair in a tight bun. She was trim and moved with speed and economy, like a small bird. When she first saw Billy, she colored slightly, then regained her composure.

"Is something wrong, Frau?"

"No. It's just that you look familiar. A bit older perhaps, Herr Fischer, but you remind me of someone I saw once when my late husband Walter and I went to the circus in Vienna. It's probably just an old woman looking back on a happier time in her life, but somehow …"

"A circus?" Frieda said.

"Yes. The man I'm talking about was very special. An American-style cowboy. His name was Billy Jenkins. He was the toast of the whole Continent. That must have been nearly twenty years ago."

Billy said nothing, but Frieda could tell he was smiling inwardly. "How did you become involved in helping Jews, Frau Plötzl," Frieda asked.

"I was married to one. My Walter was killed when the Germans occupied Vienna in 1938. I was Catholic and a widow, so the authorities accepted my papers when I moved to Berlin a year later. I fear that once the Nazis have eaten up all the Jews, the Catholics will be next, so I'm doing my small part to keep that from happening."

"You know," Fritz said, "for the longest time I couldn't believe this was happening in Germany. I watched the Nazis burn synagogues, rip Torah scrolls, plunder Torah silver, smash windows, and loot the Jewish shops, but I felt this was an aberration that had nothing to do with me. I was German, hence rational. What I was watching was not German because it wasn't rational – Polish or Russian, perhaps, because Poland and Russia had had pogroms, but not German because this had always been a country where law and order prevailed."

"No one is as blind as the person who doesn't want to see," Frieda interjected.

"Yes, but when I first met you," Billy said, squeezing her hand, "you were the one who convinced me this was not right."

"That's because we weren't 'Eastern' Jews," Marlene said. "In the little town where I grew up, except for the time and manner of our worship, nothing set us apart from the rest of the community. Oh, there were anti-Semitic episodes from time to time among a fringe element, but most folks didn't pay the brown shirts any attention. We were Social Democrats, but we were never politically active."

Dinner was elegant, despite its simplicity: potatoes, fried, boiled, and mixed with onions; cabbage, carrots, and beets roasted in olive oil; *knödlach*, bread dumplings with gravy on top; and brandy, an unheard-of luxury in these times of privation.

"How do you manage to continue living underground?" Billy asked.

"As Jews always have. By the use of our wits. After 1933, it became apparent that taking over my father's store was a short road to nowhere, so I decided to learn goldsmithing. I soon discovered I was a better businessman than a goldsmith. By the end of the year, I was making more and more trips to Berlin to trade in jewels."

"When we first came to Berlin in 1940, my husband worked at forced labor on a railroad gang for a few *pfennig* an hour, Marlene said. "What the Nazis never found out, praise God, was that he was making fifty times that at night, trading jewelry."

"You were able to do that right under the Nazis' noses?" Billy asked.

"I had many clients," Fritz said. "As German currency continued to lose its value, people who had never owned jewelry bought as much of it as they could afford. Of course, they bought it in the large, reputable Aryan-owned stores, but those stores relied on me to keep them stocked with merchandise. On a good day, I could make $5,000, American currency, not Reichsmarks."

"So your life in Berlin wasn't so hard after all?"

"Don't kid yourself. In January 1942 every 'above-ground' Jew in Berlin was ordered to surrender all their winter coats, warm clothing, and blankets, which were shipped to German troops at the Russian front. All Jewish households had to post *Magen Davids* on their doors."

"We couldn't ride public transport, or use public restrooms or telephones." Marlene added. "A little more than a year ago we were deprived of electrical appliances, cameras, typewriters, bicycles, telephones, and radios. We couldn't buy newspapers. We were allowed to buy only potatoes, cabbage, beets, and a half-kilo of black bread a week, and only between four and five in the afternoon, after all the food had been picked over."

"Couldn't you have gotten out?" This from Billy.

"I suppose, but the smaller a place you go to, the more you stand out, the more chance that a neighbor will betray you. In times like these, the price of turning in one more Jew is pretty low, a kilo of ersatz butter, a pair of shoes, a coat," Berger said. "Berlin might be a large cage, but there's always room for a little animal with a brain to survive."

~ ʃ ~

That evening, as they went their separate ways, Frieda asked Billy, "Do you think we did the right thing coming back to Germany?"

"I don't know. The 'cage' Fritz talked about is bigger when you're a *mischling*. Even bigger when you've got papers that say you aren't exactly Jewish."

"Are you, Billy?"

"Am I what?"

"Jewish?"

"Until six months ago, it would have been simple to say no. Now I believe I am."

"So what do we do?"

"We try to survive as best we can until better times come.

51

It was close to midnight by the time they reached the western edge of Nuremberg. The streets were deserted. The street lights were turned down. Leibstrasse was splotched in shadow. As they turned toward their apartment house, Billy felt a tug of discomfort. When they got to their front door, their fears were realized. The door was sealed and a bar lock had been installed. Worse yet, they stared at a letter on *Geheime Staatspolizei* letterhead addressed to Erich Otto *Israel* Rosenthal and Frieda *Sarah* Schönemann directing them to appear at the Judenhaus on *Wielandstrasse 6* for "statistical purposes" at 9:00 a.m. the following morning.

After Billy's trembling became manageable, he whispered to Frieda, "'Statistical purposes' is Gestapo shorthand for 'resettlement,' and 'resettlement' means the East and the death camps."

"What in God's name can we do?"

"I'll walk into the Judenhaus in the morning. If we're to survive this together, we've got to risk everything on one hand of cards. In an extreme emergency, I may have one trump card I can play. We can only hope he remembers me."

"Göring?"

"It's the longest of longshots, but it's our only one."

"But he doesn't even know me. As far as he knows, you died in the fire more than a year ago."

"He knows my handwriting and he's the one who arranged my defense department commission. Do you have a pen and paper?"

"Yes, in my purse."

"Good."

By the dim light in the hall, he wrote three pages, signed his name, took his commission papers, which he always carried on his person, out of his jacket pocket, and handed them to her. "We must leave this place immediately. I'm sure we're being watched. I'm equally sure they won't make their move until after nine in the morning, when we don't appear."

"Where do we go tonight?"

"Back to Frau Plötzl's. Hopefully the Bergers haven't left Nuremberg yet. Between the Gnädige Frau and the Bergers, they'll probably be able to get you to Berlin. If Fritz Peters is as resourceful as I think he is, he should find a way to get you into the Reichsmarschall's office …"

~ ∫ ~

"Herr Rosenthal, I am pleased you appeared voluntarily. Frau Schönemann did not accompany you? Where is she?"

Billy looked at the middle-aged man awaiting him at Judenhaus. He looked like the typical Nazi functionary, as far removed from the Aryan ideal as one could imagine. The *Regierungsrat* – Gestapo equivalent of Sturmbahnführer – wore an SS uniform with a blank collar patch and an SD sleeve patch. He was shorter than Billy, no more than five-foot-seven, and he wore rimless eyeglasses.

"First, Herr Regierungsrat, we need to get a few things straight. My name is not Rosenthal, it is Fischer, Erich Fischer, and if you have done your homework, as you seem to have done, you'll undoubtedly know that my professional name for the past forty years has been Billy Jenkins."

"Yes, yes, I know all that," the bureaucrat said. "You've probably bribed people for years to hide your true identity and your religion, *Jude*. It doesn't matter. Here you're the same as anyone else, one more subhuman fish caught in the Reich's net."

"I don't need to take that from you," Billy snarled. "I have friends …"

"That's what they all say," the Sturmbahnführer said offhandedly. "Undoubtedly the Führer himself is your friend and admirer, and while we're at it, why not throw in the Reichsmarschall, Goebbels, and Heinrich Himmler, too."

"Look, you upraised mouse turd …" Billy exploded.

No sooner were the words out of his mouth when he felt himself hurled to the ground by two huge toughs. Immediately afterward, he felt intense pain as his cane was ripped from his hand and the two guards slammed him in the face and on his neck with truncheons.

"Upraised mouse turd? Did I hear you correctly, Herr Rosenthal?"

"Damn right you did," Billy croaked.

"I suggest your mouth is a little too big for you," the Regierungsrat said. "Gentlemen, our guest should be taught a lesson in manners," he continued, addressing the two goons.

One of them punched Billy in the mouth, with the strength of a hammer. The other seized a pair of pliers and twisted two of Billy's front teeth out. The two guards were joined by a third giant, who commenced kicking at Billy's midsection and kidneys until he was writhing on the ground in agony.

Through a haze of pain and semiconsciousness, he heard the Regierungsrat continue, "Listen, 'mouse turd,' it wouldn't be good for you to look like that when we resettle you." The man laughed nastily and turned to his henchmen. "Throw him in solitary for a few days until some of his wounds have started to heal. Of course, if you're asked, you know what to say."

"Of course, Herr Commandant," one of the gorillas said, snapping to attention. "When we came in we saw he was drunk and he was assaulting you with his cane, threatening your life ..."

"Exactly."

~ ∫ ~

Headquarters Luftwaffe was a frighteningly forbidding pair of five-story buildings at the corner of Wilhelmstrasse and Leipzigerstrasse, less than a block from the Reich Chancellery, in the very center of Nazi Berlin. Frieda knew she must hide any outward fear she had, since Herrmann Göring held Billy's life, and her own, in his hands. Fortunately, Fritz Berger had known exactly from whom to seek out help.

Countess Marthe von Bornholm was a striking woman whom men found irresistible. She had never recognized the supposed inferiority of women: she was as strong as many men her size and a good deal more active. She was trained in judo, rode horses like a jockey, and could swim for miles. She had slim hips and walked with a man's gait, but she was feminine enough to enjoy wearing dresses that showed off her shapely legs.

She had met her gentleman friend, a Jew named Heinz Rockower, the epitome of the stereotypical absent-minded professor of romance languages, in 1939 at a soiree. At the time, she was thirty, Heinz was thirty-nine. She was more quick-witted, but he had greater experience and knowledge. The fact that he was Jewish appealed to her. She loathed the Nazis, so associating with a Jew in direct violation of the Nazis' racial laws demonstrated her defiance. They fell quickly and genuinely in love. But although they were lovers, they didn't live together until 1942, when so many of Heinz's friends had been deported that prudence didn't matter anymore. Heinz moved into Marthe's flat on Detmolder Strasse in Wilmersdorf.

When Fritz Berger first introduced Frieda to the Countess, he advised her that Marthe truly was a *bona fide* countess. Her family, originally from Sweden, had migrated to Germany where they'd lived for the past hundred and fifty years.

In the Berlin of late 1943, friendships among Jews and those who helped them – *Judenknechte*, lackeys of the Jews, the Nazis called them – were made on the spot. That precious commodity, trust, was given freely, and usually turned out to be well-deserved. Both Marthe and Fritz were aware, however, that just as there were *Judenknechte*, the Gestapo had their own "pet Jews," Jews who, in order to survive, frequently betrayed their own coreligionists to the Nazis. To decent Jews, these scum were even more despised than the Gestapo.

During their initial conversation Marthe told Frieda, "When Heinz moved in, he brought a daybed that doubled as a couch, a massive, boxlike piece built of mahogany with a lid hinged on the inside, which could be opened to store bedding. One day I told him, 'Heinz, that would make a perfect hiding place for you if you ever needed one. We could drill holes in the bottom.'"

Over Heinz's weak protests, Marthe had taken command of the situation. Using a hand drill, she bored holes, then covered the underside with loosely woven linen fabric. Inside the top, she fastened a latch, so that when Heinz climbed inside he could secure the lid; the pad on top would fall back into place. Each morning thereafter, when Marthe went off to her classes at the university – although she already had a degree in engineering, she was training to become a veterinarian – she would put a fresh glass of water and a bottle of cough suppressant inside the couch, knowing that her man would most likely forget to take these things with him if the need presented.

To the outside world, the Countess maintained the tightest connections with all the important Nazis. Indeed, an alarmingly high percentage of nobles did, since it was politically expedient. Because she was beautiful, intelligent, witty, and seemingly unattached, she was frequently invited to parties held at the highest levels of Nazi society. She'd met Herrmann Göring, who fancied himself a social butterfly, at least a dozen times and was on such close terms with Emmy Göring that she could, and did, telephone her several times a month just to chat.

Frieda felt far less threatened than she would ordinarily have felt as she approached the Luftwaffe Ministry because Marthe, who had made one of such calls to set up an appointment in the Reichsmarschall's inner sanctum, had given her a personal letter of introduction and a request for assistance to the Number Two man in the Reich. Marthe had insisted that Frieda wear appropriately attractive clothing, a chic gray wool outfit that had been tailored by Esther Thomas, a Jew whose safety was assured only because more than half of the top Nazis' wives insisted that in drab Berlin, they would wear *only* outfits tailored by that magnificently talented young woman.

Frieda waited thirty minutes in the Reichsmarschall's outer office before she was shown in. She was surprised at his appearance. Herrmann Göring looked like he weighed at least thirty kilos more than in the publicity photographs of him that regularly graced *Der Angriff*, *Der Stürmer*, and the *Volkischer Beobachter*. He also looked older and more exhausted, as though he were carrying an unbearably heavy weight on his shoulders.

"Frau Fischer." He rose to greet her and held out his hand.

There was an awkward moment where she didn't know whether he intended to shake her hand or kiss it, but that moment passed as the Reichsmarschall smiled and resumed his seat. "Our mutual friend the Countess spoke highly of you," Göring said. "You must excuse my appearance, but lately I've not been feeling well. Some years ago, I boasted that if the bloody English made inroads against our Luftwaffe, I'd change my name to Meier. Have you been in Berlin long?"

"Two days, *Reichsmarschall.*"

"Then you haven't had a chance to experience life here. The British bomb Berlin at least twice a week. My Luftwaffe forces haven't been able to stop them. The underground word of mouth is calling me 'Reichsmarschall Meier,' not that *that* bothers me as much as my worry that our civilian population now seriously doubts we can win this war."

Frieda coughed uncomfortably. "Did Countess von Bornholm tell you I'm Jewish?"

"She did, but it's nothing I didn't know before. Your late Uncle Bernhard was well known in Berlin for many years. You needn't look surprised. Not all of us are Jew-eaters, Frau … Schönemann, if I may call you that?"

"Please do, Reichsmarschall. It would eliminate much of the pretense."

"Countess von Bornholm said you had a favor to ask."

"Yes. It concerns not only me but an old friend of yours."

~ ſ ~

"But that cannot be!" he exclaimed. "He died almost two years ago! I, myself, read it in the Volkischer Beobachter!"

"Perhaps this will convince you." She handed him the commission papers and the letter from Billy. The Reichsmarschall read the letter. His eyes widened. He read it again, slowly.

"This handwriting could be forged."

"You really think it is?"

The huge Air Force commandant was silent.

"There's one certain way to find out, unless, of course, it's too late."

~ ſ ~

Billy's face was mottled with scars, bruises and deep abrasions, but after three days they were more yellow than purple. His eyes were still swollen, not all the way shut anymore, but ugly nonetheless. His jaw, where they'd forcibly extracted two teeth, was still twice its normal size. His clothing, gray workpants and a gray sweatshirt, hid most of the welts on his body.

The train had pulled into a small station twenty kilometers east of Nuremberg's hauptbahnhof, an old steam engine bearing six empty cattle cars. "How many?" Regierungsrat Voss asked his second in command.

"Only eight hundred this time, Commandant."

"Damn! We must be getting *Juden-frei* by now. At least Himmler and Goebbels will be happy. It's good sport, though. Most of those stupid Jews have no idea where they're going. The actually *believe* this resettlement crap. Where's this train headed, Theresienstadt or Birkenau?"

"Poland, Commandant."

The Regierungsrat laughed mirthlessly. "You know, it's ironic," he remarked. "Krakow was one of their largest, most important settlements. I'm told we've killed more than twenty times the number of *Yids* that used to live there, in a place less than forty kilometers from that city."

"Are you sure you're supposed to be talking about this, Commandant? The official line is ..."

"Yes, I know, lieutenant, *Arbeit macht frei* and the Jews who get sent East are 'earning their freedom.' Thirty, forty years from now, who's going to know? More important, no one's going to care. Does anyone remember the Armenians today? Or what the holier-than-thou Americans did to their Indians? What's Rosenthal look like?"

"Still ugly."

"Too ugly to put on the train?"

"Probably not."

"Do it then."

~ ∫ ~

Herrmann Göring himself piloted the three-engine Junkers Ju-52 from Berlin to Nuremberg. It took him just under two hours to get to the *Flughafen*. The Mercedes staff car arrived at the Judenhaus Gestapo Headquarters within twenty minutes after he'd landed. The Reichsmarschall had instructed Frieda to remain in Berlin. Still not entirely trusting that Billy was alive, he wanted to see for himself.

Regierungsrat Voss had received word that Reichsmarschall Göring was enroute. Although he had never much cared for the man – he felt the Luftwaffe Marshall was a pompous blowhard who put on cultural airs – he was acutely aware that although the Reichsmarschall's star had waned, Göring was still the number two man in the Reich. Accordingly, he ensured that every aspect of his operation was shipshape. As Göring alighted from the Mercedes, Voss gave a crisp straight-arm salute and the requisite, "Heil Hitler!"

The Reichsmarschall did not even acknowledge the salute, but immediately said, "Voss, I understand you have a man named Billy Jenkins in your custody?"

"I know of no such person, Herr Reichsmarschall."

"Jenkins? A famous performer?"

"I have never heard of him, Sir."

"Fischer, then, you idiot! Erich Fischer?" The Regierungsrat gave him a blank stare. "Rosenthal? Erich Rosenthal?"

"Ah!" A light of recognition went on. "One of my Jews, and a nasty one at that. Tried to assault me. Thank goodness three of my associates were here to witness his actions and quell the disturbance. You'd be proud of me, Herr Reichsmarschall. After a little discipline, we made certain he was well-groomed and healthy when he got on the train."

"He ... got ... on ... the ... train?"

"Yes. You know. One of our transports East?"

"He ... got ... on ... the ... train."

"Yes, Herr Reichsmarschall. Twelve hours ago." He looked at his wristwatch. "Should be crossing into Czechoslovakia within the next hour or so."

"I see." Göring signaled to the *Oberst* who'd accompanied him from Berlin. Turning to Voss, he snarled, "*Mister* Voss, you are demoted to SS-*Unterscharführer*, the lowest grade, effective immediately. Colonel Hoffman, you are to drive me to the airport forthwith. After you do so, you are to ensure that *Unterscharführer* Voss is immediately transported to Dachau to await a general court-martial for treason. Voss, you had better start praying that I'm in time."

~ ʃ ~

The train bearing its sad cargo was just readying itself to pull out of the Moosbach Bahnhof when a staff Mercedes roared into the station. Billy was crowded into the cattle car with eighty other woebegone human beings, men and women. Already the stench from their accumulated vomit and feces had made the smell unbearable. His bad leg throbbed. Deprived of his cane, he had been bodily lifted and thrown into the railroad car by two of the toughs who'd assaulted him what seemed a lifetime ago. He'd been unable to sleep. He'd retched up the last food he'd eaten some hours ago, and now hunger pangs were working on his insides. He had no idea where he was, since the car doors remained closed and barred.

The engine had hooted its mournful whistle. Billy felt a sharp jerk as the train lunged forward. Moments later, he heard shouting noises and the engine braked to a hard stop, throwing the inhabitants of the car forward. The doors to the car were flung open, and Billy's eyes were assaulted both by the brightness of the late afternoon sun and by high-powered spotlights. The commanding voice of a high-ranking Luftwaffe officer, a Colonel by his insignia, barked out a single name. "Jenkins! Billy Jenkins!" as he went from car to car.

The faces of his co-inhabitants were closed. No one said anything.

Was his punishment going to be still worse? Had the Regierungsrat singled him out for yet more? But what punishment could be worse than this? Wait a minute! The Regierungsrat had never once referred to him as Billy Jenkins. Billy had told Voss his professional name, but the sadistic bureaucrat had brushed it off with a curt "I know all that. You've probably bribed people for forty years to hide your true identity and your religion, Jude. It doesn't matter. Here you're the same as anyone else – one more subhuman fish caught in the Reich's net." What more did he have to lose by responding to the colonel's call?

The next time the officer called out, "Billy Jenkins?" Billy responded with a croak. He'd had neither food nor water since he could remember. His voice was weak, scratchy.

The officer had not heard him. He turned to the stationmaster. "All right, close the door! The fellow's not here."

"Wait! Wait!" Billy screamed thinly. "I'm … I'm Billy Jenkins! Wait! Please!"

"Did you hear something?" the colonel asked, turning back to the door, which was already three-quarters closed.

"I did not," the stationmaster said. "Let's …"

"No!" Billy exploded. "Please! Wait! I … Billy …!" Suddenly, he doubled over with pain as a spasm wrenched his stomach.

"Open the door, Herr Stationmaster," the colonel commanded. "It may be a false alarm, but it might be the man the Reichsmarschall's looking for."

52

"So you really did survive?"

"Like a cat, many lives. I thought this would have been my last one."

After their return to Nuremberg, Göring had hired a nondescript Fiat and driven to Saint Leonhard, close to Hitler's Berchtesgaden aerie, but still outside Germany proper. "Christmas, 1943," Göring remarked. "*Frohe Weihnachten!*" There was bitterness in his voice as he beheld the festive lights of the town. "I wonder what next Christmas will be like."

"You don't sound optimistic, my friend."

"At least you still call me your friend. By this time next year, I fear our loyal German countrymen as well as the allies will be calling for my head. So ... Billy Jenkins came full circle and decided he was a Jew after all?" He smiled wryly.

"I know what you're going to say, Herrmann. Could I have picked a worse time and place to do it?" They sat in companionable silence for several moments, each sipping a brandy. Although fate had cast them in totally different roles, in totally different worlds, they shared a genuine liking for one another, which had spanned more than two decades.

"The Jews'll survive," Göring said thoughtfully. "I'd have said the same about the Führer until Stalingrad."

"He's blaming you." It was a statement, not a question.

"For that. For the failure of the *Luftschlacht um England*. For the English breaking our secret codes, for the English inventing radar, for the English bombing somewhere in Germany every night, for their arrogance in dropping incendiary bombs on Berlin during daylight hours. For every perceived failure of the Luftwaffe. He's the ruler of the whole world, but his empire is shrinking every day, and he needs to blame everyone but himself."

"You'd dare say such things about your Führer, Herrmann?"

"Never in public. Not even to my wife. But when are you ever going to show up in my living room?"

"You know whatever you say is safe with me."

"I've known that since 1923. But what about your own safety?"

"I still have the commission."

"For all the good it will do you. I suggest you destroy it and let Billy Jenkins remain dead for the duration. I'll make sure every reference that you ever were an officer of the Reichswehr is destroyed."

"So Frieda and I would go underground?"

"Yes, but I can help you. I know some important but highly secret information. Two weeks ago, a bomb demolished the building that held all of Hamburg's official records. I can obtain official departure papers that you'll need in order to move from the city. Since there are no longer any records for the officials to check, you and Frieda could give a false name, place, and date of birth. Tell the authorities you'd lived in a part of Hamburg that was destroyed, and that you wish to visit elsewhere for several weeks."

"Go ahead," Billy said, brightening.

"The destination you want to go to would *not* be Berlin and it would not be Nuremberg, because those places are too obvious. The Gestapo, knowing that Hamburg's records have been destroyed, are on the lookout for false papers from that city. What we need to do is to get you departure papers for an intermediate city, one that has not been touched by the bombings. A few weeks later, the papers from Hamburg to the intermediate city would be converted into departure papers from the intermediate city to Berlin or Nuremberg. The police would not be likely to suspect papers from a city that had not been hit by bombs."

"But the Gestapo in Nuremberg know us by sight."

"A good reason to change your residence to Berlin. Besides, it would make it easier for me to keep an eye out for you, and for you to get in touch with me. Do you know the Countess von Bornholm?"

"I don't."

"Your Frieda met her in Berlin. It was the countess who gave Frieda the entrée to my office. I suggest you seek her out when you move to the capital."

~ ʃ ~

Two weeks later, an old man showed up on the doorstep of Frau Plötzl's house with departure papers authorizing a move from Freiburg-im-Breisgau to Berlin for Frieda Krause, born Lenz and her husband, Jenkins Krause. The papers bore recent photographs of both of them, as well as their signatures, and were exquisitely official, even down to the seal of the Gauleiter of Freiburg. During that time, Billy had found a dentist in the underground who was more than willing to trade a well-fitting permanent bridge for the furniture he and Frieda were leaving in Nuremberg.

~ ʃ ~

Marthe von Bornholm was every bit the charming enchantress Herrmann had told Billy she'd be. She quickly accepted Billy and Frieda almost as surrogate parents and arranged for an apartment for them in

Wilmersdorf. Shortly after they'd settled in, the countess approached them and invited them to tea in her still sumptuous flat. Although they'd met Heinz when they'd first come to Berlin, he was nowhere to be found. Instead, a somewhat heavyset, elegant woman, a few years older than Billy, sat in a chair adjacent to the countess's sofa.

"Herr und Frau Krause, I would like you to meet the Baroness von Artnzen."

Billy took her hand and bowed.

"Gräfin," he said courteously. Turning to Marthe, he asked, "Where is Heinz?"

"I sent him out shopping," she said.

"Isn't that dangerous, Countess?"

"Please, Herr Krause. I didn't say *where* I sent him shopping. It may be in the next flat for all I know. As much as I love my Heinz, he is not aware, nor would I want him to be aware, that I am working in another capacity with the Baroness."

The baroness had resumed her seat as Marthe continued. "My friend is the wife of a Danish diplomat. She married him after her first husband died. She's German by birth and certifiably Aryan, so the Nazis pay her no mind."

"I trust you're not particularly partial to the Nazis, Baroness?" Frieda asked.

"Frau Krause, I detest the Nazis as much as Marthe, perhaps even more. Since Marthe has told me you both can be trusted, I will come straight to the point. For the past two years I've been involved in an operation that's managed to get two hundred Jews and another hundred undesirables out of Germany to Sweden."

"Heinz doesn't know?" Billy asked.

"Heinz neither knows nor suspects any of this," Marthe said. "And please, you must never disclose it, for the good of all of us."

"Why tell us?" Billy asked.

"Herrmann told me you are a good man and a damned resourceful one – 'Nine lives' he said. When I told the Baroness such a man was moving to Berlin, she said she wanted to meet you and hoped you might be of assistance to her."

"Is there a reason you haven't enlisted Heinz, Baroness?" Frieda asked.

It was Countess von Bornholm who replied. "Heinz, God love him and *I* certainly do, is such a bumbling sort that if he knew, he might forget and blab it to others."

"Blab what?"

"The Baroness' *real* calling."

All this time, the Baroness was looking at Billy strangely, tilting her head sideways and squinting. "Forgive me, Herr Krause, but have we not met before?"

"I think not, Baroness von Arntzen, but in this day and age everyone seems to have led many lives. Why do you ask?"

"It's just that you remind me of a man I once knew many years ago. A famous cowboy – well, he wasn't really a cowboy, but …"

Billy felt his cheeks flush. Simultaneously he felt his hands grow cold and clammy. "Oh, my God," he breathed. "Hedy?"

"Billy?"

"Uh-huh."

~ ∫ ~

Within a week, the Baroness von Artnzen, née Hedy Dietrich, his erstwhile lover, had enlisted Billy and Frieda into her clandestine operation. Neither woman exhibited the slightest hint of jealousy toward the other, which put Billy at his ease. What they were engaged in was far more important than rekindling ancient amours, and the two women quickly established a genuine liking for one another.

Late one afternoon Billy and two men in their twenties took a train from Berlin to the west. Billy knew nothing about the young men, only that they had been assigned to accompany him. They got off the train at Friona and walked north through the square, its lush lawns faded and covered with dead leaves. The air was crisp, but not cold. There was almost no movement on the streets. Billy had been worried about encountering patrols, but Hedy had assured him there'd be none this night. The three men walked a mile from town to the beginning of a forest. Then they turned off and walked into the woods. A hundred meters in they found the people.

It was dark now, but not so dark that he couldn't see twenty of them. Billy motioned them to come close. As they approached, he noted they were of all ages. Some appeared to be Jews, others didn't. All looked haggard and badly frightened. "You must walk very carefully," Billy began. "More carefully than me." He held up a wooden walking stick. His attempt at humor met no response. "Take care not to stumble or step on anything that will break. Don't walk on the road. Stay in the woods. Just follow the person in front of you. Be brave. This is the last short step to freedom."

They walked for a mile in the woods. Then Billy silently halted the column. He motioned for the two young men to approach. "I can't explain it, but I've got a bad feeling. I want you to go home."

One of the men began to protest, but Billy held up his hand. "I'm in charge. Please do as I say." Without another word the two young men left. The column moved on. To Billy their footfalls sounded like the pounding of kettledrums.

At last they came to a clearing. Billy held up his hand once again and they stopped. He beckoned and they came closer and huddled next to him. He pointed to the clearing. "Look," he whispered. In the broken light he pointed out a tiny shack next to some railroad tracks at a point where a dirt road crossed the tracks.

"Hide in woods on the other side," he said softly. "When the train comes, stay hidden until someone fetches you. Then do what you're told. Now move out, one at a time. God be with you." One by one they crossed the clearing and disappeared into the woods. All was still.

Billy ducked into a shallow trench immediately ahead of him to watch what happened next. As he waited, he thought, *Who are these men and women? Where do they come from? What did they do before the war? Most of them look like Jews, but a few don't. Probably political dissidents. They know nothing about what's going to happen. They only know they're being smuggled out of Germany.*

At that moment, a slow-moving freight train, drawn by an old, coal-fired locomotive, passed in front of him and chugged its way a hundred meters past the tiny depot. As it reached the desolate stretch of track that cut through the woods, it slowed to an unscheduled stop. Suddenly a group of men rushed from the woods and opened one of the boxcars. As Billy watched wide-eyed, they broke the seals on a number of large crates and carefully pried them open. They started dumping furniture from the crates onto the siding. Moments later, the illegals ran from the woods, where the same group of men who'd emptied the crates lifted them into the boxcar, and directed them to get inside the empty boxes. As soon as each man or woman entered a crate, three men nailed the carton shut and affixed counterfeit seals to replace those that had been broken.

Their clandestine work done, the men jumped from the boxcar and closed the door. With not so much as a whistle, the train started down the track once more, bound for the port city of Lübeck. Billy knew from talking to Hedy that in the morning the crates would be loaded aboard a freighter. Next day they would be unloaded in Sweden. The furniture would have long since been hauled into the woods and destroyed.

The operation had originally been Hedy's idea. She was the one who had smuggled a Jew out of Berlin to Sweden a month before in a crate that was supposed to contain a piano. The operation had worked well. Suddenly, her idea became more practical because the Germans had unexpectedly given the Swedish diplomats, whose families were being evacuated, permission to ship their furniture back to Sweden.

"To make the plan work, we needed the cooperation of the train's crew. We told them nothing about the plan. They didn't know what it was about, and they didn't *want* to know what it was about. All they were asked to do was to stop the train in the woods outside Berlin for the amount of time it would take to make the switch."

One of her subordinates, a fellow of thirty-five with a shock of red hair, had added. "Usually the crews are made up of poor, elderly pensioners. They aren't younger, pigheaded Nazis who've been sent off to war. Amazing how much a ham, a carton of cigarettes, a kilo of butter, or a dozen eggs is worth in Berlin today."

"How did you handle the broken seals?" Billy had asked.

"Simple enough," Hedy had replied. "We copied a counterfeit stamp from a used seal. The more difficult problem was providing for the stowaways while they were crated in the vans. They'd need food, water, and waste pots. Even codeine to suppress coughs."

Billy, who'd had years of experience moving circuses all over Europe, had suggested, "Don't forget that human beings weigh far less than furniture. You'll have to add some weights.

"Good idea," Hedy said. "I hadn't thought of that."

Billy had been brought into the operation only toward the end. The counterfeit seal had been obtained, the railwaymen had been bribed, all was in readiness. It was then that Hedy had asked Billy if he would lead the illegals through the woods. Now with the train gone, Billy retraced his path to make sure no one had followed them. If he encountered a patrol he'd sidetrack it somehow, so he could protect those people now on the slow-moving train.

Billy was nervous. It did not seem logical that they'd get away with the operation so easily. There were forced labor camps in the area. The laborers were forever breaking out and the Germans invariably tracked them with dogs. If it happened tonight, the dogs could easily pick up the group's scent.

Now that part, at least, was over. Billy walked back through the woods in a stillness so deep he could hear his own breathing. Just as he reached the edge of the woods, he heard the sound of barking dogs. And then – was it his imagination? – the thud of boots marching on pavement. Suddenly, the darkness was pierced by a curtain of light thrown across the clearing fifty meters ahead of him. He knew then that it wasn't his imagination. Seconds later, another curtain of light appeared behind him. He was caught in a quadrangle. By the sound of their baying, he concluded that the dogs had picked up his scent.

Less than twenty meters in front of Billy there was a brook. Beyond it, if his sense of smell told the truth, there was a pile of manure. As quick as he could, Billy limped to the brook. Since it was shallow, he half-waded and half-pushed himself through the water. Once on the other side, he buried himself up to his neck in manure. When he was sure his body, which was still sopping wet, was covered with the fertilizer, he caned his way back to the brook, effectively having stopped his scent at the manure pile. As quietly as he could, he waded with the current until he reached a pond that was overhung with trees. He swam to the far side and waited under the trees until the sounds of the frustrated dogs became fainter. Only then did he lift himself onto the shore.

But Billy's problems were by no means over. He had no idea where he was. Even if he did, in his condition he'd have to wait out at least the night and then figure out a way to get back to Berlin. He hoped the illegals had fared better than he. He worried about Frieda, who'd be alarmed when he didn't come home. His wet clothes clung to his skin. He was shaking uncontrollably from the cold, but at least he was alive and, for the moment, safe.

~ ∫ ~

Dawn came. Billy, frozen and now quite hungry, was still afraid to move. Whoever had tracked him through the night would be waiting for him to leave the woods. With his wet and filthy clothes, he would give himself away. He waited through the day, praying for an air raid, the only thing he could imagine that would enable him to escape. As darkness fell, the four searchlights came on again. He was still trapped, still hunted.

And then he heard the sirens. The sweet, sweet sound of air raid sirens! Moments later, the curtains of lights went out. He heard the bombers droning in and then the whistling, followed by the thudding explosions. *It's now or never*, he thought. Crouching and weaving, his bad leg throbbing with pain, he made his way through the trees until he reached the edge of the forest. Just then, there was a tremendous explosion as a bomb hit a nearby factory. Soon the factory was blazing, turning night into an eerie reddish-orange day. Billy could see that the road was empty. The moment the all-clear sounded, he limped as quickly as he could toward the factory. As he had hoped, everyone was much too busy with the fire to pay attention to a half-crippled old man caning his way down the road.

For an hour, Billy helped fight the fire. Soon his clothes were no more wet and soiled than those of the others around him. As soon as the fire was under control, he approached an official. "I'm not from here," he said. "I was visiting friends and got caught by the raid. I helped put out your fire. Can you give me some kind of paper saying that's what I've done?" He got the paper without question.

By the next afternoon, Billy had made his way back to Wilmersdorf.

Frieda took one look at him and drew him a hot bath. Then she insisted he immediately go to bed, where he slept for the next twenty-four hours.

53

By November 1944, Billy couldn't tell what was more terrifying, the increase in the volume of bombs dropped or the constant pounding that had intensified his perception of the raids. Already the bombs had destroyed part of the roof and broken a number of windows in his apartment house. Even if he and Frieda were spared a direct hit, there would be questions about bodies uncovered in the ruins.

Day after day, without reprieve, the Allies attacked their area. Incongruously, the radio broadcasts from the Deutsche Rundfunk were filled with Strauss waltzes and operetta music, *Tales from the Vienna Woods, Die Fledermaus,* the *Emperors' Waltz, Morning Journals,* and, of course, the almost incessant *Blue Danube.* Conspicuously missing from the mix was Strauss *Vater's Radetzky March.* Even the Propaganda Ministry realized that martial music was not what Berliners wanted to hear.

In the apartment, Billy tracked the approach of the bombers with the help of an army map. He would listen to the military broadcasts locating the planes on the grids. As soon as it became clear that the planes were coming their way, he and Frieda would run for the near-est shelter.

One day, as Billy followed the route of the bombers, he noticed they had bypassed Berlin. But just as he was about to relax his guard, the next coordinates indicated that the bombers had suddenly turned back for a surprise attack. Billy grabbed Frieda and raced from the apartment. The first bombs hit before they reached the shelter. They were pelted with flying dirt and pebbles. Frieda fell. She tried to get up. So paralyzed was she with fear that her legs would not respond. Finally, he lifted her to a standing position and half dragged her to the shelter, where they cowered in a crowd of people, all of whom were as panicked as she was.

When the bombers had gone, Billy and Frieda returned to the apartment, marveling that they had survived another day. After each heavy bombing, Billy would find out which areas had been destroyed, then go to those areas and stand in line for the emergency ration cards being handed out.

One day, shortly after Christmas, a private wearing a Wehrmacht uniform appeared at their door. "Herr und Frau Krause?" he inquired politely.

"Yes," Billy answered.

"I was told to bring you regards and a gift from an old friend," he said, handing Billy a flat, wrapped package.

After the soldier had left, Billy tore open the outer wrapping. As he looked at the gift and read the letter accompanying it, he began to weep. Frieda came over and put her arms around him. "What is it, my darling?"

In response he handed her a yellowed photograph with frayed edges, displaying a much younger Billy, who was clearly in his prime, and a slightly older man dressed in chaps and vest. The two of them stood on either side of a tall, stout, dashing-looking young man. The almost illegible handwriting in the lower right hand corner of the picture read, "Billy, Tom Mix, and me, München, November 1923."

Her hands shook as she read the letter from the Reichsmarschall.

"Dear Billy –

"What a difference twenty-one years makes. I fear I am now nearing the end of my trail. I fully expect I will be dead within the year, and that I'll be reviled as one of history's great villains. I didn't mean for it to be that way. I don't say I'm blameless. I was as much hypnotized by the Führer as anyone. Power is the greatest narcotic and the greatest aphrodisiac, and don't let anyone tell you otherwise. I lived for the power and the glory. I lived to put my little toy airplanes into the sky and watch as the little men flying them killed other little men flying other little toy airplanes.

"We don't always choose the path we want to take in life. Sometimes life is thrust upon us and most men succumb to the narcotic or the aphrodisiac. The Germany I know will soon go up in flames and so will I.

"Please remember, Billy, that I always considered you my friend and I still do. Remember that the fat, sad old man whose photograph you now see in the newspapers was a soldier once and young … Look at this picture, my gift to you, once in awhile, and remember that once upon a time there were three friends in the summer of their lives, in a much younger, more innocent, and happier time. I give you my hand and my heart in friendship and love.

- Hermann Göring "

54

The final scene of the tragedy was about to be performed. The Yalta Conference had just ended. It was no secret in Berlin that Roosevelt, Churchill, and Stalin had pledged to make a final coordinated attack on Germany from all sides. In the east, the Russians had already penetrated the Reich. In the west, the Americans and British had launched their massive assault on the Rhine. There was no doubt whatever about the outcome of what lay ahead. It was evident from everything that had gone before that Hitler would fight to the end, regardless of the cost. Fortress Berlin would be defended and fortress Berlin would be destroyed. For thousands of helpless Berliners the one overriding task was to avoid being destroyed with their city.

Early in April 1945, Billy and Frieda invited Marthe von Bornholm and Heinz to go on a day's drive to Tempelhof airfield with them. "Why Tempelhof?" Heinz asked.

"Hedy got her exit visa to leave Germany, and I'd like to say goodbye to her. The Church of Sweden said they'd let me use its DKW."

After Billy had secured the automobile, he picked up his three friends up at the apartment house and they started out for the airfield.

The daily Allied bombings had been as much a part of their lives as anyone else's, but there was no way any of them could have imagined the devastation that had come to the capital. As they drove the four kilometers through Schöneberg to Tempelhof, passing street after street of gutted buildings, Heinz could only exclaim over and over again, "My God! My God!"

There was almost no traffic, but their progress was incredibly slow because the streets were clogged with fallen trees, rubble, and wrecked cars. Twenty minutes passed before they reached the field. When they came into the departure lounge, they saw Hedy smoking one cigarette after another. Ten cigarette butts were lying at her feet when a reedy woman's voice came over the loudspeaker to announce that ABA, the Swedish airline, was boarding its flight to Stockholm.

When they returned home late that afternoon, the news on the *Berliner Rundfunk* was desperate. The Russians had reached the Oder River, fifty kilometers from Berlin. In the West, the Americans were approaching the Elbe River, eighty kilometers from the capital. At the rate the Allied armies were advancing, they'd be at the outskirts of Berlin within a week.

Now, another problem reared its ugly head. Food supplies in Berlin were virtually nonexistent, even on the exorbitant black market. There seemed to be only one recourse. Marthe von Bornholm had a second cousin whose family had a farm near the Elbe. As courageous as she was, Frieda was petrified by the bombs. The raids on Berlin had been bad enough, but at least there she could go to a shelter before the bombs began to fall. If she made the trip, she'd have no shelter and no advance warning of the raids.

But someone would have to go or all of them would starve. Marthe volunteered that since it was her relative, it only made sense that she should be the one to go. Billy's sense of chivalry and his appreciation of everything she had done for them, moved him to say he would go with her to ensure that she was safe, at least as safe as could be expected. On the appointed day, they left the apartment house and walked toward the Bahnhof Zoo.

That morning, the British dropped hundreds of bombs. With practiced strides, Marthe and Billy walked calmly into the shelter, then boarded the train as soon as the all-clear sounded.

In Stendal, the first stop on the journey, the town had just been hit hard by bombers. The station's waiting room was so jammed with people trying to get out of town that the countess and Billy could scarcely move. The power lines were down. There was no electricity. The room was lit by candles, which cast a drab, unearthly light over the people and made them seem like ghosts. A soldier standing next to Marthe asked her if she was hungry. When she responded that she was, he gave her an apple and some bread. At last, she and Billy found a space to rest next to some exhausted children.

Then another fleet of bombers came over the town and began dropping their cargo of death and destruction. The station emptied quickly. Marthe and Billy left with the others because they were sure there'd be no trains going anywhere from Stendal that night. They walked to the main road, where they waved down an army truck. The driver took them a few miles along the road. Then they hitched a ride in a horse-drawn cart. It had been hours since they'd had anything to eat. They went to a restaurant in the next town where Marthe told the manager she had money but no ration cards. The manager served them potato soup.

Finally the train for Werben came. They boarded and the train set out, but they were scarcely out of town when the bombing started again. The train braked so quickly that the passengers were thrown violently forward. Billy and Marthe fled to the woods. With the greatest of good fortune, the bombs missed the engine. They reboarded the train, and were soon in Werben. From there, they walked the rest of the way to Marthe's cousin's farm.

All the following day, as Marthe and Billy rested for the return journey, Marthe's cousin, argued strenuously against the trip. "The Americans will reach Werben any day. When they do, the war will be over for me – and for you if you stay here – regardless of what happens in Berlin."

"But Heinricus," Marthe staunchly replied. "Heinz and Frieda are in Berlin."

"I understand. But the battle for Berlin will be the worst one of the war. If you return, you could be killed in the fighting or by the bombs. If neither of those things happen, you'll starve to death or you'll be raped by the Russians. The Russians won't let even a rat out of Berlin alive. At least wait for the Americans."

Heinricus' advice gave Marthe no comfort. For weeks, the *Volkischer Beobachter* had screamed headlines about the savage treatment of German women by Russian troops. A seventy-year-old woman raped. A nun ravished twenty-five times. Marthe had no illusions about these headlines. She was sure they were fabrications, part of Goebbels' relentless propaganda machine. Still, the subject had been raised frequently among her friends in Berlin. The specific word "rape" was never used. The women always referred to "it." Surely "it" had happened to German women along the Russians' path. Surely the Russians had in mind the treatment accorded *their* women during the German Army's invasion of Russia. Even assuming Marthe could avoid "it," she was more worried about a second rumor: when the Russians arrived they would seize all available food and starve the Berliners.

They left the following evening with bags of food strapped to their backs and bundles in their arms: mutton, chicken, bacon, eggs, potatoes, onions, and flour, the kind of food no one had seen in Berlin for months. The flour was full of sand from the grinding stones, but it would do. They took the train as far as Goldbeck, where they were told it would not go any farther. Billy and Marthe walked to the road and stopped an S.S. truck loaded with hay, which took them a bit closer to

Berlin. Aircraft flew above them dropping flares to illuminate targets on the ground, but neither Billy nor Marthe had any idea whose they were. Suddenly what they thought was lightning flashed across the sky following by more lightning.

"Thunderstorm?" Billy asked.

"No," the driver said. "The Americans."

So Heinricus had been right about how close they were to the war. All they had to do was to wait and they would be in an American-occupied zone. Thousands of Germans were on the road, walking west, toward the Americans. By the time the truck got to Stendal, the town was deserted. There was no train. Soldiers advised Billy and his friend to flee to the west.

"What are you going to do?" Marthe asked.

"Go back to Berlin."

Marthe shook her head. "I think Heinricus was right. I'm staying. The Americans will be here soon and the war will be over for me. Please, Billy, take all of the food with you. Can you manage?"

"Do I have a choice?" he asked, grinning wryly.

"Bring the others back as soon as you can. Before the final battle starts."

After they parted, Billy walked out to the road and tried to hitchhike, but no vehicles stopped. Finally, he stepped into the path of an oncoming truck. "If you hadn't have been so crazy, I might not have stopped," the driver said. "You going to Berlin?"

"Yes."

"You really *are* crazy." He popped the passenger door open and said, "Come along then. I can use the company. Maybe Lady Luck will smile down on me for giving a poor crazy man a lift."

The truck was carrying munitions. It stopped at an armament depot just outside Berlin and Billy gave the driver half a ham, which the fellow seized appreciatively. The driver hailed another truck for Billy, which took him to Charlottenburg. As he got down and handed that driver the other half of the ham, Billy spotted a pay telephone. *Why not?* he thought. *I've been lucky so far. Perhaps the telephone will work.*

It did. Any doubts he may have had about his decision to return to Berlin was erased the moment he heard the joy in Frieda's voice. It took him two hours to reach Wilmersdorf. He could not believe the devastation: buildings crumbled, trees uprooted and lying across streets, streets strewn with brick and pocked with craters. People shambled along slowly, their hair gray from the powdered brick and plaster, their bodies sagging, their faces drained by fatigue.

It was growing dark when Billy arrived home. Frieda had used the last of their comestibles to prepare Billy one of his favorite dishes, potatoes Lyonnaise. But just as Frieda finished cooking, the air was filled with a terrible sound. Hissing and howling, Russian artillery shells ripped the air overhead and hit their targets with such force that neighboring buildings shook. From the streets came the terrified screams of pedestrians caught in the sudden bombardment.

"Come to the basement!" Frieda screamed.

"No," Billy said calmly. She looked at her lover in astonishment. "I'm going to eat my potatoes Lyonnaise. I spent two days and three nights waiting for you to cook such a meal and now I'm going to eat it."

For a few seconds, Frieda regarded Billy as though he were a madman. Then, without another word, she loaded her own plate up with the aromatic meal. The two of them took their dishes to the window and watched the flashes from the guns in the distance and the shells exploding in Pankow, several hundred meters away.

~ ∫ ~

The Russians advanced to the outskirts of Berlin, but the city center was still, technically at least, in German hands. During daylight hours, Russian air attacks made movement impossible. Berliners, driven by hunger to stand in line for food, were mowed down by strafing aircraft that flew too low and moved too fast for the civilians to take cover. Whatever needed doing could be done only at night. Even then the hazards were enormous. One evening, late in April, their cache of food depleted to almost nothing, Frieda and Billy, who'd sent Heinz packing to Werben, left their flat to forage for food. All about them the city seemed to be exploding, as though there had been a chain reaction in a munitions dump. Shells screamed and whistled through a sky so filled with crisscrossing patterns of light that they could have read a newspaper. The air was so thick with smoke and the cordite smell of explosives that they could taste it, so hot from the fires that it singed their nostrils and parched their throats. An elderly woman, her hair turned white by plaster and dust, walked by them, as oblivious to where she was as of the blood running down her face. On the wall of a building a blood-splattered poster warned that anyone who surrendered would be shot or hanged on the spot.

Suddenly, as they approached a horse-drawn ammunition truck, Billy tackled Frieda chest-high and crashed with her through a door and down a flight of cellar steps. An instant later, there was a deafening roar as a Russian shell hit the truck, blasting the vehicle, the horses, and the driver into small pieces.

Nowadays, almost all military supplies were moved about the city by horse-drawn vehicles because there was no longer any gas. The streets were littered with dead horses. At night, many Berliners crept from their shelters, knives in hand, to cut up the horses for food. Everyone seemed to have the same idea, to stash away a supply of food in anticipation of the Russians. Once they arrived, everyone was convinced, there would be no food for some time. When they could, the S.S. patrolled the streets looking for deserters, shooting anyone whose papers seemed the least bit suspicious.

And then one morning the shooting stopped.

55

They waited for several minutes, almost unwilling to express the joy and relief they felt. Billy signaled Frieda to come to the window of their second floor apartment, lest their celebration was premature. Peering outside, he pointed. "Look! Russians are walking down the nearby trolley tracks!"

They were, but shortly after they'd disappeared around a corner, Polish and Ukrainian forced laborers, who'd been freed, rushed into the town and began to plunder stores.

"Come, we must help Schultz. He was good to us," Billy said. She agreed. Within moments, they stood at the front of the small grocery store, barring the entrance.

"Leave this man alone," Frieda said sternly. "The man who owns it is a Jew."

The laborers backed off, but instead of being grateful, the store owner scowled, "Are you trying to get me killed? What if the Germans counterattack?"

"Don't worry, they won't," Billy said.

But an hour later they did. As soon as they saw the Russians falling back, Billy and Frieda hurriedly packed a bag apiece and fled on foot in the direction of Grünewald, five kilometers away. Neither of them even tried to count the number of bodies the S.S. had strung from lampposts and trees.

~ ∫ ~

When even the German radio stations acknowledged there was fighting within Berlin, Billy smiled grimly. Here and there pockets of resistance still kept up the fight. He and Frieda walked from one side of the shattered city to the other. Suddenly they found themselves staring into the cannon barrel of a Russian tank.

"Don't fire!" Billy shouted. He pulled a white handkerchief from his pocket and waved it frantically. He and Frieda raised their hands. The Russian soldiers came forward.

"*Jude! Jude!*" Frieda shouted. "*Ich bin Jude und meine mann ist auch Jude!*" She looked over at Billy and saw that he was sweating.

The Russian soldiers apparently understood that much German, but they shook their heads and trained their guns on him. Just then a Russian officer rode up on a bicycle. "What's the trouble?" he demanded. He listened to the troops, all the while staring at Billy. At last he approached. "You're a Jew?" he asked in German.

"Yes!" Billy said.

"Say the *Sh'ma*."

Thank you God and Avram! Billy thought. Out loud he promptly and forcefully recited, "*Sh'ma Yisroel Adonay Elohenu Adonay Echod. Bo'ruch sheym k'vod malchuso, l'olom vo'ed.*"

The officer turned to his troops. "He's a Jew," he announced.

The soldiers smiled, nodded, and shouldered their rifles. The Russian officer, a major, turned back to Billy. "These soldiers are from a division that found many S.S. who had sewn on Jewish stars. They had orders to shoot them all."

~ ∫ ~

By evening the Russians had reoccupied Wilmersdorf. When Frieda went into the kitchen the following morning she saw a Russian in the garden with a sack over his shoulder. When the Russian saw Frieda, he made signs for her to open the gate. She did and the Russian left. When she turned around, she realized that the hens they'd kept in a coop were gone.

"Let him have them," she told Billy, as she savored the first silence she'd heard in months.

Later that morning, she and Billy decided to visit an elderly couple they'd befriended a couple of blocks from where they lived. When they got to their friends' building they found the basement filled with Russians, sturdy and well-nourished, wearing starched, clean uniforms. They were orderly and businesslike, and paid the two visitors scant attention.

"Herr und Frau Blaustein?" Frieda asked among the Russians. Finally, she found an officer who spoke German. "Please, Officer, I'm looking for by friends, Karl and Sarah Blaustein. *Jude.*"

The officer shrugged and shook his head. "The Germans still hold the other side of the building. Your friends may be over on the German side."

The apartment building, built on a slender triangle of land, was shaped like a ship, its narrow bow at the point where two diagonal streets converged. The two wings of the building fanned out from that point. In the basement, the wings were separated by a thick wall. The Germans were holed up on the other side and would have to be blasted out, the officer explained. "I don't think we'll see your friends again."

"Oh, my God!" Frieda cried. "To think these poor old people survived the war only to die now!" Then she saw some neighbors. "Sarah? Karl? Have you seen them?"

A woman told her she had heard someone yelling on the other side of the wall. "It might have been the Blausteins."

For Frieda, the next hour seemed like the longest of the war. She and Billy waited helplessly while the Russians blasted the Germans from the other side of the basement. She had never been this close to gunfire.

Every explosion reverberated in her head. When the fighting stopped. Billy and Frieda clambered over the rubble. Hearts hammering, they searched among the bodies. The Blausteins weren't there.

As the Russians moved on, Frieda and Billy moved with them, believing their only chance to survive was to remain with the side she was sure would eventually win. Then suddenly it was quiet. The couple left the last building in which they'd taken refuge and began to walk the streets. They could not begin to count the bodies.

A warm wind was blowing, pushing along swirls of brick and plaster dust. Petals from blooming fruit trees mixed with the dust, lending a fragrance to the smell of the fires, but that fragrance was obliterated from time to time by the smell of death. In the distance they could hear the booming of the big guns, the *rat-tat-tat* of strafing and the popping of flak, but the area in which they were walking was calm, for the moment at least. Some of the Russians were setting up bivouacs in abandoned yards under the blooming fruit trees. Frieda could hear their voices and their clanging mess kits and, far in the distance, a melody from an accordion played in a minor key.

Several miles away, the city was on fire. Billy said, "It must be the city center. Hitler's bunker is there." The center of Berlin was northeast of Wilmersdorf.

Suddenly, they saw the elderly Blausteins near the bivouac, eating what appeared to be soup. They motioned Frieda and Billy over and the four of them embraced as if they were the last people in Berlin. Some Russian soldiers offered Billy and Frieda some food.

While they were eating, Billy asked the couple, "Your apartment house?"

"Blown apart," Karl responded. "Nowhere to go. We've lost everything."

"I'd hardly say you lost much. The few sticks of furniture you had can easily be replaced. You have your lives …"

"Yes, but …" the elderly Sarah Blaustein burst into tears. "We'd managed to keep the photographs from our wedding, and the time we honeymooned south of Vienna, and the picture from two days after our son was born. He's dead now, of course. So many memories, and that's all they are now, memories."

When they'd finished eating, Billy and Frieda insisted that the Blausteins remain with them as long as they needed to.

The next morning, it was so quiet that Billy could hear a water pump handle squeaking somewhere nearby. He peeked out the living room window. The street was filled with people, all of them with white bandages and handkerchiefs wrapped around their arms. They looked gray, wrinkled, and tired beyond remedy.

~ ʃ ~

Later that morning the four of them heard the clumping of boots. Two soldiers had entered the courtyard and were mounting the stairs. Sarah Blaustein rose from the sofa and was about to speak when Billy put a finger to his lips. He went into the bedroom and returned with two old pistols he had saved from his performing days. He handed a pistol to the aged Karl Blaustein and signaled for the older man to follow him silently. They found the soldiers in a corner of the building, setting up a machine gun post. With all the firing going on, the soldiers could not hear Billy's and Karl's footsteps. When the older men were two meters from the soldiers, Billy shouted, "Hands up!"

The soldiers were too startled to do anything but throw up their hands. "Now turn around," Billy ordered. They did. They were S.S. men, both in their early twenties with blond hair and pleasant features. "I'm not going to have this building shot up," Billy told them. "I'll give you your choice. You can give me your weapons and your uniforms and stay with us, or I can shoot you right here and now. Which will it be?"

"You can't give up!" one of the soldiers shouted back. "You can't win the war if you give up!" The other man nodded in agreement.

"You stupid idiots, the war is lost," Billy said calmly. "Now make up your minds."

For another minute the soldiers struggled with themselves. Then, simultaneously, the adrenaline seemed to drain from their bodies and their faces showed relief, as though someone had forced them to a decision they'd wanted to make but had been incapable of making alone.

Billy and Karl marched them down to the cellar, took their uniforms, and locked them up. Karl took the uniforms to the courtyard and burned them.

A few hours later, Frieda went out into the street abutting their apartment. A group of Russians gathered around her. A Russian, obviously an officer, approached. "Soldiers?" he asked in German, pointing into her building.

"No. Only four old people." She went on, calmly. "I'm a Jew. I want to thank you." The Russian shook his head and shrugged. He obviously didn't understand. So Frieda repeated the words she had found in a Russian-German dictionary in anticipation of this moment. "I am a Jew," she said in Russian.

The officer shook his head and spoke in broken German. "No Jews in Germany. All dead."

Carefully, Frieda reached into her purse and slowly pulled out her Jewish identity card, which she'd hidden for over a year. The officer looked a the card incredulously. Suddenly he said, in clear Yiddish, "You're really a Jew?"

"I told you so!" Frieda exclaimed in the same language.

They were both astonished. Of a moment, they reached out and hugged one another. The Russian grinned at her. He reached into his pocket and pulled out several men's and ladies' watches. "You said there were four of you? Here's a watch for each of you, *Mazel tov!*"

And thus did the nightmare of World War II come to an end for Frieda Schönemann and Billy Jenkins.

56

In the summer of 1945 Billy was now nearly sixty, with very little money left. There were few prospects for an aging circus cowboy, whose star had been eclipsed when he'd "burned to death" three years before. Still, he and Frieda managed to survive.

"Can you believe it?" Billy said angrily to Countess von Bornholm one day in early June when he and Frieda were visiting her family's farm in Werben. "I never fought for the Reich, I risked my life during the Warsaw uprising, and no American will even talk to me."

"Eisenhower's non-fraternization policy," Marthe replied casually. "That won't last long. Americans are much too friendly for that. Give it a couple of months and it'll blow over."

"But why blame a whole country for the insanity of the Nazi regime? It's like the government treated the Jews when the NSDAP first came to power."

"At least you're still eating," the Countess said. "I read in the *Stars and Stripes* that the average German gets twelve hundred calories a day, while American and British soldiers each consume three times that many calories."

"The talk in our neighborhood is that people in the Russian sector are starving," Frieda said.

"Not only in the Russian area," Billy added. "The Americans are making sure we don't get any help from outside sources. The Russian Bear and the American Eagle are partners now, but things'll change when their two systems come up against one another. One thing's for sure: There's no choice between being a Communist on two thousand calories a day and a believer in democracy on a thousand."

"I had no idea things were so bad in Berlin," Marthe said. "Out here in the country, we might not have money, but we grow our own food and we eat well."

"I'd give a lot to be able to live and work on a farm."

"Not that you have that much to give," Frieda said, squeezing his arm affectionately.

"Would a sophisticate like you really work on a farm?" Marthe asked, raising her eyebrows.

"Why not? Unfortunately, you don't seem to need extra hands here."

"No, but I have another cousin who's got a farm outside of Hof. They always need help there."

"Never heard of the place."

"Most people haven't. It's in the northeast corner of Bavaria, near the Czechoslovakian border. Good food there, even now, mainly sausages and strong beer."

"Near the Czechoslovakian border? This side of the Soviet zone?"

"You can get to Berlin or Munich on the autobahn."

"Ah, yes, the autobahn," Billy said cynically. "The fallen regime's great military road. What do they grow on your cousin's farm?"

"*Ach*, Billy, what does anyone grow in Germany? Potatoes, cabbage, carrots, beets, barley. Also a lot of chickens and pigs."

"Ugh!" Frieda said. "And to think I was raised Orthodox."

"My dear," Marthe replied, "If you haven't had meat for awhile your religious scruples may have to give way to practical necessity."

~ ʃ ~

"Well, darling, it's certainly not Berlin," Frieda said, then added, "Thank God."

True to her word, Marthe von Bornholm had put them in touch with her cousin Rolf Gmund, a strapping young man of thirty, whose beefy, red-faced wife looked as strong as her husband. Their farm, adjacent to the Franconian forest, was rich and fertile. As Marthe had predicted, Rolf and Helga Gmund needed all the help they could get.

The war had hardly touched the city of Hof, twenty kilometers to the east. Now that the hostilities were over, there was more demand for food than ever and this year's crop was the best it had been in half a dozen years. In addition to their usual spring planting, the Gmund's had sowed hops, wheat, and rye.

"You are a godsend!" Rolf exclaimed when he first met the couple. "We have four fields and many hands with few brains. Slovaks, Poles, and even a few Turks, hard workers but not too bright upstairs. What we really need is a supervisor, a field boss."

"I've had experience supervising people," Billy said.

"A shame you can't ride a horse. It would make you much more efficient."

Billy stretched his bad leg out and bent it back. It didn't seem as stiff as it had in the months following the fire. *I wonder? ...* he thought. "It's been awhile since I've ridden, but I'd be willing to give it a try."

"My man is far too modest," Frieda said. "Have you ever heard of Billy Jenkins?"

"Sure. That's *his* name," Rolf replied, pointing to Billy.

"Not quite what I meant," Frieda said. At that moment, she felt dreadfully sorry when she saw the expression on Billy's face.

"*Sic semper gloria,*" he said softly.

"Don't know of anybody named Gloria," Rolf remarked.

"Mind if I look at your horse?"

"Happy to have you look. Be better if you could ride."

The two men walked to the barn, which held four milch cows and three horses. Gmund pointed to a large, solidly-built gelding. "That there's *Pferd.*"

"A horse named *Horse?*"

"Couldn't think of a better name. He looks big, but he's gentle as a lamb. Want to try him out?"

"Maybe."

It had been three years since he's last sat astride a horse and he'd been much stronger then. Rolf tossed a saddle and bridle on the gelding, tied it down, and hitched reins to Pferd's head and neck. As soon as he'd mounted the gelding, Billy knew he was back where he belonged. It was as if he'd been off a horse three hours instead of three years. "Do you mind if I walk him around?"

"Go ahead. If you really can ride, you'll be doing *me* a favor."

Billy gently tapped the horse's flank with his toe. Pferd walked slowly out of the barn. As soon as the gelding was out of the paddock area, Billy clicked his tongue at the same time his legs touched the horse's flanks more insistently. Pferd broke into a trot, then into a canter, then into a sprightly gallop. His gait was as clean, steady, and as natural as that of a show horse.

Billy felt the cool breeze on his face. He smelled the exhilarating aroma of trees and felt the fluid, muscular motion of the several-hundred-pound beast as it thundered along the gravel roadway which circled the fields. He was *home* and it felt *good.*

Ten minutes later, when he pulled up in front of Rolf Gmund, the younger man was grinning broadly. "I guess you can ride all right," he said. "I've got a little secret I didn't tell you, Herr Jenkins. I've had three other supervisors this year. None of 'em could ride that horse like you. Looks like you found yourself and your woman a new home here."

~ ∫ ~

Three months passed. By the end of the harvest, Billy's frame had filled out once again. The hard physical labor, ample food, and lack of stress had taken years off his face. He was starting to resemble the Billy Jenkins of old. One day, as he and Frieda were walking in the gentle warmth of a late fall day, Billy casually remarked, "I've been practicing."

"I know," she responded.

"You do?"

"Yes. For a month now."

"Two."

"In the barn?"

"For the roping. Out in the woods with the pistol."

They continued walking in comfortable silence. A flock of geese passed overhead, flying south, squawking noisily. "You can take a showman off the show, but you can't take the show out of the showman," he said.

"You're really thinking of going back? At your age?"

He chuckled, but the chuckle was melancholy. "I doubt if any *real* show'd have me. As the Americans say, I've gotten 'a bit long in the tooth.' But there are all kinds of places where they'd welcome *any* entertainment, old age homes, orphanages, church functions … I wouldn't need to make a lot of money. I'd continue to work on the farm most of the time. But it sure would make me feel needed. Besides, sixty's not *that* old, woman!"

"No big top? No large theater?"

"Don't need one. I can't do voltige anymore, but I can still shoot while I'm in the saddle and that ought to give folks a thrill. Besides, who knows? There might even be one or two people who'd remember Billy Jenkins."

She smiled, reached up and caressed his whiskered cheek. "You'd need an assistant, of course?"

"Mmm-hmm."

~ ∫ ~

That night, Frieda wrote three letters, one to Switzerland, one to Palestine, and one to California.

~ ∫ ~

The Jewish holiday of Purim, the happiest day of the year, which commemorates the deliverance of the Jews from the first attempted Holocaust, the one that had been planned and almost successfully carried out by Prime Minister Haman during the reign of King Ahashuerus of Persia, takes place on the fourteenth day of the Hebrew month of *Adar* each year.

In 1946, which corresponded to the Jewish year 5706, this was a day of monumental significance for the remnant of European Jews who had escaped the jellied fires and Zyklon-B gas "showers" of the most recent incarnation of Haman. Six million of their brethren – more than a third of all the Jews in the world – had perished during the *Thousand Year Reich,* which had lasted twelve years.

Of the thousand Jews who'd lived in Hof before the war, fifteen were left, most of them elderly widows and widowers. "Fifteen may not be a large audience, but it's a start," Billy had told Frieda two nights before the scheduled show.

"Are you nervous?"

"Of course. It's been three-and-a-half years. Back then, I had the birds and the other performers. I was younger and there'd been no fire ..."

"I talked to an actor once," Rolf said. "He told me there was an easy way to get over your nervousness. You just look out into the audience and what you see, but they don't, is that they're wearing nothing but their underwear." The farmer chortled. "Hell, you got only fifteen people to worry about, and they're all older than dirt. Shouldn't be too hard."

"Would you be able to do it, Rolf?" Frieda asked.

"Nawww. That kinda' stuff ain't for me."

~ ∫ ~

Sunday, March 14, 1946, promised to be an especially bright, unseasonably warm pre-spring day in Hof. While the trees had yet to bloom, the aroma in the air was one of rebirth and new life. Billy was up by seven that morning. The show, which was to play at Hof's tiny, half-ruined Jewish Community Center, was to start at two in the afternoon.

"I'd have thought you'd want to sleep in," Frieda told him. "Do you want to ...?"

"No, my dear. I'll need all the energy I've got for this afternoon."

"You've never suffered from lack of energy in *that* department," she smiled. "But I can understand that you want to get on your way."

By nine, the four of them, Billy, Frieda, Helga, and Rolf, were on the road to the city, one-and-a-half hours away. Billy rode Pferd. The others were seated atop a farm wagon drawn by the other two horses. All of Billy's paraphernalia – plates, gourds, show pistols, and boards for a makeshift ring, were stored in the back of the wagon. The road from the Gmund farm into town was a narrow gravel path, wide enough to accommodate two wagons side-by-side, or even a tiny motorcar, but no more than that. Aside from the surrounding forest, the land was so flat it was impossible for them to see the city itself until they were within a kilometer of the town center.

It was Billy who spotted it first. "Damn!" he swore. "A circus tent! Big one, too. It's awfully early in the year for a circus to be playing. Must be a warm-up show. Funny, I never heard there was going to be a show here. No paper, no word of mouth. That'll pull most of the crowd away from my show. I'll be lucky if five people attend."

"That'd be a terrible shame, Billy," Frieda said. "All those months of work for a handful of people. Maybe a few of 'em will catch both shows."

"Maybe." But Billy looked despondent.

He was so busy feeling sorry for himself that he didn't see the look Frieda gave the others.

~ ∫ ~

"That's odd," Billy said. "The tent is all set up but there are still no signs anywhere, You can't even tell what circus it is."

"It's almost noon," Helga said. "Why don't we go over and have a look? It's less than a kilometer from here."

"Might as well," Billy said sourly, as he looked around the empty courtyard outside the Jewish Community Center. "I'm already dressed for my performance and this place is emptier than a tomb."

~ ∫ ~

Ten minutes after they'd reached the big top, people started to arrive. As Billy walked around the tober, he heard a dull rumbling. More people were coming from all directions. For the next three quarters of an hour, a steady stream of men, women, and children continued to arrive. By twelve forty-five, more than a thousand people filled the town square where the circus had pitched for the show.

Billy had the uncomfortable feeling that everyone was looking at him. As he turned first in one direction, then in another, there was absolute silence, except for the persistent chirping of a songbird in a nearby tree. Then a very soft voice started to say "Bil-ly Jen-kins, Bil-ly Jen-kins, Bil-ly Jen-kins." A moment later a second voice joined in, then another. Within a minute, the chant picked up throughout the audience. It never rose to a shout. Rather, it had the quiet force of an ocean wave surging along a coast. As Billy walked silently toward the tent, the crowd parted to let him through. Just before he entered, he paused for a moment and looked skyward as the sudden realization of what was happening hit him. "Oh, my God!" he said softly. "Oh ... my ... God!"

A tall, elegant woman in late middle-age, her hair still pale blonde, approached him. "Wanna' buy a book, Mister" She held out a handful of paperback books. *Billy Jenkins* novels.

"Tara?"

"No, Queen Nefertiti of Egypt! Of course, Tara, you dunce!" She hugged him hard.

"Gregory?"

"Present," he said, coming from the side of the tent. "I brought along a friend I'd like you to meet, a fellow from New York. His parents immigrated from Byelorussia. I just produced a movie in which he had a role. He's told me what he really wants is to act in cowboy movies. When I told him you were one of Tom Mix's great friends, he couldn't wait to meet you. Billy, I'd like you to meet Issur Danielovitch."

Billy shook hands with a man of thirty, his own height, with a cleft chin and a pleasant, open face. "What am I supposed to call you?" the circus performer said. "Mister Danielovitch? Issur? Izzy?"

"Kirk, if you please."

Gregory grinned. "If I can go from Grigori Migdalowicz to Greg Migdale, he can call himself anything he wants. There's another fellow who's stopped by to say hello."

When a man emerged from the other side of the tent, Billy thought he was seeing a ghost. "Jürg? Jürg Knie? But you died a decade ago!"

"My father did," the man said. "I'm his youngest son, Hubertus. And I'd show a little respect for your youngers if I were you. It's my tent you've borrowed and you're appearing on my show!" He guffawed. "Well … maybe for today it's *your* show."

Moments later, Frieda appeared. "Darling, I hate to interfere, but I think you'd better get ready for your show. It starts in an hour. Besides, it'll give you time to talk with some of the others."

"Some of the others?" a deep voice growled. "Why would I want to perform with an old *ferta* like that?" The head was bald, *really* bald now, and the man had put on twenty kilos in the years since Billy had last seen him, but the gravelly voice was as distinctive as ever.

"Sammy?"

"In the flesh, a lot more of it than you remember. Abrielle's here, too, as are the boys. And I don't want you to get a heart attack and keel over, so I may as well tell you now – the gorgeous apparition you're going to see doing the voltige act later on today is not Brenda Lee and it's not Abrielle, even though she'll be wearing the same outfit. It's my *granddaughter*, Hannah, and she brought a fellow along with her who says he knows you, Avi Blutstein. So you finally decided you were a Jew after all?" He pounded Billy on his shoulders.

"Why not? If I've survived the last few years and I see what's going on today, maybe there is a God after all."

Promptly at two o'clock, the doorman let in the huge crowd, most of whom were elderly and among the last Jews in Germany, but some were youngsters as well. The lights dimmed and there was the loud roll of tympanis, which grew in volume and ended with a sudden *BOOM!* A loud trumpeting issued from the top of each aisle. Two elephants, each clad in red and yellow silk with the words "Billy Jenkins – King of the Cowboys!" – paraded down the aisles to the ecstatic cheers of the audience. When they reached the twin side-pistas, each went to one of the rings where they first established themselves on tublike platforms, then raised themselves on their forelegs, doing, in effect, a handstand. After the thunderous applause died down, they faced each other across the pistas, raised their trunks toward one another, and trumpeted once again.

Between them, Billy Jenkins, King of the Cowboys, strode out wearing western jeans, a spangled orange shirt, a green bandana, and boots. He looked like he had walked right off the cover of a Billy Jenkins novel.

Sidling up to the stage, where he knew his voice would carry throughout the huge tent, since four of the most modern Telefunken microphones and an equally modern speaker system had been set up, he started speaking in a relaxed, casual tone. But for the fact that he was speaking fluent, accentless German, albeit in a faux-western drawl, he might have just come in from a gunfight in the American West or stepped from the pages of a *Billy Jenkins* novel.

"It happened one night about ten years ago ..." he started. "It was a hot summer evening in the Texas Panhandle. There was a crescent moon that evening, and it was hanging over the Pecos, all lovely and silver. The stars were piled up so thick you could've reached out and touched 'em."

From somewhere in the band section, a harmonica hummed *Shenandoah,* while a dim electric "fire" wavered in the center of the pista.

As Billy continued his slow, drawling narrative, he picked up first one lariat, then another, doing an impressive array of rope tricks while he kept talking the whole time.

~ ∫ ~

"That was quite a show," Hubertus Knie said, hugging him.

At that moment, they were accosted by a lad who was a head shorter than Billy. He had curly blond hair and eyes so blue they looked unreal. "*Enschuldigen, bist Sie der Herrscher von das Zirkus, Herr Jenkins?*"

"Yes, I am, er, I *was* a Governor once. The Herr Knie is the Governor of this show. And you are …?"

"Wilhelm Baldur Stark," the boy snapped, clicking his heels together smartly.

"I'm pleased to meet you, Wilhelm. Is there something I can do for you?"

"Yes, Herr Jenkins. I would like to join out with the *zirkus*."

"How old are you?" Knie asked.

"Thirteen years."

"You live in Hof?"

"No, sir. I was born in Berlin. My mother died shortly after I was born. My father was killed on the Eastern Front. I was raised by my grandparents, but they're old and poor and it would be a mercy if I found my own way in the world."

Their conversation was interrupted by the nearby trumpeting of the two elephants who'd been in the show. As the lead bull approached Billy and young Wilhelm Stark, she stopped in her tracks, lifted her trunk up and down in the boy's direction, and softly whuffled what sounded like a respectful greeting.

"Well, I'll be damned," Billy said, his eyes widening as he looked toward Wilhelm.

"Who would have believed it?" Hubertus Knie echoed. "The old tradition isn't dead after all. Of course he'll need a mentor and a teacher, an old cuss who knows how it's done. What do you say, 'old timer?'"

"I'm game if you are."

"Looks like we've got the newest First of May." Knie addressed the boy. "Willy Stark, enjoy your rest tonight because tomorrow you are going to start working harder than you've ever thought possible."

EPILOGUE

From October, 1949 until a year before his death, Billy Jenkins, who now used the name Billy Jenkins-Rosenthal, traveled with his Wild West Show throughout Germany. He eventually settled in a suburb of Cologne, where he died on January 21, 1954. Four days later, he was buried in Cologne's Melaten Cemetery.

Issur Danielovitch, who at one time had been known as Izzy Demsky, kept his newly adopted name and later appeared in numerous American western movies, including one of the greatest – if not the greatest – western movie ever made, *Gunfight at the OK Corral*. He became known to worldwide audiences as Kirk Douglas.

Imi Sde-Or (né Lichtenfeld) was a real larger-than-life character who is credited with founding **Krav Maga**, the Israeli hand-to-hand self-defense system. The definitive **Krav Maga** series is published by Dekel Publishing House of Tel Aviv, Israel, so far in English, French, Spanish, Dutch, German, Czech, Hungarian, Polish, and even Japanese.

The rights to the *Billy Jenkins* novels were sold by Werner-Verlag Deutsch to Uta Publishing House, which published them from 1949 until 1963, nearly a decade after Billy Jenkins' death. They remained the most popular and successful Wild West novels published in Germany.

Billy Jenkins never visited the American West, or even the United States. Instead, he created his own America, based on his own dreams and on the dreams of his fans. The circus, the world of adventure and the dime novel were his means of transforming the sadness of everyday experience into a magical world: Billy Jenkins, the mythical Man of the West, and Erich Rosenthal, concerned with fame and fortune, are two realities whose contrast a tolerant spirit can endure.

THE END

AFTERWORD AND ACKNOWLEDGEMENTS

Although I have used numerous references, the four that stand out are the article *The Nazi Cowboy: A New Exhibit Explores the Life and Work of Billy Jenkins* by Ruth Ellen Gruber, which appeared in the *Forward Newspaper* (formerly the *Jewish Daily Forward*) of New York on January 2, 2008, and which gave me the idea for this book; *Billy Jenkins: Man and Legend, An Artist's Life* by Michael Zaremba (2000), Husum, Hansa-Verlag, the definitive work on the life of the real Billy Jenkins; *Spangle* by my late friend and literary mentor, Gary Jennings, the finest circus novel I've ever read; and a series of hundreds of black-and-white photographs taken of the Circus Knie in 1975 by the incredibly talented photographer, Lawrence Migdale.

With the exception of certain anchors of fact, this work is fictitious. As in all novels, much of what occurs in this book originated largely in my own imagination.

As always, I am grateful to Zvi Morik, for his friendship and his extreme patience (he had two other books he wanted me to write ahead of this one, but graciously "gave me my head" and let me write this labor of love first). I was blessed with not one but *thirteen* editors, Pnina Ophir, Tom Burns, P.D. Cacek, Herbert Chelner, Bill Daniels, Walter Gourlay. Arlen Grossman, Paul Karrer, Joyce Krieg, Charles Watnick, Katharine Ball, Anne Canright, and Dennis Alexander. I was so very fortunate to have the brilliant Lisa Peaks of *DesignPeaks* as graphic designer, cover artist, and typesetter.

Dick Gorman, my law partner for over 30 years, and his wife, Claire, have been among my closest friends for 53 years. Colleen Miller has been my paralegal, secretary, and friend for more than three decades. The late, great Gary Jennings, author of *Aztec*, was my first true mentor. He taught me so much about the historical novelist's art.

As I move closer to the center of my Universe, I thank my late father and mother, Alfred and Trudy Gerstl, my brother Ted, his wife Candy, and their family, my sister Margie, her husband Harmon, and their family, my son Jeff and his wife Rachel, my daughter Tracy, my stepchildren Greg, Karen, and Roslyn, who are as close to me as if they had been my blood, and my six grandchildren, Jake, Abrielle, Oliver, Ryland, Fineas, and Vivian who are our future.

Finally – and eternally – I thank and love the center of my Universe, my wife Lorraine – without whom there is nothing, and with whom I have truly found paradise on earth. God bless you all.

– HNG – January 25, 2019.

* 9 7 8 1 9 5 0 1 3 4 0 4 5 *